INDIA
THE ASHES

Mark Tufo

Copyright 2014 Mark Tufo
Discover other titles by Mark Tufo
Visit us at marktufo.com
and **http://zombiefallout.blogspot.com/** home of future webisodes
and find me on FACEBOOK

Editing by:
Joy Buchanan

Dedications: To my wife, to another chapter!

To Kimberly Sansone, thank you for taking the time to help make this book be the best that it can!

To James Cummings, who put a face to Drababan, thank you for that! Please visit him at webpages.charter.net/zerostrife As always to the brave men and women of the United States Military, Thank you all for your sacrifice for our Great Nation.

Table of Contents

Prologue
Chapter 01 - Mike Journal Entry 01
Chapter 02 - Genogerian Encampment - Outlands U.S.
Chapter 03 - Mike Journal Entry 02
Chapter 04 - Paul
Chapter 05 - Mike Journal Entry 03
Chapter 06 - Paul
Chapter 07 - Mike Journal Entry 04
Chapter 08 - The Guardian
Chapter 09 - Mike Journal Entry 05
Chapter 10 - Mike Journal Entry 06
Chapter 11 - Mike Journal Entry 07
Chapter 12 - Tracy
Chapter 13 - Mike Journal Entry 08
Chapter 14 - Tracy
Chapter 15 - Alex
Chapter 16 - Tracy
Chapter 17 - Paul
Chapter 18 - Mike Journal Entry 09
Chapter 19 - Tracy
Chapter 20 - Paul
Chapter 21 - Drababan
Chapter 22 - Paul
Chapter 23 - Mike Journal Entry 10
Chapter 24 - Tracy
Chapter 25 - Mike Journal Entry 11
Chapter 26 - Tracy
Chapter 27 - Mike Journal Entry 12
Chapter 28 - Paul
Chapter 29 - Mike Journal Entry 13
Chapter 30 - Drababan
Epilogue

Prologue

My name is Michael Talbot and I'm a Colonel in the United Earth Marines Corps. (Okay, *Lieutenant* Colonel, but it sounds way cooler to say Colonel.) It has been three years since I was part of a revolution of Genogerians (a supposed sub-species to the Progerians) and more importantly, the repelling of a hostile alien takeover of our planet. We were able to overthrow the command inside the Scout Ship Julipion and take control. Once the necessary repairs were completed, we renamed it the Guardian. For three years we (and I use that liberally—I really mean man in general) have torn apart and rebuilt damn near the entire ship as we learned the Progerians' advanced technology. The Genogerians we have come to ally with have proven far more useful than the Progerians ever thought them capable. They had only ever used the Genogerians for basically their grunt work—lifting heavy stuff, guarding things and expendable ground troops as planets were discovered.

Earth had the unfortunate luck of being found by the Progerians some five years previous. During the attempted takeover, I spent nearly two years aboard the Progerian scout ship competing in fights to the death with my fellow humans, all of whom had been attending a Widespread Panic concert at Red Rocks. At first, I had fought merely for survival, then I fought to save the lives of my "spoils", human women the

Progerians had given to me after every round. Then ultimately I fought to win back the Queen of the Games, my girlfriend, Beth.

Before my final bout I had hatched a half-assed plan (famous for that, by the way) to escape, never truly believing in any success. The alternative, however, was to fight a man that I probably couldn't have beaten with a grenade launcher. I had been more successful then I could have ever imagined due to the ultimate sacrifice of the Space Shuttle Liberation and her brave crew as they detonated a nuclear device inside the hold of the scout ship. I thought the nightmare was over as we landed on terra firma only to discover I hadn't even fallen asleep yet. I had no sooner decided to throw my lot in with the Marines and hook up with my best friend on the planet, Paul, who had formed a highly organized militia in Colorado, when I found myself whisked off to France where I received some much-needed tracker removal surgery. I was still in recovery when Paris was leveled in an attempt to find me.

I had given myself up before they could kill any more innocent people. I was going to have my dance with Durgan; a human that had been taken in the initial invasion on Red Rocks and forced into battle along with the rest of us. The aliens had quickly fallen in love with his success and willingness to shed others blood on the arena floor. Come to think of it, he'd probably been subjected to the same chemicals the Devastator mutants had. Durgan had been pretty muscle-laden when he'd started his first bout but by the last one, he was freakishly large to the point where I was convinced he could take out a Geno in a straight up fight. (Look in Journal One for more about the psychotic steroid ingesting, murdering megalomaniac.) A higher power apparently deemed me worthy the day we fought. I bested him and my reward was not another woman but the right to fight Drababan, the Genogerian champion. Drababan was somewhere in the neighborhood of eight feet tall and six hundred pounds, which made Durgan look like a hobbit in comparison. The beast probably ate meals that weighed more than me.

The Progerians had circled our planet long enough to pick up some tricks, drama being one of them. Our fight was to be aired worldwide as we fought in the crater where the Eiffel Tower once stood. Our weapons of choice for the match were swords and we parried for a few moments. Okay, scratch that, Drababan had parried and I was blocking his potential deathblows. Somehow I had found an opening in Drababan's attack and was able to cut him, nothing that would require more than a stitch or two, but it had enraged him to no end.

For the sake of my honor Drababan had been prolonging the fight so that I would die well. (Stopping there for a second, who the fuck dies well? Dying is dying, the end result being death, right? To die with dignity is what Dee wanted for me. Oh, and while I'm already on a tangent, I started calling Drababan 'Dee' because he was sick of me butchering his name; it's a hard 'D' with a rolling 'R', it was ridiculous trying to say it properly. He seemed alright with it, this I know because he hadn't eaten me yet. Back to the original tangent, I fucking basically wanted to live with indignity if it came to that. There is no recovery from death—no laughing, no loving, nothing! Sorry, had to get that out.) So there I am, holding up this sharp toothpick as a charging T-Rex is barreling down on me when all hell broke loose. I know you're thinking what more could happen. Well, plenty actually. My buddy Paul, who had forsaken me in France, picked the most inopportune of times to attempt a rescue. Or opportune, really depends on how you look at it. Marines had attacked the ring of Genogerian guards who had been completely caught unawares. And this is where it gets strange; Dee, the charging T-Rex I told you about earlier, scooped me up like a bellhop grabbing a valise and ran full tilt for the opening the Marines had blown in the side of the crater.

    Bullets whined by me, as did the blue arcing fire of the Genogerian rifles. I remembered this all vividly as I bounced around on Dee's back. I probably should fill this in a little more. I had been in recovery after the fight with Durgan for, maybe a month, and in that time Dee had visited on numerous occasions. We talked many times during my recovery and even played some games, which he consistently trounced me in. I learned that he was a truly spiritual being; he had been imprisoned and forced to fight due to his beliefs. He was as much a victim as me. It was there and then that I learned the Genos were not so enamored with their lot in life.

    When Dee saw a chance to escape he took it, no questions asked. I hadn't realized that at the time and neither did my rescuers who almost shot him to death (he had already been shot a couple of times). A sub picked us up off the coast of France, and while we were traveling back to the U.S., the Progerians released their military might. To give you an idea of the enormity and severity of the attack, picture the U.S. in its heyday with all of its military might going on a full-scale invasion against the island nation of Guam. There was nothing we could do to stop it. We were helpless as destruction was unleashed upon our planet. It was that brutal. The only thing that most likely saved the planet was that the Julipion in its truest form is only a scout ship meant to find habitable planets and report back to the home world. Destroyer and Cruiser Class ships are then sent to complete the job.

    The Julipion did not have enough ground troops to effectively control the planet and at least for now they wanted to protect Earth's most precious commodity - people. We were the perfect slaves, ruthless in war and apparently tasted delicious.

Chapter One - Mike Journal Entry 01

"Holy shit, when did he start to walk?" I asked.

"Mike, he's two and a half and he talks as well."

"Get out of here!" I said disbelievingly.

"Maybe if you spent more time at home you'd know that. His first words were, 'Who that man?'" Tracy laughed as she came into the living room. She kissed me and wiped her flour covered hands on the sides of her pants.

I grabbed Travis, gave him a kiss and spun him around a couple of times before putting him down.

I wasn't gone nearly as much as our long running joke would lead one to believe, but, out of necessity, I did spend a lot of time away from home. It was my goal to ensure that Travis lived as long and fruitful a life as he possibly could. There was no doubt the Progerians were coming back. For a while the military had received transmissions of the Progerians progress, but I think when we stopped sending anything back the Progerians thought better of broadcasting their whereabouts.

I'd been back up to that friggen scout ship three more times since the takeover. The first time was more of a photo-op, a way to rally the world so to speak. Although, if the threat of slavery and death wasn't already enough, then my smiling mug wasn't going to tip the scales.

"Dee!" Travis squealed.

I turned to see Drababan, my bestest, biggest, baddest alien friend who had come to visit. It really wasn't that big of a deal as he lived next door in a special house retrofitted to his enormous size. When I let him in, he immediately leaned down and picked up my son by his outstretched arms.

"That still scares the hell out of me, Mike," Tracy said as she headed back into the kitchen, where I was also headed. I lingered for a moment as the eight-foot, six hundred pound Croc-beast picked my son up and nuzzled him close. Travis was laughing as he wrapped his left hand around one of Dee's teeth. With his right he was attempting to smack Dee's snout.

"You will be a fighter like your father, Travis," Dee said with a Genogerian version of a smile.

Out of necessity Dee's words might one day ring true, even though I was going to do everything in my power to ensure that would not be the case.

"You know, your big green friend out there still refers to me as, 'small female that mates with Mike.' At least he calls our son by his name."

I smiled (inwardly). This was a sore spot with Tracy. Dee would only use the names of those he respected and for some reason I garnered a coveted spot with him. As far as I knew he used mine and now Travis's actual names; everyone else was a descriptor.

I was helping Tracy prepare dinner when we noticed it had quieted down in the living room.

"I can finish up here. Could you please make sure your friend hasn't eaten our son?"

"Sure." It was a sight to behold as I walked into the living room. Dee was stretched out on our over-sized sofa with Travis resting comfortable on his chest, nearly lost in the steel iron of Dee's arms. Dee lifted an eyelid.

"He is exhausting."

"Tell me about it."

"He also punches harder than you."

"Okay, now you're just being mean."

"I would like to talk with you," Dee said as he tenderly moved my son off of his chest and onto the sofa.

"Sure. Let's go outside."

"Mike," Tracy called from the kitchen entryway. I turned just in time to see a two-liter bottle of Moxie hurtling in my direction.

It would have slammed off of my nose if not for Dee's large hand swiping it out of the air. His eyes lit up as he snagged what was undoubtedly his favorite drink on the planet.

"I have once again saved you, Michael Talbot. Thank you, small female who has birthed Travis."

"You're welcome," Tracy sighed.

If not for Dee I wouldn't spend any time hunting down the caustic drink, but it was worth it just for his reaction. The plant had shut down after the initial attacks. I was having a horrible time imagining what three-year-old bottled soda tasted like but the big guy didn't seem to mind.

I walked outside and when Dee finally met me there he handed me an empty plastic bottle. The belch that issued forth from him rumbled like a freight train.

"Better now?" I asked him, taking the bottle. "This shit is going to kill you."

"It will be worth it," he replied in all seriousness. "It is good to have you back in this vicinity, Michael."

"You as well, Dee. How did your trip to the Outlands go?" I was referring to where the vast majority of freed Genogerians had decided to make a settlement in the U.S. It was near a town called Hyder in Arizona. After Phoenix had been leveled, most of the remaining human inhabitants had left the state completely. Our informal census had the Geno population at a few hundred thousand, which meant they now outnumbered humans nearly four to one in the region. They'd first wanted to set up shop in the Middle East. It had taken numerous conversations to steer them away from that. History was rife with conflict in that area. Peace across the planet was at an all-time high at the moment. If we were able to somehow repel the next wave of attacks, and the world was once again safe from outside invasion, then I was sure that we would revert back to our natural state soon enough. Mixing the Genos within that type of scenario would be like adding Napalm to a forest fire. Plus, I knew there was still a fair amount of justifiable hatred directed toward the Genos. The largest group had settled in the States, that way I'd be in a much better position to ensure their safety.

"They are much like unsupervised children," Dee said in all seriousness. "It is good that they did not all settle in the same place."

That had been by design. We'd separated the Genos and placed them around the globe so that there would not be any one place that had a huge concentration.

I shuddered, thinking of the damage my son could do in thirty minutes on his own. Multiply that by a factor of a million or so for the Genos and you get the picture.

"They know not what to do with their new found freedom."

It was a volatile situation. Dee and I had worked with some of the natural leaders like Tantor, but once the Genogerians had discovered they no longer had to listen to their overseers, they took that to the next step and didn't want to listen to anyone at any time. Add to that the fact that they'd somehow developed a new alcoholic beverage called Krakas, which was like gasoline-infused tequila. Two shots would put a man on his ass. Yes, I was the test subject for that particular experiment. The Genogerians thought it hilarious the Earth champion could be dropped so easily.

It is impossible to pigeonhole the entire Geno population, though. They are a dynamic and divergent group as any populace will be. There were some that traveled down Dee's path for inner peace and religion, and some wanted to mate and raise families, although not in the traditional American way—Genos' weren't really the domesticated type. Can't imagine any of the brutes wearing a tie and going to their accounting job in the city. A good number joined up with the new coalition military forces because they knew the fighting wasn't quite done. It was like any populace, but with two distinct problems: they had no leadership and no police force to keep them in check. If a fight broke out it could go on for days among multiple groups. Luckily, most of the injuries only revolved around broken bones. Deaths were rare, but without a common goal or a unifying force it was going to be difficult, if not impossible, to rein them in.

Urlack, the Progerian/Genogerian shunned hybrid, who had basically led the rebellion and brought me back to the scout ship for our final showdown with the Progs, lived there now. A couple of the Progerian pilots including Iserwan, who was the first to force Kuvlar the Interim Supreme Commander to surrender, stayed aboard the ship. The Genos that stayed aboard were becoming very adept at what the pilots were teaching them. More than once I witnessed Iserwan shake his head at the ease at which a difficult concept was passed on to the "lesser" species. If he had ever thought the Genos were less than he himself was, that had long ago evaporated. That isn't to say all of the old prejudices had melted away as well, but it was a start. They were not the ignorant mindless beings he had expected them to be.

It is still strange to me to think that bigotry travels the stars. Possibly that is a necessary way of thinking for a planetary conquering species, or for any conquering species in fact. Maybe it's the justifying of a hostile take-over by believing that you will be doing the "savages" some good, protecting themselves from themselves, I guess.

In contrast to the Wild West style of the Geno Outlands, the Progerian settlement was as regimented as I imagine Sparta had been. They wanted nothing to do with man or especially Genos. They also knew help was coming and they could not wait for the salvation, retribution, and revenge it would bring. We monitored them as best we could; we'd recently got a few satellites back up into orbit using the troop transports as couriers. And we'd sent flybys as needed.

The last envoy of humans and Genos we'd sent had been treated with contempt and nearly open hostility. The Progs had settled on the very tip of Florida and my hope was a giant fucking tsunami would take them out. I wonder what the alligators down there thought of them. It wouldn't surprise me at all if the Progs started rounding them up and tried training them to serve them. *That,* I would pay to see.

I'd had many discussions with military leaders around the world and the consensus was really to go in and just destroy them. Trust me, I was onboard with that. I just couldn't see myself pulling the trigger, though, literally and figuratively. The Progs were combative assholes but they had surrendered, sure with the ultimate hope they'd be rescued and returned to the fight. But the fact remained, they *had* surrendered and to just go in and obliterate them didn't sit well. I'd fought vigorously against killing them, so much so that my best friend and Earth Coalition leader, Paul Ginson, and I had nearly come to blows. He could not for the life of him understand my desire to defend them, and really neither could I. I was convinced this was going to go one of two ways: either I was going to be hailed as a genius when for some unforeseen reason the Progerians helped us to an ultimate victory or deemed as a traitor for all-time and to all of mankind when the Progerians defeated us. That was a razor's edge I did not like balancing on.

Paul and I had since breached our gulf, but I did not think for a second that he would hesitate to destroy the Progerians if I ever let my guard down. Trust me, there were times that seemed the much easier path. Then you start throwing in all those inspirational poster quotes: "The road less traveled...", "The easier path is not always the right path...", "An alien in the hand is worth two...", yada yada yada, you get the point. When it came down to Paul and me, sometimes I didn't think it was really the aliens' situation that was our main problem.

Beth and Paul had married shortly after the aliens had

fallen. I don't know what was weirder, that Beth had supposedly gotten over me so fast and married my best friend, or that I'd had to stand up at the wedding as Paul's best man. *That* had been uncomfortable as hell. As for the bigger slight, Tracy had been put at a table, as far removed from the wedding party table, as was possible, and still have her at the ceremony. That was a no-brainer on my part as I'd spent the majority of the evening in the cheap seats with her. Beth had cornered me into a dance and had smiled happily the whole time. I could feel laser burns contacting my body from Tracy and Paul's stares alike.

"This should be our wedding," Beth had said as we'd twirled about the dance floor.

"Are you insane? You just got married to my best friend," I'd said with no small amount of shock.

"And why do you think it is that I married Paul?"

"Oh, I don't know, maybe because you love him?"

She'd outright laughed at that. I knew Beth could be manipulative, narcissistic and definitely egotistical but only up to a point—certainly not the levels she was displaying now. We never really sat down and talked about what she'd gone through while she was out on the road and Deb had died. Whatever it was, had amplified some of Beth's lesser qualities. Sometimes I caught glimpses of the girl I'd fallen in love with, like when she rescued a bunch of kids from some catacombs out by the Quabbin reservoir. She'd said they had saved her and she needed to do the same. Although, in reality, the little buggers seemed to be doing pretty good for themselves, especially Max, the kid who had become their leader after some kid named Sammie had died driving Beth to Worcester.

Mostly, she was becoming this new creature that I was convinced was going to sprout horns at any moment. That she was going to hurt Paul was without question, and I hated her for that. If I thought for the minutest of moments that he would listen to me, then I would have said something.

As it was, I had to make sure that she in no way harmed my family and with everything else that was going on it was a distraction I was not overly thrilled about having. What's the worst one woman could do? And then, the name Helen of Troy just kept popping up in my head. Beth had the ear of arguably one of the most powerful men on the planet. Paul had been thrust to the forefront when he had come out of the super fortress known as The Hill with its thirty-five-hundred or so inhabitants.

    The planet's military forces had been nearly destroyed; the Pentagon was a memory as were all other HQs around the globe. Air forces and tank battalions were a thing of the past and the ground troops had suffered a serious beating as well. What little of men in uniform that had survived, were leaderless and more concerned with preserving their own lives as opposed to leading a rebellion. Paul had stood atop the smoking ashes victorious and the world had rallied behind him.

    I don't begrudge him that at all. I had done what I did in the battle arenas mostly for selfish reasons, primarily to save my life and the lives of those around me. I did not want to go through the pain of losing any of them. Paul had created, recruited, trained, and built the only viable force against the aliens on the planet. And he'd done it for the noble cause of preserving our species. There had been a little friction in the beginning when some around us had advocated me becoming the Commander in Chief. I had steered *that* ship as far away from that course as was possible. I wanted nothing to do with the political bullshit that was sure to ensue. Paul had graciously accepted. The funny part was that those few who had thought I'd be a better leader were now gone. Nothing as nefarious as say murder, but a few were now in charge of remote posts that were as tactically necessary as Hawaii during the American Revolution. I didn't have proof, but my money was on Beth being responsible for those assignments. Paul just wasn't that petty.

Early on we had hoped that transmissions from the Julipion had never reached their home world Aradinia. Our hopes were crushed when we picked up their call. They'd dispatched three ships of battle, the names nearly unpronounceable and mattered little anyway. We changed them to Moe, Larry and Curly. The change did little to ease our hearts about the threat they posed. We had a couple of pluses in our corner—the Battleships they were sending were smaller than the Guardian and we had the element of surprise. That was about it. Pathetically short list but, at least, we had something. According to Iserwan, the battleships were more maneuverable, better armored, and had much bigger weaponry. The odds were not in our favor.

Luckily, they generally did not carry troops for land based operations, as the mop up duty would be assigned to the scout ship once the battleships crushed any sort of resistance. When we began to formulate our defense plans we had thought about creating another Scout. But the sheer size of the task, coupled with limited resources, made attempting this ridiculous in the time given. Industry on Earth had come to a standstill during the invasion and it had taken more than a year to get up and running. We now had the ability, and the capacity, to churn out some fighters, thanks to our new allies. It had taken two years, three months and six days to roll out that first alien fighter. The controls had been scaled down to fit a man but everything had been kept the same after reverse engineering. However, some did have cockpits fit for the bigger Genos. None of the Progerian pilots who worked with us would fly again or so they told us.

We'd almost been stopped in our tracks from the onset when the engineers removed the starting mechanisms from the fighters. The Progerians had created them as a failsafe so that only one of them could power up the machine. This had been due to an earlier Geno uprising when some enterprising rebels had stolen some fighters and turned them against their masters. Thus far no one could figure out how the system was integrated, but it was somehow such an integral part of the entire design that even the newly produced ships could not be flown without it, there was no work around and we didn't have the time to try and figure it out.

It was a lab-tech that had found the key. He had remembered that the Supreme Commander (the one I kidnapped) had some strange genetic markers in his blood. I'm not going to go into detail, mainly because it will highlight my ignorance, but I'd been told that the Progs had a strange enzyme that they secreted through their palms. So when they placed their hand on the starter the machine would fire up. It was this enzyme that we synthesized and had Geno and human pilots alike use. Some had argued we should just cut off the Progs hands and place one in each fighter. The Progs had lucked out when it was determined that only a live host could make the marker.

Chapter Two - Genogerian encampment – Outlands, U.S.

"I hate this place!" Junguar shouted. He was in the minority, but it was a growing sentiment among the younger Genogerians.
"We are free," his friend Xackrid replied.
"Free? Free to do what? Watch as the sun travels across the sky? Free to watch as birds circle our heads? Tell me, Xackrid, what are we *free* to do? We do not work, we do not fight, and we cannot go *anywhere*. Tell me what it is that we are free to do?"
"We are no longer under the rule of the Progerians, Junguar."
"We fight, Xackrid, we kill things. We have traveled the galaxies."
"Join the hu-man forces if you are desirous to fight."
"Pah!" Junguar spat.
The rebellion aboard the Julipion had heated the Genogerian blood to the boiling point. The Geno leaders had been able to convince their species to fight, but now that the heat of battle had cooled, many of the Genogerians had lost their taste for it against their former masters. Their masters, however, had not forgotten.

***

"Are you sure about this Tom?"

"I told you, Lemmie, the aliens promised us gold and safety."

"For what Tom? Just to drop this truck off in the center of the Geno city? It doesn't make any sense. We make the same supply run every month. Why is this one different?"

"Them ugly things said they put a surprise in here for them other ugly ones. What do I care what it is if it gets us off this run. Do you like being around those things? I'm always afraid they're going to forget their manners and eat us."

"And they said we can't check the cargo?"

"They forbade it. Now normally I wouldn't listen to them but they gave me this as a down payment if I promised." Lemmie held up a small gold bar.

Tom ogled the brilliant metal. "Who am I to argue?" He laughed.

A package roughly the size of a Volkswagen thrummed in the back of the truck.

Chapter Three – Mike Journal Entry 02

"Mike, you just got home a few days ago. It would be nice if you could stay and maybe help raise your offspring," Tracy said. She wasn't mad, but she certainly wasn't happy.

I was sitting on the couch and I had Travis up in the air. He seemed somewhat bored at the height I had achieved. What kind of hope did I have against Dee's outstretched arms? The kid was nearly in orbit when Dee did it.

"Tracy, it's only for two days. It's just a chance to show off all the new fighters docking on the ship. Paul thinks it's an important photo opportunity."

"He certainly likes to have his picture taken doesn't he?"

I shrugged and put Travis down. He had made a 'pffft' sound and dribbled spittle all over my forehead. "You think that's funny?" I asked him as I tickled his belly. He was squealing in delight from my ministrations. "Honey, you know what's going on. People want to believe everything is all right, that there isn't still a war imminent. The Genogerians are grousing and the Progerians just keep stirring up the shit. We need to keep this in the forefront and if it's just a matter of my wonderful mug getting snapped again then it's worth it. You know you can come, right?"

"And bring Travis?"

"Of course."

We'd had this talk before; it wasn't going to go anywhere. Before Travis was born Tracy was the penultimate warrior, first in last out. After having Travis, her protective gauge had ratcheted to maximum. She was becoming one of those that chose to believe the worst was over. She couldn't imagine a warring world for her child.

"He doesn't like to fly, hurts his ears."

Travis must have known I was leaving the next day. We played hard up until his bedtime and then he slept throughout the entire night, affording Tracy and me some alone time. I was surprised the following morning when I awoke and Tracy was already out of bed and sitting in the dining room staring at her steaming mug of tea.

"Everything alright?" I asked as I walked over and kissed the top of her head. She reached over her shoulder and grabbed my hand.

"Bad dream. I don't think you should go." She turned to look at me.

Even in the dim light it was easy enough to see the look of concern in her eyes. A light knock on the door pulled my gaze away. "That's...that's my ride. I'll be back on Friday." I leaned down and kissed her. "It'll be alright." She turned back around.

"Lieutenant Braverly? Since when did you get on shuttle duty?" I asked after answering the door. The Lieutenant was one of Paul's top handpicked men. He was of Australian descent, which in itself was unremarkable. It was his damn eyes—they were as flat and emotionless as a reptile's. His loyalty to Paul was without question; it was just the cold and calculating way he went about his business that made one stop and think.

"General Ginson wanted me to personally look out for your safety, sir."

Dee was exiting his house and coming across the lawn. It was such a strange dichotomy watching such a foreign being leaving such an ordinary dwelling. I wasn't sure if I was ever not going to chuckle when I witnessed it.

Pointing at Dee heading our way I said, "If that big guy couldn't keep me safe then I'm not sure anything or anybody could."

"As you say, sir," Braverly said as he sized up Dee. I knew he was thinking I was wrong, but I just kind of wanted to see if he would say anything.

"Hello, Michael," Dee said. "I would have been ready sooner but I was having trouble with my hair."

I snorted. Braverly was not amused. "Gentlemen," he said, sweeping his arm towards our ride, which happened to be a large truck flanked by two Hummers stuffed full of armed personnel.

"How concerned is the General?" I asked when we started to roll.

Braverly did not respond.

"How are Travis and your mate?" Dee asked.

"He was hoping to see you last night."

"It was my evening of prayer."

"I've been meaning to ask you. Do you think at any point you will stop referring to Tracy as my mate or some other variant?"

He cocked his head to the side. "But that is who she is."

"Fair enough." I dropped it. It was only another ten minutes or so before we got to the official airfield. In reality the transport could have landed in the empty lot across from my house and picked us up but Paul was never one to let an opportunity slide. Press from around the globe was on the tarmac.

"Fuck." I stepped out of the truck. Beth was smiling and waving to the cameras.

"Former love interest that walked with bears is here," Dee said as he looked upon the same scene I did.

"When you address her could you maybe not use the "former love interest" part?"

"Is it not the truth?" He was looking at me.

"Regrettably yes, but we don't need the constant reminder anymore."

"She still has feelings for you. However, I am not

sure if I could classify it as what you humans call love."

That was another of Dee's fantastical qualities. He was able to tell almost anything about a person merely by the scents they gave off. He damn near got me kicked out of the house one week, the previous year, when he had come in and declared me frustrated. He then asked if it had something to do with the menstrual cycle that my mate was going through—right while Tracy was sitting next to me at the dinner table. Yeah...*that* went over real well in the Talbot household. Thought I was going to end up with a fork in my thigh.

"Yeah, I think you're smelling revenge."

"You need to be careful around her."

"I didn't need your nose to tell me that." We were walking up to the podium and I had a large smile plastered across my face for the cameras. It slipped somewhat when Dee spoke again.

"You must also be wary of the General."

"Of Paul? Why? It can't be because of Beth, I'm more than happily married."

"Part of it is the jealousy he feels towards you for having been with her first. That is another strange trait of you humans—Genogerians rarely mate for life. And to be angry that a partner has lain with another makes no sense. Procreation is the main reason living beings exist at all. Spreading seed and eggs ensures the prosperity of any species."

"Yeah buddy, let's not get down to the nuts and bolts of this okay?"

Dee reached out and stopped my forward progress. "I said partly, Michael," he stated as he spun me around to face him. "He is dizzy with his newfound power and has a great dislike toward anything or anyone that could threaten it."

"I'm that threat?"

Dee nodded.

"I've told him before I don't want anything to do with

running the planet."

"There will always be those who think what you have done was of greater importance than what he has done, and that is something he fears. It radiates off of him every time you two are near."

"I had no idea."

"I know."

"And what do you propose I do about it?"

"I think the safest course of action would be for you to kill them both."

He said it so dryly and matter of fact, he wasn't kidding. Dee was learning about human humor but this, unfortunately, wasn't one of those moments.

"I don't think that's going to work out so well, Dee. Besides him being one of my best friends, I think there would be more than a few pissed off people if I killed Mr. and Mrs. Planet."

"Then you had best be careful." He stepped past me and up the dais.

"Well, you're about as helpful as legs on a fish," I said as I followed him.

"Hey Mike! Good to see you!" Paul said as he vigorously shook my hand. He was all smiles and sure seemed sincere enough.

I almost choked when I looked up to see Dee drag a large claw across the front of his neck. Was the alien fucking with me?

"Good to see you as well," I told Paul as he pulled me in close and gave me a hug.

"Michael," Beth said, extending her hand for me to take. She really was working the Jackie Kennedy angle. I had to admit she looked good, but a broom shoved up her ass couldn't have made her stand any more ramrod straight. I was pretty sure we were on a live feed right now and that Tracy would be seething just watching me hold Beth's hand. I debated turning to the cameras and mouthing 'I love you' but odds were that would only make it worse. As much as Dee understood humans, especially women, I was in direct contrast in the knowledge department.

She held my hand two heartbeats longer than was socially acceptable. Out of the corner of my eye I was able to see Paul as he gazed over, the photo-op face he had been portraying faltering for a moment. As I quickly pulled away, Beth laughed.

Crazy ass bitch was what I thought. She was playing a dangerous game with some very dangerous people.

"Ahh, they're here. Almost time to go," Paul said merrily enough.

I watched as another convoy pulled up and was happy to see Tantor and Urlack as they got out of their respective rides. My stomach soured, though, like it knew something my brain didn't. Then it dawned on me. Some of the most prominent and influential humans and aliens alike would all be together on one shuttle ship. If anything were to happen, the world would fall even deeper into chaos. Could this have possibly been what Tracy dreamed of? I wished now that I'd spent a moment more and asked. I generally didn't believe in prophetic dreams but one can never be too careful.

"Paul."

"In public, you will refer to me as General. Is that understood, Colonel?" Paul replied frostily.

"Well, it is now." I wanted to tell him not to get his shorts all in a bunch that I remember when we were tripping in college and he was looking in the bathroom mirror making monkey noises while he brushed his teeth. Although thinking about that now, I'm pretty sure I would have ended up at the wrong end of a firing squad for that. "Um, General?"

"Yes?" He softened his shoulders, sagging a bit. Maybe he was remembering a better time or he realized I had an excessive amount of dirt on him.

"Is this wise to have all of us together like this?"

Paul looked around. "Absolutely. I think it's the

perfect time. The Progerians are being their normal asshole selves, the Genogerians garner hatred just for existing, and most of the planet is having great difficulty figuring out where their next meal is going to come from. We are on the brink of a war, even our most optimistic models don't think we can win, and I miss all that I've...we've lost. We finally have a sufficient number of fighters rolling off of our assembly lines to restock the Guardian bays and I'm going to celebrate that fact. I want to show the world that they were right to have faith in me, that I...we can somehow pull off the impossible."

"My concern, Paul, er General, is that if anything were to happen to this group, the world would be leaderless."

"Your concern is unfounded. We go up to spend the day touring, shaking hands, sending live feeds down to a populace hungry for some good news, and tonight we dine at our respective homes."

"Sounds good when you say it like that," I told him.

"I'm...I'm sorry for earlier."

"Don't worry about it; we're all under a bit of stress." I clapped him on the shoulder and stood behind him as camera flashes popped off; it was like the 4th of friggen July. Reminded me a little of the battle on the scout ship with all the flashing.

"I can hear you sighing back there, Mike," Paul said in between waves. "It'll be alright, man. This'll be over soon."

It was twenty minutes later when we were finally in the shuttle and then all I could think of was how easy it would be for an RPG (rocket-propelled grenade) to take us out. I looked over to Urlack, who had become the emissary to the Progerians—although, in reality, that did not entail too much. They wanted less to do with him than with us. At least we were the true enemy. As a highly unlikely hybrid between the union of a Progerian and Genogerian he was considered an abomination in their world. Add to that fact, he had turned on their rule and was less of a being to them than we were which was difficult because they once used us as food.

Paul was heading up to the cockpit when a crewmember came over and handed him a black object that was about the size of a brick. The shuttle hadn't fired its engines yet so I was able to hear the man speak clearly enough.

"The interrupter is ready, sir."

Paul looked around guiltily as if he had just been handed a cloaking device that would allow him to go into a women's locker room undetected. At least that's how I saw it. "This will do exactly as I asked?"

The crewmember nodded. Well, that was curious. I was thinking about going up to ask him what it was, but he quickly stuffed the interrupter into his briefcase and retreated into the cockpit. I guess that was going to be a conversation we had later. It was obvious enough he did not want to share the knowledge.

I pretty much forgot about the thing the moment we took off. My last thought of it was if it was a cloaking device, then I wanted in. I immediately went back to my original train of thought. I was unsure what was going to happen to the Progerians because they abhorred contact with us. They could have Florida for all I was concerned, but did anyone truly want an aggressive, deadly, smart species roaming around unchecked? If I thought the coming attack force would at some point admit defeat, then part of the armistice terms would involve them taking the Progs back with them. Urlack had a heavy look about him. I knew he was wrestling his own demons; he was an alien divided, his foot in two worlds but belonging to neither. The Genogerians were wary of him because of his Progerian half. We'd talked before and I knew he felt that freeing the Genogerians and stopping the wholesale slaughter of humans was the right thing to do. I had thanked him for that. But, being considered a traitor to all those you worked for and fought beside was no easy feat.

Now they would always believe that his heritage had weakened him somehow. I tried desperately to let him know that it had done the opposite by strengthening him enough to make a stand. I don't know if it helped any but he thanked me for it.

Tantor, easily my second favorite alien, sat directly across from me. I liked Urlack but he just tended to brood too much. I didn't need anyone, especially an alien, mellowing my high so to speak. Tantor was very influential among the Genogerian populace, even amidst the chaos in their settlement. The Genogerians were hesitant to accept any kind of rule even from their own kind. It was leading to a Wild West type mentality out there. Eventually something was going to need to be done there as well. Even without much weaponry, the Genos could do a serious amount of damage before a big enough military response could be garnered to deal with them.

"You look tired, Tantor," I said.

He growled at me. "If I knew fighting alongside you, Michael, would mean I would become a custodian of my people, I would have just eaten you."

Dee laughed. "He speaks the truth."

"That's funny to you?"

Dee turned away from me but I could see his shoulders rising and falling.

"Dealing with my people is a lot like your earth children. They run around wild, smashing all that they can and moving on," Tantor replied.

"They'll learn," I said hopefully. "They just won their independence and they don't know what to do with it just yet. A lot of countries here, that have finally won their freedom from outside rule, take a while to adjust. They go through their own growing pains."

"Perhaps you should come and speak."

"I'll think about it." I lied, I wasn't going anywhere near them. Shit, if Tantor wanted to eat me and we were friends, well, the rest goes unsaid.

"Bring Tabasco," Dee blurted out.

Tantor gave him a confused look. Just because Dee was becoming adept at humor didn't mean the rest of his species were as well.

"He fears being eaten," Dee explained. "Tabasco is a spicy flavoring that would give taste to something that would most likely taste as bad as Michael on the palate."

Tantor paused for a moment longer, then his mouth opened wide and a loud hiss issued forth. Apparently, he thought it was hilarious as well.

"I'd kick both of your asses if I could reach," I pouted.

Paul poked his head out from the cockpit. "Almost there."

I was glad he'd taken Beth up there with him. It was bad enough I had Genogerians laughing at me; I didn't need her glaring (leering) on top of it. My heart skipped a handful of beats as the massive ship came into view on our starboard side. Okay, who am I shitting, I have absolutely no idea which is starboard and which is port. I just figured it made me sound like I knew what the hell I was talking about. Although, by the time Travis reads my journals he'll know better. Let's just say I could see it out the window I was looking through.

I fucking hated going on that ship. My palms were sweating, my heartbeat increased, I felt a sense of vertigo. It could be one hell of a panic attack if I let the reins go. So much death and cruelty had bled onto those decks. I still mourned for a good portion of those people. And, I was convinced Durgan's ghost *still* roamed the bulkheads seeking revenge for his final loss, unable to come to grips with it even in death. The shuttle thudded down, the artificial gravity pulling on my limbs. But it was more than that, which weighed heavily on me. This ship had fundamentally altered my being and I struggled with anxiety just thinking about it.

I'd thought about seeing a therapist for what I figured was a heavy dose of Post-Traumatic Stress Disorder, but I knew the fragility upon which my reputation and perceived power lay. If anyone smelled weakness, I'm sure it would be exploited to its full extent and I could never let Paul down when he needed me the most.

It was the quiet times when I reflected the most, when I saw Stephanie die or any one of the men who had stepped into the ring with me. I could feel my arms shiver as I thrust a spear or sliced with a sword meeting friction when I hit bone. Even the vast myriad of life threatening injuries I had received would come rushing back in to fill the gaps of my 'quiet' time. Travis was a blessing in more ways than one because he gave me a reason not to sleep. There were times I would wake him up just so I wouldn't be alone. Sorry Travis, but just remember you were probably going to wake me up soon anyway. You sleep so little that I sometimes in my darker thoughts wonder if it's because you know the end is near and you want to enjoy as much of life as possible.

"You are coming?" Dee asked. It was then I noticed the shuttle was empty.

I looked up with what I would imagine a state of confusion laced across my face.

"Michael?" Dee asked, stepping back in.

"Sorry, sorry," I mumbled, shaking the cobwebs from my mind. I stood and followed him out. The main procession was nearly out of sight with the gaggle of reporters following. "At least I know my place," I said sourly.

"You have a mate at your dwelling that emits chemicals that lead her to believe she is in love with you and a child that adores you. You, Michael, have very little to feel sorry for."

"I sometimes wish you weren't so adept at knowing our inner feelings."

"Humans are the equivalent of an open book, as you put it. Your multitude of facial muscles and pheromones make it incredibly easy. How any of you lie so successfully is the true mystery."

"Don't ever let Tracy know that it is merely a mixture of chemicals within her brain that makes her think she loves me because she'll find some medication to rid her of the condition."

Dee looked at me for a second. "That is the Talbot I know." I nearly went sprawling from the hit to my shoulder.

As we meandered our way to the bridge, Paul had already started his speech in regards to the rebuilding efforts. Beth gave me a look that could have cut glass when we walked in late. Iserwan was there as well, looking mighty uncomfortable with all the cameras pointing his way. He was probably afraid that the Progerians would somehow get a hold of a television and witness his treachery firsthand.

"Mike, Mike, nice of you to join us, come on up here!" Paul was waving enthusiastically.

I had been just about to sit down. "Wonderful," I muttered.

"Have fun." Dee was smiling.

"Kiss my ass, Godzilla."

I was halfway up when an alarm blurted off to my left. It wasn't like the one that rang through the entire ship during the takeover, but more like an alarm clock at 6:30 a.m. on a Monday morning, so yeah, still pretty fucking irritating.

I found it humorous when the man monitoring the ship said "Sir" and half the room turned towards him. His next words, however, contained nothing to laugh about. "There is an imminent displacement."

Iserwan was, for all intents and purposes the interim supreme commander, although we were just calling him Commander to avoid any negative connotations. But that's beside the point. I think if he were capable of paling he would have done so.

It was a reporter that asked the next question. "What does that mean?"

"Battle stations!" Iserwan yelled.

The lights changed from white to red.

"Launch all fighters," was Iserwan's next command.

"Is this part of the tour? Let us get a feel for the power of this ship? Because I've got to tell you it's working," another reporter said.

I saw Paul look over towards Iserwan, maybe wondering the same thing.

"Clear the bridge," Iserwan stated.

Two Marines stepped forward. It was Sergeant Stone that requested that all non-essential personnel please move towards the exit.

"I'm going to say that this is not a drill," I said as I began shoving the slower moving reporters. I was planning on following them.

"Where you going?" Paul asked.

"What the hell am I going to do in here? I don't know how to fly this thing."

"You're going to be my moral support."

Iserwan was sitting in the Commander's chair staring straight ahead, waiting to hear the next news.

"Imminent displacement?" I whispered to Dee.

"It is the signature an incoming ship displays as it moves through space."

"Any chance it's a shuttle?"

"Shuttles do not have the capability to buckle."

Buckling was how the Progerians traveled over vast distances in space before their crews died of old age. It had something to do with folding space and traveling over the crease before space had a chance to unfold. Like I said, I have no clue how this was achieved. I basically like shiny shit and blowing stuff up.

"How are they detecting this and how much time do we have?"

"Like an Earth ship that pushes through water and leaves a wake it is much the same in space."

"A space wave? Can you surf it? Sorry," I added when Dee looked at me crossly like a father might to a wayward son. "I'm nervous."

"As the ship is coming out of the buckle and space is redefining itself it creates a disturbance that the sensors on board can detect. As to the second part of your question, seventy-two minutes, twelve seconds."

"Umm, that's pretty precise."

"It is the same, it has always been the same. Of course we have used different forms of time measurement but that is what it is in human time. We actually call it two partians."

"So two partians comes out to seventy-two minutes and twelve seconds."

"And four hundred thirty-six milliseconds but I did not think you would care about that."

"Are you kidding me? Four hundred thirty-six milliseconds could mean the difference between life and death."

It didn't take Dee long, not long at all. "Sarcasm?"

"Nailed me. So mostly likely this is a..."

"Battle Cruiser," he finished.

"What do you figure are our chances?"

"Without you onboard, I would say one in three. With you here it has to be fifty percent."

"Dee, that makes absolutely no sense. I have no authority on this ship and I certainly can't fly it or a fighter for that matter."

"Does not matter, Michael. You will somehow find a way to change the tide of the battle."

"I wish I had as much faith as you."

"So do I Michael. Do you wish to pray?"

I truly was going to tell him that I didn't think now was the time. I was still unsure of my belief system and then it pretty much came down to 'screw it'—what did I have to lose? We got away from the hustle and bustle of a bridge preparing for war and found us a quiet piece of bulkhead. Dee and I got down on our knees. We both prayed, me to God and Dee to Gropytheon. (Odds were they were one in the same…is that sacrilegious?) I honestly don't know if either heard but I have to admit I felt better for it.

"Five minutes," the radar operator stated.

Five minutes? We must have had a whole Mass over in that corner. We all had our eyes trained on the large viewing screen; the thing was as huge as a screen at any football stadium and it was full of fighters. I was wondering how anything could survive what they were about to unleash.

"Tell the fighters to leave enough room for our cannons," Iserwan stated. "Weapons?"

"On target, armed and awaiting your command, sir."

"At two seconds to arrival, launch everything," Iserwan stated calmly.

"Will that be enough?" I asked Dee.

He shook his massive head. "It will certainly cause damage but not enough. All intelligent species have the capability to detect imminent arrival."

"Is that a slight?" I asked, interrupting him.

"One of the greatest minds of your world said that human stupidity is infinite."

"Who the hell said that?"

"Albert Einstein, Michael. How is it that I know more about your species than you?"

"It's the sexual thoughts, Dee. It's difficult to concentrate on anything else when you see a perfect female ass."

"You are the one that will lead us to salvation? Perhaps I should have remained a slave."

"Sarcasm?"

He didn't answer. "Back to your original question. The Progerians know that their approach can be detected and have engineered their ships to withstand nearly any initial onslaught until they can engage and return fire. The fighters will hopefully be a large enough contingent that the Battle Cruiser will not be able to return all fire on us."

"We're going to get hit?"

"Without a doubt."

"What if more than one Battle Cruiser comes through the arrival?"

"You have prayed, there is naught more we can do."

"Have I ever told you how much fun you are?"

"Sarcasm?"

I decided not to answer him. Those next few minutes seemed to take forever; I was thinking about Tracy and Travis mostly. If I could do something up here that would ensure their safety I would die happy. Not sure what that was going to be, not, at least, until Iserwan looked over at Deester and me.

"Drababan and Michael, could you please go to the armory? I will send troops to you, please arm them all."

I was about to ask him why when I felt my feet vibrate. We had just fired everything in our arsenal. Blue, red and some sort of purplish streak arced across the vast openness of space. For a long second I thought the rays would travel infinitum, possibly slamming into some poor farmer's land on a planet four hundred thousand light years from here. It would be in all the newspapers—the strange lights in the sky—and now he'd have a bunch of dead alien cows and sheep all fried up. Reporters would come from all over to look at the huge gaping holes in his south fields.

Suddenly, it was there. A ship, just like those old television shows with the horrible special effects. You know the ones, one frame there is no evil man, in the next he appears and everyone in the shot is trying to maintain the pose they had when they 'cut' him in. It's generally pretty cheesy. And maybe that would have been the case here but I was too scared shitless to think that. The fucking thing was massive. I guess I wasn't expecting it to be that big. I knew the Guardian was bigger but certainly not as badass looking.

Our scout ship basically looked like a giant Chevy Station Wagon compared to the Battle Cruiser, which looked more like an Apache Helicopter. It was sleek and just oozed menace.

I only had a moment to stare at it before our barrage slammed into it.

"There's no way anything could survive that," I said aloud just as klaxons blared.

"Incoming!"

Dee grabbed me and we headed for the armory. We had no sooner left the bridge than the ship was slammed to the side. If not for Dee's bulk I would have smacked my head off the wall. As it was, hitting him was no great bargain.

"How could they strike back so fast?"

"This is all they do," Dee said, righting me. We began to move a little quicker.

"And you call humanity stupid?"

He didn't answer.

We were rocked twice more before we got to where we were going.

"Any personnel not directly involved in the defense of this ship please head to the armory. Colonel Michael Talbot will be your troop leader." This came over the ship intercom.

"Who the hell are we going to fight, Dee? I'm sure as hell not going to don a spacesuit and fight like in some crazy James Bond movie."

"Moonraker."

"You saw that?"

"It is entertaining for me to watch what humans believe to be advanced technology."

"I have a hard time picturing you sitting on a couch eating potato chips and watching a movie. And I've been meaning to ask you, what's with all the cats? Do you keep them around so that if you get a little hungry and want a snack you can just grab one and pop it in your mouth?"

Dee looked aghast. I thought it comical I could elicit

that response from him.

"They are endearing little creatures and I would never harm any of them!"

He was getting pissed. I was glad Genogerians and humans alike were showing up to get rifles. They had most likely saved me.

"It looks like we will once again be fighting side by side on this ship, Michael," Tantor said as he walked in, a smile on his face.

Urlack was behind him.

"Urlack, can you tell me what the hell is going on?" I asked.

"The Battle Cruiser will send over landing parties in an attempt to take back this ship. It is too valuable an asset to fall into enemy hands. Failing that they will then attempt to destroy it and us."

"Glad I asked. Should we get down to the hangar then and await our guests' arrival?"

"The hangar will be the last place they come. The docking ships have the ability to latch on to any part of the outer hull. They can cut through the composite material in under a minute with troops immediately running through the resultant hole."

"Holy shit." A chill went up my spine. "Tantor, any chance we can convince them to lay down their arms?"

"Unlikely in the time we will have available. I would imagine it would give them pause when they see Genogerians shooting back at them. However, they will have Devastator troops with them and you know as well as I do they care for little, even themselves."

Devastator troops were genetically mutated Genogerians who were larger and somehow more deadly than the originals. I just liked to call them 'mutes', seemed derogatory. In my mind they were not worthy of a better name.

"If they can strike anywhere I'd just as soon be on the

bridge so I can see which way the tide is turning." Genos and men alike parted as I headed for the door.

"Sir?" Tantor asked.

"Right, right, I'm in charge. I'm married with a kid, not used to giving orders or anyone actually listening to them."

The Genos looked at me blankly. The men looked scared as hell, my joke doing little to appease them.

Dee, however, snorted. "It is true. I have seen his much smaller spouse completely ignore his entreaties!"

"Okay Dee, there wasn't much need to elaborate."

"Even his off-spring will at times ignore him completely."

"Dee!"

Dee had not wrested any response but he seemed to be having a grand old time.

"You and I are going to have a talk when this is over," I said, pointing up at him.

"What makes you think he will listen?"

"Oh come on Tantor, you too?" I just shook my head and headed to the bridge.

The lights flickered at irregular intervals as we were once again struck by whatever the Cruiser was shooting our way. Within a few minutes I found myself once again on the bridge with Dee. I had the rest of the troops waiting outside.

Iserwan looked over, acknowledging our arrival. Paul was busy looking at the screen. He seemed calm enough but I could see his death grip on the console in front of him.

"We're ready, Iserwan," I said. "Will we have any type of warning other than shooting sounds in corridors?"

"You will, but not much. How many soldiers do you have?"

"Thirty."

He took in a sharp intake of air.

"I take it that's not enough?"

"Each Breacher will have up to a hundred troops on

it."

"Each one? How many do they send?"

"They have ten."

"A thousand to thirty, we should be fine, right Dee?"

"You are horrible at math, Michael."

Iserwan had been in the process of completely manning the ship. At present it was at somewhere in the neighborhood of seventy percent. That number, however, did not include troops. No longer was it an inter-galaxy explorer and plunderer so much as a planet defender; everyone on it was here mainly for that reason. I'm sure at some point they were going to put troops on it to repel a pirate boarding but they were the last on the list. It truly was essential personnel on board at the moment. Although in reality the troops would now be very much considered essential personnel. I wondered for a second if it would be possible to convince the reporters to fight. Lord knows there were enough of them.

My gaze was glued to the screen much like Paul's. The fighters in comparison to the Cruiser looked like gnats flying around the head of a person. And like gnats they were being swatted out of the air with impunity. The loss of so many lives was staggering; add to that the fact of so many thousands of man-hours spent creating the machines and it was truly disheartening.

"Can't we do something?" I whispered.

We were doing all we could, trading punch for punch with the more heavily armed and armored vessel.

"Their Breachers have deployed, sir."

I'd yet to like anything the radar operator had to say. Maybe I should punch him. I saw five ships deploy from the Cruiser; they looked to be somewhere in the size of a traditional sea battle ship and they were huge. Even they dwarfed the fighters.

"Major Templeton, deploy Red Team Six," Iserwan told his communications officer.

I saw three Campaign Class ships leave the Guardian.

These were comparable in size to what was heading our way. There had been a huge debate about rebuilding these planet busters, primarily because of what they were used for and the resources that would be necessary to build them. Right now I wanted to give a big wet kiss to whoever had been an advocate for them. They'd been renamed to Campaign Class but it didn't take a rocket scientist to figure out what they were for. Cannons and gun turrets lined every available meter of their outer hulls and right now they were streaming fire. It was so thick it looked like a swath of colored death.

The Breachers began to return fire but for the first time since this started the invaders were outgunned. Then from the rear of the Cruiser a fighter escort emerged.

"Son of a bitch," I think I said, although it may have been Paul.

The invading fighters were oblivious to all around them except the Campaign ships that were now diverting some of their resources to the new threat.

I had an idea. I turned to see if Iserwan was going to pull some of the fighters off to help. "Iserwan, you need to help those Campaign ships." Explosions began to wash over us as they suffered heavy damage.

"There is no help. I have nothing left."

"Listen, you said they want this ship back, right?"

"Yes, that would be their initial goal, destruction if they cannot achieve it."

"Let them have it back."

I don't know who protested first, Paul or Iserwan, but it didn't matter; I quieted them down quick.

"I don't mean hand it over, just let them think that. We cannot afford to lose those Campaign ships or many more fighters either. Have the fighters pull back and attack the Breachers."

"If the Battle Cruiser is left unimpeded it will destroy us when they lose their breaching capability," Iserwan stated.

"That may be the case but they won't lose their

capability, not entirely anyway. We destroy four and let the fifth make dock. We have to let them believe that they still have a chance to win this ship back over."

"What will that accomplish?" Iserwan asked.

"It buys us time," Paul said, "and that is something in diminishing supply right now. Have the fighters engage the Breachers, Commander, and let one get though. You can handle your end, Mike?"

"Piece of cake," I lied.

Even with all our fighters pulling back we lost two Campaign ships. Two Breachers burned intensely in a hell fire, with a third disintegrated into a thousand pieces, a lot of which peppered the Guardian like seasoning. The ship rang out as one of the Breachers finally leeched onto us, heavy materials grinding and clashing as the ships 'kissed'.

"Deck 33, section 2 G as in Golf," the radar operator said as I looked over toward him.

"Iserwan, you need to stop that last Breacher from docking. Dee, Tantor, let's go." We were in full on sprint mode and I was tempted to ask Dee for a ride. If I stumbled now I was going to end up as a stain on the bottom of a Genogerian foot.

The ship rang like a bell again. The last Breacher had made a landing. "Fuck," I muttered. This was immediately followed by explosions.

"That's us," Dee said, turning to see how far behind I was falling. "Our fighters are shooting at the Breacher before it can cut through the hull.

"That sounds safe."

"I can assure you it is not. If the Breacher makes even a slight hole in the hull and is then blown apart, anyone or anything caught near the breach will be sucked through the hole. It is not a pleasant way to die."

"Is there such a thing as a pleasant way to die?" I asked.

"Some are better than others." With that he turned

and redoubled his efforts.

It couldn't have taken us more than two minutes to get to where the aliens had set up dock. Iserwan was correct in his estimate of how long it would take them. I grabbed a hold of Dee's prayer bag to get his attention. I motioned with my hand for him to stop. He touched Tantor's shoulder to halt him. The deck plating rumbled with the footfalls of the Devastator troops as they raced toward our junction in the hallway. As of right now they had no idea we were there. If I could have possibly hidden in a room and let them run on by I think I would have.

"Down," I hissed, getting into a crouch. I quickly poked my head around the corner and took a glance before leaning up against the wall. They were about twenty-five yards away and coming fast. I took two breaths and then spun, resting my rifle against the wall. I began to pull the trigger as quickly as I could. Blue shots raced across the corridor, death riding the beams.

Genos and humans came around me as the Devastator troops began to return fire. It looked like an Ozzy laser show in that hallway. The shield plating each Devastator had seemed to absorb a fair amount of our weapon's discharges. It wasn't bullet proof so to speak but it gave them an advantage. They could take two, even sometimes three hits before being down for the count. We'd surprised them, but they'd recovered quick enough and it wasn't like we'd been able to set-up a tactical ambush; we were in a fucking corridor.

Instead of falling back like you'd figure a normal enemy would, they pressed the attack. Oblivious to the death we were dealing them, they were in a rush to get to the forefront and accept our gift. I got the impression they were expecting some fair number of virgins on the other side. A human and Geno went down beside me, the former nearly cut in half from her wounds, the latter had caught a discharge to the side of the head, charring it like a long forgotten steak on the grill. We were killing more of them than they were of us, but they had the numbers.

"Fall back!" I shouted over the din. Dee was right behind me, Tantor off to the left. I was swinging my head back to the enemy when I saw Tantor crumple. Shot in the thigh, it had sliced him open, his leg no longer able to support his body as muscle ends split and cauterized. I could hear him grunting in pain as he folded over. It was a short-lived suffering as a red bolt caught him in the neck. We were getting shredded and would not have the opportunity to pull back because they were almost on top of us. Red and blue shots ricocheted off the walls, floor and ceiling. Someone nailed a control panel causing sparks to arc out as the lights went on and off wildly.

The smoke was so thick it was nearly impossible to see anything. Something hit me hard in the back, forcing the wind from my lungs. I was driven to the ground by six hundred pounds of brute force. 'Oh Dee,' I thought. My friend had been shot and I was more concerned for his well-being than I was for the fact that I was being crushed under his bulk. Just when I should have become a much thinner version of myself I saw Dee's arms brace on either side of me.

"Quiet, Michael," he grumbled, his huge maw no more than an inch from my ear. He was breathing heavy and I could tell by the way his mouth was open he was highly stressed. Lord knows I had half a dozen smartass responses to give him, but I thought better of it. What was left of our defenders were dead, dying or hopefully running the hell away. From my position I stared into Tantor's lifeless eyes. I'd miss the brute, not only had he been a hell of a Genogerian, he'd also been a hell of a being, plain and simple. It seemed he was just beginning to turn the corner on the whole humor thing. Blood ran down the deck toward me, washing over my cheek like a red tide.

The invaders stopped only long enough to finish off

those who were still groaning. Best I could figure was that we'd killed somewhere in the neighborhood of fifty of them. But who would stop them now? There were no traditional troops on this ship; it was all mechanics, pilots, operators of various kinds and officers in charge of the whole affair, what we truly needed and we did not have were the people or Genos that knew how to use a rifle.

"You alright, Dee?" I asked when the last enemy troop loped past.

"Yes," he said as he pushed up. "We must get back to the bridge."

"Won't do any good, there's too many of them." Dee helped me up. "I've got a better idea." I looked down the hallway at the gaping hole in our hull and into the Devastator transport. The Breacher was still attached like an over-sized blood-fat tick.

"Michael?"

"What will happen if we destroy that ship?"

"It will fall away and everything in this section of the ship will be sucked out into space because of the depressurization. Including us."

"What if we're in the ship?" I asked.

"I like that idea better."

"Come on, before those Devastators get too far."

"There will likely be crew onboard."

"Good. I will consider them partial recompense for Tantor," I said as I began to sprint down toward the ship. I was slowed somewhat as I either skirted or jumped over bodies but I still beat Dee, which I considered a victory all on its own. I'd no sooner bridged the docking gap than I opened fire. The Progerian officer checking the seal wasn't wearing the armor so I guess he never figured to get in the fray. Two Genogerians came up on my left—where the hell they came from I didn't know. Why I wasn't cut in half instantaneously I was to find out momentarily.

Dee was directly behind me and had once again saved

my life. At this rate he was going to start charging me interest. The Genos to my side began speaking loudly, their rifles trained on me. I was pretty sure I heard Dee's name in his native tongue. He was now speaking rapidly back to them. I just stood and watched. I was convinced that to make any movement would make my life forfeit. There was more shouting—although really they could have been reciting poems—it all sounded like swears. Out of the corner of my eye I was thinking that possibly their rifles were coming down a bit. So instead of having my brains liquefied they'd just lop off my head neatly at the shoulders, not a vast improvement.

"Dee?" I breathed quietly.

"Do you not see me talking here?"

I suppressed a laugh. He sounded so much like my mom when as a youth I would interrupt her while she was on the phone.

"Something is funny here, Michael?"

"You can tell? Oh that's right. You're the human whisperer. Sorry, just now you sounded like my mom a bit. What's going on?"

"They know who I am. I have told them of you and what has happened on this world and the Julipion. They are deciding if they wish to become part of the resistance."

"If they decide against it?"

"You will not feel a thing."

"You suck, Dee."

We got our answer soon enough when their rifles once again raised up, but not for me.

Another Progerian came from the cockpit but he did not have a weapon in hand. His eyes widened when he saw us, hostility becoming the dominant feature when he saw the betrayal from his own guards. I watched as one of the Geno's large knuckles whitened on the trigger. I didn't know if this was going to cost me my forearm but the Prog was a pilot and I was going to need him. I placed my hand over the end of the Geno's rifle. I shook my head, but who is to say that's a universal symbol of negation? I might have just told him his mother sleeps with goats and I photographed it. I think I got my point across when he looked down at me much the same way Dee does, as if to say, "What is wrong with you?" and come to think of it, it's a lot like Tracy looks at me. I felt like a fucking elf looking up at all those tree stalks. It was like talking to Ents. (Those are basically tree-like guardians of Middle earth forests for all of you who are not Tolkien fans.)

The Progerian pilot garbled his undistinguishable language to me and everyone else.

"Ask the asshole if there is anyone else on board," I said to Dee.

Dee spoke their native tongue.

"He will not talk to me," Dee replied.

The pilot's mouth dropped open as I pointed my rifle at his skull. "How about now?"

Dee spoke again, the pilot replied this time. "He seems much more affable now, Michael."

"I figured he'd warm up."

"He says there is no one else worthy on board now that you killed his co-pilot and his guards have gone insane."

"Tell him I'm real sorry about that. Actually hold that thought, he'll think I'm serious and I'm not going through that whole thing about teaching him sarcasm. Tell him to get in his seat and move this bucket."

I waited a moment for the exchange and the inevitable denial. I didn't even wait to hear Dee's response to me before I clipped the officer's side. The round sizzled into the panel behind him, doing a considerable amount of damage to the electronics beneath it. He hissed in rage and pain. The Genos behind me winced almost as loudly. I didn't know if it was in commiseration with their previous leader or chagrin that they had not been able to dole out the punishment.

"Let my new friend know the next round is going in his stomach and I'll take my chances flying this thing."

Dee paused to look at me. "Really?" he asked.

I shrugged. "Sure, why not?" I can't be certain because the alien language sounded like German spoken underwater while gargling sharp rocks but I'd swear I heard Dee say, "For the love of all that is holy please don't let this human fly this ship" or something akin to that. Whatever it was the pilot immediately changed his earlier stance and got back into the cockpit with us close behind.

There was a heavy whirring sound as the Breacher door shut and then a loud popping sound as if someone had opened up the largest soda can in the world. We pulled away quickly, debris rocketing out of the gaping hole in the Guardian. I watched as dead Devastators were pulled out, then I was horrified when it was our own dead being sucked into the abyss. I had a sort of sick satisfaction as I watched the soon to be dead Devastators do everything in their power to not be sucked out into the vacuum of space.

"It will not get them all," Dee said as he sat in the now vacated co-pilot seat.

"Will the remaining ones quit fighting now that their ship is gone?"

"Perhaps. Should I have this pilot dock in our bay?"

I was a hair's breath away from telling him yes. "No, have him go to the Battle Cruiser."

Dee turned to look at me. "Michael, I had truly hoped that you had found a new level of sarcasm but I can see by your facial features you mean the truth. Your pheromones indicate high levels of anxiety and excitement, which I find to be a very confusing mixture—it should be one or the other but not both. Excitement leading to conflict is generally reserved for sociopaths."

"Looks like I forgot to take my meds today."

"What do you propose we do when we get there?"

"I've always wanted to add a Battle Cruiser to my

collection."

"If insanity has an odor I do believe I am smelling it for the first time." Dee turned back towards the front.

Chapter Four - Paul

The bridge's attention was rapt on the battle in corridor C-47.

"They are in trouble," Iserwan said as his hands tightly gripped the edges of his chair.

Paul watched in horror as Mike's position was soon to be overrun. "Get out of there you fool," he said as he stood.

Beth's hands were over her mouth. Shots flew around wildly, the camera feed flickering and going black.

"What happened?" Paul demanded.

"A junction box was destroyed. I am trying to reroute the connection now," a technician replied.

"Iserwan, we need to send more troops down there!" Paul yelled.

"It is not that I wish to hold them back, General. It is that I have none to send."

"Help him....them, Paul!" Beth nearly cried.

"Iserwan! Any personnel that can carry a gun needs to do so, now!" Paul said forcibly.

"We need these men and Genogerians to fly the ship."

"There will be no ship to fly if we do not stop them!" Paul shot back.

Iserwan was about to issue the command when a vibration and a loud puckering sound reverberated throughout the entire ship. The Guardian minutely canted to the side and then righted itself.

"Hull breach, deck 33!" the damage control officer shouted.

"Again?" Paul asked.

"The Breacher ship has pulled away."

"That had to be Mike," Paul said as he hung his head.

"What? What happened?" Beth begged.

Paul was too lost in his distress to notice how deep Beth's concern went.

"He knew he'd lost so he must have damaged the Breacher ship so it would detach, knowing that the hull breach would pull everything in the area out into space." Paul braced his arms on the console in front of him.

"Mike is drifting off into space? You...you have to help him, you need to pick him up."

"It's already too late. He died to save us; we can't let that be for nothing."

Beth began to openly sob.

"Sir, I've picked up the Breacher on radar. It's under power and flying towards the Battle Cruiser."

"Target the Breacher," Iserwan stated.

Paul went over to the panel. "Why, why would they do that?" he asked, perplexed. "Why would they leave their men in a battle they were obviously winning?"

"Target is acquired, sir."

"Belay that order," Paul said staring at the machine. "Can we talk to that ship?"

"Not without everyone else hearing us," Iserwan said.

"That cagey fucking bastard." Paul beamed.

"Sir?" Iserwan asked.

"The only reason that ship left is because Mike is on it. He knew they'd lost the battle so he commandeered it and had them disengage from our hull in order to kill the invaders. For some reason only he knows he's headed for the Cruiser."

"Isn't it possible they had a malfunction or were possibly recalled for a different purpose?" Iserwan posed. "We have the opportunity to destroy them and I think we should take it."

"That's possible, but this just reeks of Mike. Let's make sure they have safe haven until they get to where they're going."

"What if he's been taken prisoner?" Beth asked.

"Well then that certainly lends credence to not shooting it out of the sky."

Chapter Five- Mike Journal Entry 03

"We can't just land in the hangar, Michael."

"I know, I know, I'm thinking."

"Perhaps you should think faster." The hull of the Battle Cruiser was dominating our field of vision.

"Are the Genos trustworthy now?"

"They will fight alongside us if that is what you mean. I only wish they could have perhaps tasted freedom longer."

"Dee, are you thinking we are going to die?"

"Every day I stay alive around you is a blessing for my Cravaratar."

"Hilarious. Ask them how many Progs are on the bridge."

"You mean to breach the bridge?"

"Say *that* ten times fast. And yes, I think that is exactly what I plan on doing. Seems the easiest, most direct thing."

The Progerian pilot seemed more stressed out with Dee exiting the cockpit. I happily sat down next to him, wearing the biggest shit-eating grin I could manage without my cheeks hurting too much. He kept glancing over and then quickly looking forward. I probably scared the hell out of him. I'd had an opportunity to get used to the Progs and Genos. Who knows? To him I was probably like a giant, hairy spider to a kid with arachnophobia. I thought about touching his shoulder to see if he would shriek like a little girl, but I had to remember this thing outweighed me by about three times and could rip my arm off with his mouth.

He might be scared of me, but how many petrified kids had found the nerve to squish spiders under their feet?

I could hear arguing behind me. Dee and one of the Geno guards came back up.

"He says we cannot attempt to breach the bridge. There are gun emplacements all around it and as soon as we attempted to land they would blow us from the sky."

"I guess they figured if they could breach hulls so could others. Shit, maybe we should go back to the Guardian."

"He says there is another way."

I perked up. "I'm listening."

Fighters were engaged in battle all around us. The Battle Cruiser and her darker colored fighters were steering clear as were the Guardian's.

"Paul figured out what's going on," I said thankfully.

Dee was looking down at me with a scowl.

"What's the matter?" I asked, looking up.

"You took my seat."

"Really? Well, maybe you shouldn't have gotten up. Fine, you big baby." I stood, feeling the pilot stiffen as my thigh came in contact with his shoulder.

Dee looked like a kid let loose in Legoland as he sat down. I thought about going back and sitting with the lone Geno guard but he looked hungry and I didn't see a whole bunch of food on board. Dee began telling the pilot where to go as the other Geno guard standing beside me pointed.

"At what point will they start shooting?" I asked when we slid by the hangar.

"We can only hope they are distracted enough as to not consider us a priority or perhaps they believe us to be returning to the ship after suffering some damage." As if on cue a volley of incoming something struck the Cruiser on the far side.

"Thank you, Paul." He had launched the much-needed distraction.

"Agreed," Dee piped in.

We flew to the bottom of the ship. There were more gun emplacements but they seemed entirely too busy with the fighters whizzing around. The Geno guard tapped his former leader on the shoulder and pointed to where he wanted him to go. The pilot hissed in return. I thought for sure the guard was going to shove the stock of his rifle through the pilot's skull. Dee diffused the situation, though. I stepped away just in case. I'd be like a baby caught in between two pit bulls if they decided to go at it anyway.

It was a tense moment as the Breacher magnetized itself, or whatever it did, to the hull. Could have been super glue for all I knew. We could hear the torches or lasers I guess, doing their work and then the airlock was secured. I was heading for the door as the Geno guard wrapped an arm around me. For the briefest of moments I thought this was all some sort of ruse and the Earth Champion had finally been corralled. Then I let the egomaniac part of me go when I realized they had not a clue who I was.

Dee rose out of his chair and checked his rifle. "Michael, the depths with which you will go to get yourself harmed are almost limitless."

"You should see me with power tools," I retorted. "Could you call off the guard?" I asked, not even bothering to struggle with the iron arm around me. I didn't want the guard to know just how much stronger he was than me. He might regret his decision to fight with us if I did so.

"Michael, the Genogerians have no idea of what has transpired. If you were the first to walk through that door they would most assuredly kill you. The guard just saved your life."

"Well, I could have figured that out on my own. (Belatedly, was my internal thought.) Could you please thank him for me."

Dee did as I requested. The guard let me go and may have nodded at me as he did so. I noticed that he made sure to block my egress though, as if he didn't quite trust me. Smart Genogerian.

The two Genogerians stood shoulder to shoulder in the opening as I peeked around the lip of the airlock. There were at least a couple of dozen Genos with rifles in the corridor. The truly troubling part was the Devastators peppered among them. The two guards did not seem to be conveying their message clear enough because there was a lot of confusion on the regular Genos' faces and the Mutes seemed to be getting pissed off at the traitorous talk. That all changed when Dee showed his face.

I had no idea just how famous my friend had become. Almost every Geno, in the corridor, hushed down. I knew, to the word, what Dee was saying about living free, out from under the rule of their oppressive leaders. But to see just how swift a reaction it caused in the warriors was dumb-founding. It was amazing just how close to the surface their rebellion had been—that a few uttered words could sway them from nearly everything they had ever known for their entire lives.

I'd always known that the pen (or in this case - the spoken word) was mightier than the sword but sometimes you just don't really get to see it in that swift of an action. I guess it didn't hurt that Genogerians weren't duplicitous; there was no underlying hidden agenda in Dee's words. What he said was the truth and they would accept it as that. Anything human leaders said to their populaces was always taken with a grain of salt, and we would always look for what he or she really meant from the words that were spoken. That was something the Genos got right in their evolutionary tract. Although when Mrs. Geno asked if she looked fat in her armor...well that led to its own pitfalls.

The Geno rifles pointing at us were either going down, as they wrestled with this new promise, or up as they celebrated their impending freedom. The Devastators realized when the corner was turned, though, as one of them shot at Dee. The shot went wide and caught the guard in front of me. The heavy bolt cut completely through him and struck the back of the Breacher. The metal peeled back from the hit and I wondered just how many layers were left before the void of space was exposed. I did not want to be extruded through a hole no bigger than my fist. I'd look like human Play-Doh as I drifted off into the darkness.

The second guard was already shooting, with two of his shots striking his companion's killer. And, just like that, it was on. It looked like pro wrestling in that hallway as pairs, trios and even quads of combatants squared off. There were a few shots taken but for the most part it was all paw-to-paw combat. The Devastators held their own for a bit, but the far superior Geno numbers turned the tide quickly enough. It wasn't long before the Genogerians were lining up to honor and give praise to Dee. I was completely forgotten in the shuffle, except for the sidelong glance from time to time. I think they thought I was his pet or maybe his personal porter, I'm not sure.

It was the pilot that almost screwed everything up and I guess for good or bad got me noticed. I saw him get up from his chair to see what was happening and then just as quickly head back to his seat when he realized it had not gone as well as he'd hoped. I ran to the front as he was messing with buttons and controls. He was meaning to dislodge from the ship and kill everyone in that corridor. I think it was my shot neatly slicing off the side of his face that dissuaded him from his course of action. He slumped down, the top of his head smacking the wheel, or whatever you call a steering device in a spaceship. The Genos began to look at me like they'd seen me for the first time. Dee would later tell me that he then told them I was the Earth Champion come to liberate them. At the time, I did not know what the hissing and cheering were for.

First things first though, I suppose. We were knee deep in enemy territory and I didn't have the remotest clue on what to do. Communicating quickly was going to be difficult considering none of them spoke English. If Dee had been hit by that shot instead of the guard, besides losing my best friend, (which would have been horrible in its own right) I would have been trying to communicate complex battle plans with hand gestures and who knew if they would pay attention to me at all. The whole thing could have fallen apart right there and then. If I made it through the day, I was going to have Dee teach me how to speak his language. I wondered where I was going to find rocks that felt comfortable in my mouth.

For ease of writing in my journal or at least until I learn alien-speak, Tracy or Travis or whoever ends up reading this please realize that all communication still had to go through Dee. It's just easier to write it as thus.

"How many Devastators are on this ship?" I asked.

"Michael, I have already told you."

"Yeah, I just didn't like that answer. I was hoping if I asked again you might change it."

"Please do not pass too many of your traits on to your son."

"That's actually pretty good. Okay, so there's just somewhere south of five hundred Mutes after the Breachers were destroyed and only a couple hundred Genos. How many Progerians again?"

"Are you just not listening?"

I shook my head as Dee did his version of a sigh. It was fairly comical to see those huge shoulders sag.

"Best guess from my brethren is eight or nine hundred."

"What a strange displacement."

"This ship is designed to destroy from space or air, not ground. There is a lot of need to pilot the fighters and control this ship, including mechanics. The Devastators are used primarily for breaching and the Genogerians are here to do all the distasteful and dangerous jobs."

"Who knew the term 'illegal alien' would travel the

star ways."

"The Julipion, and ships like it, can patrol space for up to twenty years at a time, hence the need for so much personnel. When they discover a habitable planet they are merely there to enforce first rights."

"Yeah, I'll say. I just don't get why the scout ships wouldn't be smaller and faster. It seems like such a drain on resources to carry around that many beings everywhere."

"Many years ago it was like that but the cosmos are more populated than your people are willing to believe. When the Progerians realized their ships were being followed and the subsequent discoveries seized, they began to assemble Planet-Class Scout ships that could sustain themselves while also repelling nearly any attack. A scout ship is its own occupation force and colonization populace."

"A giant planted flag."

"Basically. The Battle Cruisers are built to beat a planet into submission, offering the necessary air support that the Julipion does not have."

"Why though? Why not make the scout ship an all-encompassing dirge? Not that I mind because it gave us more time to prepare but it doesn't make much sense from a tactical stand point."

"How many highly qualified pilots are in your populace?"

"Oh, I get it."

"There is still a need to protect our own home world and the Progerians can ill-afford to have these skilled pilots gone for two decades. Whereas the supply of ground troops is nearly limitless."

"So why not send them off? I'd really like to meet whoever is threatening the Progerians. You know, the whole "the enemy of my enemy is my friend" thing."

"The God-less are no one's friend. The Stryvers would turn on you the moment they encountered your kind. It is more likely you and the Progerians would strike an agreement against them."

"Holy shit! That is not a world I want to live on."

"And apparently neither do I or any of them. Now what, Michael Talbot? Your people await."

I looked over the growing number of Genogerians. Well, that's not necessarily true—I didn't really have a vantage point that I could look over them—but I could tell from the press that more were coming.

"Well, the bridge is as good a place as any."

"No," the Geno nearest me replied.

I'll be honest. I was thinking that I was about to die as the shortest rebellion ever recorded came to a halting conclusion.

"The bridge will be heavily guarded by Devastator troops and we do not have the numbers to win a sustained battle."

I eyed the brute, for what I don't know. Maybe I was looking for a sign of cowardice, although they had as much penchant for that as they did for lying.

"What about the nerve center?" Dee asked.

"Yeah, what he said. What the hell is the nerve center?" I asked, turning back to Dee.

"It is the junction spot for all the controls throughout the ship. It is housed as deep as it can be in an effort to protect it against damage in battle," Dee informed me.

"Is it guarded?" I asked my new hesitant friend.

The Progerians were more concerned with their personal safety, which made sense considering all I knew about them. What fear to their equipment did they have from two subservient sub-species that would have no access to it?

"Yes, but lightly. First I will need to gain a way to enter. I will need an access...(he struggled with the next word) card." That is how it was loosely, and I mean loosely, translated. I'll explain later. The Genogerian passed me by and went into the shuttle ship. He came out a minute or so later, I guess having found what he was looking for.

"Well lead on, Geronimo."

"My name is Trill."

"You had to tell him that last part?" I asked Dee. He'd told him about the Geronimo piece.

He was once again wearing a smile.

"Yeah, you're really a funny bastard. When we get home I'm going to tell Tracy you would like to change one of Travis's diapers."

Sheer terror rippled across Dee's face so much so that the Genos closest to us picked up on it, their jaws dropping in sympathetic stress. There was something about baby crap that scared the living hell out of him and I liked to tease him to no end about it. I was no fan of the stinky things myself but Dee had some sort of phobia in regards to it. I'd yet to test it on any others of his kind but it might be worth looking into. Who knows? Maybe the fear was part of their genetic make-up. We could possibly end this whole war with just a few strategically placed shitty diapers.

"I am deeply sorry that I have offended you," Dee said with a nod. The even funnier part was he meant it.

"I'll let it slide this time."

He looked relieved.

"Lead the way, Trill," I said as we made a path through the Genogerians so we could get out in front. The Genos were funny; they crowded close to get a look at Dee as he approached but backed up when they realized there was some little being by their feet. I felt like a mouse among a bunch of scared housewives. Sure they were scared, but being the mouse was no bargain either.

For all that had happened on this ship thus far I was in shock that alarms weren't going off. We'd breached the hull and had a small but intense skirmish in a hallway. Now I was leading a rebellion, yet everything seemed relatively calm even if a war was being waged inside and out.

"You are not supposed to be here Geno-scum!" shouted one of the Devastators as Trill and a couple others rounded the corner.

"Pecking order even among the dregs. Makes sense, though. No one wants to be low man on the totem pole, no matter how tall the damned thing is."

"Do you talk merely for the sake of pushing airwaves?" Dee asked.

I wondered if the Mutes understood the dig, but I did remain quiet while we waited to see how Trill's plan worked out.

"At least I am not altered from a lab," Trill taunted.

"Altered? I am enhanced! I am superior to you and your worthless kind in every way!" the Devastator's voice boomed.

"You are an abomination to all manner of living things," Trill replied.

I was concerned for Trill's well-being and was pretty sure he'd ruffled enough feathers to get a violent response. So when I heard heavy footfalls, it came as no surprise. Trill ran past our junction spot, his three possibly dumber than brave new enemies quickly in tow. The floor vibrated as the heavier and larger Mutes pursued. So focused on the pursuit they had nearly passed up our ambush before even noticing us. I know Dee would have preferred a peaceful solution but they were the Genogerian equivalent of Durgan.

I didn't feel bad for Durgan when I killed him and I sure as hell didn't care when I pulled the trigger repeatedly as the Mutes ran past. Blood sprayed across my face and down my throat as I yelled. I nailed one Mute across the thigh. The shot traveled deep enough that white bone was exposed for a moment before blood and tissue moved back into place. The smell of burnt skin dominated the small enclosure. As the Mute tried pivoting to get at me, I shot him in an approximation of where I figured his belly button should be. The bolt sliced along the front of his stomach, ribbons of intestines falling to the ground as his external casing was cut open. Still he had only one thought in mind, which was to get to me. He might possibly have succeeded if his legs hadn't gotten tangled up. My third shot blew open the top of his skull as he thudded to the ground no more than a foot or so away.

The two to his side suffered similar fates, though only one of them by my hand. I'd been so intent on killing the one I'd been shooting at that I nearly joined him as I stepped out into the open. A red bolt nearly separated my nose from the rest of me. It was so close I could literally smell the heat as it blazed by. My eyes must have been the same angry red as the discharge, because when I turned to look, the Mute paused for a moment. In reflection it probably had more to do with what he was looking at. Odds were huge he'd never seen a human before. I heard Dee shout "NO!" I raced towards the brutish guard anyway, my gun firing wildly as I ran. Bolts blew all around him, even a few into him. I may have surprised the guard but he was no fool; he was matching me shot for shot. The only advantages I had was that I'd hit him early on and with me being so much smaller, I was a difficult target.

The Mute's head had no sooner hit the deck than the alarm sounded.

"Fool!" Dee shouted, coming up behind me.

I figured he was angry because I'd somehow set off the alarm.

"How will I ever tell your mate if you were to die on this ship?"

Trill had turned back, caught up and passed us just as I was about to tell Dee I was all right.

"We must hurry before they seal the access!" He kept running.

I was expecting some giant door to come slamming down and we were going to have to do some cool Indiana Jones sliding type stuff just before the door tried to crush my skull. Now that I'm really thinking about it, it sounds way cooler watching it on the big screen, rather than potentially living it. Trill hit something on the wall and a small panel slid down. Without a ladder and a personal jet pack I could not get high enough to see what was there. Best I could figure was a slot for the security card. At least that was what I thought right up until he pulled out an eyeball still attached to about a foot long section of optic nerve. Can't tell you how happy I was that it'd been a few hours since I'd last eaten.

When the hell was that? Breakfast with Tracy and Travis on Earth seemed about a month ago. I was expecting to see blue laser lines as Trill held the eyeball up.

"Retina scan," Dee elaborated.

"Yeah I got that. Where's the laser beams? Should I ask where he got it? Forget it. Knowing your species' propensity for violence, why wouldn't the designers of that security device somehow make sure that the eye it is scanning is attached to a living body?"

"I could ask the same of your security designers. And there are no lasers Michael, why would anyone want to have a laser shot into their eye?"

"Yeah, well, I guess that's true."

"It is an unspeakable thing for a Genogerian to commit a crime against a Progerian. It just doesn't happen."

"Well at least not without a little prodding. I'm still amazed the Progerians are still as clueless as to just how willing the Genogerians are to rebel."

"My former masters are only concerned with my former masters. The hunt for more resources along with fending off the Stryvers leaves little time for other distractions."

There was a low humming and then a foot thick blast door rose up into the ceiling. Trill ushered us in and I quickly stepped over the threshold. If that thing came down as fast as it went up it would get messy soon.

"Even Indy wouldn't fuck with that," I mumbled.

"What, Michael?" Dee asked.

"Nothing. Holy shit," I said as I looked at the room. It

was huge, like the size of a decent super market, and it glowed in a variety of iridescent colors, from violet, blue, yellow, red, orange and green. What looked like servers lined one whole wall. Cables as thick as my thigh were running along the ceiling like streets on a map. I could feel the hair on the back of my neck beginning to stand from all the juice that was flowing around this place. There were some video screens and work stations near us as we entered.

"This place runs the ship?" I asked Trill.

"It is the bridge that runs the ship but everything comes through here."

"Can they re-route past this?"

"Re-route?"

"The Earth Champion wishes to know if we disable functions here is there any other way our former masters can restore functionality."

"The way I said it was easier."

"The way I said it will get a response."

"No," Trill answered. "There is no other way."

"Do you know how to take the weapons system offline?" I asked. It was worth a shot, but the fact that Trill knew as much about this place as he did was already a bonus. There was no way he would have that sort of technical expertise.

"I do not."

"Michael, the smell of it is coming off of you in waves…you cannot just randomly shoot up this room. There is a possibility you could permanently cut off life support."

My first response would have been, "Awesome". Then I realized Dee and I were still here. I still had no great love for other Genos, Mutes and especially Progs.

"Now what? Because we've already burned through a lot of time and we need to help out the Guardian and get off this bucket. There might only be one way in but that means there's only one way out and I really don't want to be trapped in here."

Dee went over to look at the markings on the monitors and panels. A small murmur went up among the Genos.

"What's got them all excited?" I asked, coming alongside.

"It is unusual that one of my kind can read."

"Oh, I could agree with that assessment. It's kind of like going to the zoo and seeing an elephant open up type. Can you imagine the reaction that would get?"

"I used to think you were funny," Dee said as he sat.

Chapter Six - Paul

"We cannot take too many more hits like that." Iserwan had just righted himself in his chair.

"What is Mike up to? Whatever it is he'd better do it soon." Paul was wiping the blood off the side of his head where he'd struck the corner of the station he was trying to hold onto. He extended his hand to help Beth up. She had a trickle of blood coming from her mouth where she'd bit her lip.

"Do you think he's still alive?"

Paul really had no idea because he'd lost sight of the Breacher that Mike had hijacked. He'd put the word out to his fighters to not attack, but even all those eyes in the sky had lost sight in the maelstrom. As more and more of the Guardian fighters fell to the superior firepower of the Battle Cruiser, the heavily armed ship was able to divert more armament the Guardian's way. At this point they were trading punch for punch at a rate at which the Guardian would not be able to sustain for very much longer.

"General, I suggest we engage the buckle drive," Iserwan stated.

Paul knew that to do so would leave the fighters and Mike at the mercy of the Battle Cruiser and last he'd checked that ship had been mighty low on that particular trait.

"Can we recall the fighters?"

"There won't be enough time and they are all that stands between us and the Cruiser following immediately. If we depart now we may have a chance to escape."

"What of Earth? Should we leave it to its own devices as well?" Paul spun, looking at the ship's commander.

"We will do no one any good if we are strewn about this galaxy."

"Five minutes Iserwan, just give it five minutes more."

"What will change, General?"

"It's just something Mike told me once. He said if you are waiting for something and have finally come to the point that you will wait no longer, add five minutes from there. Something about you being able to pick up on the universe aligning itself. More times than not what you are waiting for will come to pass in that time frame. Personally, I think he's smoked too much pot but damned if it doesn't work."

Four minutes and three barrages later, damage reports began to flood in from all areas of the ship. A fair portion of the structure was on fire or exposed to the hostile elements of deep space. Paul was rapidly losing faith in Mike's assumptions.

"Iserwan. Time?" Paul asked. The Commander had been marking time for the departure.

"Four minutes, twenty-four seconds."

"Shit."

"Sir?" Iserwan begged to give the order.

"Thirty more seconds," Paul said through gritted teeth.

"Respectively, General, we don't have thirty seconds. As it is, we may not survive a buckle jump with the ship damaged to this extent."

"Then it has been my honor to serve alongside you, Iserwan."

"Paul, what are you saying?" Beth was looking up at

him.

"Ten, nine, eight..." The drive operator was counting down.

"I love you Beth and maybe you love me a little bit, at least I hope. It's no secret to me that you've always wanted to be with Mike. Maybe it's best this way."

"Three, two..."

"HOLD!" Paul shouted.

"General, your five minutes has now elapsed. If we want to have any chance of survival we must depart now."

"Iserwan, stop for a second. When was the last time the Cruiser shot at us?"

"One minute twenty-two."

"And what was the rate of fire beforehand."

Iserwan's damage control officer spoke. "Every forty nine seconds and increasing in frequency."

The bridge was tense those next couple of minutes. Paul figured he was going to need to see his dentist from clenching his teeth so hard when he got back Earth side. He eased up a bit, finally letting go of the board. "The son of a bitch did it," he said quietly and laced with hope, although he was not entirely convinced.

Beth was crying.

"Well this makes my admission awkward, doesn't it?"

Beth ran off the bridge.

"They've stopped shooting at our fighters!" the radar operator said.

"Should I target the Cruiser?" Iserwan asked.

"Absolutely not. My best friend is still on that thing. But blow those fucking fighters up!"

Chapter Seven – Mike Journal Entry 04

"I wonder if that worked?" Dee and I were staring at the destroyed remnants of the work station that was labeled "weapons."

"I, perhaps, could have figured it out in a few more moments had you not shot it up."

"Dee, the Guardian may have not had a few minutes, and besides, we can't stay here. Once we left, how long would it have taken the techs on this ship to turn it back on?"

"Valid points Michael, but your 'destroy first, ask questions later' attitude could at some point prove detrimental."

"My mom used to say something like that, I mean not with all the fancy words and it used to involve a backhand or two but something like that. If you could find the one for the ship's drive that would be fantastic."

"It is the station two over from you but..."

I blew a series of holes through it. The lights immediately flickered, went out and were replaced by a soft glow that emanated out from the walls themselves.

"I did not quite realize that my words would be so prophetic and so quickly."

"What's the matter?" I asked.

"Much like an Earth automobile, all of the systems on this ship are operated from the power of the drive, from a fully functional operating drive."

"Umm *all* of the functions?"

"Yes, Michael." Dee did a very human gesture as he sat and placed his massive head in his massive hands. I thought about going over and consoling him while rubbing his back but he looked über pissed off and I didn't want to get too particularly close.

I waited what I figured was an appropriate time. A good ten seconds at least. "How are the glow lights operating?"

"It is like a battery but more of a capacitor that has stored power and is now releasing it to be used for essential functions like scrubbing the air."

"How much time do we have?"

"Sixteen, possibly eighteen hours."

"Aw hell, that's plenty of time to figure out how to get off this ship."

A deep pounding began to resound off our exit door as troops on the other side looked for a way to get in. It would only take one officer who could access this room and we'd be in the midst of a firefight we could not win. To disable the door, though, gave us no way out. It was death by suffocation or death by bolt. Whereas the firefight was much more glorious, dignified and quicker, once we were out of the way there was a good chance the Progs would be able to get all the systems back on line in a relatively short time. I could not allow that.

"Trill, disable the door."

He nodded once, understanding the implications. The pounding stopped a few minutes later, to be replaced by a Progerian officer demanding we open the door. Once that stopped, the pounding began anew, but whatever that door was made out of was pretty stout. It sounded like hammering from a city block away. It wasn't much of a distraction. Only when I thought about who was trying to get in did I get a shiver up my spine. For the most part, my group had come to terms with their lot in life. I was sitting in a chair with my feet propped up; occasionally closing my eyes to see what picture shows were on the back of my eyelids. Dee was pretty much in prayer mode—he had a few of the Genos around him, some who still practiced in secret and others that wanted to know what the forbidden ritual was all about.

Still others were talking animatedly. They looked excited and somewhat happy if I knew anything about the species. It mattered not to them that they were going to die soon, they'd come to terms with that thought from their earliest memories. They'd been taught they were nothing more than a tool for the Progerians, and when their usefulness was done so were their lives. Under Progerian rule dying was easy enough. Living was the hard part. Now that they had a small taste of freedom (ironic considering we were trapped - but that's just perspective I suppose) they were going to enjoy it.

Chapter Eight - The Guardian

All was silent. The Guardian fighters with help from their mother ship had quickly defeated the Battle Cruiser's fleet. What was left had slunk back to their own hangar.

"It's been four hours. Why haven't we heard anything from him?" Paul asked, more to himself. No one within earshot had an answer.

"How is it possible that he disabled a Battle Cruiser?" Iserwan asked and not for the first time.

"No clue but I don't put too much past him."

"It is not possible. How could one human disable an entire Battle Cruiser? Nothing like this has ever happened."

"Do you doubt one man's resolve, Iserwan?" Paul was looking for something in the alien's features. Iserwan had told Paul flatly that he would not fight his own kind when the time came. That he would only command the ship as it was being rebuilt. Paul wondered for a moment what Iserwan might have done had he not been on the ship for the press tour. Iserwan had given his word he would no longer fight against the humans but would handing over the Guardian have broken that promise?

"I do not know what to think. There have been many times over the last few years I have wished we had never found your planet."

"Why did you engage in battle, Iserwan? Certainly it

wasn't to protect Earth."

Iserwan paused long and hard, his gaze fixed on Paul. "I do not like humans. You are savage little beasts. I think the universe would be far better off with your kind extinct or under dominion. I fear I have done a great evil by allowing this ship to remain intact. I have given an intergalactic ship to a species that I believe will make the Progerians rule look like an act of kindness."

"Then why, Iserwan? Do you fear death?"

Iserwan 'hurrumphed' and stirred in his seat, looking somewhat agitated. "It is not my death so much as it is the chance that I may never see my family again. Although I am already a traitor twice over to my people, my mate and children will want nothing to do with me and will need to distance themselves as far as possible just to survive. It would have been far better for me to have died in vain I suppose. I have made their lives that much more difficult."

Paul wanted to argue that Iserwan had a jaded view of humanity if he was just going off of what he'd seen in the arena battles, but human history was strife with conflict, betrayal and murder. Odds were that if they could repel this attack that mankind would indeed strike out on a quest to colonize other planets and it would not be benign exploration like in *Star Trek*. "Iserwan, you did not do a completely selfish act. You, in part, did what you did to protect the lives of the pilots under you, to give them an opportunity to live out the rest of their lives."

"In virtual prison."

"It's more than you would have allowed us. I do not harbor much love for your kind either, Iserwan. You came to my planet unannounced and uninvited and threatened to take everything from us. If I didn't need your help as bad as I did, you'd be down in Florida with the rest of your kind."

Iserwan stood, for a moment appearing as if he was going to let the words instill a red-hot anger into the pit of his heart. He then sat back down, looking deflated. "You are right. No matter your faults, they are yours to work out independent of outside rule. We have no right. It was once, not so long ago, that we would not interfere with sentient beings. The Stryvers changed that, though. They cared little for any populace and we could not afford to let them gain too many resources."

"Keeping up with the Stryvers? Now that's rich."

"I do not understand the reference."

"Incoming message," interrupted the communications officer.

"Put it over the speaker," Iserwan told him.

"Ummm, big ass Battle Cruiser to whoever is listening, hopefully the Guardian. Can you hear me?"

"Mike, is that you?" Paul asked.

"Hey Paulie! How you doing?" Mike asked excitedly. "Great to hear a friendly voice!"

"Is not my voice friendly?" Dee growled behind Mike.

"You keep working on that tone." Mike turned his head.

"Mike...Mike?"

"Yeah sorry, the natives are surly over here."

"You alright?"

"We are for now...not sure for how long though. We've got enemy at the gates so to speak. Sure could use a little help."

"Name it, Mike."

"Any chance you could beam us over?"

"Like in *Star Trek*?" Paul asked. Paul looked over to Iserwan. "Can we?"

"I do not understand 'beam us over,' " Iserwan said, confused.

"You would tear apart a person to the molecular level wherever they are, have them travel across a beam of light and then reconfigure them in a portal on this ship."

"You have that kind of technology?" Iserwan asked.

"That is incredible. Why have I not seen it before?"

"Ah Mike, I'm going to go with a 'no' on the beaming you aboard."

"Shit. Thought so, figured it was worth a try."

"Could you give me an idea what's going on over there?" Paul sat, staring intently at the box, waiting for Mike to speak.

"We got to the nerve center of the ship."

"Brilliant," Iserwan interjected quietly.

"I was able to destroy the weapons and because of Drababan's tardiness I also took out the life support systems."

"Not so brilliant," Iserwan stated.

"You dare to blame me for your impetuous actions?" Dee bellowed.

"Well I'm sure as hell not going to blame myself. Maybe next time I'm in a highly sensitive area you'll act a little quicker, instead of lollygagging about."

"Perhaps I should take that weapon away from you and bend you over my knee..."

"Boys! This is General Ginson. Can we get back on track here?"

"Sorry, General. He started it," Mike stated.

"I will destroy you," Dee rumbled.

"I won't say it again!" Paul shouted.

There was silence, Paul knew without a shadow of a doubt Mike had just stuck out his tongue at Dee and Dee had returned the middle finger—a gesture which he had just recently learned and thought hilarious to use. Inwardly Paul smiled. "How can we help, Mike?"

"Well that's the tricky part, buddy. We're in the middle of this tin can with a bunch of hostiles trying to gain access through the only entry or exit point. We do not have the forces to repel them should they make it through. I'm really calling so I can pass on some final messages."

"Don't you fucking dare, Talbot. I will not sit here

and listen to your Swan Song. How many do you estimate to be at the doors?"

"All of them I would imagine."

"A number, Mike. A fucking number. Why do you always have to be a smartass?"

"Hey man, I'm stressed out, sarcasm helps me cope."

"Why don't you just drink like everybody else?"

"Four or five hundred or thereabouts."

"How much air time do you have? And if you say something like 'until my last breath' I'm going to come over there and kick your ass myself."

"Well I was going to say twelve hours but your answer is pretty good as well."

Paul sharply sucked in some air through his teeth.

"Well that certainly did not sound good." Mike said.

"Iserwan, could we land shuttles with troops in their hangar?"

"We could certainly land the shuttles but little else. They are heavily guarded with nearly impenetrable embattlements. The personnel and resources we would expend on the endeavor would not be worth the rescue."

"How about you let me weigh the scales," Paul chided the Commander. "Maybe I'll just send up shuttles loaded with Progerians and we'll see what happens."

"Boys, boys!" Mike exclaimed. "When you're done, there are some things I would like to say to my wife and child if that is at all possible. Could you maybe get Tracy on the line?"

Beth had taken this inopportune time to come back onto the bridge, her eyes puffy from crying. "He's alive?"

"Don't get your hopes up, it won't be for long," Paul said sourly. He was angry with himself for his pettiness but he was about to lose his best friend and he now realized the false premise upon which his marriage was built.

"How could you?" Beth asked.

Neither Paul nor Mike knew to whom she was

speaking.

"Mike, I am going to get you out of there."

"Buddy, I appreciate the sentiment, I truly do and I more hope you're right. But just in the off chance that I somehow find myself dead in the next few hours I would really like the opportunity to talk to my family."

"You've got it. Give me a second so we can make a connection."

"You planning on breathing down my back like that, Dee? I'm getting soaked in your exhalation."

"I also wish to speak to my Godchild."

Paul had tried his best to not take offense when Mike asked if he would share co-God parent rights with Drababan. He'd almost let his prejudice get the best of him and just tell Mike that Drababan could be the sole heir and then had thought better of it.

"Sir, we're ringing through to her home line now," the communications officer said to Iserwan.

"Any chance of some privacy?" Mike asked.

As Paul looked to the comm, the officer shook his head. "That's a negative, Mike."

"Well, so much for my man-card. Although I won't have to live with my shame for long."

The chiming ring echoed throughout the now silent bridge. Tracy's apprehensive voice answered. "Hello?"

"Hey, baby," Mike responded.

There was an audible sigh of relief. "You're alright. I was so worried. The news is reporting on a huge battle going on up there. You can even see it with the naked eye."

"I'm okay for now, hon."

"For now?" A waver shimmered her voice.

"I've got myself in sort of a pickle."

"What's happening, Mike, and how serious is it?"

"A Progerian Battle Cruiser showed up. We were going to get our asses kicked and I made an executive decision."

"Spill it, Mike, don't sugar coat it."

"The Progs have these things called Breachers that rip through the hulls of ships. Well, I sort of borrowed one and went into the Battle Cruiser."

"Oh, Mike."

"We disabled the ship, hon. We won the day."

"At what price, Mike?"

Mike paused. "I'm so sorry hon, I'm so sorry to you and Travis. I don't think we're going to be able to get out of here."

"What is it with you saving the world?" she hitched as she spoke the words. She was on the verge of tears.

"It's sort of my thing. I guess I've been typecast."

"You said 'we'. Who's with you?"

"Dee and a bunch of new Genogerian recruits. Tantor died today."

"Drababan can't get you out of there?"

"If I could, Tracy, know that I would," Dee said.

For the first time since the call began Tracy sobbed.

"What is it? What's wrong?" Mike begged.

"I...I just know it's bad now. That's the first time in the three years Drababan has known me that he's used my first name."

"I have enjoyed my time with Travis, please tell him that his Uncle Drababan loves him very much."

"Do you mind? This is kind of my time to say goodbye. You're stealing my thunder."

"I am merely making sure that my feelings are expressed while they still can be. I do not want things unsaid when I go to meet Gropytheon."

"Are you done then? I'd really like to talk now."

"Tracy, your company has been enjoyable as well. I wish to express my gratitude to you for always opening your door to me. I know that you have not always harbored good tidings for me and it is a reflection of your character that you were able to overcome that."

"You're really not going to let me get a word in edgewise are you? Friggen lizard."

"I do not think this is a time to get personal, simian."

"You have got to be kidding me!" Paul interjected.

"Just how many people are on this call, Mike?" Tracy tearfully asked.

"Well, let's see, I'm sure the bridge of this Battle Cruiser. What, Dee? He says definitely, the Guardian bridge is also here and then I've got Dee so I'd say we've pretty much fleshed out a decent sized party line."

Tracy was silent as she collected her thoughts.

"Tracy, I've never loved anyone like I've loved you. Everything seemed to fall into place that first time we met."

"I wanted to shoot you the first time we met, Mike."

"Well, see? We got past that! And then when I found out you were pregnant, I can't even begin to tell you how great I felt inside."

"Is that why almost the very next day you once again went on a mission to save the planet?"

"It's what I do. You knew what you were getting into the day you said 'I do'."

"I did, oh God I did. I sometimes feel like our love burned so brightly because it was going to be a short-lived flame. I've cherished every moment we've shared together, Mike."

"Tracy, I can't afford to cry right now. There are way too many people listening. My man-card would be revoked."

"Your human trait of letting salt water flow through your tear ducts is a perfectly acceptable form of communication right now, Michael. With the heightened levels of stress in you, it would be a beneficial release."

"Don't you have a remote village somewhere you can terrorize?" Mike asked.

"I do not know how you have lived with him these three long years, Tracy," Dee stated. "It must have been as close to your Hell as was possible on Earth." He walked over to the console next to Mike and sat down heavily in a chair.

"Is Travis there?"

"He's with your father. They went out for ice cream and he spent the evening at his home."

Now it was Mike's turn to sob when he realized he would not get some final words with his son. "Will...will you tell him that his daddy loves him very much and that I will keep a watch out for him, for both of you?"

"Tracy, we are under the gun here. I'm sorry, that was a poor choice of words," Paul apologized. "I have no intention of letting Mike die today or any day in the foreseeable future. I'm going to end this call so we can see about bringing him home."

"Please don't let me down, Paul," she pleaded.

"Wait, so you have a plan and yet you let me get all soft in front of a full audience?"

"Shut up, Mike. I am going to get you out of there. Tracy, do not tell Travis anything that you will have to recant."

"Well, fantastic. Dee says he wants anchovies on his pizza."

"You know I do not like those little fish—they are entirely too salty. Pepperoni, however, would be nice."

"Well, my love, according to the General we should be home for dinner. In the off chance that I am late, will you wait for me?"

"You know the answer to that. Mike, please don't leave me. I don't want to do this alone."

"I'll be with you always in one form or another."

There were loud crashes over the line.

"What's happening, Mike?" Paul asked with alarm.

"General, perhaps it would be wise to continue this call at a later time," Dee said.

"Mike..." Tracy was cut off.

"It seems our hosts are adamant about rooting out their pest problem. They're cutting through the door, Paul.

We're seeing the sparks on our side."

"Iserwan, what is the ETA on the shuttles?"

Iserwan looked at his screens. "The shuttles have just finished loading up and should be here in a matter of hours."

"I don't know what you were planning, buddy, but I can guarantee you we don't have hours. Dee thinks they'll be through the door in under one."

"Fuck. Iserwan, give me an open channel with the wing commander of the fighters."

"It is yours," Iserwan spoke after a few moments. "His name is Captain Taggert."

"Captain Taggert, this is General Ginson aboard the Guardian. Can you hear me?"

"Four by four, General," the Captain responded.

"I want to thank you for your fine work today, although we're not quite done."

"Lost a lot of good men and Genogerians today, sir."

"I realize that Captain and they will be mourned and celebrated in due time. Right now I'm trying to save a few more from having to be celebrated and mourned."

"The ones aboard the Breacher, sir?"

"Yes, they were able to disable the ship but now they're trapped in it and I'm going to need some help convincing the Cruiser to let them go."

"Just let me know what I need to do, sir."

"I want you to get about ten fighters arranged around the bridge of their ship and then just keep your channel open. We'll see what happens from there."

"Aye aye, sir."

Chapter Nine - Mike Journal Entry 05

"Hey, Mike? You still there, buddy?" Paul asked.

"Yeah, I've got nothing else going on right now."

"Any way you can give comm back to the bridge?"

I'm sure Paul could hear some murmured talking in the background as I asked Dee if this was possible.

"Dee thinks that may be a bad idea. They might be able to get off a distress signal or something, or possibly a warning to those coming behind them."

"Shit, okay can you relay messages then?"

"Dee shrugged."

"Could you maybe get a clearer response from him?"

"Okay, he thinks so."

"Mike, my plan hinges on being able to talk to the bridge."

"Alright Paul, Dee believes he has tapped...(there was a loud squelching sound that made everyone within earshot cover their ears)...yup he's definitely in the intercom system. Nice one, big guy. I will never get over how funny it looks when a Geno flips me the bird."

"Mike," Paul said with no small measure of exasperation.

"Sorry."

"Okay, have Dee translate for me. Battle Cruiser, this is the UE Guardian."

There was a moment as Drababan spoke the words, then the loud surprised grunting of the Cruiser's commanding officers, followed by what sounded like a litany of swears. Again for ease of relating this story I will forego having to mention that everything said here needed to go through a clearinghouse to be translated.

"This is Battle Cruiser Gount. Who is this? We demand that you give control of our ship back to us immediately!"

"Damn, they sound pissed." Even before I got the actual meaning of the words it was not difficult to tell what was going on by the tone.

"Shut up! I am in charge here!" Paul bellowed. "My name is General Ginson and I am in command of the United Earth Guardian."

I did a small fist pump. "Go get 'em, man," I said softly.

One thing the Progerians can understand is authority; they were not quite so gruff the next time they responded even if it still sounded like a bunch of expletives coming over the speakers.

"We require the knowledge of what has happened to the Supreme Commander of the Julipion, Vallezt."

"He was delicious," Paul retorted.

I had to move away from the microphone so that the sounds of my laughing would not be heard, although in reality they really wouldn't even know what that sound meant.

The shock and outrage on the bridge of the Gount was evident as the officers talked animatedly.

"Now you will listen to me. Your kind came to my planet with the intent of taking it over by hostile force. We have since taken over your Scout Ship Julipion and decided to make it ours. We have destroyed your mutated Genogerian Devastators and imprisoned your Genogerians. The Progerians that survived *our* hostile takeover have been allowed sanctuary upon our planet."

'Good one, buddy,' I thought. He was giving them an out. Without one they would have no reason to capitulate to his demands. "Paul, our hosts are making some serious headway. If you've got an idea you might want to play that card soon," I said as an aside.

"We have now rendered your ship useless while also implanting an explosive device that will destroy you."

"You did not contact us just to let us know. What do you want?"

"I would rather have your ship and the men I still have onboard it intact."

Dee turned to me after making the translation. Softly, he said, "I would have believed that at least *you* would have been at the forefront of his request."

"It's a display of power. He doesn't want to look weak in the eyes of the Progerians. He needs to make us look almost like an afterthought. Getting this ship would be a boon." And that got me thinking—maybe, just maybe, there was a part of Paul that was thinking just that. I decided not to dwell on it.

"We will soon have your men and they will be dead or in captivity. Our ship will be online and then we will destroy you while we await for our Destroyers to come!"

"Captain Taggert, open fire."

I could feel the Cruiser rocking back and forth from the blows. It was a full minute or so before Paul gave the order to cease fire.

"Do you believe you can do all of the things you presented to me *before* I destroy your ship?"

It was difficult to hear the Progerians response over the blaring sound of klaxons. A bolt of red blew past me. As close as it was to me it was nothing compared to Dee, whose tunic got singed.

"Defensive positions!" I shouted. We returned fire to the Devastators that were trying to gain entry. It was a small hole that opened up but enough to send rifle blasts in.

"What's going on?" Paul demanded.

"Taking fire, Paul."

"Battle Cruiser Gount, you will remove your

personnel that are attempting to enter the nerve center of your ship or the next time I tell my Captain to open fire on your bridge, I will not have him stop until molten pieces of you are drifting away into space. You have until the count of three."

I nailed the rifle barrel of the one shooting at us. Hopefully I was able to take off a couple of his fingers as well. When he pulled back, two more fought their way to the access point and still whoever was attempting to torch their way in was still at work.

"ONE!" Paul shouted.

Two Genogerians off to my side fell over as they took mortal wounds.

"TWO!"

The firefight was intensifying. I could only hope that it was because they only had one more second to do so.

There was shouting beyond the door. The Devastators shooting at us turned. It sounded like there were a few shots being fired out there as well. I decided to add as much chaos into the maelstrom as was possible.

"Michael, what are you doing?" Dee asked as he rose up from behind his place of concealment. I was heading for the rift in the door. I was nearly touching the backsides of the soldiers as I placed the barrel of my rifle through the hole. I began pulling that trigger as fast as my finger would go. Even the Devastators started running away from the destruction I was causing. From this close of range I could not miss as the bolts sliced into and through the soldiers whose armored plating was only protecting their fronts. Their backs were exposed and suffering my full wrath. Flesh and organs alike shone on the floor as I nearly covered it in alien viscera.

"Mike, what's going on?" Paul asked before he got to the decisive three.

"Michael, stop," Dee said as he gently placed his large hand on my shoulder.

"Nobody, Dee. Nobody is going to stop me from

seeing my family again," I said, looking up to him. I must have had a pretty intense or insane glaze to my features because even he backed up a step.

"General, they have evacuated the corridor," Dee replied for me as I regained some semblance of control. "We will still require assistance in exiting this room."

"Got that part under control, Drababan. Is Mike alright?"

"General, he is unharmed physically."

I took note that he avoided my mental state. Paul did not pick up on it.

"You two hold tight. I have the Calvary on the way."

"I do not know where he thinks we could go," Dee said to me.

"Still here and I think that you've been around Mike too much. I have shuttles with troops coming. I'll have you out of there in a few hours. Out for now, call me if you need anything."

"I'm better now," I told him. "Could you tell a couple of the Genogerians to keep an eye on that hole to make sure none of our hostile friends come back?"

The Genogerians that got guard duty looked back at me with concern when they got to the hole and saw the damage I had wrought.

"Ahh, Michael, look at you. Winning friends and influencing people wherever you go," Dee said when he noticed the same nervousness. "If they were not completely convinced of my words earlier they will be now."

One by one the Genos in the room would go up to the hole, take a good long look, and then look over to me. Some would put their hand to their head and bow; others would put as much distance as they could find in the confines we found ourselves in.

"Do you think the commander will capitulate?"

"Are you asking if they will allow the shuttles to land and rescue us?"

I nodded.

"I do not see what their options are. Progerians are not very much into personal sacrifice of their well-being. We put them in a powerless position and they are as angry as rabid dogs, yet I do not see a way in which they can prosper by not letting us off this ship. It is possible they believe they can fix this damage quickly and still destroy the Guardian or hide until help arrives in the form of the heavier Destroyers."

"You know we can't just leave this ship, right? The Guardian isn't a match for this thing and they have bigger ones coming."

"Letting us out of here so that they can repair and continue their mission is one thing. Handing over this ship is another. They will have a self-destruct installed in case they are afraid that it could fall into enemy hands. It is generally reserved for an abandon ship order so that the technology cannot fall into the hands of others, but I do believe if they were pushed to the brink they would execute the order to destroy themselves and all aboard it."

"We are going to have to take that chance, Dee."

"Undoubtedly."

"So you're with me?"

"I have answered this question before, Michael. I may not always agree with your particular plans but I will always be by your side while I can be."

"Is there any way to disable the self-destruct from here?"

"If we had the codes perhaps, but without them I fear we would only succeed in initiating the countdown prematurely."

"Not much good comes from the word 'premature'."

"I know that you have a second meaning associated with that response, but I as of yet have not discerned it."

"Maybe we should just leave that one alone. We're walking a fine line now. I am torn between wanting to destroy everything in here beyond repair and wanting to temporarily disable it so it's still usable when we take it to use against the Destroyers."

"Mike, you there?" Paul asked.

"Not sure where else I'd be," I answered a little peevishly. "Sorry man, I just get real apprehensive when I get trapped on alien spaceships."

Paul completely blew me off. "Mike, we need that ship."

I didn't say anything for a bit. "Yeah I know. What's your plan? And before you answer that are you sure we have a closed connection?"

"That I don't know but I don't think it matters much. They can't understand what we're saying."

"Dee, do you agree with that?"

"I would. The Julipion studied your Earth languages for weeks before deciphering them."

"Just so you know, you need to factor in a self-destruct into anything you have planned."

"Well, that makes it much more interesting."

I wanted to rage at him. "Interesting" was how he put placing our lives in danger. "I guess that's one way to put it."

"Paul, you can't seriously be suggesting this. You need to get him out of there." It was Beth's voice. She was putting a lot of strain on Paul's and my relationship. Shit, she was probably half the reason why he wanted to try this. No, that's not fair. We did need this ship. I was one life against the weight of the world.

"Beth, this is a military operation, and the last time I checked you did not wear a uniform." Paul told her curtly.

"No sex for him tonight," I whispered to Dee.

"That is a very juvenile response to a very serious matter, Michael," Dee admonished me.

"What's that, Drababan?" Paul asked.

"Nothing, General. We were discussing tactics," Dee told him.

"Nice save."

"I will not do it again."

"Party crasher."

"Mike, I have two hundred plus rescuers coming your way."

"We'll still be outmanned and that fucking bomb is a game changer."

"Can you get any local help?"

"The Genos are a minority here. The ship is dominated by Devastators and Progerians, neither of which is going to change sides any time soon."

"Mike."

"I know, I know, we still need to try. I should have eaten that second piece of french toast Tracy made for me. Dee, can you set up the intercom to broadcast throughout the ship?"

"What do you mean to do?"

"I want you to convince the Genos on board that they should side with us."

"It is a risky maneuver, Michael. The Progerians will have the Devastators descend on the Genogerians in a moment's notice if they believe there is some form of mutiny."

"Dee, I would not put your people in harm's way unnecessarily. The price of freedom, however, is a rather steep one. You yourself have told me that you would rather die than live one more moment under Progerian rule. Do you not think we should give the rest of your brothers and sisters the same choice?"

"How can you go from wise-ass to wise in a matter of moments, Michael?"

"It's a talent," I told him with a lopsided grin.

"There will be much blood spilled today I believe, in the name of freedom."

"Better than in the name of religion I suppose. Paul, how long until the shuttles get here?"

"Shouldn't be more than a couple of hours."

"Sure wish I had a deck of cards or something."

"When do you wish me to make my attempt?" Dee asked.

"Let's wait until the shuttles arrive so that they can at least have a safe haven should they decide to join with us."

The intercom crackled and then harsh alien speak came through. Dee's features immediately changed to extreme anger. I looked over to the Genos who were with us. They were looking around at each other. Some displayed anger but most looked absolutely terrified.

"Dee?"

He stood, flipping over the console, sheering heavy bolts in half as he did so. He roared. I'd not seen him so enraged since he'd been trying to kill me and I was just as nervous now as I was then.

"Dee, talk to me, man." I made sure not to get too close lest he lash out. He could break me in half without even trying.

"They have rounded up the Genogerians, Mike!" he raged. "They plan on slaughtering them like cattle unless we leave this area."

"Paul, you hearing this?"

"Loud and unfortunately clear," he acknowledged.

"We have got to help them!" Dee demanded, his eyes wild.

"Dee, I get it, I do, but we can't get out of here and even if we did, what then? Forfeiting our lives will do them no good."

"Would you be so cavalier if it was your people?" he demanded.

"That's not fair, Dee. We're in a no-win situation right now."

"I will tear this ship in two!" he said in English then louder in his native tongue.

He was rewarded with the sound coming over the speaker of a plasma gun being discharged. I had to imagine it was at the kneeling form of a Genogerian. Dee moved quickly to the door and began to hammer on it.

He did this for a few moments, his fists turning bloody and then he leaned his head up against the metal.

"Michael." He turned to me.

I had the distinct impression he was recanting all he had sworn to me and was now going back over to the dark side so that he could save his brethren.

"Whoa, buddy. Hold on, man. I'm really not liking the way you're looking at me." I had my rifle at my side and was thinking about pulling it up so I could get an accurate shot off if the need arose. Would I be able to get twenty clean shots off though? As soon as I hit Dee, the shaky alliance I had with the Cruiser Genos would be off. I'd never be able to convey a message to them to save my ass.

He advanced, I gripped my rifle tighter. When he spoke I wished he'd just killed me because it would have been easier and cleaner.

"You will fit through the hole."

I let go of my rifle. "What?" I asked, standing straight and cocking my head to the side like a confused dog.

"You can fit through the hole," he reiterated.

"The fuck you say?"

"You can help them!" he said excitedly.

"Dee, by myself?"

"You honestly can't be thinking about this, Mike?" Paul asked.

"What in my tone even remotely conveyed the idea that I want to go out there on my own, Paul?"

"Because I know you, Mike. It's not that you want to; it's that you'll feel compelled to. Drababan just played the hell out of you and now you are going to feel compelled to prove his words."

"Mike, they're big crocodiles! You cannot risk yourself for them!" Beth shrieked.

"Get her off the bridge," Paul said, pained.

"She didn't mean it," I told Dee.

"I care little for what the deceptive one said. Will you help?"

"Dee, you are asking me to single-handedly take on a Battle Cruiser."

"It is only one less than when you originally set out."

"Well, you've got me on that one. Shit, why do I have to befriend a smart croc?"

"Mike? Come on man, you can't do this."

"Aw hell, Paul. I threw my life away the second I stepped on that Breacher. I've just been waiting for the end to come since. I've already said my goodbye to Tracy, what more could I ask for? My only regret is not eating a bigger breakfast. I'm fucking hungry now."

"At least wait for the shuttles, Mike. They're on the way."

"The Genos don't have the time and I'm pretty sure they'll be the first to go." I turned to Dee. "Okay, let's play pretend now. Let's say I somehow get the Genos free. How am I going to tell them what the hell is going on?"

"Word of this has already reached them. They will know who you are." Dee was pointing to the intercom.

I'd been wondering why Dee kept repeating everything twice.

"Great, give me a map back to the Genogerian wing and then to the bridge."

"Mike I will demote your ass if you disobey my orders!"

"You never gave me any," I told him resignedly.

"I told you to sit tight until reinforcements come. You can't go running around that ship on a suicide mission to save captives that for all we know are already dead."

"Paul, I get it. You need me to perform your suicide mission to take hold of a ship that is destined to explode in space. Either way, buddy, I end up with a twenty-one-gun salute and a hero's funeral. Unfortunately I won't get to have my ashes spread over the Rockies but I guess all over space is pretty cool, too."

"Michael, there will be no ashes. Perhaps some of your tissue will survive the explosion though, to forever roam the vast cold area of space."

"Well, that's much better Dee. Thank you for that."

"You are most welcome."

I stood on my toes to look out the hole. I didn't see anything. "Help me up. If I die, Dee, I'm going to haunt your ass in perpetuity."

"I look forward to it," he said as he lifted me up easily. I caught a couple of times on the jagged metal but as luck would have it not enough to impede my progress.

"Maybe if I'd eaten more breakfast I wouldn't have fit."

"Fuck the breakfast Mike, come back here alive and I'll buy you an IHOP."

"You heard him, right Dee? He promised me a restaurant. I'm going to hold him to that."

Dee deposited me gently enough on the ground outside before handing me my rifle. I immediately got down on my haunches, although if anyone had been out here watching they could have shot me a half dozen times by now.

"I sure wish you could come as well, Dee. Maybe if you didn't like Tracy's meatloaf so well you could."

"It is indeed a delicious meal. Be safe, Michael and go with your God."

"I'll take yours as well, no sense in not doubling up. Cover me for as long as you can, please. Wait…give me your knife, too. What the hell is this thing? Looks like a damn broadsword," I said as I strapped it to my leg and then began to gingerly make my way down the hallway, doing my best not to slip in the remains of the Mutes. The stink was fierce and I could only hope it was the worst I would have to deal with for the day.

I looked back just before I took my first turn. Dee had

stuck his hand through and waved. I don't think I'd ever felt so acutely alone as I did the moment I was in that new corridor. "This is insane. What can I possibly do?" I muttered to myself. I was tempted to kill a Prog, take his eye, and access a boiler room or something and just wait until the shuttles came. I could tell Dee that it was too late. But he'd know—he'd be able to smell it on me. Stupid pheromones. I wish I knew what the markings on the doors meant. I wanted to go splash some water on my face, take a deep breath and maybe a whizz or seven. Odds were I'd open up the Mute barracks instead.

Yeah, it was going to be better to just stick to the corridors. Didn't really need the map, just needed to follow the bloodstains back, either from those we'd killed or those of us that had been killed or wounded. I could hear running footsteps and the labored breathing of something moving fast down an intersecting hallway. I got as close to the wall of approach as I could and got low to make a smaller target of myself.

A battered and bloodied Genogerian ran past, his eyes widening as he got sight of me, but whatever was chasing him scared him more than me. Mutes, it had to be, and they would not run past. I waited until they were completely in the intersection. They were so entirely focused on their prey they did not see me. I waited as long as I could, trying to ascertain if there was more than two. When I was fairly confident there wasn't, I fired. My first shot caught the mute behind the knee, almost completely severing the bottom of his leg from the rest of him. He fell over, crashing hard to the wall on his right. The second mute turned and was firing before he'd even acquired a target.

I had to roll away as the thick red bolt slammed into the wall, barely over my head. I shot wildly, more instinctually than anything. The round spun the alien; I'd caught it across its broad back, splitting the skin wide open but more importantly severing its spinal column. I could have almost felt bad for it as it slammed to the floor, its legs unmoving. It did little to stop the murderous rage in its eyes, for some twist of fate had allowed its upper body to still work as it attempted to swivel around and get a lock on me.

"You're kidding, right? Who thinks about killing someone when they have just become a cripple?" I was firing while I asked my questions aloud. One or two nailed it in its shoulders and the one that finally stopped him was the one that hit him in the top of the skull. Funny, of all the shots that I thought would do the most damage, hitting it in the head seemed the least likely. Because there was no way this thing had a fucking brain housed in there.

I'd been so intent on killing the Mute that for some unfathomable reason didn't like me that I'd not been keeping track of the other one. I needn't have worried. The Geno they'd been chasing had at some point turned and lodged a three-foot piece of something sharp through the side of the mute's neck. It had not quite come out the far side but was bulging like the beast had swallowed a baseball bat sideways.

"Bedark narr," the Geno said to me.

I was pretty sure that translated to, "You look tasty". I spun my gun on him. He eyed me warily, leaned over slowly and grabbed one of the Mute's weapons and then stood. Calmly he walked over to the other, grabbing that one's discarded weapon as well. The whole time the muzzle of my rifle followed. Never once did he make an overt gesture of hostility, but you'll have to excuse my lack of manners in that particular moment in time. It was when both of us realized neither was going to shoot, the Geno began heading down the hallway. It had taken a few strides before looking back at me as if to ask, "Are you coming?"

"Fine," I said as I got in line behind him. It was as we were walking that I noticed the amount of damage he'd taken. A fair amount of the skin that was showing was a deep purplish color, signifying some serious bruising. There were heavy abrasions and some fairly significant cuts all over its body. It looked more like a situation in which torture was involved rather than a fight. So when he began to stagger I reached out to steady him, which was about as effective as a child trying to keep a tree from falling over in high winds.

He marshaled his reserves and we pressed on. He needed a doctor but I had a feeling we would have a hard time finding quality healthcare at this particular moment. Something needed to happen, though. The beast was leaving a blood trail, and as of yet I wasn't entirely sure where we were going, because, thanks to the crude map one of the Geno's had drawn out, I was pretty sure it wasn't to the bridge and it wasn't towards the Geno quarters. Although, I'd sort of lost track. It was difficult to hear much of anything with the Cruiser's alarms still blazing so I was constantly turning around to make sure something wasn't coming. I quickly realized my mistake when I felt a large meaty paw wrap around my shoulder and lift me off the ground like so much chaff.

I had just enough time to wonder what it would feel like to have my body bounce off a hard metal wall when I found myself thrust into a small room. With my new friend/ally/potential killer right behind me, the confines shrunk down immensely when he was all the way in and the door closed. A soft glow came on as the door shut. It was as if a sensor realized we were in there and illuminated the room, although in fairness it was more like a closet. Well, technically it was a closet; it was filled with rows of Devastator armor and uniforms. But once you got past the push of the nearest uniforms the "closet" (for lack of a better term) was probably somewhere in the neighborhood of five hundred square feet.

The Geno urged me further into the tangle of clothing. For a moment I smiled as I thought of donning one of the uniforms and trying to blend in. Even this Geno as big as he was would look like a kid trying to wear his father's clothing. I'd be lucky if I could even hoist the damn stuff.

The Geno waited until we got to the far wall before slumping against the hull. I grabbed a pair of Mute pants, placed my rifle down and grabbed my knife. I cut the material into thick swaths. I wished I had some water or antibacterial cream, something, but that was going to have to wait as I wrapped some of his more serious wounds. I'd just finished tying off the second one when we heard the door open. I grabbed my rifle and spun quickly. I again felt the Geno grab my shoulder, though this time was much gentler.

I turned. His eyes were half closed and he did not have such a great hue going on. He shook his head from side to side. "Is that a universal gesture? How do I know you're not telling me to get up and run or maybe dance? Yeah, my dancing would definitely scare the hell out of them."

I shut up so that I could hear whoever was approaching but as of yet I could not see them. The only thing that was not making sense was how quietly they were coming. Devastators aren't much on stealth. A large foot stepped no more than a few inches from my location. The beast was looking down at me. I think I actually caught a momentary pang of surprise course through its features. And then it quickly went by me to look at its fallen comrade. I was watching the new Geno fumble around in a small pack when I about released my bladder and colon. In the same instant, another Geno had come up behind me as silent as a cat, another reason to hate the vermin. The cats, I mean. The Genos could be useful.

The Geno on the ground and the one helping were talking quickly, and occasionally my traveling companion would point over to me, probably discussing how I would complement a red wine or something. The Geno administering to the hurt one looked over at me a couple of times with large eyes. It could have been in disbelief that I'd killed a Mute or maybe it thought I stunk to high heaven—it was like looking at a lizard and trying to know what it was thinking. Give it a go sometime and you'll know what I mean. The first new Geno (whom I'm going to call 'Doc') undid my makeshift bandage and applied some sticky salve it had pulled from its little pack. Had to have been the same stuff I'd literally been bathed in to heal my wounds when I was doing my gladiatorial battles.

Normally I was too wounded to take much notice of how well the stuff worked but being able to watch it was like special effects in a movie where the wound just immediately begins to knit itself up. I knew now because of the studies Earth scientists had done on the stuff that it combined with the DNA of the injured party and threw the repair process into over-drive. It used the body's own healing process but just sped it up to speeds it wasn't used to. It was generally best to include a lot of sleep and a lot of fluid intake to maximize the results. The color came back quickly to the Geno, and that unexpectedly made me feel better. I'm not entirely sure why, I guess maybe it had to do with we'd already saved each other once. It's a distinct possibility.

The whole process only took a few minutes; it was just that I was under a very restrictive clock. Would they just let me leave? Could I somehow convince them to help with just hand gestures?

Then I saw it, the inner ship communication device. Okay, intercom. It just sounds way cooler calling it the former and because it looks very little like the latter. I went towards it when the third (I'll call him 'Chaplin' because he was so damn silent) growled at me. Yeah that pretty much ratcheted up the fear factor. I stepped away. The injured Geno looked angrily at Chaplin and then at me.

He made a rectangular outline on the floor with a large finger and then pointed to a spot within the large rectangle. Made absolutely no sense to me. Then he pointed to the inner ship communication device. The light came on after the third or so time, from him pointing to the intercom and back to that same single spot on the floor. I had to believe my alien guide was thinking I was a little thick by this point, probably trying to figure out how we had taken over one of Prog ships.

"Oh, I get it now. If we use the intercom they'll be able to tell where we are." Chaplin looked a little anxious when I pointed to the intercom as if I might try to get past him and push on it anyway. "Well that sucks. I'd really like to talk to Drababan."

"Drababan?" And then a bunch of alien speak came from the rapidly healing Geno. "Drababan?" he asked again.

I just nodded, but he really could have been asking if Drababan was dead and I was merely confirming it.

"Stirrix," the alien said as he stood, pointing to his chest. Doc didn't seem all that thrilled that his patient was getting up just now.

"Hello, Stirrix. I'm Michael," I said, pointing to myself.

I'm pretty sure Stirrix butchered my name more than I did his. "Immichel," he said, pointing at me.

"Close enough, now what?"

Stirrix tilted his head.

"You almost look cute for a six hundred pound, chew-my-face-off type of behemoth. We need to find the Genogerians."

That word perked them up but it had no context.

Chaplin grunted something and Doc replied. The way they looked around I could only assume they wanted to go to wherever they had been planning on going before I arrived. Doc turned to me and I could tell he was thinking about something. Then he did something I wasn't expecting; he picked me up just as Chaplin turned around. Chaplin grunted, snarled and spat as Doc placed me on Chaplin's back. It looked like I was going for a piggyback ride. Doc grabbed some parts of uniforms off the racks and then began covering me up.

"Well isn't this going to be fun," I whispered in Chaplin's ear. I was inches from those meat-tearing teeth and

I was about the size of a piece of beef jerky to him. Sometimes I have all the brainpower of a hamster. No, that's not fair. Hamsters don't mess with the things that want to eat them.

We quietly left the closet. As Chaplin was hauling ass down the hallway, my teeth were slamming into each other from the violent shaking. "Fuck man, I feel like a backpack."

Chaplin growled, I think to shut me up.

We traveled a little further in this bone-jarring manner until Doc, Stirrix and Chaplin stopped to talk. Wherever we were going or whatever was about to happen was soon. Chaplin was making motions like he wanted to pluck me off his back, as if I was a leech that had latched on to him. Stirrix, I believe, was telling him no and sternly. It was tough to tell the hierarchy among them but I think Stirrix was a little higher up the ladder as I ended up staying put, for better or worse.

Some things translate well from Geno to human without ever being said. We were going into battle. Doc and Stirrix both checked their weapons. Chaplin was putting on a brave front but I could feel his muscles bunching. I almost started liking Chaplin because I thought he maybe wanted to put me down and tuck me away safe. Then it dawned on me he probably didn't want me there because he thought I'd get in the way. Maybe that's how I'd feel as well. If as a person I'd joined an alliance with a being the size of a garden gnome...that's close enough to the size discrepancy.

I pulled my rifle off my back and slid it over Chaplin's shoulder and then moved the myriad of material I was under so that I could see clearly. I may or may not have received a grunt of satisfaction from him. This wasn't going to be easy for either of us. He had his elbows close to his body and holding on to my legs, so he had limited mobility with his rifle. I had one arm partially wrapped around his neck and with the other I was aiming. Luckily there was nearly no recoil on the weapon or I'd end up with the back of my head smashing into Chaplin's ass every time I fired, and I can guarantee he would not be a fan of that.

Doc went to a door. There were no codes required so it slid open easily enough. I knew what it was immediately—a mess hall. It wasn't overly large, forty feet by thirty feet at the most. I think the one at my high school was bigger. It was quite possible this was one of many but that didn't matter right now. What did matter were the dozen or so Mutes standing guard over fifty to sixty Genos. Two disemboweled Genos lay on the floor unmoving, a third recently gut shot and writhing in pain. The Mutes attention was adhered to the suffering mass on the ground. They seemed to be thoroughly enjoying it.

Doc brought his rifle up and was about to fire. I beat him to the punch, sending blue bolts of death towards the Mutes. My first shot caught the closest Mute right under his helmet, blowing the protective gear along with a significant portion of his skull to the ground where the rest of him immediately followed. Chaplin grunted again. I think he liked my marksmanship. Doc and Stirrix were now firing, but things were beginning to get interesting as the Mutes regrouped. I tapped Chaplin on the shoulder. When he looked at me I pointed down with my index finger and mouthed the word "down" (like that was going to help).

He got the idea though. My feet had touched down just as Doc took a lethal blow. Stirrix was like a demon possessed, firing and screaming and advancing. I was giving him as much firepower cover as I could manage. Chaplin started to fire but it was clear that he'd never held a rifle before. He was as much a threat to the Geno prisoners as he was to the Mutes. Stirrix must have stirred something within the subdued Genos because a fair number of them launched at their guards. I was appreciative of the help, I really was, but now it made it impossible for us to continue shooting at the Mutes. We'd taken out three by the time the other Genos had gotten involved and I'd gone over to Doc to see if there was anything I could do. I couldn't shoot and I sure as hell wasn't going to get in the middle of the scrum that was now going on.

Blood had trickled out of Doc's mouth. Without a beating heart it wasn't moving any more. His eyes were glazed over, his face relatively serene. Not the normal mask of pain I associate with the rifle blast. There were a few more rounds fired but soon the sound of snapping bones and grunts began to dominate. I looked up over a table. The last of the Mutes were being dealt with. Two Genos were each holding him up by an arm as a third shoved some sort of skewer through its chest. Still it nearly had the power to pull away from its captives. The third Geno just kept pulling the long strip of metal out of its chest and plunging it back in until the Mute finally stopped struggling. The Genos let him fall unceremoniously to the floor.

Chapter Ten - Mike Journal Entry 06

When it was over, sixteen Genos including the original three that were gutted plus Doc lay dead or dying. Four more were injured, one seriously as the lower portion of its arm was shot off. All thirteen of the mute guards were dead. "Well, it's a start I suppose," I said arising from my hidden spot. I nearly got my head shot off for my trouble.

Stirrix held up his arm to halt any further aggression. It was then I learned Stirrix was not a "he" as a small Geno ran towards her and began to shout "hubardtar". I'd heard enough of the Genos die in combat to know they were crying for their moms when they were wounded. Again, not for the first time and certainly not for the last, the similarities in our two species were striking. I'd thought Stirrix was a little smaller than Doc or Chaplin but I didn't want to say anything. Sometimes short men have issues with that.

There was a lot of commotion as the Genos were trying to figure out what I was. None of them knew the species of the planet they were heading to. Dee had told me for the most part, the Genos on board here were servants. They cleaned and cooked or were mechanics, basically the support staff for the Devastators and the Progerians. This was not set up like the Guardian had been, where there were millions of Geno troops and the Mutes were only used as internal guards. The Cruiser itself was the weapon. For all the power the Guardian possessed it was a support ship for the Battle Cruiser and the soon to be coming Destroyers.

The scout ships, which the Progerians had three of, well, two now, were sent out on missions that could span generations as basically its own sovereign country. This was why a Supreme Commander was chosen to rule over the voyage. Once a habitable, albeit populated planet was located, it then became the mission of the Scout to send back coordinates and then set up a defensive perimeter around the planet, kind of like pre-flag planting protection. When the Cruisers and the Destroyers were in place and had rained down all the fury they could muster, it became the job of the Scout to send fighters and foot soldiers down to mop up for the coming colonists housed on the Destroyers.

As big as the Guardian was, the Destroyers dwarfed it. According to Iserwan, the difference was like a jet fighter to a Commercial airliner. It was difficult to fathom something quite that big. But it made sense because it was full of colonists and supplies for them, plus enough armament to tear asunder a planet or three. We had been on the losing side of battle with a Cruiser. How we ever thought we'd be able to take on a Destroyer still eluded me.

After I'd received my fair share of poking, prodding and hair ruffling, Stirrix decided it was time to go. Again, I had no clue but it looked like whatever she had in mind closely mirrored my own agenda. Chaplin decided he liked me on his back. He picked me up like a loaf of bread and placed me on his back. He grunted—this came as no great surprise. I was somewhere in the middle of the group as we headed for the doorway with Stirrix and her child next to us. I don't know who the poor bastard in the lead was, but he'd no sooner stepped through the door than he was shredded by gunfire. The parts of him still remaining were hurtled back into the quickly retreating group behind him. Three more fell before the door could shut.

I was going to ask if there was another way out, but Stirrix shouted out some commands and then began running toward a door on the far side. Some Genos pushed over tables and set up a defensive perimeter while still others followed us through the other door and into the galley, which was surprisingly hygienic looking considering the monsters that were baking in there. There was another door that led out to the corridors, but it was already opening and Mutes were contemplating coming through until I gave them a reason to reconsider. Chaplin grunted. I think we were officially besties now.

Stirrix once again spoke animatedly as she looked around. I knew that look. She didn't know what to do. We were effectively trapped. I did the down gesture to Chaplin who complied immediately. I knew where I wanted to go—a control panel over by what looked like some sort of meat storage box. I really didn't want to know what kind, it'd have to suffice that it most likely wasn't of human origin.

There was some shooting from the mess hall but it was a quick burst. It appeared the Mutes were looking for a soft spot to come in. I placed my hand over the intercom, which glowed softly. My voice came from overhead and throughout the entire ship.

"Hey, Dee."

"Michael, it is good to hear your voice. I was concerned for you."

"Your concern is well founded."

Dee paused.

"It's a good thing you can't smell me now, buddy. I think you'd get a little more than you bargained for."

There was a long pause before he spoke. I could sense the tension in his voice. "Is there anything I can assist you with?"

"Yeah. Get on the horn with Paul and have him pull the plug on the whole thing."

"Michael, you know that I do not yet understand all of you colloquialisms. Could you please say that again in American English."

"Grammar Nazis everywhere you go," I said to Chaplin, who grunted like he understood.

"Tell Paul to blow the bridge to hell and back. I'm

pretty pinned down where I am. I have some new friends. One is kind of cute—you might like her."

"I do not believe if Paul blows the ship up that I will have the opportunity."

"Well, that's probably for the best. She's got some baggage anyway. And to be honest I'm not sure if she's single, it's not like you guys wear rings or anything."

Stirrix spoke over my shoulder to Dee. I thought it was particularly rude but I refrained from calling her out. I'm smart like that.

"Stirrix agrees with your assessment," Dee said to me once they were finished.

"And if she hadn't?"

"Well, you are in the kitchen. I suppose she could have baked you into a nice frittata."

"Fuck you, Dee. Call Paul, say your prayers and I'll see you on the other side. Wait…do they let different species intermingle in the afterlife?"

"I will call Paul and ignore the rest."

There were no more shots while I waited for a response. It seemed the Mutes were content to keep us bottled up for now. Oh, I'd imagine they were asking the higher ups if it would be possible to use some explosives. This might have been the only time I was happy we were in space. No commander in his right mind is going to risk a hull breech. So that meant we probably had a few more minutes before the Progerians acquiesced.

The intercom came back to life just before Dee spoke. "I have spoken to the General."

"And?" I prodded.

"He is not of the same mind."

"Well, he's not here now is he?" I was hot. "Maybe if he got his ass over here he'd feel a little differently!"

"Michael, I have seen this from his view point. This ship is a valuable asset and you are also asking him to kill his best friend. Neither are enviable choices."

"Dee, I get it but the alternative is that the Progs get control of this ship back and destroy the Guardian and then Earth. That's not even including the innocent Genos that the Mutes are taking out."

"Regardless, he will not fire on this ship until it is absolutely necessary."

"It might be too late at that point. Dee, okay, you remember that neat little trick you did with a rifle?"

"I do not like the topic of this discussion."

"Would you be able to walk me through that?"

"I believe you house enough intelligence to be able to replicate my commands."

"Either great sarcasm or one hell of a back-handed compliment. Nice. Now let's get to work."

"This will cause extensive damage to lives and material."

"Well that would kind of be the point, don't you think? Buddy, I hope we meet up again. Do you think they have chess in Heaven?"

"If my Cravaratar should once again see you, I would rejoice, but Heaven, Michael, is the end of all suffering, so I would imagine chess would not be there for you."

"Dee, you need to take your show on the road. All right, let's get to work."

It took a little longer than I'd expected, Dee was impressed that a hairless ape was able to perform the task at all, so there's that. A low whine came from the rifle, which was beginning to pick up in intensity. I held it as far from my body as I could as if that was going to do a damn thing.

Stirrix was looking at me strangely. She did not know what I was doing, at least until she spoke to Dee. After that the look of concern came across her features. She grabbed my arm and was about to pull me away.

"Dee, what the hell is your girlfriend doing?"

"She is not my girlfriend, we do not have courtship on our world like you do. We procreate and if our mating is pleasing we will stay together through a season before parting."

"Dee, man, she's stronger than I am!"

There was quick chattering between them.

"She wishes for you to throw the explosive at the Devastators."

"Well, that was the plan. How much time do I have left?"

"From the vibration soundings of the rifle I would say seventeen seconds plus or minus three seconds."

"You do know what happens if I'm on the minus side of that, right?"

"I cannot give you any more accurate reading than that. My suggestion would be to toss it NOW."

The time for banter was done. I was so scared I thought my asshole was going to swallow me whole. Strange, but that was what I was thinking. My hands were dripping puddles of sweat. The Genos quickly got out of my way as I ran across the hall. Looking back it probably would have been a lot wiser to go to the galley entry since it was much closer. That's how scared I was. I couldn't even think straight. The thought of being blown into bite-sized chunks was having that effect on me.

The only thing that saved my life as the door opened was my height. At least two red bolts streaked by my head. There was a good chance I'd received a Mohawk haircut. I turned to the side and planted my feet, swiveling as quickly as I could to get as much arc on the rifle as possible once I released it. It all happened incredibly fast from this point forward, although it felt like it took the span of a lifetime to do so.

I watched in high definition as the rifle reached its apex. The Devastators barely noted its presence as they sought a target to release their anger on. I swear I saw the beginnings of a blue explosion no bigger than the head of a pencil. I was then tugged from behind like those pulley systems they rig on stunt men in Hollywood when a shotgun (or an explosion in this case) is blowing them back. I lucked out, though. It was actually Stirrix who had grabbed me and pulled me to the side. The door was about midway shut when we all felt the concussion. At this point I didn't need Stirrix to send my body sprawling. For ten feet I was Superman, well more like the Orville Wright of super heroes. I was off the ground but not for long. I smacked the floor face first, my nose exploding in a spray of red. I'd busted the damn thing again, at that particular moment I couldn't have cared less. My ears hurt worse, and if the trickle of blood going down my cheeks was any indication, I'd just shattered both of my eardrums.

  The ringing in my ears was so intense it was disorientating. I turned over just in time to pull in a large chunk of smoke and debris into my lungs. Genos were lying all around me, some sitting up, others would never do so again. The door was twisted and hanging askew of its normal location. I struggled to get my wits back. I needed my rifle although at this point I had no idea why. I was like a boxer who had been knocked down and nearly out. I knew I needed to get up and that was my sole mission in life. I just couldn't figure out what for. Stirrix was laying on the ground, her back to me. I couldn't tell if she was alive or dead. The life I still possessed was due to her sacrifice, I could only hope I didn't waste it.

  By degrees my surroundings began to come back, although not my hearing. It was like I had the world's largest tuning fork shoved in my ear and some asshole kept smacking it with a hammer. Probably Durgan. I crawled over and grabbed a rifle. It felt good in my hands—I wasn't quite sure what to do with it yet but the composite material still felt good.

  I rolled over onto my back and I laid the rifle on my stomach, it was pointed toward the door. Nothing was coming through, not yet at least. We'd had the twelve-inch thick door to protect us and we'd still suffered some damage. Whoever was on the other side was now facing judgment or reveling with their virgins or divining the secrets of the universe. Could the Mutes even conceive of an after-life? Then I decided I didn't give a shit. I sat up, my head simultaneously as light as a feather and as heavy as a piece of granite. When it wasn't trying to float off my shoulders it was trying to slam into my chest.

There was movement to my right. Stirrix was also sitting up and holding her head. Hands grabbed me from behind. Chaplin was helping me to my feet. I couldn't hear him but I felt the breath of a grunt pass by my neck as I got wobbly to my feet. He then moved over to Stirrix and helped her up. She in turn checked on those fortunate enough to make it through this round. What lay ahead, none of us knew. It had seemed like hours since the explosion, but it was more like seconds. And we had no time to spare, the Mutes would either try to gain entry through the galley or come to the explosion. Neither was a good alternative.

I stepped over to the door, noting the blast had removed some of the floor. Parts of Mutes coated everything else; it looked like it had been spray painted with some grisly formula a gothic lover would get at Home Depot. I avoided the still smoldering hole in the floor and looked for anything coming our way. Chaplin was beside me doing the same. Stirrix thankfully was next.

"Drababan," was all I could say to her. I think I must have yelled it several decibels louder than necessary because she placed a large hand to her head.

She got the meaning along with the survivors and we were on the move back the way we had come. Each step I regained some of my former self. By the time we got back to the area Dee was in, I was pretty much good to go, except for the hearing and the blood leaking from my nose and ears.

"Dee!"

"Michael, it is indeed good to see you on this plane."

"Can't hear much!" I told him, although I could see his mouth moving. He repeated his words at a louder volume.

"Gonna blow the door! Get back!"

"I do not think that wise!"

"Yeah, me neither." I was already tearing my newest rifle down and reversing the discharge. He had pulled back from the door and I would imagine was telling those with him to seek cover.

I was holding the rifle wondering why it wasn't working when Dee came back to the hole.

"Run, you fool!"

That, I heard. Whatever pitch the rifle was humming at was completely lost to me. I dropped the rifle and hauled ass away and down an offshoot. Chaplin was smiling as he picked me up and ran further and faster. We were both airborne as the concussion rippled through the ship. Luckily we were far enough away that I didn't suffer the same damage as I had previously. Most likely my brain would have just leaked through my nose if that had been the case. The part of the ship we were now in was encased in a fog of smoke that made seeing past your fingertips impossible. Coupled with my deafness, that made for an eerie feeling. I felt like I was in *The Fog* and the monsters that would come out here were easily as bad as anything Hollywood could dream up.

Faintly I could hear the Genos talking. Didn't matter, I couldn't understand them anyway. Chaplin at some point had put me down…not sure when that happened. He lightly pushed me to my knee, and what I could see of the Genos around me showed that they were on one knee as well. Those who had weapons had them pointed outwards. Until the dust settled, moving was not a good idea. The cover was our protection for the moment. I felt slight vibrations in my legs and thought something was running. Or more like some *things* and it was getting closer. Wisdom dictated it was Dee but I wasn't sure. Even if I went out to greet him chances were I'd get trampled like a Black Friday shopper trying to get a television for cheap. There was more conversation and no firing so odds were increasing it was Dee.

"Michael, I have seen you look better!" Dee was nearly in my face. He'd startled the hell out of me.

"Yeah, I've felt better, although it is good to see you."

"What now?"

"Do you really believe that I've thought this out past this moment?"

"No, I did not. It is nice to hope from time to time."

Faintly I heard garbled talking over the intercom. It could have been because this area of the ship was in serious need of repair or my damaged eardrums. In the end, it didn't much matter. Alarm spread throughout the Genos around me. I looked to Dee.

"The Progerian Command has authorized the murder of the Genogerians held captive in their housing area."

Stirrix was getting ready to bolt and go help.

"It's a trap, Dee."

"You know that, I know that. They all know that, Michael. What else would you have them do?" I shrugged. "These are their kinsmen."

"Can we get to the bridge? Seems to me they want to pull our focus away from there."

Dee thought about it for a moment. "I do not believe Stirrix will wish to stray from the course of action she is discussing."

"She's so willing to die?"

"To save the others? Yes. You do not truly understand the gift you have given them. Just the small taste of freedom that has slipped past their lips is the sweetest of ambrosia. You have been free most of your life…how did it taste when you were off the Julipion the first time?"

"You're going to make a damn fine lawyer someday. Fine, first we free the Genos then we storm the bridge."

"Excellent," Dee replied.

The high-pitched whining in my ears was slowly fading. My equilibrium, which had been sketchy, was also returning. I'd stopped, stumbling into Dee's legs a good fifty feet previous. I think at first he thought I was playing with him as I kept falling into him. But then once he noticed I was also bouncing off the wall with as much frequency, he stopped shoving me away and just kind of set me straight. We had only a couple of dozen Genos, most of them unarmed. Chaplin had given me his weapon after I'd blown up my last one. He'd thrust it into my hands, nearly breaking them as he did so. He'd grunted in satisfaction when I finally was able to shake the pain out of my fingers and grip the rifle correctly.

"New friend?" Dee had asked.

"I sure do know how to pick them."

"That is wonderful sarcasm, Michael. Because now you are implying that I am a less than desirable companion."

"I'm not implying."

"Even more! You are a master at your craft!"

"Funny, how we can create our own realities. Does Stirrix have a plan that doesn't involve us all getting killed?"

"Of course she does, she is not you," Dee said in hushed tones as we approached the Geno housing area.

"How is this whole scenario even remotely possible?" My statement was met with a disapproving stare from Stirrix.

"She wishes you to be quiet," Dee translated unnecessarily.

"I got that."

Stirrix now looked like she was going to rip my lips off. I put my hands up in a placating manner, whatever the gesture translated to in Geno-speak seemed to take the focus off of me, or it could have been the Devastators coming. Looking back that was more likely the cause.

It was their armor that saved us, as strange as that sounds. The helmets they were wearing wrapped nearly around their entire faces, destroying a large portion of their peripheral vision. A column of them passed us by on a hallway that angled away from ours. I thought that crap only happened in movies. How many times had I seen that exact thing? I always cried, "bullshit". It would have just taken one soldier to turn his head over his left shoulder and there we would be, like a herd of deer caught under a huge spotlight. We were frozen, we dared not move. We looked like a picture, stuck in time like that.

There was humor there, maybe not at that very moment, but when I had a chance to think back on this I would remember seeing Dee, mouth open about to tell me to be quiet, one hand coming up with an admonishing finger. His left leg hovered above the ground. He swayed with the movement of the ship. When the Mutes had passed so had the immediate danger. There was a collective sigh of relief, well at least from me. The sight of the Mutes seemed to infuriate the Genos. It was a death squad dispatched to kill their friends and for some unknown reason they were taking that pretty personally.

I knew the hallway we were supposed to take because the Mutes had just gone down it. Stirrix had other plans. Good for her, I could only wonder how she did it. She brought us to a door. This was it, time for another round. I wasn't quite sure which one; I'd been sort of out of it when the cute girl holding the round card had strutted around. Always miss the good stuff.

When the door opened up and there were no immediate shots I had a surge of hope. Or more likely it was the flood of dread leaving me. Both were welcome feelings. It was a closet and a utility one at that. Apparently ships across the galaxies needed to have their decks swabbed. This one was automated but still needed to be serviced, new water put in and old water taken out. Unless the bucket doubled as a bomb I didn't see the sense in why we were all trying to stuff ourselves inside. And speaking of bombs I was getting pretty sick of the damn things. What I couldn't see from the forest of Genos was the door on the far side. I only noticed it because of the light that was now spilling in from it.

"It's a bathroom," I mumbled, and then it dawned on me why once again we weren't being fired upon. The Mutes didn't guard this area because they didn't know about it. Why would they? Service closets were below their station. At least some of them were definitely going to pay for their transgression. There was some whispering, which is sort of difficult for an eight-foot croc but they were pulling it off well enough. The huddle began to disband.

"What gives?" I asked Dee.

"Genogerians with rifles will run through the door, killing the closest Devastators and then the unarmed ones will run out to collect their weapons."

"I should probably go first, since I'm the shortest."

"Stirrix does not wish for you to go at all."

I was about to unleash some expletives on her when I looked to Dee. "You lying sack of shit. Besides you, I'm easily the best shot here. She wouldn't let that kind of asset sit on the sideline. She's one tough croc."

"Michael, we've been through this. Calling us crocodiles is like us calling you apes."

"You do it all the time."

"This is true."

"I'll go through first."

"As you wish," Dee replied, but he looked pissed about it.

The door was wide enough for a couple of humans, definitely not Genos. This was going to be dicey for a little while. Oh, who the hell was I kidding? This was going to be dicey the entire time. Stirrix looked down at me as I pushed my way to the front. Dee was so close on my back he could have been my shadow—a very large, heavy, green shadow. Chaplin grunted and I was happy that his noise was now louder than the screeching in my ears. Odds were though all the progress that my hearing had made was about to go to the wayside as soon as the bathroom door slid open.

"Poztrinic?" Stirrix asked.

"She wants to know if you're ready?"

"No. Open the fucking door."

"Sarcasm?"

"I wish."

Stirrix hit something on the side of the wall, the door slid open quietly. Shit, it could have sounded like it was grating on glass, my heart was hammering so hard I could hear nothing else except the slamming of blood in my temples. What I took in was absorbed in a fraction of a second. The barracks was much like the mess hall had been, only more. There were more Genos huddled in a mass, a bunch of Devastators were guarding them and dozens more dead Genos blanketing the floor.

I came out directly broadside to the event and fired into the mass of Devastators nearest to me, about twenty feet away. Fish in a barrel without water would have been harder to hit. Dee was firing directly over my shoulder. The savagery with which we were hitting them was repelling them at first, especially as more and more armed Genos came out behind us. Dee and I moved to the left, staying close to the wall. This also gave us better firing angles on the Mutes as they regrouped and began to fire back. Two Genos never made it clear of the bathroom door as they were cut down.

Their weapons were immediately picked up and rejoined back into the fray. The Mutes were too bunched up to be able to direct their full firepower in our direction. I heard Dee yell out. I turned to see that a round had singed his side, the smell of chicken dominating. My mouth watered of its own volition. I had to remember to apologize later for that Pavlovian dog response. As I was turning back, I noticed Chaplin had jumped over the fallen Genos and was sprinting headlong towards the Mutes with nothing more than a nasty snarl and I would imagine a series of grunts.

"Geno with a death wish? I thought only humans did that." I started lining up shots on the Mutes that had taken note of him and were trying to stop his progress. A bolt nailed him in the shoulder. He hardly flinched as the molten beam traveled through him.

"Dee, gotta help Chaplin!" I quickly pointed.

Dee fired in that direction. We killed the first line of Mutes on that side so by the time Chaplin arrived, the Devastator soldier he ran into had no clue he was coming. Chaplin grabbed for the weapon and had nearly wrestled it away before the more powerful Devastator pushed him clear. As Chaplin went sprawling to the floor, I hit the Mute with two quick rounds, one in almost the same spot Chaplin had been hit, with the other hitting his mouth. For a brief second he looked like a fire breathing dragon as the flame lit him up. Sure, a dragon that spewed blue fire but the effect was still pretty cool. Chaplin scrabbled to grab the rifle. He was going to have to be on his own for a minute as we were under increasing fire.

"Garvund!" It sounded like Stirrix.

Whatever message she had been trying to deliver worked its magic as the huddled Genos broke apart and began attacking the Devastators' exposed side and flank. It was a good thing too; we'd lost half our number by this time. Another Geno died as he was coming to our position. He must have been a primary target because he was shot three times before his body could make it to the floor. With the captured Genos joining in the cause, we now had the numbers. But the Mutes were bigger and a lot better armed. The Genos had a cause, though, and that had to count for something, right? The Mutes were merely mercenaries but the problem was that they liked to fight. That was their primary and possibly sole purpose in life.

I had to switch from rapid firing to precision as the Genos closed in on the Mutes. Initially, it wouldn't have mattered as Genos were being torn apart in the melee. Body parts spun in the air as they were ripped free of their moorings. Had they been humans I would have had to pause to quell the rising gorge, even as it was, it was brutal. Genos were screaming in rage and pain. The Mutes were merciless; they shared genes but not compassion. If they had so little compunction with their own kind, people were in a world of trouble. The room looked like a damn disco club from the late seventies with the red and blue streaks flying around. The chaos had initially been widespread but now it was pairing down to small groups fighting as is often the case in hand-to-hand combat.

Why I'd felt bad for the Genos was a mystery. They were just as ruthless as their cousins. When the opportunity struck they would bludgeon the Mutes to death with heavy handed blows using anything they could grab, blood misting in the air like a heavy rain. Brain matter clung to walls where it was flung. The carnage was gruesome. I could tell Dee was chomping at the bit to get into the mix but he was reluctant to leave my side. I was in just as much danger of arbitrarily getting trampled as I was shot. More than once he had shoved combatants away, as well as placing a well-aimed shot if the chance was there. Even with the superior numbers we were getting our asses handed to us. Gun versus bare hands, there really isn't that much of a competition.

The Mutes looked absolutely pissed off that their charges would dare raise a hand against them. They turned with such a savage fury on the prisoners we were all but forgotten for a moment. This battle was going to go down to the last man standing and the ground I found myself on was shaky at best. The Genos looked like they wanted to break and run and they may have, but there was nowhere to go. It was forward into the teeth of the enemy or backwards to the wall to be shot like condemned men. The Genos were inflicting damage but not at a sustainable rate and once the Mutes turned their attention back on us, it'd be over. Our dozen or so guns weren't going to do shit. If I thought Dee or

Stirrix would go for a tactical retreat I would have suggested it. Funny, when I woke up this morning I did not think it would be a good day to die.

I began to ponder just how long it would take to convert my rifle to a bomb. Would I be able to do it while getting shot at? If we did not make it, I could not allow the Mutes to make it either. And then I felt it, that telltale sign of something heavy moving quickly. The floor shook like cheap bleacher seats at a high school championship football game. You know the kind, the cold metal ones that freeze your ass off. More Mutes were coming. Yea though I walk through the stupid valley of death...more rifle fire broke from across the room. Heavenly bolts of blue radiated out from the doorway as human and Genogerian coalition troops quickly fanned out from the opening. The Mutes were now surrounded on three sides, although they didn't seem to mind all that much. They didn't run and they certainly didn't give up. If anything they fought harder.

The Mutes had been pushed against the far wall and I did not have a shot that I could take. The unarmed Genos were pushing the attack, unleashing centuries of pent up repression on their oppressor's puppets. We were winning now, though I still didn't feel confident enough to leave my relative place of safety. I didn't want to be that guy that ends up as a footnote in history. "Michael Talbot was the last combatant to die in the Human-Progerian war". I always felt bad for those poor bastards, especially the ones that die AFTER a cease-fire was reached. War generally seemed purposeless to me anyway and a death at that point just highlighted the uselessness of it all. Another wasted life.

A short three round alarm came through the sound system. I figured the Progerians had found out how this battle was proceeding and were getting ready to muster up whatever defense they could.

"Proximity alarm," Dee told me.

"Paul?"

"Possibly."

Cheers erupted as the last of the Mutes was being drawn and quartered. There were two Genos on each appendage, including the unfortunate brute's head. They grunted as they all pulled away simultaneously, the tearing and rending of flesh, bone, cartilage and tendon was about all I could handle for the day.

"We need to get back to the nerve center."

Dee was transfixed on the scene in front of him. "It seems our propensity for violence mirrors your own," he said to me sadly.

"Universal cancer, I suppose. Somewhere, Dee, some race has transcended this shit, but not here, at least not yet. Let's make sure we survive long enough to see if it can happen."

He finally pulled his gaze away, a deep sadness in his eyes as he looked down on me.

"More of your people won their freedom today, Dee. Let that be the thought you take away from here."

He didn't say anything as we left the barracks. The nerve center was eerily quiet as we approached. I went to the comm board. "Hey General, you in the vicinity?" I asked. I purposely did not use the familiarity of his name, as I was still a little pissed at him. It was tough though to be overly ripped. I was still alive and he was partly the reason for it.

Well, if I thought I was being formal, Paul took the cake.

"Colonel, are you in command of the ship yet?"

"Yeah, I walked right up to the bridge and they handed the keys over."

"Colonel, we have reason to believe a Destroyer's arrival is imminent. I don't need smartass remarks right now."

"Sorry, General. Things have not been particularly cake-walkish down here."

I could almost hear Paul purse his lips. "I'm sorry,

Mike. You're right; I don't know what's happening over there. I do know we have a world of hurt hurtling towards us though. The Guardian has lost nearly half its fighters and at least a third of our systems are off-line. Without that Cruiser we don't have a chance."

"General," Dee spoke, "this ship is not fairing much better, and even at full complement she is no match for a Destroyer, even with the element of surprise," he added to end Paul's next argument before it even began.

"That's it then," Paul said with deep resignation in his voice. "All we've struggled for these last few years is all for nothing."

I cared little for myself or for the countless millions that were about to die. I was concerned solely with the cherub face of my child and the angelic face of my wife. They were all that mattered, they were the sole reason I existed. That I had failed them weighed heavily upon me.

"General, how much time do we have?" Dee asked, looking around the room.

"A little under seventy minutes now."

"You hoping to get a good long marathon prayer session in?" I asked him sourly.

"While I would certainly like to, no, that is not my reasoning."

"I'm sorry, that was in poor taste."

"You are learning. General, you must demand the bridge surrender. If they do not, fire on the bridge until it is destroyed."

I knew Paul probably had twenty questions.

"There is no time for answering questions, General." Dee was moving towards the control panel. "There is a chance we could still win the day but we must either own the bridge or it must be destroyed. Once that is done, sir, we will need a pilot and some technicians."

Paul was talking to the bridge when I asked Dee what was his plan. "I am breaking honor with what I am desiring to do, Michael."

"What exactly are you 'desiring' to do, buddy?"

"The best analogy I could use from your Earth history would be kamikaze."

"What? You plan on ramming the Destroyer once it shows up?"

"No."

I blew out a gust of air. "Woo, thanks man, you scared the hell out of me."

"I plan on ramming the ship *before* it comes out of its buckle. To do it after would be like driving a car into a tank. We would not win. It is against all manner of treaties to do this. Even some of our most bitter enemies have vowed to never interfere with a buckle. To do so is catastrophic."

"I'm not thrilled with the prospect of dying today, Dee. But if there is *anything* we can do that allows my wife and kid another chance at life, I'll take it. Honor be damned. All's fair in love and war. And now that I've said that, it finally makes sense. Never really did right up until now."

"I am glad you were offered an epiphany."

"Sarcasm?"

He didn't answer.

"Mike, I think with the defeat of their Devastator troops all the wind is gone from their sails. They have vowed revenge but for now they are acquiescing to our demands. However, they will not formally surrender until they are face to face with the leader of the rebellion. It does sounds like a trap to me though." Paul added.

"Normally I'd agree with you, Paul, but the aliens are seldom duplicitous," I replied.

"I asked you once before to stop using those fancy words with me," Paul half joked.

"I don't have a choice. I have to sound vaguely intelligent in front of Dee."

"You have yet to succeed," Dee said dryly. "I do agree with Michael on his assessment. Once a word is given it is kept."

"You guys just be careful. Iserwan has volunteered along with some techs to come over. We have a chance now! With that ship in our arsenal we just might have a chance."

"You going to tell him your idea?" I asked Dee softly.

He shook his head tersely. "He would not agree."

"Agree with what?" Paul asked.

"Talk louder next time why don't you," I hissed at him. To Paul I said, "He's saying cherry Pop-Tarts are the best food earth has to offer and for some reason he thinks you'd disagree."

"Really? You're having a Pop-Tart discussion right now? And no, Drababan, cherry Pop-Tarts are not the best. I'd say something more along the lines of a chicken Parmesan sub."

"I'm starving."

"Just get to the bridge and be careful."

"Yes dad," I said, then I smacked Dee on the arm. "General, I'm sending the freed Genos your way. Some of them are going to be in some serious need of medical attention, so please send a shuttle pilot with the group so that he can fly them back."

Paul responded with 'uh-huh'. I knew all of his thoughts were dominated with the newest war ship he had at his command. I was not going to tell him it was to be a short-lived responsibility.

Dee and I ran back to the Geno quarters. He told Stirrix what needed to happen. She did not look too entirely pleased.

"She is concerned for what is to happen when she gets to the new ship. The games are widely known among our people. She would rather take her chances here."

"And she knows your plan?"

Dee nodded.

"Tell her to get her ass on a shuttle."

Stirrix snorted in anger when Dee told her.

"She and her off-spring will be safe, for now."

The offspring part got her, as I knew it would. The Genos were in full-throated celebration and mourning. Their freedom was hard fought and the price paid steep. Leading the cheer was a familiar face. Chaplin was grunting his satisfaction, thrusting a Devastator rifle over his head.

"It is good to see you again!" I shouted. "I thought you'd been lost."

He'd not a clue to my words but the conveyance of meaning was clear enough. Chaplin elbowed his way through the crowd. He placed his rifle down and snatched me up. The crowd instantly quieted as he held me up. I felt like Simba in *The Lion King* the way he was displaying me. Stirrix said a few words and then a chant started up.

"They are honoring you, Michael," Dee said, coming up alongside.

"I feel like a rack of ribs about to get devoured. Any chance you could tell him to put me down? We've got a lot of shit to do before we die."

"Surely a minute more will not hurt either way." Dee was smiling.

"You're an asshole. He's squeezing me like a tube of toothpaste."

He waited a few moments longer before he spoke. Maybe he could tell I was losing the ability to breathe. Chaplin put me down, it was then I remembered he'd been wounded. Blood was running from his shoulder although he seemed relatively nonchalant about the whole thing.

Stirrix got the group moving towards the hangar level.

"Will they be alright?" I asked Dee.

"They will once we acquire the formal surrender from the Commander of this vessel."

"Well, let's get it done." It took some convincing to get Chaplin to go with the main group. I think it had more to do with the blood loss than any true desire. Once Stirrix told everyone where to go, she refused to leave. Grabbing a rifle, she said that she'd lived her whole life wanting to witness a Progerian bow to someone else and she'd be damned if she was going to miss out.

"She really said damned?"

"Loose translation. I improvised," Dee elaborated.

I kept expecting to be ambushed at some point along our journey to the bridge. Dee looked tense but I think it had more to do with the confrontation that was about to take place. Whereas Stirrix had a look of anticipation upon her stony features, if I was to apply a 'loose' translation, I would say she looked like a kid on Christmas morning about to unwrap a coveted present. I just kind of felt like I wanted to crap. Not a very heroic feeling, but it's my journal. I might as well be honest.

There were seven Devastators on the bridge along with the eight Progerian commanders. Apparently they weren't as trusting as we were. I don't even think anyone glanced in my direction as we walked in, all eyes were on Dee. He was known far and wide for his exploits. I guess it'd be like Mike Tyson walking into a room. There was shock and anger on the Progerians' faces. Shock that Genogerians had rebelled and anger that the Progerians had somehow let them. I felt like the forgotten kid among a room full of adults; they were talking and I was just looking around at all the pretty lights. The instrumentation used to run this thing was beyond my skill set.

"Michael!" Dee said harshly. "Come back and try to act regally, will you? I am having them surrender to you."

It was then I noticed that the bridge had gone quiet and the Progerians and Mutes were looking at me. I'd seen that look before—plain, unadulterated shock.

"Why me, Dee?" I asked out of the corner of my mouth.

"They can see you. They said they would only surrender to the leader of the rebellion and that, well, that is you. Plus it gives me great satisfaction to see the look of disappointment on their faces that they lost to someone of your stature."

"Are you saying I'm short?"

"Do not turn your back, it is a sign of weakness."

I abruptly stopped what I was doing.

"The Devastators will now lay their weapons at your feet. They will attempt to intimidate you. If they feel they are succeeding there is the possibility they could attack, no matter the orders from the Progerians."

"Just knowing they exist intimidates the hell out of me, Dee."

The first Devastator began to walk towards me, his weapon still in his hands. He was snarling, rage contorting his features. I lifted my rifle up and pointed it at his head. He snarled more.

"I'm not playing this game Dee. Tell him to drop his weapon."

The Mute was still coming my way, his rifle not exactly pointing at me but in the blink of an eye he could be firing a shot. If anything my words taunted him more.

"Fine, have it your way." My shot burned through his eyeball and somehow found the brain. Apparently I was a better shot than even I knew. He fell back, nearly taking a commander with him.

"Michael, this is not honorable! They are surrendering!"

"They're not surrendering, Dee. They're trying to make me scared, which I am. And if they can pick up on that a tenth as well as you can then he was going to rip my fucking head off my shoulders. Sorry, but I'm pretty fond of its present location. Tracy may or may not agree with that last statement. And don't give me any shit about honorable, these assholes came to my planet unannounced and nearly destroyed it. Forgive me if I don't play by their skewed rules. Tell all of the Mutes to put their guns down or my next shot goes to one of these Progerian pigs with all the shiny shit on their shoulders."

Dee spoke, the Mutes did not look like they were going to comply, at least until the commanding officer spoke. They did not hesitate at this point. The Mutes nearly threw their guns to the ground. The officer, who made the Mutes do as I told, did one of those backhanded surrenders. Something along the lines of, "you have won this round but we will destroy you in the end. We will reduce your cities to ashes and rape your luggage". Yada yada yada.

"Could you please ask him if he is done? He's boring me."

The officer's mouth clamped shut.

"I do not believe him to be a fan of your insolence." Dee had delivered those words with humor. I would have loved to turn and see his expression but I didn't need to give the Mutes any other reason to attack.

I was unsure what we were going to do with the captives. Then Stirrix stepped forward and took charge.

"She is taking them to the hangar to be transferred to the Guardian," Dee explained.

"Good riddance. Think we could take this thing for a little ride before Iserwan gets here?"

"I believe the best you could hope for would be a fiery crash."

"Come on, Dee. There's nothing even out here."

"Yet my original statement stands."

"You mad at me for killing the Mute?"

"You had your reasons. I wish I had fought as ruthlessly as you when the Progerians took everything of mine away."

"We're doing it now, bud. We're making them pay for every wrong they've committed. Earth is the rock they are going to wish they'd never crashed up against. And, Holy Man or not, I know you are enjoying the revenge."

"Retribution."

"You call it whatever you want, if that lets you sleep at night."

"I do enjoy it, though."

"That's my over-sized cowboy boots!"

"Would you like it if I wore monkey mittens?"

"I get it. Sorry and please don't get monkey mittens. It would take like three of the poor things to cover your hands."

I walked around the room a few times. It was extremely difficult for me not to touch all of those instruments. All the lights and displays captivated me. I noticed that Dee hovered extremely close, especially when I got close to what I figured was the drive or possibly the self-destruct.

"What if I pushed that?" I said, lunging.

Dee swiped to grab my shoulder.

"Having fun?" Iserwan asked from the doorway. "Permission to come aboard?"

"Permission granted," I told him, wiping the smile from my face. I felt like my parents had just caught me teasing the dog.

Iserwan stepped through with a couple of Progs and humans I recognized from the bridge of the Guardian.

"Who commands the Guardian?" Dee asked.

"I have put it in the capable hands of Colonel Bailey. He will command her until such a time that I can train someone properly on this vessel. That is if we make it through the day. My technicians should be able to have the drive back online in twenty minutes."

"That soon? I really thought we'd messed that thing up indefinitely."

"All Progerian technology is predicated on over-redundancy. It will merely be a matter of re-routing past the damaged consoles."

"I'll remember that next time." Iserwan stated.

"How many ships do you plan on boarding?"

That was a good question. I really hoped this was the last.

There was a moment of silence as Dee figured out his next words. "Iserwan, I need you to show me the basic operation of this vessel."

"For what purpose?" Iserwan asked him suspiciously. "You could not learn enough in the short time available to sway the inevitable outcome."

"It is possible that I could."

"Oh fuck, enough dancing around. We plan to meet the Destroyer head on while it's in its buckle," I said. Dee looked at me so hard I thought it quite possible he was hoping I'd wither.

"This cannot be done!" Iserwan shouted. "It is against every conventionality of war."

"It's against your conventionalities. I personally don't have a problem with it. Well, that's a lie. I'm not enamored with the thought of dying. But if it saves my planet then I'm all in."

"The General does not know about this," Iserwan stammered.

"And he won't 'cause I don't plan on telling him. He wants this ship more than just about anything, except maybe that one girl up at college in his history class, and I can't really blame him for that, she was smoking hot. Dee, don't tell Tracy."

"I am unsure, Michael, when you thought I might have the opportunity."

"Oh, yeah."

Iserwan was looking back and forth at us and then at the bridge. "Does not suicide condemn your Cravaratar, Drababan?"

Dee looked down. "Indeed, I am fearful for my soul, but I consider this more as a selfless act of sacrifice than of suicide."

"This is not like driving an earth vehicle, Drababan. I

cannot show you enough of what you need to know before it is time."

"We'll have to take our chances, Iserwan. Show us and maybe between the two of us we can figure it out." I'd no sooner said the words than I knew the lie I'd spoken. Dee was magnitudes of order smarter than I was. The best I could offer him was that I liked shiny stuff and I could push buttons.

"No."

"What?" I asked him incredulously. "This isn't open for debate, Iserwan! As soon as that Destroyer figures out what's going on, the Guardian and then Earth will be reduced to rubble. I have a wife and child and I will not let that happen."

"I said no, Colonel Talbot. I will not attempt to teach you something in thirty minutes that can take up to three years. The mission would be destined for failure before it ever began."

"That is unaccept..." I was shouting until Dee placed his hand on my shoulder.

"Sometimes, my friend, you need to not only listen to the words that are being spoken but also the manner in which they are being delivered."

"What? Are you going Buddhist on me?"

"There are a lot of qualities within the Buddhist religion that I find very similar to my own. Look." Dee physically turned my head.

Iserwan looked like a whipped dog. He was sitting heavily in the Commander's chair. His gaze shifted downward. Then he spoke. "I admit it, Drababan. I never understood what your kind saw in the need for religion and the praying to a God you could neither see nor hear. Yet right now, I inexplicably feel that I would like to talk to your God. Would you show me how?"

"What is going on?" I whispered to Dee.

"Sacrifice, Michael." Dee walked over to Iserwan and

clasped hands with the Progerian. "Kneel with me." Iserwan did.

"Oh," I said softly. Iserwan was planning on piloting the ship himself. I had a surge of hope flood through me. Drababan and I were about as useful as horns on a gerbil at this point. Cool looking, maybe—useless, definitely. I'm all for going down with the ship if the need arises, but apparently right now, there was no need. Dee and Iserwan spent what seemed like an inordinate amount of time praying. I was debating how rude it would be to interrupt them when they finally stood.

"Thank you, Drababan," Iserwan stated with a slight bow. "I feel better now, my heart is lighter somehow. Will God forgive me my actions against my own people?"

"You are helping to preserve an innocent species against the wrongful acts of our superiors. You will be heralded as a hero both on Earth and in Heaven."

"I will be labeled a traitor."

"Only by those committing these travesties."

"There is not much time, Drababan. You should get any remaining personnel off of this ship."

I was in total agreement. My heart nearly bottomed out when Dee spoke.

"I will stay with you."

Goddammit, if Dee stayed then I was honor bound to stay as well. Damn honor, I'd like to go shove it up a donkey's ass. Is that a redundant statement? Think about it.

Iserwan turned to look at Dee. "You would truly do that? I was a fool for so many years to look down upon your kind. You could have taught us so much if we would have only listened."

"It is not too late."

"Perhaps not. No, my friend, I will not have you sacrifice yourself. You have given me so much I will do this in return. I will beg at Gropytheon's feet for his forgiveness."

"He does not want your groveling, Iserwan, just your

love."

"That I can do. Now go…and take the puny hu-man with you."

"It has been an honor, Iserwan," I said as I strode towards him and extended my hand. He gripped my hand in his large paw.

"Likewise, Colonel Talbot. You are all that your species should strive to be."

"Oh, I would wholly disagree, but thank you for the compliment."

"Please tell the General that I am sorry that I will not be able to return to my duties."

"That is not a conversation I am looking forward to. You will be sorely missed." And I meant it. His expertise would be difficult to replace. I felt for the creature. He was being torn in two inside. He was helping what was once the enemy to defeat his own kind, it couldn't be easy.

"Go, time is short."

Dee bowed. "Let us go, Michael."

We were halfway to the hangar when the suspicious side of me reared its ugly head. "Is it possible he's lying?"

"I have thought of that as well."

"And just now you are figuring to voice your concerns? He's been around humans long enough, he could have easily picked it up."

"Perhaps if we had not prayed. It matters little either way, Michael. With or without this ship we cannot defeat that Destroyer."

I wanted to go with the classic "comforting" retort, but it didn't seem to have the kick I was hoping for.

"Come, I am confident Iserwan will do the right thing."

"But for whom?"

"That is a much better question."

The techs and a pilot (thankfully) were waiting for us when we arrived at the hangar. The place was like a wasteland. I half expected tumbleweeds to go rolling by. Iserwan's voice came over the system.

"I can see that you have not left yet. There are only seven minutes until contact."

Seven minutes. That was not that long a time, whether you were trying to save your life or were racing toward its end.

"This is it? Everyone else is off-ship?" I asked.

"The last prisoner ship left about ten minutes ago, Colonel," one of the techs replied.

"What of the Commander? He will need help piloting this ship," our pilot said.

"Not where he's going," I said vaguely. "Let's go."

We were off ship and had the Guardian in sight within a minute.

"Guardian, this is the shuttle Patriot, permission to land?" the pilot asked.

"Patriot, this is General Ginson. Is Mike aboard your vessel?"

"Shit, time to face the music," I said softly.

"I hear no music." Dee was looking around.

"Just a saying."

"It does not make sense, this saying."

"Yeah, it really doesn't. All the same, here goes nothing. Yeah, General, I'm here."

"What the hell is going on with the Cruiser? Iserwan will not respond to my hails."

"You sitting?"

"No, dammit, I am not sitting, now tell me what is going on!"

"You remember the movie, *The Enemy Below*?"

"Mike, do not go getting all ambiguous on me. What does a World War Two Destroyer and German u-boat movie have to do with anything?"

"You remember how it ended?"

There was a pause, and I know it wasn't because Paul

was trying to remember how exactly the movie had finished. We'd both watched it about four or five times. I think he was probably trying to figure out how not to blow a major blood vessel in his head. For those of you who may read this and have no clue, the Captain of the American Destroyer had no choice but to ram the German U-Boat. It results in the destruction of both. If, by chance, the habitat you live in is actually up and running or you have a generator and can spare a few hours from surviving you should definitely check it out.

"Just report to the bridge when you get back," Paul said tersely.

I wasn't expecting a marching band when I got back but I sure as hell wasn't expecting an armed escort either.

"Nice gun. Want me to shove it up your ass?" I asked the Sergeant who told us to follow him.

"Michael, I am detecting elevated levels of stress coming from you."

"You think, Dee?"

Paul did not turn when we entered the bridge.

"Sir, I've brought Colonel Talbot and Drababan," The sergeant at arms announced.

"General, imminent arrival in two minutes, twelve seconds," the radar operator spoke out. Although to be honest, I'm not sure if it's actually radar, but that's beside the point.

Paul finally turned. I was nearly frozen by the look of disgust he sent my way. "You see that big Battle Cruiser sitting there, Mike?" he asked, pointing towards the viewing screen.

"It'd be hard to miss," I answered honestly.

"I've talked to my officers. They said ramming the Destroyer would do very little damage. The Cruiser, however, will most likely be a total loss. You want to tell me how that is a good idea? With the combined fire power of the Guardian and the Cruiser we might have had a chance."

"Two rifles against a tank, Paul."

"It's General."

"Fine. Two slingshots against a machinegun nest, General. That better? And just so we're clear, Iserwan is planning on meeting the Destroyer in the buckle."

There were gasps among the Genos and Progs on the bridge.

"What does that mean?" He made sure not to ask me.

"Sir, the ships are traveling near to the speed of light. This causes space to fold over, making traveling vast distances..."

"Did I ask for a physics lesson? I just want to know what is going to happen."

"Sorry sir, both ships will be reduced to the atomic level from the resulting collision. It is a practice banned in the known universe."

"Well, look at you, Mike. Your crime has gone universal. You know what's screwed up, Colonel? That Destroyer will be here in under a minute yet MY CRUISER is still sitting there in space. You ever think that quite possibly Iserwan snowed you? That maybe he's going to hand that ship back over to his superiors? Did that ever cross your fucking mind?!" He was damn near to shrieking. I hadn't seen him lose it this bad since that one time in college when he thought one of those sorority girls he screwed around with was pregnant.

"Yeah, I thought of that, right up until Dee and Iserwan prayed."

"Oh, that's rich, buddy." The "buddy" part came out as sarcastically as I think he could manage. "They prayed. I can't tell you how much better I feel now. Damn, you put my mind at ease. How long do you think we're going to last as soon as the Cruiser AND the Destroyer turn their guns on us? Maybe you should go pray on that."

"Paul you weren't there..."

"I know I wasn't because if I had been, I'd be getting

ready to target the Destroyer, not the Cruiser." He turned back to the crew on his bridge. "I want everything we have targeted on that Cruiser. If she's not fighting with us then she sure as hell isn't going to fight against us."

"General, you cannot!" Dee spoke and stepped forward.

Paul whipped his head around. "Sergeant, detain the prisoners."

"Prisoners? Are you kidding me! You lay a fucking hand on me I'll tear it off and shove it up the General's ass," I told the Sergeant. He stopped his movement. Dee looked just as mad as I was and he was probably the real reason why the Sergeant wasn't approaching. "It'd really be nice, General, if you took me out to dinner before you tried to fuck me. How about a nice little thank you for disabling the Cruiser and saving your ass? How about that?"

"Save? You didn't save shit. Near as I can tell the Cruiser will be blowing Toyota sized holes in us soon enough."

"Sir, ten seconds until the Destroyer arrives."

"Sir, we have a confirmed firing solution."

"Fire on a five countdown."

"Nine for Destroyer."

"Five for fire."

"Eight for Destroyer."

"Four for fire."

"Seven for Destroyer."

"Three for fire."

"Six for Destroyer."

"Sir, the Cruiser is gone!" the radar operator shouted.

That was easy enough to confirm by looking at the void of space where the ship had been.

"Brace, Michael," Dee said quietly as he moved towards a railing that encircled the entire bridge. "Gropytheon's speed, Iserwan," Dee muttered.

"What he said," I repeated solemnly.

What I saw next is difficult to put into words. I have nothing to base it on and I will never be able to convey the vividness with which it burned itself into my brain. I think a poet might be better able to capture the moment. Space ripped open. At first it was a hole, definable only because it was darker than the space around it. Then it began to grow lighter to the point it became painful to look at. The sphere was an iridescent blue which glowed and pulsed. It was beautiful. If I stared long enough I was positive it would yield all the answers to the universe. An angry red blotch appeared in the center of the vision before me. It was easy to tell it was something that was completely out of place to the grandeur of the event, like someone had splotched paint across the Mona Lisa. Not that I'm an art buff but I still recognize beauty and am saddened at the needless destruction of it.

The blue pulsed one more time brilliantly, but, like a spectral balloon that had been popped, it collapsed in on itself to be replaced by that angry red, that in its own way had answers but those were all laced in anger, pain and death. Dee grabbed my hand and placed in on the railing; I'd completely forgotten. My eyes were as big as my jaw-dropped mouth. I'd seen God, I was convinced of it, and he was pissed!

Alarms blared all around us. "INCOMING!"

Paul sat at the ship's main console and strapped a harness over himself. The wave of whatever it was hit us, rocking the ship. My feet were horizontal to the floor as I held on for dear life although if I remembered correctly the Sergeant was right behind me and was sure to break my fall whether he wanted to or not. The ship's systems tried desperately to stop the spinning and bouncing we now found ourselves in. I felt like were one of those lottery ping-pong balls in that air-blowing machine. We were bouncing around like a super ball on espresso shots.

The sound of groans and broken bones reached my

ears as those not lucky enough to find a safe haven slammed into just about everything. And almost as fast as it started it was over. The red-eyed demon closed its massive eye and the gyro-scopic motors in the Guardian once again placed our feet solidly underneath us. Alarms still rang as widespread damage throughout the ship was soon to be assessed. But first, the many wounded were going to need to be tended to.

The bridge crew came through relatively unscathed. The Sergeant who had escorted me looked a little worse for wear but other than that, we were in good shape. Paul looked as pale as a snowflake, well, that was right up until he turned slowly to look at me and then his face flushed with anger.

"That," he said, pointing to the screen, "Was the useless destruction of valuable assets."

I was going to say something like "prove it". There wasn't so much as a sprocket of evidence. I, at least, had sense enough to not open my mouth.

"You will be held accountable in a military tribunal. Sergeant."

"We've had this talk before, Sergeant," I said, spinning on him, my finger nearly popping him on the cheek. I spun back to face Paul. "You know what, General? I quit. I renounce my commission, take all this shiny shit," I said, ripping my Colonel silver leaves off, "and melt it down. Go make yourself a little tin man that does whatever you command him to do. I'm taking my family and going to find a little corner of the world and enjoy it while I can."

"I am ordering you, Colonel Talbot..."

"See, that's where you're wrong. I'm not playing Marine anymore. Oh, and I know what you're thinking. Yeah, you're thinking you can still toss me in the brig. But you know what, pal? What do you think is going to happen when the Genogerians find out what you did to their liberator? Shit, man, you'll have a mutiny on your hands in a matter of minutes and then if you're lucky enough you'll end up in my now vacated cell. I mean, if they don't tear you apart that is. So this is what I'm going to do. I'm going to grab me a pilot and a shuttle and I'm going home where I'm packing up and finding as remote a place as I can and do my best to completely forget all of this. And one more thing, General. If you ever fucking disturb me I'll destroy you. So are we clear?"

Paul was glaring at me. I had gotten so close to him our noses were nearly touching. When I figured I'd made my point I turned, nearly colliding with the Sergeant who had come up behind me. I didn't even think as I grabbed the barrel of his rifle and twisted it with enough torque that he released his grip. He was grabbing his wrist in pain as I slammed the flat of the butt stock up against his skull. As he recoiled to the side I kneed him in his jewels. He fell over quickly, having a difficult time trying to protect all the areas that now hurt.

I leaned down. "I don't think I could have been any clearer." I tossed his rifle to the ground.

"Sir?" the other two guards asked Paul. They were barring the exit.

My back was to Paul and I was as tense as a coiled snake.

"Let him go. Drababan, what of you?" Paul asked.

"Where Michael goes I will follow, General."

Initially I was happy because it was another triumph over Paul. Plus, I would miss the jolly green giant if I were living out the rest of my life in the Himalayas without him.

"Let's go Dee. I think there's about a case of beer back home and I'd really like to go work on that."

"I would rather have Moxie."

"Yeah, we're going to have to work on that," I told him.

I wondered while we were on the shuttle if Paul would just blast us from the sky. Maybe he would have if it wouldn't cost him a shuttle and a pilot. Both were in short supply and he couldn't afford any more losses. There was another Destroyer out there and according to the Geno pilot, they would be able to tell what happened to the first one and would not make the same mistake.

"Meaning what?"

"Now that they know, they will pull out of their buckle early and come here using their more conventional drive system. They will not spare their fury. They will reduce this planet and its inhabitants to ashes," the pilot said, in that arrogant way pilots deal with just about everything in life.

"What's the range on this shuttle?" I asked Dee.

"The day of our death is of little concern, Michael. It is how we are prepared for it that matters."

"Dee, your wisdom is invaluable and I appreciate it greatly. I care not much for my own life—it's Tracy's and Travis's that I want to preserve."

"Then we must find a way."

The shuttle dropped us off and barely waited until we were clear of the back blast before he lifted off, presumably to head back to the Guardian. I snagged a Hummer without even thinking about it, been doing it for a few years now. I had two 'uh-oh' moments within a few seconds of each other.

"Shit!" I blurted out.

"Are you meaning that you need to defecate or is this an expletive to signify a problem?"

"The former, wait I meant the latter."

"I am unsure of which I would rather it was."

"Dee, I quit the Marines so that means I pretty much just stole this ride."

"That could be bad."

"Yeah, and that's only the half of it."

"What is this other part?"

"Tracy thinks I'm dead. With so much going on I forgot to tell her that I'm alright."

"That is much worse than stealing a military vehicle."

"I know."

"What are you planning on doing?"

"The only thing I can…drive faster."

"You sometimes are blessed with a wisdom I do not give you credit for."

"Sometimes I forget just how much you've picked up from me."

"That was not sarcasm."

I nearly ran over four schools kids, three grandmothers, two English bulldogs and something that looked like a yeti. If I hadn't been in such a rush I would have stopped to check out that last one. Tracy was at the door with Travis in her arms before I could even get out of the Hummer. Even from this distance I could see that her face was washed out from a decent sized crying.

"Did you miss the sale at Shoe City?" I asked, doing my best to diffuse a situation that was most likely going to entail several punches to my shoulder.

"I thought…" she swallowed hard. "I thought you were a military notification of your death."

"That would be something if I came to tell you of my own demise."

"Don't make light of this, Mike. I thought you were dead. I've had a bad few hours trying to hold it together for Travis."

She placed Travis down, he came waddle running over to me. I picked him up and spun him around, much to his squeals of delight. "Oh boy," I said as I handed him to Dee. "His diaper is dirty."

Dee growled. Travis pulled on his snout. "If it were not for you having to grovel at the feet of your woman I would hand him back to you," he said as he headed into the house. He hesitated, and then turned to Tracy. "Do not be too severe. When he called you, our prospects of survival were indeed dim. Once again the charm that encircles your mate was able to find a way to salvation."

Dee had done me a serious solid. Tracy, who had

looked poised to pounce, seemed to have all of the fight drained out of her. We met halfway, each of us holding the other up in a long embrace. The only interruption was Dee's moans of bewailing as he dealt with Travis's diaper and my son's squeals of delight as he put his uncle through the ringer.

"He is flatulent as I am changing him!" Dee roared. "It is burning my olfactory senses!"

"That's my boy," I mumbled in the tangle of Tracy's hair. "I'm so sorry to have put you through that. It was touch and go for a while."

"What happened?" she asked, pulling back a bit so she could look into my eyes.

"I bought us some time. We destroyed a Cruiser and a Destroyer today."

"That hardly seems possible."

"Yeah, I have to agree with you. Dee and I went on a suicide mission."

Tracy gasped.

"Sorry, bad phraseology. How about high risk mission?"

"Why, Michael? Are you in such a rush to get out of our marriage and fatherhood?"

"Don't you ever say anything like that again. It was the thought of you two and you two alone that spurred me on to even attempt it. The Guardian was getting its ass handed to it. We were in serious danger of dying aboard that thing and I'd be damned if I survived everything I'd done on that ship only to have it end that way. Dee and I found a way to get onto the Cruiser and we took it over."

"Just like that? You landed and said something like, 'I am Lord Michael Talbot and I now command all that I see.' "

"Yeah. Something like that."

"It really feels like you're leaving out a vast part of the story."

"Do you really want the number of rounds that were

shot in my direction? Because that was one hundred and twenty six. Do you want to know how many bombs I detonated? That was two. Do you want to know how many Genogerians and humans I saw die today? It was..."

"I get it, I'm sorry."

"Iserwan died."

There was another sharp intake of air from Tracy. "How? Who will pilot the Guardian?"

"He was training Bailey."

"Bailey? That idiot couldn't fly a kite."

I shrugged my shoulders. "Iserwan gave his life. He flew the Cruiser into the Destroyer during a buckle."

"Is that even possible?"

"I guess, because he did it. The sight of it was beyond description. I think I saw God and the devil today." I drifted off in thought.

"What now?" Tracy asked.

"Ultimately I only bought us some time. There's another Destroyer coming and it's going to be firing first and not ever bothering with questions."

"Is Paul coming up with a battle plan?"

"Well, see, that's where it gets a little sticky."

"*That's* where it gets sticky?"

"I quit."

"Quit? Quit what?"

"The Corps."

"You can't quit."

"Well, let's see. Paul was going to bring me up on charges of disobeying orders and destruction of government property and I guess now he could add assault. So I told him to fuck off and I tossed him my leaves. So that's insubordination as well. Not enough rocks in Leavenworth for me to crush—they'd probably have to ship them in from Arizona or something."

"What is wrong with you?"

"I want to move."

"Move where?"

"Somewhere remote. We have maybe a couple of months before that Destroyer is parked on our doorstep and maybe we could hold out if nobody knew we were there."

"You said it yourself, Mike. There will be no place remote enough. If they drop those planet busters we know they have, nowhere will be safe."

"Your mate speaks the truth," Dee said as he emerged from the house in a much more pleasant mood than when he had gone in. He was dangling Travis over his head by one leg. My son was punching the knobs atop Dee's head, long ribbons of drool hanging from his mouth. "It is lucky for you God-son that I do not eat meat." Travis and Dee were face to face, albeit Travis was upside down.

"So we just sit here and wait for the end?"

"Once we are born, Michael, all that we are ever doing is waiting for the end."

"Buddhists. Got an answer for everything."

"We should enjoy the time we have left together." Tracy hugged me tight.

"Well, that's not the worst idea I've heard today," I said, wrapping my arms around her.

"No. The worst ideas of today all came from your mouth."

"Don't say another word, Dee. You're going to ruin this for me."

Chapter Eleven - Mike Journal Entry 07

That night was among one of the most peaceful I'd ever felt. We sat in some chairs in the back yard with Travis running around like a banshee with Dee growling behind him. I drank a few beers, spending most of the time with my head back looking up into the sky, Tracy's hand intertwined with mine. There was a shower of bright white lights that streaked across the sky. I didn't even let the fact that they were charged ions from the massive collision destroy the illusion of it being my very own fireworks show.

I more than half expected Paul to show up that next day, with either a Military Police escort (I still had the Hummer) or by himself to see if we could work through this. Honestly, that next day had he come with hat in hand I may have. Each passing day, though, my resolve set harder. I was really getting into the swing of being on perpetual vacation. I'd been at it a solid week and not once had I pissed off Tracy. Dee was another matter because I had spent a fair amount of time over at his place. He had a garage full of experiments and I always liked to see what he was doing. So it was one small beaker…you'd think I knocked over the answer to world hunger by the way he'd chased me out of his place. I'm not going to lie—it felt a little like the time he was going to kill me in France. Had I known what was waiting for me at my house I may have just stayed put and suffered my fate. Dee was cursing as he slammed down his garage door behind me.

There was another Hummer in my driveway. I couldn't really tell from where I was but it looked like the

Sergeant who had tried to detain me was sitting in the driver's seat. I got closer to confirm.

"Hey buddy, how you doing?" I asked, startling him by tapping on the glass. "How's your head? Do you have any headaches? How about them balls? Will your dog still lick them?"

"Fuck you, Talbot."

"That's really the best come back you have? Get out of my driveway."

"You're on a military base. I'll damn well park anywhere I want."

"I'm going to drag you out of that thing and..."

"Mike, get your ass in here," Tracy said from the doorway.

"You're a lucky bastard," I said, pointing my finger at him.

"Look at you running with your tail between your legs. Do you do everything she tells you to?"

"Of course I do. Just because I'm an asshole doesn't make me stupid."

The Sergeant raised his eyebrows and pursed his lips. "Makes sense," he said softly and rolled his window back up. Guess he couldn't argue with that logic.

"You have company," Tracy said with no small degree of flare in her voice. "We need a few things for dinner and I'm taking Travis with me. I'll be back in half an hour and I'd appreciate it if our *guest* (that word was laced with ice) was gone by then." She then walked out.

I wondered what Paul had said that had her so upset. And then I realized it was Paul's lesser half. Beth arose from her seat to turn and look at me. "Your baby is cute."

I didn't need her to say it because it was written on her face. "Our baby would have been beautiful."

"Beth, why are you here?"

"We could leave—just me and you. It could be the way it was always meant to be."

It was not lost on me in the least that she said "me" first in her statement. It wasn't as intentional as it was just hard wired in her to always think of herself first.

And people are always asking me, "What's wrong with you? Fucking weird. I'm getting a beer, want one?"

"Didn't you hear me? We could finally be together."

"Oh, I heard you." I closed the fridge door and twisted the cap off my beer. I took a long pull before I responded again. "Let's see…I am happily married to a woman I love dearly. Then there's this little being about yay big," I held my hand up to about my hip, "who I'm just fascinated by. Then, and this is a big part, there's this other being…" I held my hand way above my head and jumped a little, "who would be seriously disappointed in me if I ran away. Oh yeah, then there's this guy, he's like a General or something who for a fair portion of my life held the best friend honor and strangely enough is also married to you. And now for the kicker, Beth…I don't love you. Why you haven't figured that part out yet is a mystery to me."

Her face flashed anger and then bewilderment before abruptly switching to an all-knowing smile. "You don't mean that."

I took another pull from the beer before sitting down. "And I really thought my time aboard the Julipion screwed me up. What the hell did it do to you?"

She seemed undeterred. I wasn't sure how much clearer I could make my point. She reached to touch my face, I pulled away. That anger came back; I think if she had a weapon she would have used it.

"I'm here for another reason."

"If you're pregnant, it's not mine."

"Paul is my husband, your friend. He needs you."

"I know who he is, pretty sure I didn't need the reminding. Oh, wait. Sorry, you probably did that for your benefit."

"Funny." The words did not match her tone.

"If Paul, my friend and your *husband* (I stressed 'husband') needs me so much, why isn't he here instead? My guess is he doesn't even know you're here. After your outburst aboard the Guardian, which I'm sure did wonders for all of our relationships with him, I'd think he wouldn't want you within a country mile of me. Not that I even know what a country mile is, but it sounds far."

"You're right. He doesn't know I'm here."

"I'm like psychic or some shit."

"Mike, this is serious. Colonel Bailey is having a difficult time taking over the helm of the Guardian."

"Not much I can really do about that," I said, kicking back and placing my feet up on the table. "Oh hey, could you not tell Tracy about this?" I asked, pointing to my feet. "She'll get pissed. You know, I'm really getting into this vacation thing. I almost beat Dee in a game of chess. The downside is I've been changing WAY more diapers, should probably ask for hazard pay or something. A real good thing, though, was I didn't have to kill anything at all within the last seven days and the bonus is that nothing was trying to kill me. I mean, with the exception of Trav's diapers." I finished my beer and let the front chair legs hit the ground as I stood up. "Sure you don't want one?" I asked, swishing the empty bottle in her face.

She shook her head. My next beer shattered on the kitchen floor with her next words. I would mourn for its loss later. "Paul is planning on bombing the Genogerian settlement."

"What? What the fuck for? I'll kill him. Come on," I said, grabbing her hand and dragging her behind me.

"Where...where are we going?"

"Getting back up." I was dragging her towards Dee's house.

"Mrs. Ginson, are you alright?" The Sergeant stepped out of the Hummer.

"She's fine. We'll be right back." I didn't turn to

respond. "Keep the engine running."

I slammed my fist against Dee's garage door.

"Only you, Michael, are crazy enough to disturb me in this fashion!" Dee bellowed from behind the door. Beth was attempting to shrink back but I held her fast.

"We have to go."

"Important?" His demeanor changed with the question.

"That's an understatement."

The door flew open quickly. "Does it have something to do with small female who travels with bear?"

"Her mate."

"Is the General not well?" he asked, stepping out and shutting the garage door behind him.

"He won't be when I'm through with him. He's looking to end the Geno settlements, violently."

"Should I retrieve my weaponry?" Dee was about as ripped as I'd ever seen him.

I had to think about it for a moment. I was afraid if we had anything on us, we might be tempted to use them, and by "we" I meant Dee. "If we need anything we'll take it from the armory."

"Where are we going?" he asked as we walked back over to my driveway.

I honestly had no idea and looked over to Beth.

"He's on the Guardian."

"We're going to the Guardian."

"Would it be too much if I inquired as to why?"

"I don't know all the particulars. Beth here is going to fill us in on the way, but suffice it to say it involves the wholesale slaughter of Genogerians."

The Sergeant must have seen the anger Dee was emanating because he involuntarily reached for his sidearm.

Tracy pulled up just as we crossed the street.

"Mike?" she asked, rolling down her window.

"It's not what it looks like," I said, letting go of

Beth's hand, which I had been squeezing tight. Beth sighed in relief as I let it go, vigorously rubbing it to get some circulation back into her purpling digits.

"It looks like Beth is terrified and you and Dee are about to start blowing things up."

"Friggen nailed it. How do you do that? I've got to go the Guardian."

"Is the second Destroyer here already? I thought we'd have more time."

"No, something different. I'll tell you when I get home."

"And when will that be?"

"I don't know." I leaned in the window and kissed her like it might be my last time. And who knows, maybe it was. With only a few exceptions, did you ever truly know when you might have kissed the one you loved for the last time? And I'm not talking about while they're in a casket, that doesn't really count. Just like all those stupid flowers people feel the need to buy for the dead. The deceased sure as hell doesn't give a shit. Probably would have liked it a lot better if they'd received them when they were alive. Well, that's my two cents anyway.

"I'm only authorized to drive the General's wife," the Sergeant said, looking at me as Beth and I climbed up in the back seat.

"Tell him that," I said, pointing to Dee who was sitting up front.

"Right. Everyone's going to the airfield I take it?"

"Out with it," I said, turning toward Beth. "What possible reason could Paul have for wanting to bomb the Genos? And please don't tell me this is some sick way to get back at me because if it is, I'll put him down like a rabid dog."

The Sergeant shot me a glance through the rear view mirror.

"Figuratively, figuratively," I repeated, trying to

appease him.

"No, he's not trying to get back at you. It's not always about you, you know."

"In my world it is."

"I did not take you for a narcissist," Dee stated.

"I only let it out occasionally—sometimes I can't even stand myself."

"That makes more sense." Dee said.

"Two men drove a supply truck into the settlement and detonated a bomb."

"Did they say why or who sent them?"

"No. They died in the explosion."

"Suicide bombers? What would be the reasoning behind that?"

"How was the bomb detonated?" Dee did not turn because he really didn't have the room in the tight confines of the Hummer.

"Trigger switch in the passenger's hand."

"Something stinks here. Why not just put a timer on it, drive the truck up, park and walk away? Okay, that's something we'll have to figure out eventually. What in that scenario necessitates bombing the Genos again?"

"They've gone nuts," the Sergeant added. "At least forty Genos bought it in the blast, seven of them were young. They've gone on a rampage, saying that they've got the right to protect their borders. There have already been a few skirmishes, with some outlying folks who haven't fared so well. The General sent an emissary and they shot him. Without Tantor they have no one to settle them back down."

"When's he planning on bombing them?"

"They were in the middle of their strategy session when Mrs. Ginson came and got me."

"What's his plan?"

The Sergeant looked a little torn. It wasn't like we were buddies and now that I was no longer in the service there was a chance he could be brought up on charges for talking to me about this.

"Bomb them into submission." Beth bailed him out.

The Sergeant nodded his head in agreement with her words.

"They will not submit, Michael. They will all die attempting to defend what is theirs and to also protect themselves from what they would feel was an unprovoked attack."

"I know that, Dee. We cannot allow him to perform what will ultimately become genocide."

"And what exactly are you planning on doing? I cannot allow you to harm the General. In fact, I cannot allow you on a shuttle no matter what you threaten to do to me." He looked over at Dee as he said the words.

"Shit, you're right. As big of an ass as you are, I don't want to be responsible for getting you shot."

"Gee, thanks."

"At least he is somewhat concerned with your well-being. That is more than most get," Dee explained.

"Beth, you need to go up there and convince him to give me a chance to stop this before it gets any worse."

"How will you get out to Arizona? I believe he will want to strike soon."

"Sergeant, can you have the shuttle swing by Arizona first before going up to the Guardian?"

"I could have some plausible deniability .The pilot owes me money from our last poker game."

"You're not that bad. Now I kind of feel bad about your balls."

"Kind of?"

"Take what he has given you, Sergeant, and run with it. I am amazed he apologized at all."

"You're really starting to become a pain in the ass, Dee."

He laughed. If you didn't know what it was you were hearing, you'd swear that he was coughing up a whole cat.

The Hummer swerved and Beth tried to meld into her seat.

***

We were in the shuttle and halfway to Arizona when Dee finally quit. It wasn't that he had such a long laughing bout—it was more a testament to how fast the shuttle was. It had easily shaved five hours off of any conventional flight time.

"I can't get any closer," the pilot told us as we looked out over the horizon, which was glowing the red of a setting sun. Unfortunately it was only about noon. "It's restricted airspace."

"On whose command?" I asked.

"The Genogerians. They're shooting down anything that gets within five miles of them."

"Where are they getting this type of weaponry?" I asked Dee.

"Do not look at me. I am not an arms merchant."

"What are all those experiments you've been doing in your garage?"

"These men will not think your false accusations humorous."

"Fine, but where could they have gotten anti-aircraft guns?"

"Sir, they're using alien technology," the pilot told me. Obviously he hadn't gotten the memo yet about me not being active military anymore.

"Well, isn't this interesting? Dee, any theories? Is this something they've been working on?"

"If so then they were keeping it secret from me. I saw no such endeavors."

"Something stinks here. We have a bomb that goes off nefariously and then somehow the Genos have been equipped with some heavy duty weapons. Seems like someone wants this little side drama to play out. Who gains from a Geno war?"

"Land owners?" the Sergeant offered.

"Normally I might agree with that, but no one was particularly interested in this land before the Genos came so why would they be now? Plus, there's more than enough acreage to go around." The rapid depopulation of the planet had left vast areas devoid of people the likes of which hadn't been seen since the ice age. I kept talking, hoping that at some point I would strike across a chord that rang true. "Paul? Could this be a set-up on his part to wipe out a populace he's not overly fond of? Why go through so much trouble? He could strafe the shit out of this place and no one would be the wiser."

"He would never do such a thing," Beth protested.

"No? He's told me numerous times about the resources he has to use to defend and supply them. Makes life a lot easier if they're gone. Now ultimately I don't believe he'd do it, but right now he's a suspect. Beth, just have him hold off for a little while."

"I'll try, Mike, but if they keep attacking villages he'll have no choice."

"All right."

"Be careful."

"That's my middle name," I smiled.

"Is that sarcasm?" Dee asked.

"Over confidence or sarcasm—either work." We landed, I grabbed two rifles from a rack as Dee hopped out, I joined him before moving away from the shuttle as it took off again.

"If there is indeed a war going on, the shuttle is surely going to attract attention."

"Do we have something to worry about?"

"It is my understanding that there are casualties in war."

"Fair enough."

"Will the General abate?"

"Doubtful. We may have bought twelve hours or so. If he doesn't do something soon to protect people he will be seen as weak and possibly a traitor to his species. Even if he didn't want to squash this uprising he will be compelled to do so."

"Then we must get moving."

I had a lot to thank for my son; he'd kept my cardio at optimum performance. Even so, keeping up with Dee without an engine of some sort was difficult. He was holding back on his full gait but by the third mile I was beginning to lag and flag.

"Should have paid the extra fare to get closer," I said between intakes of air. Dee had stopped again and was waiting for me. He looked like he was out for a leisurely stroll on a nice fall day. I, however, was covered in sweat and dragging in breath.

"You would have never defeated me in the games."

"Really, Dee? That's what you're thinking at this very moment? Not cool man, not cool at all. Maybe you should just put on a clown outfit and really terrify the shit out of me."

"I do not think I could find a red nose that would fit." The bastard was smiling.

"I wonder if they could make footballs from your hide? I'd sure like to get in a little punting practice."

We thankfully began walking the closer we got. Fires were raging, flames leaping from building to building. We were traversing a pile of rubble when we came across the first Geno since we'd landed. He was a younger one, adolescent maybe, he still dwarfed me. He had a pipe in his hands, looked like it was a signpost once, it still had the bulb of cement attached to the bottom. Thing had to be close to a hundred pounds yet he wielded it like a kid does a plastic sword. The cement ball whistled by the top of my head, if it had connected, I wouldn't have had enough time to even register my death. Dee shouted something and the young

Geno took off.

"Dee, he nearly took my head off." I rubbed the top of the head expecting to feel some stickiness there. I shook away a couple of pieces of gravel that had come loose from the makeshift mace.

"Yes, that would have been unfortunate."

"That's it? That's your response?"

"You are still alive and unhurt, is that not good enough?"

"You've got to work on your empathy a little bit. I just had a near death experience. I was expecting a little more solace."

"I am not your mate."

"Keep talking like that and you never will be."

Dee snorted.

"He's going to tell his friends." I once again rubbed my head. One does not get over nearly having their skull caved in too quickly.

"We have to find some leaders and stop this madness. I fear for my safety as well."

"What do you have to fear?"

"I am traveling with a human; that will make me a target."

"Is that supposed to be funny?"

"No, I take my personal safety seriously."

"Why do you always show these obtuse sides of yourself when we're in danger?"

"It is nice to see you expanding your vocabulary. Come, we must move away from this place."

Another half mile went by. The streets preternaturally quiet as if the encroaching tension was pushing noise out of its path.

"I believe we are surrounded," Dee said, looking around at the structures to either side.

"What are they waiting for?" I was looking around for any sign. I was in agreement with Dee; I could feel the eyes upon me, I just couldn't see them.

"It is possible that you and I have been recognized. It is my belief that now would be a good time to put our weapons down."

"I hate this part," I told him as I pulled the sling over my head and slowly bent over to place the rifle by my feet. I made sure it was pointed outwards with the safety off. If I needed it I was going to make sure I could have it up and firing in a moment's notice.

The young Geno that I must have pissed off in a former life showed himself. He still had his weapon of choice and was standing across the street. He had come out from behind a large blue dumpster. He ran towards us, more specifically, me.

"Dee?"

"Do not move."

"That's easy for you to say."

My aggressor had halved the distance.

"Dee, man."

"If you reach for that rifle you will be shot."

"Better that than split-pea brains." I moved nearly imperceptibly.

"Michael."

"Fine but I'm not going to watch. Mom, save me a spot." I outstretched my hands and leaned my head back, my eyes closed. "My Father, who art in heaven..."

The young Geno was screaming, sounded like a war cry. I'd heard those enough to know.

"Stop!" Dee said forcibly. "We mean you no harm."

I could hear the wind being pushed out of the way as the cement ball arced through the air.

"This is going to fucking hurt..." my teeth were gritted.

The impact as the club smashed into the ground, lifted me off my feet a good three or four inches. I opened my eyes, fully expecting to be standing in front of St. Peter, desperately trying to explain why I warranted a spot on hallowed ground. What I got was a snarling greenish mask of teeth and hate not more than half a foot away, looking down at me.

"I am Drababan, young one. We have come to seek peace and to stop further bloodshed."

"There can be no peace with the hu-mans!" the Geno raged.

"Do you know who I am?"

"I know you as Drababan, Champion of the Games, leader of the rebellion and friend to the Earth Champion. Should that make me quake in my feet? Should I grovel before you like a worm begging for your attention?"

"Teenagers are teenagers no matter the species," I said through gritted teeth.

The young Geno got closer, his growling punctuated with long ropes of spittle.

"I said that out loud?"

"I am not asking for your obedience. If you know me then you know I would not come here with the intention of harming my people."

"*Your* people? You live with the vermin. One word from me, Drababan, and you will both be spilling your innards onto this accursed ground."

"Then why have you not already done so? Your words are beginning to bore me."

"Let him talk some more," I bemoaned.

The Geno raged for a moment longer and bounded off.

I let out a breath I'd been holding since seemingly the whole thing had started.

"Now what? King of bright ideas."

"We wait." Dee sat down and unwrapped a granola bar.

"Got another one of those?"

"You should be more prepared." He didn't offer me

one or a bite of his as he ate with some lip smacking satisfaction. "That is payment for the last diaper you made me change." And with that he began his humming and chanting as he went into a meditative state.

I sidled closer to see if I could look in his small backpack. A large eye rolled open to look at me.

"You'd think they were made of gold." I moved away, doing my best to scan the area without making it appear as if that was what I was doing. The Genos now seemed less concerned with stealth because I caught sight of at least a half dozen, most of them armed. "Well, this is a good time."

Dee was just stretching out of his last session when my new bestie showed up again. He was dragging his face smasher behind him, an older Geno by his side.

"Drababan." The older Geno bowed slightly.

"Jurtillion, it is good to see you." Dee returned the nod of respect.

"It was not wise of you to bring a human here, even one as worthy as him."

"It was he who brought me here."

"Hmmm, most unusual. We should get out from the open. There are some among us that will shoot first and deal with the consequences later."

"I like his idea, Dee."

"Hello, Michael." Jurtillion nodded in my direction. The young Geno scoffed. "Forgive my son Cythion, he does not fully understand the role you played in the freeing of our people."

I thanked the stars that he didn't. If he knew that freeing the Genos was more a means to an end he might hate me more.

"The bomb that destroyed our gathering place extinguished the life of his mother, my mate."

"I am sorry for your loss," I told him solemnly.

"It is your kind that did it!" Cythion exploded.

"The act of a few does not condemn the many!" Jurtillion shot back.

Cythion scoffed again and bounded off, taking that friggen street sign with him. I was going to shudder every time I came across any kind of traffic sign for the rest of my days, although that really didn't seem like any type of extended sentence.

We walked relatively slowly but with a purpose. Jurtillion was tense, he might be a leader but he did not have absolute control. There was a physical relaxation in him as we entered into what used to be a gas station.

"Step away from the windows, please," he said, urging me forward. "It is customary on this planet that I should offer you a beverage. Prune juice, perhaps?"

"What the hell is it with Genogerians and laxatives?" After Moxie, prune juice reined in the number two spot on Dee's favorite drinks.

"I thank you, Jurtillion. I would like some please," Dee said as he walked past, making sure to bang the back of my head with his hand.

"Make sure his has pits." I rubbed my skull.

"Is it true that the Progerians have returned?" Jurtillion asked, handing Dee a pitcher of the purplish liquid. My stomach gurgled wildly just looking at it. Watching Dee quaff it down almost had me running to the bathroom in sympathy elimination.

"It is. They returned with a Cruiser and a Destroyer."

"Then time is short."

"Not as short as you may think. The one whose life your son tried to end has destroyed them."

"This human has beaten a Cruiser and Destroyer? This is not possible! This is cause for celebration!"

"Got anything better than prune juice?" I asked once I was able to stand straight again. Jurtillion had nearly knocked me over.

"The battle is not quite over, Jurtillion. There are

more pressing matters to be concerned with. What has happened here?"

Jurtillion's earlier merriment evaporated quickly. "It was the time of our prayer. As a leader of the community it was my mate's duty to get things ready. There were some others there as well. She had just sent Cythion away to get more supplies when the truck carrying the humans and their bomb arrived. Dozens died."

"Was it normal for humans to come here?" I asked.

"About once a month your kind would come, sometimes with seeds or equipment for farming."

"Same truck every time?"

"Same truck, and the same two men."

I watched in fascination as Dee placed his now empty pitcher down, my thoughts racing from bomb to stomach, with both seemingly on the edge of explosive results. (Sorry—prune juice does this to me.)

"Wait...you're saying this was also the same truck AND the same men?"

Jurtillion nodded. "Most humans want nothing to do with us and quite honestly we prefer it that way."

"Something stinks."

"It is not I, Michael!" Dee raged.

"Whoa, Dee, I meant metaphorically, not intestinally."

"That is acceptable," he said, calming down.

"Why would two men who have been doing the same supply run for years all of a sudden go suicidal? I won't deny the fact that potentially they harbored some deep hatred for your kind, but why wait so long to exact revenge and why take themselves out as well? They may have not known the bomb was on the truck. And that seems more likely, given that they did not have an opportunity to escape. Dead men tell no tales."

"It still begs the question, why?" Dee stated.

"Well I think it's fairly safe to rule out Paul. He

would have just leveled this place. Who would dislike Genogerians even more than humans?"

"Progerians?" Dee asked. "But how? They are across the country in Florida and heavily guarded."

"More like heavily watched. Paul placed them in that location with the hopes that the territory would be more of a barrier to their movements."

"I agree with your premise that the Progerians have no love loss for Genogerians but it still comes down to why? They must have known their bomb would cause only minimal casualties."

"Maybe they had an idea of what would happen after the bomb was exploded," I said.

"Chaos and war," Jurtillion expressed sadly. "That one bomb could be our undoing."

"With Genos declaring war on everything around them, Paul and the military will be forced to act."

"It is brilliant in its brutality and simplicity. That is most certainly the Progerian way." Dee looked pissed off. "How could we be so naive as to think the Progerians would finally leave us alone?"

"They are without spirituality, Drababan, and as such only know one way to deal with their world."

I figured Jurtillion and Dee were about to go down prayer mode so I wandered around a bit before going to the window. I hoped Beth was able to convince Paul to delay his strike or else we were going to be crispy critters soon. A mass evacuation was sort of out of the question. First off we were talking in the neighborhood of a few hundred thousand Genos and secondly, where could I lead them that Paul's bombers wouldn't find us? This wasn't going to be a localized disaster; this one would travel with us.

"Shit." Cython was coming back, twirling his street sign like a baton, and he had friends this time. "Um, guys?" No response. I stepped back. "Guys, this really isn't the time for some meditative relaxation. We (and by 'we' I mean 'I') have a serious problem right now."

Jurtillion snorted as he came up beside me. I followed him outside with Dee close in tow.

"What are you doing?" Jurtillion questioned his son.

"I am eliminating the threat that has walked in among our people," Cythion said brashly.

"Michael Talbot has proven to be our friend. He has freed us from the Progerians."

"Yes, to live on this reservation waiting for handouts. That is what true freedom is all about. Father, can we leave this compound? Can my friends and I explore this vast land? No! We stay here to rot like unpicked fruit. The humans did us a favor with that bomb."

"Do not say such a thing!" Jurtillion shouted. I thought I saw Cythion shy away a tiny bit.

"We are now truly free to forge our way into this world—with fire!"

"Why then are you still here, Cythion? Why have you not joined this liberation cause? No, you have stayed here under the guise of protecting our borders. You attack one man and when it does not immediately go your way you run. Now you have enlisted the help of your friends to once again try and kill this one man."

Cythion looked like he was going to blow some major blood vessels.

"If you are so truly brave and ready to fight for a new existence then why not take on this man by yourself?"

"Hey, wait," I said softly.

"Just know this is the Earth Champion, the man that defeated all other men on his planet."

"Well, that's sort of an exaggeration," I mumbled.

"The man who had Drababan on his knees!" Jurtillion continued.

"That is most assuredly an exaggeration." Dee echoed my earlier words.

"Just so you know, Cythion, he also defeated a Star

Scout, a Battle Cruiser and a Heavy Destroyer. What bigger way to prove yourself than by killing a hero of this magnitude by yourself?"

"I'm not really liking the line this conversation is taking."

Cythion looked scared—I could see it in his features. Jurtillion had painted him into a pretty serious corner and in front of his friends no less. As a matter of fact he'd done the same to me. If he was trying to get rid of one of us he had done so very deftly.

Cythion stepped back before stepping forward. "I accept the challenge."

"Whoa! I never agreed to this," I said.

"This is madness," Dee said. "We came here to prevent further bloodshed, not spread more."

"I had not expected this response," Jurtillion said with regret.

"Bullshit, you knew exactly what you were doing. What are you going to do when I kill your offspring? You move closer with that stick in your hands and I'm going to blow your fucking head off, lizard boy!"

Cythion hissed. A crowd was beginning to gather.

"Jurtillion, you must gain control of your people," Dee warned.

"It was my mate!" he shouted.

"Oh, shit."

"We were attempting the Earth custom of staying together for more than just procreation. I found solace in her nearness, and now she has been taken from me."

"Jurtillion, your grief is deep and perhaps you are not thinking clearly, but this man had nothing to do with your loss. His death, if it were to come at the hands of your off-spring, would bring you no comfort, only more death."

"Yeah, what he said." I was holding my rifle up to my shoulder, scanning the growing crowd for an even bigger threat than Cythion.

"We came here to diffuse the situation not add to it, Jurtillion," Dee offered. "However, if it is blood you require as payment for blood, then you shall have it."

"Hey, big fella, don't you think that maybe we should have talked about this first?" I pulled the rifle away from my face so I could look over at Dee.

"You must, however, bind yourself to the laws of our duels."

"I do." Jurtillion nodded.

"If Michael is to win, we walk away with no further confrontation."

"Done. And when Cythion wins?"

"Well, you will have the blood you feel that you so desperately need. We have naught more to offer."

"Those terms are acceptable."

"Dee, man, what did you just get me into?"

"Nothing that I cannot handle, for I will fight in your stead."

"What?" Jurtillion and I asked at the same time.

Cythion looked like he was going to wet whatever he called the thing he was wearing. Looked like MC Hammer pants.

"It is our right within the guidelines of a duel for a champion to be chosen, and I am just such a champion." Dee pulled off his rifle, rolled his shoulders back and puffed out his chest. That was the warrior that scared the hell out of me.

Cythion was looking wildly from his father to his friends. He'd really stepped in a big fresh pile of shit this time.

"Hold on, Dee."

"Now is not the time, Michael. He may be an adolescent Genogerian, but he is still easily twice as strong and fast as you. I will dispatch of him quickly and mercifully. Then we will leave this place."

Jurtillion looked crestfallen and desperate. Dangerously desperate, enough so that I think he was going to "damn" the rules of the engagement.

"I'll fight him, Dee. If he wants a piece of the human race I'll give it to him."

"Michael, what are you doing?"

"Something that needs to be done. You have to trust me on this one."

Dee nodded, as well as he could sense what humans were going to do it amazed me that he could miss the signals that Jurtillion had been throwing off.

"Weapons?" I asked. Bare-knuckled was not how I wanted to go down, the idea of punching that leathery covered thick boned hide was making my knuckles ache.

"It must be weapons of agreement," Dee shot out before Jurtillion could make something up on the spot. Maybe he had sensed something.

"I chose this!" Cythion thrust his sign above his head.

"I don't think I can even lift that."

Cythion and his friends snorted in derision. The youth had gone from wanting to flee to ready to kill in a matter of heartbeats.

"Puny hu-man. What can you use?" Cythion snarled.

"A grenade would be nice." Unfortunately they didn't know what those were.

"Michael, you must take this more seriously."

"Trust me, buddy, I'm taking this pretty seriously. Bow and arrow?" I asked.

"I decline," Cythion shouted. "Hand to hand?"

"I decline."

"Because you are scared of my might!"

"No. It's because I'll bruise my hands on your fat head."

That got him riled up.

"Steel!"

"He means swords," Dee explained when I looked confused.

"Sure. Steel it is then." I probably should have been

more specific. The thing tossed my way was a crudely formed broad sword. Weighing in excess of twenty-five pounds, it was like wielding a car bumper. For Cythion he most likely could have spun it fast enough to take off like a helicopter.

I was dragging the point of my sword behind me. Cythion had his held high above his head. The crowd fanned out into a circle. I noted that Dee was standing close to Jurtillion. I knew at some point if things got desperate for me he was going to take matters into his own hands, for good or bad. I might die out here today but I didn't want my friend to join me. I sized up Cythion. He was bigger, stronger and faster than me, what he lacked was experience. I can't imagine he'd done any true training.

"The duel commences when my words come to a stop, and ends when only one of you can walk away," Jurtillion announced.

"So if I was to sprain an ankle and had to hop?"

"The duels are to the death," Jurtillion clarified.

"Always to the death. Does your kind need to be so serious about everything?"

"Cythion, do not take this man lightly, he is dangerous. I have watched him fight on many occasions," Jurtillion added.

"I am dangerous, father!"

"I think the lady doth protest too much," I said as I pulled the tip of my sword off the ground.

The earth was shaking as Cythion pounded towards me. I'd expected Jurtillion to say something like "let the games begin", I was wrong. For the second time that day Cythion nearly took my head clean off my shoulders. The steel blew past my head; I barely had enough time to pull my sword up to thwart his back swing. The crash of metal on metal rang through the air. The shock of the vibration traveled up my arms and through my skull. I stumbled back four or five feet, trying to regain my footing.

Cythion was faster than I was expecting. He had not the time to get his sword back into a killing position, however, he was able to slam into me, sending me sprawling. The buzz of the crowd was deafening as they began to smell blood. My adversary was coming again. He was going to punt my head like a football and he was attempting an NFL record seventy yarder. I was able to roll away just as his foot swung out, a claw from one of his toes ripping my cheek open. I lost part of my facial movement as he cut through skin and muscle. This was something I would note later as I had not the time to worry about so inconsequential of an issue. A millimeter or two deeper and I would have been able to stick my tongue out the side of my face.

His pursuit of my rolling body was relentless, the only thing I had going for me was that he wasn't using his "steel". I didn't know how long I could keep scrambling without him getting in a kick that would cave in my ribcage. My hands were torn up, small pebbles embedded under the skin. My jeans, which had been relatively new before the day had started, were now bloody and shredded at the knees. I was also suffering the same skin condition on my hands. Then he struck as I got hung up on a rock. I didn't quite get the distance he'd been hoping for—some but not enough. The front of his foot caught me in the ribs, propelling me up and over my obstacle. The pain crashed into me in waves.

"Michael! Now would be a good time to fight back!" Dee shouted.

If he thought I was playing possum with my opponent he was pretty far off base. However, it did buy me a second as Cythion took his eyes off of me to look towards Dee. I moved further away and simultaneously began to stand. It was nice to finally have a perspective where I wasn't flat on my back. Cythion again charged; at least he was predictable. I stayed low, as he seemed to have a problem swinging his sword at that angle, and this was no exception. I moved slightly so that I did not take in the full weight of his body as he tried to drive me once again to the ground.

His forward momentum took him past me where he began to pinwheel his arms. He had been expecting to hit me and when he mostly missed, he was leaning too far forward to stay upright. He crashed into the ground head first, ten feet away. I moved as fast as I could and still he was able to spin onto his back, his legs pointing towards me, kicking back and forth. If any of his attempts had connected he would have broken my spine. I had both of my hands on the hilt of the sword down by my hip so that the point was straight ahead of me. I had meant to drive it into Cythion's back but he'd been too quick. As he lashed out with his right leg, the tip of my steel blade caught him dead center in the foot. Between my running toward him and him kicking out, the blade easily parted flesh, muscle, sinew and bone. He howled, pulling his leg back wrenching the sword free from my hands. I stepped back as he wildly swung his left leg out, seeking purchase. The Genos quickly quieted down as Cythion raged on. Jurtillion moved forward as Dee shook his head.

"He cannot fight anymore, Jurtillion. Is this battle done?" I asked. I wanted it to be, as pain flared up my side.

Jurtillion was tight-lipped, well, as tight-lipped as a being without lips can be.

"Duels are to the death, Michael," Dee filled in.

I was pissed at my big green friend. I thought I had given Jurtillion an out from this battle and further bloodshed but that didn't seem to be the case. Fat droplets of blood fell from my face, splashing heavily onto the ground. Cythion was trying to remove the blade from his foot. I had not so much as a knife on me and getting that close to Cythion was still a death sentence. He might be one leg short, but his other plus his arms were more than enough to crush the existence out of me. I circled slowly around; he made sure to follow my movements, never letting me get behind him. His mouth was open in stress and pain and maybe even a little bit of panic. There was Geno-speak going on all around me as his friends tried to urge him on. If I didn't end this soon, odds were that one or more of them would jump in, regardless of the rules.

I kept my head up as I leaned down and grabbed a decent sized chunk of brick and cement, the heft of it feeling good in my hands. Now I had to get into a position in which I could use it. I jogged around Cythion just to see how quickly he could spin. It was surprisingly fast. I picked it up a notch as I noticed the crowd begin to press in. It would only take one errant elbow or shove to send me into Cythion's mouth or arms. I was running about as fast as I could in a circle, with Cythion twirling like a friggen top. There was a small rise of rubble that I used as a backstop to change my momentum and direction. I was relatively surprised when I didn't tear a MCL or an ACL as I changed direction. Cythion was a moment too late as I ran towards his approaching head. He had just stopped his direction as I came down onto his skull with my left knee. That may have dazed him a bit, but it was when I brought the brick and cement rock down on his snout that I changed his outlook on life.

I heard the bones in his nose shatter as I drove the rock down. I was able to get one more powerful hit in before he reflexively tossed me off. I must have been airborne for close to ten feet before landing with a heavy grunt. Blood was beginning to choke Cythion as it flooded into his nasal cavity, throat, stomach and lungs. His screams were muted with the wet, thick fluid, making them sound more like heavy mucous-laced coughs.

"Is this not enough, Jurtillion?" I asked in a shout. If looks could kill, my heart would have stopped at that moment.

"Finish him, Michael. To not do so is an insult," Dee implored.

My chest heaving, I grabbed a heavier rock and once again brought it over my head. I was ready to smash his skull repeatedly until I heard the bony armor crack and shatter.

Then I realized Cythion had let go of his sword to shield his destroyed face. I bent down and reached for it, at this point realizing that his friends were beginning to crowd in. A warning bolt from Dee's rifle sent them back a few feet.

"If they attempt to impede again you are within your rights to harm them," Dee said to me very matter-of-factly.

I know he was trying to put the fear of Gropytheon into them, but if he thought I could take on even one more juvenile Geno without suffering some grievous wound or wounds, then he had more faith in my skills than I did.

Cythion was mewling, he was in a lot of pain and scared I was about to send him to his after-life. I would imagine he was feeling a large portion of betrayal as well. Here he was, surrounded by his kind about to get murdered by the enemy and none of them were able to lift a finger. I had no doubt that sentiment would change if I lingered too long. I raised the sword above my head like I was going to plant a flag in some particularly hard packed dirt. The tip broke through his skin just above his sternum. There was a sickening crack as the blade broke through bone. He blew blood from his mouth as I forced air from his lungs in a rush from the impact. I could tell I had sliced into a lung as air bubbles made of blood formed around the wound. His chest cavity began to sag down as he thrashed around wildly. He began to slice his hands up as he gripped desperately at the blade, trying to wrench it free from his body. I twisted it back and forth, not in malice but in the hopes that it would end his suffering. I placed a foot against his neck and pulled the blade free. I had a feeling I might potentially need it before we were able to leave.

The crowd slowly closed in. "Is this what your word is worth?" Dee asked of Jurtillion.

I think Jurtillion was about to say 'to hell' with honor. I don't know what clicked or most likely broke in the Geno but he told them to let us leave. I think it was the heartbreaking loss of his offspring. Killing us would do little to bring him back.

"If you are anywhere near here by sundown, we will consider it an act of war. Now go."

Dee and I looked at each other. We shouldered…well, *he* shouldered his way through and I followed closely. We left at a decent pace, not taking our time but certainly not running. I think if we had started jogging it would have triggered a chase response in them. We weren't more than a mile from the outskirts of the Geno city when something dawned on me.

"Did you notice anything strange about that Geno crowd?" Dee hadn't said more than two words to me since we'd left. My battle and subsequent killing of Cythion had affected him deeply.

"I did not," he offered up after a few moments, not bothering to ask me to fill him in. He just clammed back up.

"A bunch of the Genos were armed, Dee."

"That is what happens in war, Michael."

"Yeah, Dee, but if you stopped and thought about it for a second, where in the hell did they get all those weapons? Those aren't old shotguns they were slinging around. Those were state-of-the-art Progerian war-machine firearms."

Dee stopped. "Someone is supplying them."

"It's like I said, someone wants them on the war path—someone with contacts either at the armament factories or on the Guardian. Either way, Paul has some serious problems."

"We need to move further away. We are being followed."

"Really? I somehow missed the fact that huge Genos are pursuing us?" I asked, turning around but seeing nothing. I may have seen a shadow but it felt more like I'd imagined it to make it seem that I wasn't completely unaware.

"They will follow us until night descends, thereby honoring Jurtillion's request."

"That's not really even straddling the line, that's just plain shitty. How many are there?" I once again turned around as fast as I could in an attempt to catch one in mid-stride out in the open.

"At least ten."

"How the hell can you tell?" We both had rifles, but outnumbered ten to two was not odds one could take lightly.

"I do not like this, Michael. I will fight them tonight to honor my pact with you and to also preserve my own life. However, going forward should we survive I cannot participate in this upcoming war in any manner. I will not fight with or against my people."

"I get that, Dee. Let's just try to focus on getting through the night and we'll talk after."

"My stance cannot change."

I didn't say anything else—what was there to offer? If the roles were reversed and I was on his planet I most assuredly could not fight against other humans no matter the situation. I'd also have a problem with the not joining up with them aspect. I'd known for a long time that Dee had a much higher functioning moral compass. I wasn't going to beat myself up over it, though. I'm sure he was on par with Gandhi in that respect. We were at least five miles out of the Geno settlement by the time the sun set. Definitely far enough to not be considered in the territory. Still it was no surprise when that first shot came our way. It wasn't particularly close, but then again how close do you want projectiles to be?

We'd stopped a half an hour before sunset when we realized we weren't going to lose our tail. We found a small depression in the ground and expanded it. I'd rifled through an abandoned car earlier on our trek and grabbed a tire iron. It was perfect in breaking up the soil and Dee, with his powerful arms, was able to claw it away. By the time we were done, it was big enough for Dee and I to lie down comfortably. We had a slight rise around the entire rim. It was a pretty decent fighting hole for the limited amount of time spent building it.

"We really didn't think this through," I told Dee as I rested my rifle on the berm. "Didn't bring a radio or tell our driver to come back and get us."

"Perhaps we should have planned a contingency, but I would not have predicted this outcome."

My body hurt and my cheek was throbbing. It burned so hotly it felt like someone was holding a lighter to it. I fought my way through the aches and pains, keeping still as I waited for the first Geno to expose himself. The sun had just set in front of me, the glare of it no longer affecting my shot. A Geno rose from the ground, nearly invisible, camouflaged perfectly in what I can only describe as a Geno version of a gilly suit. It's basically a net with fauna from whatever area you are in fitted through the weaves. It wasn't going to save this particular Geno, but damn.

I fired, the bolt illuminating his shocked features. I was a little to the left. That side of his face melted away under the assault of the round. I thought about asking Dee if wind and distance affected the shot but thought better of it as he was deep in prayer. I had to imagine that would give the Genos pause before they considered an all-out assault.

"One down, nine to go," I muttered just as Dee's barrel rested next to mine. "You alright?"

"Not at all," he answered honestly.

For the briefest of insane moments I almost let him off the hook and told him he should go. I don't think he would have, but that point zero zero one percent was still entirely too high.

The Genos had fanned out, intense firing heading our way, but again, not really too close. They had an idea where we were but not an exact location yet.

Two more Genos exposed themselves and two more Genos got to meet their maker. I noticed Dee's first few shots were high, as in warning. The only thing that was going to dissuade them from their present course of action was death, and I let him know that.

There were now three dead and at least two wounded, hopefully dying. Dee had gone from shooting high to shooting wide. He'd winged a couple of the Genos, but this wasn't a pellet gun round. Getting brushed by a Geno rifle could still kill you or sever a limb.

"Dee, man, they're playing for keeps. You're a better shot than I am. You can ask for forgiveness later."

Rounds increased in tempo and by this time they had a pretty good idea where we were. Dee and I both pulled back into the deeper part of the depression as dirt and gravel was blown all around us from the impacts. I was staring up at the night sky, my rifle on my chest, with Dee in the same position.

"Did you think it would end like this?"

"Very much so."

"Yeah, me too, I guess. Although, in reality, we all want to go out in our sleep or maybe have a huge heart attack while we're having sex. Wait, is that just me? Don't look at me that way."

We lay like that for another ten minutes, the barrage constant.

"Something is up." My danger radar was beginning to register. "They haven't stopped firing. For all they know they could have killed us when they began. I would think at some point they would cease fire for a minute just to see if we return fire. Or..."

"This is covering fire." Dee rolled quickly to his side of the hole and looked.

I followed suit. There was nothing on my side. The beauty of the Geno discharge was that it was lighting up the battlefield pretty well. I turned to see how Dee was doing and saw his rifle was shaking. There was a Geno not more than fifteen feet from our hole. Dee had him dead to rights, but he wasn't firing and the Geno wasn't moving.

"Dee?"

No response.

The Geno was moving as slowly as possible while trying to get his rifle into a firing position.

"Dee!" I said forcibly.

"I heard you the first time," he growled.

The Geno saw his opportunity and took it, bringing up his rifle. I spun and pulled the trigger as fast as I could. The first came dangerously close to Dee as I brought the rifle higher, "walking" a trio of rounds into the dancing Geno's body, his only shot stopped by the earth halfway between him and us. Dee sagged down, resting his head on his rifle. I clapped his shoulder and got back down. He followed.

The shots slowed in frequency but did not stop. It seemed at this point we were going to try and starve one another out of our positions. The sun was going to be up in a few hours, I wasn't overly hopeful of what the dawning of the new day would bring. Dee hadn't said anything since I'd shot that Geno. It was like I was alone and I wasn't fond of the sensation.

"I think we should try and leave right before dawn," I told Dee. "Historically that is when an enemy is at his least alert."

"It is already too late."

"Don't go getting all philosophical on me, your Cravaratar can still be saved."

"No, the soldiers will have sent someone back for reinforcements once they realized they could not kill us as easily as they'd hoped."

"You just figure that out?" I asked as I scurried up, quickly scanning the area for any signs of a vast army besieging our location. There was nothing, at least nothing I could see. I slid down and looked over at Dee. "You didn't just think about that. You've held onto that thought for a while now, haven't you." It wasn't a question. "Listen, Dee, just because you either made peace or have a death wish doesn't mean I want to go down either of those paths with you."

"I am sorry, Michael. You are right. I should have told you about my suspicions much sooner."

"Dammit. We have to go now." I thought Dee was going to resist and I'm not sure what I would have done at that point. It wasn't like I could drag him. I was on the fence. I don't know if I would have left him there or not. Thankfully he didn't allow me to make that decision. He crawled out the back of the depression. I low-crawled about twenty or so feet off to the right of our hole before standing in a crouch. When Dee was up, I ran. We made some pretty good distance and with no shots coming our way I was feeling good about our chances, especially when just as the sun was beginning to make its ascent we came up on the outskirts of a small town.

I was saddened somewhat when I realized it was abandoned, whether from the initial Progerian attack or the subsequent settling of the Genogerians in the area. It mattered little. I slowed to a walk as we came up on a gas station, then a post office. A small church and meeting hall were the only other structures of significance.

"Not like they were leaving much behind," I said aloud, but it was more of an internal thought.

"All of these buildings are stick built," Dee said.

The implication was easy enough; the blue bolts caused fire. "They're still following?" I turned.

"They will."

"Where's a good armory when you need one?" I was losing hope. I was hungry, tired, my body ached and I'm pretty sure my cheek was burning with infection. It was only a matter of time until I was seriously compromised with a heavy-duty fever and the weakness accompanying it. "Well, buddy, I can't say I'm really all that ready to die, but going out in a church seems like the right thing to do."

He nodded. The church had been looted of anything of value; the pews were stacked in the center as if in preparation of a bon fire. Not sure if someone thought better of lighting a place of God on fire or just couldn't find a match. I walked over to the window facing the way we had come. The sun had bridged the horizon and it was easier than hell to see the line of Geno soldiers approaching. Had to have been hundreds.

"Well, that's a good old fashioned screwing."

Dee came up to view what I was looking at. Would he shoot at all? I mean really, what was the point? The conclusion was foregone. Each kill for him now just brought him further away from his inner peace. The Genos were still a good five hundred yards out. Even still, missing them was impossible because there were just too many of them. But the sooner I shot the sooner they realized our location and began to fire back. Dee went to a window about ten feet from mine. He busted out the glass, crouched down and placed the barrel of his weapon on the sill. I guess that answered that question.

"It's been an honor, Dee," I said as I also broke out my window. I wondered if the Genos could hear that from the distance they were at. Then I realized how loud an army on the move could be, the heavy footfalls, the worried breathing, the small murmurs among friends, weaponry scraping against clothing. I could probably belt out "Holly Holy" by Neil Diamond right now and they wouldn't hear it. Didn't seem quite fair to Dee, though, if I did that. My singing had been equated to dying cats in heat.

"That is not the first time you have said that to me, Michael, and perchance it may not be the last."

"Well, if it is a good luck omen you can guarantee I'll use it again. It would, however, be nice if it was on my death bed, say some seventy or eighty years from now, surrounded by my family and friends and you."

Dee looked over at me, arching his eyebrow ridge. We waited until they were about two hundred yards away. Easy enough shots that, at least, in Dee's case did not allow for any distinction in facial features. I hoped for his sake they looked like cardboard targets. Return fire was instantaneous, glass from other windows blowing out all around us. I smelled smoke as the first licks of flame took hold.

"This is kind of like the Alamo." My mouth sometimes engages before my brain.

"That did not end so well for the side I would think you imagine to be on."

"No I guess not, but all these years later people still know who Davy Crockett was. Maybe my name will be said with the same reverence."

"You will care nothing of that legacy once you are dead."

"I haven't really thought this through. I'd mostly intended on finishing a picture puzzle today of the Disney castle."

The Genos knew what they were up against. Two versus an army, they weren't overly concerned, this I knew because they were sprinting towards us. Not an iota of caution in any of them. Our time left was measured in seconds. It was the stomping of so many feet on ground that at first masked the sound of traditional fire. The brass falling from the sky looked like it was down-pouring metal. We had air support and they weren't fucking around. The only thing I'd seen that could fire at that rate were mini-guns mounted on helicopters. At nearly a hundred rounds a second, they were devastating.

For all the pluses of the alien rifle, nearly unlimited ammunition and low to no serviceability, it had some major drawbacks. First off as a human weapon, it was heavy. The original design was close to thirty pounds. It had since been reengineered to be just under twenty but any foot soldier will tell you that's twelve pounds too heavy. Most of that heft was the power supply needed to charge the bolt. Another drawback was the system could only be fired as fast as the trigger could be pulled. There was a nanosecond between pulls as the rifle charged back up, so making it into a fully automatic rifle was impossible. Trust me, there were enough blown up labs around the world to attest to that fact. Every effort to tweak the system had failed, it would overheat and blow up much like the rifle would when the feedback was reversed. It was a brilliant weapon but it had its limits. I'd been to a class on it but once I realized we wouldn't be shooting anything I'd zoned out and basically doodled the entire time.

What I had learned was that it could never achieve the devastation that was raining down from above. Genos were falling in vast swaths as the gun laid them to waste. They were still firing but they were also pulling back.

"Colonel Talbot?" A voice came from above.

"I didn't think God would address me by rank," I said to Dee. I was so happy my cheeks hurt from smiling.

Dee was not feeling of the same ilk as he watched the Genos get cut down like wheat.

"Mike, get your ass out in the open so we can pick you up!"

"Looks like the General came down to say hi. I'm telling him this was all your idea." I hadn't realized it but the entire top half of the church was engulfed in flames. When the shuttle crew saw me they immediately landed in the roadway. Dee came out a few moments later, head hanging low. The machinegun operator was waving us on. I hopped on board, for a second I thought Dee was going to stay. He looked at me and then back toward the Geno line that was reforming.

The shuttle was about a foot off the ground when Dee hopped in; we dipped down to that side. I grabbed his arm as the shuttle rocketed straight up. An alarm blared.

"We're being painted!" the gunner yelled.

Dee looked at me confused as the statement made no sense to him.

"Anti-aircraft."

That he got.

Paul was absolutely glowering at me but he was going to have to wait to see if we survived before he chewed me a new one.

"Buckle up, evasive action!" the pilot turned to let us know. The gunner's door closed. As the shuttle turned at forty-five degrees, I felt significant g-force as he must have had the pedal to the metal. That's all figurative, I don't really know if there's a pedal or not. I think at one time we were upside down. It was tough to get my bearings as I was doing my best to make sure my internal organs didn't come flooding out of my mouth. The alarm, which was already at ear splitting decibels, sped up as whatever was shot at us was gaining. We were pushed violently to the left as we were struck. Thankfully, the alarm stopped. Then I realized that was because all systems had failed. We'd basically become a brick, a very fragile brick, very high up in the air.

The ship began to plummet towards the earth ass first. I would gladly have screamed if I could have pulled in enough air to do so. My stomach felt like it was being squeezed in a big greasy fist. We were going to crush like a beer can under the heel of a heavy boot. At least now Paul was alternating between glowering at me and being pissed off at our predicament. There was one positive to come from our crash.

"Brace for impact!" The gunner shouted. "In five..." He held up his hand with fingers extended.

I thought he had either balls of steel or marbles in his fucking head. Bracing for impact was like a nice way of telling us to kiss our asses goodbye. Plus, I knew we were about to die—he didn't have to fucking announce it with a countdown.

"...four."

There was a half 'braaap' as the alarm kicked in for a millisecond.

"...three." A small light came on over Dee's head and then winked out.

"...two." Passed without a glimmer of hope.

On 'one' I flipped the bird. I figured to go out in style. Everything suddenly kicked on, the alarm deafening after the total quietness of free falling. The engine whined like a spoiled brat leaving a toy store empty handed. We still hit the ground with a significant thump, but nothing like the crushing blow we'd all been expecting. The rear right split open, dirt and debris swirling about all of us as the pilot attempted to regain control. I could feel as the ship tipped forward, we were once again horizontal. We weren't more than two or three feet off the ground and by the way the pilot was moving rapidly, twisting dials and punching buttons it was easy enough to tell he had not regained control. Power yes, control no. We were listing heavily to the side that had struck the ground. And by the screeching of rock on metal I could tell we were scraping the ground. Although, out of all the problems we were looking at, at that very moment stripped paint was the least of them. We were approaching a good-sized town and some very solid looking three to five story buildings.

I looked over to the gunner. "You say brace for impact again and I'm going to have him hit you," I said, pointing to Dee, who looked like he was going to rip the armrests clean off his seat. Fairly uncharacteristic of him to show fear in the face of death. Everyone has his or her limits, I suppose.

"Land this damn thing!" Paul shouted as if his words alone would restore order. Funny thing is I think it worked. The horrible grating sound stopped and the ship began to slow down.

Within another thirty seconds we had finally, and thankfully, stopped. I can't remember if I'd taken a breath since the whole thing had started but I noticed the one I took now was choked with dirt and smoke. "FIRE!" I rasped out.

The gunner hit the emergency exit handle. The door fell off its hinges and away from the craft as a large inflatable ramp quickly extended away. It was kind of funny considering we were only about eight inches off the ground. Dee stood up with the straps still attached. He had ripped them free from their moorings. I think he would have taken the chair with him had the material not given way first.

"Come on, man!" I shouted to the pilot. I couldn't see him anymore as the smoke billowed into the shuttle.

The gunner waited until I was out then the pilot before he hopped down. He ushered us further away from the shuttle as it burned.

"Looks a lot like your Buick," I said to Paul, hoping that he would remember I pulled his ass out of a burning car once.

"What the fuck, Mike!"

I was pretty sure, at this point, my tactic hadn't worked.

"You leave me high and dry and then you tell my wife to delay a strategic bombing for what? We are about to have a war on two fronts, I am spread too thin for that."

"Paul, I didn't know how bad it was. I didn't go there with the express desire to screw with your plans, I went there hoping to save lives."

"How did that work out for you?"

"You saved our asses back there so I think you know full well how it went. I learned something, though. Something you don't know yet and that might have been delayed further if you'd struck when you wanted to."

"What?"

"Someone is supplying those arms and some serious ones, too. Most of the Genos have Geno rifles and obviously they have anti-aircraft weaponry as well. Who knows what else they have. So they either have contacts at the armories or from the Guardian.

Paul immediately looked up as if he could see his ship circling overhead.

"Somebody has stirred the bee's nest all into a frenzy

and then set them free. Armed as they are there isn't a town or city organized enough to deal with them. They'll lay waste to what little infrastructure remains."

"I should have just fucking blown them away when I had the chance," Paul grumbled, making no apology even as he looked at Dee. "This is on you, Mike!" Paul was pointing his finger at my chest.

"I'm sorry I gave sanctuary to a species that helped save our planet. What a huge asshole I am for that!"

Paul looked on the verge of a meltdown. I watched as he reeled his anger in. It was like watching a man swallow a live eel—disgusting and sort of fascinating at the same time. I waited until the thing was writhing around safe and secure in his belly before I spoke again.

"Dee and I think it's the Progerians because they have the most to gain from a war. Revenge against both of their enemies."

"Mike, I have Progerians aboard my ship."

"Yeah and some of them are probably working against you."

If I thought Paul looked pissed before...

"Drababan, what of the Genogerians I have aboard the ship?"

"Once they hear of the unrest down here you will begin to have problems."

"Paul, how were you planning on bombing their city without your crew finding out?"

"Human pilots."

We backed up further as the ship began to pop and groan from the blaze.

The jarring impact of the ship had sent a sharp pain where Cythion had kicked me. Whatever had been bent seemed broken now.

"Did you activate the transponder?" Paul asked his pilot.

"The collision set it off, I checked to make sure," he

answered.

"Mike, if I remove all the aliens I won't be able to pilot that ship correctly."

"You don't have a crew you can trust. How you're going to quietly remove them from their stations is going to be a neat trick."

"Sir, the morning briefings would be the best time to get most of the crew in one place," the gunner spoke. The cafeteria was the assembly area.

"There is a lot of intermingling these days…it will be difficult to separate them without anyone taking any undue notice."

"Shots," I blurted out.

I think Dee thought I meant rounds.

"Inoculations. Any medicine administered would have to be different for humans and aliens."

"What do I tell them the shots are for?" Paul asked.

"Shit, does it matter? Tell them it's for Space Plague. Line them up, have them walk into a nurse's station, hit them with a sedative and bring them out another door and down into holding cells."

Dee harrumphed.

"Buddy, this has to be done for now. If you have a better option, I'm listening.

"And what of after?"

"If there is an after we'll deal with it then."

"This is a clusterfuck. I do not have the personnel on board to deal with this. Mike, I'm going to need you on the ground."

"With what army?"

"I can get you five hundred troops by tonight."

"A whole five hundred? You do realize there's potentially a couple of hundred thousand pissed off Genos running around, right?"

"They're not all armed, they can't be. We'd have noticed losses of stock like that."

"Well, I guess it's not like the Genos are dangerous without a weapon so I guess five hundred should be plenty then."

"Can't Drababan talk some sense into them?"

"We tried that route, didn't work out so well. Plus my big green friend here has decided to sit out this little party."

"What?" Paul turned towards Dee.

"I cannot in good conscience fight against my people or for that matter my adoptive people."

"Convenient," Paul said snidely.

I wanted to deflect some heat off Dee. "Paul, I've got an idea, once I get those troops and a ride."

"Dust on the horizon," the gunner told us. He had been patrolling our perimeter.

"Shit, Mike, why is it that most things either love you or want you dead?"

"Probably because I don't do anything half assed. If I fuck up its feet first, and if I win, it's because I'm all in."

We heard sound to our right and turned. Five armed men were coming our way. They looked pretty concerned, probably because of Dee's presence.

"We saw your crash," the man in the lead stated. "I'm Mayor Duncan of Olde Town."

"Well, gee thanks for coming out with assistance so quickly," I said sarcastically.

"We don't get visitors here very often," he continued as if he hadn't heard me. "Very protective of our borders since his kind came."

"Who, the General? Yeah, I wouldn't let him in if I were you either."

"Shut up, Mike," Paul spoke and walked forward. "I'm General Ginson."

"Hello General—I recognized you, that's why your large friend isn't dead yet."

Dee was as taut as a guitar string and nearly thrumming with tension.

"It appears as if we are going to have some unwelcome guests soon."

"We're aware of that as well. That is why I've come out to get you all to a more secure location."

I looked up at Dee who looked none too pleased.

"And what of the approaching horde?" I asked.

"I'd hardly call sixty-seven a horde," the Mayor said to me. "When they get to within five hundred yards we have snipers set up to deal with them. We've learned that the alien weapons are only accurate for three to four hundred yards and then that blue crap tends to get all squirrelly. If we keep them at arm's length we can take them out easily enough. Let's get inside before bullets begin to fly or someone might mistake your friend for an enemy."

I wanted to tell him to kiss my ass. For some reason I had yet to ascertain, I really didn't like the man although he'd done absolutely nothing wrong as near as I could tell. He was going to protect us against a threat we had brought to his front door, no questions asked, and I wanted to make his nose bleed. Sometimes I don't even get myself so how the hell Tracy deals with me is a mystery.

We walked into the Arizona National bank, the lobby full of armed men and women. The Mayor led us past the throng and towards the back of an emptied out bank vault full of children and the old.

"Not a chance," I told him. "Claustrophobic." That was a semi-truth, but I'd been locked up for far too long in my life, I was going to avoid it at all costs.

"It is for your safety. It would not look good if dignitaries such as you were killed while in our care."

"I appreciate the offer but no thanks." That was when things went a little awry. I could feel the eyes of the Olde Town citizens on me.

"I insist," he said as his eyebrows furrowed.

When I heard the hammer of a pistol cock back, I shoved the barrel of my rifle under the Mayor's chin.

"Mike, what the hell are you doing?" Paul said in alarm. Our pilot went down when someone pistol-whipped him in the back of his head.

"Anybody moves and I'm melting this guy's head!"

"We mean you no harm," the Mayor spoke, sweat beading off his forehead. I had his head pushed up and back from the force of the muzzle under his jaw.

"I'd say our pilot is harmed. Wouldn't you?" I asked, forcing him to look over at the crumpled form. "Someone either knocked him out or he's really tired."

"See Mike? This is the shit I'm talking about. You take an offer of help and turn it into a hostage situation."

"Paul, I'm pretty sure all of us would have been fine save one. I'm thinking Dee had about as much chance of making it out of here as a donut at a cop convention. I'm thinking that the proximity to the Geno city has really tainted their views of our interstellar friends."

"You blame them?"

"No, really I don't. But see," I said in the Mayor's face, "this here big brute, well he's my friend and he's saved my ass so many times, I have to pull off my shoes and socks to count that high. And if anyone is going to get the pleasure of killing him it's going to be me."

"I am not sure if I should be honored or horrified," Dee spoke.

"Sorry man, I'm really pissed off right now and that didn't come out quite the way I'd expected."

"Apology accepted."

Rifle fire started up, luckily not within the bank. It was the controlled shooting of marksman as opposed to the frenetic shooting of the scared.

"Everyone here with a gun is going to get into that vault."

"Mike, you can't take the town hostage."

"I beg to differ. I've got to imagine this guy is fairly popular and that the good townsfolk would not like to see him harmed and if they don't GET THEIR ASSES MOVING NOW, I'll be forced to do something violent. And considering I spent all that time under alien dominion and fought and killed all those humans in a deadly contest for their amusement, I REALLY AM HIGHLY UNSTABLE! The doctors said the medication has been doing wonders BUT I HAVE THESE LAPSES! I get this pressure behind my eyes." I squeezed the bridge of my nose. "They call it post-traumatic stress syndrome, sometimes I think I'm back in the games and that everyone is out to get me. It really fucks with my mind," I hissed, pulling the Mayor in close. I didn't mean it but I think my eyes may have rolled independent of each other.

If the Mayor had been sweating previously, he was now beginning to marinate in his own juices. The shooting outside began picking up, as the Genos must have begun running towards the area. Inside it was quiet except for the ravings of a madman. It's not always easy to step outside of oneself and see you for what you are. I'd like to say it was all an act, it wasn't. I was as scared of that crazy man as was everyone else in that room.

"Everyone in the vault," the Mayor said. I could tell he was hoping that he was well loved enough that the people would heed him.

"We can take them, Mayor," the one with the cocked gun said.

"Wait, we're not the enemy here," Paul spoke up.

"Doesn't look that way from where I'm standing," the gunman said.

"Listen, dipshit," I started.

"Fuck, Mike, why don't you just take a piss on everything." Paul bowed his head and pinched the bridge of his nose much like I had.

"I might afterwards," I told him. "Back to dipshit, we radioed for help. Do you think they're just going to leave a crash site without their General, especially since it's already been reported he's alive? Don't go looking to your vault over there. That shit ain't going to save you when they lay waste to your shitty little community."

"Vern, listen to the man." A voice came from in the vault.

"Yeah, Vern, listen to your mom."

"That's my wife."

I swallowed hard. "You're a lucky man, now listen to your, umm, wife."

We all heard the familiar whine as the Geno return fire streaked through the air. Concussions from explosions blew out the bank windows. Everyone ducked down except for Paul, who now had his rifle leveled on the lone gunman.

"Drop it. I have no desire to spill blood here but I also won't hesitate. There's much more at stake than you know and I won't further jeopardize it or my mission. Are we clear?"

Vern slowly released the hammer on his pistol and gently placed it on the ground. More concussions and the distinct smell of things burning wafted through the door.

"Mayor, I think whoever did your long range reconnaissance grossly underestimated the strength of the enemy. Now, I can lock you all up in this vault or we can defend this town from insurgents. Which way would you rather have it?" Paul asked.

The Mayor licked his lips. I had to think his neck was hurting from the sharp angle I had his head tilted at, but he was still able to get the words out without too much difficulty. "We fight."

I pulled my gun down, clapped him on the shoulder and smiled. "I figured you'd see it our way."

He moved as quickly away from me as he could.

"Oh yeah, before I forget, anyone shoots at my friend here and I'll butcher their family."

"Colonel, stand down!" Paul shouted.

"You forget yourself, General. I'm not in your army

and if I want to threaten the good citizens of Olde Town, I damn well will. Now could we please go take care of the invasion before it takes care of us?"

Paul sighed. I made sure Dee and I were among the last to leave the bank. The smoke was so thick it was difficult to see anything beyond a few feet away. Rifle fire had stopped completely. Even through the thick as fog haze it was easy enough to see the blaze was that of the hotel the snipers had once been perched on. It was safe to say that they were permanently out of the equation. I don't know what new weaponry the Genos were bringing to bear but it had been effective. There was an intense flash of blue off to my right, followed immediately by an explosion that sent me to my ass. The strangled cries of wounded men came next. Dee grabbed my shoulder, pulled me up, and we ran in the opposite direction. The Genos had some sort of blue bolt grenade launcher and were using it with great effectiveness.

"Did you see the General?" Dee asked.

"I see smoke and dust," I told him as I peeked my head around a corner. There was a momentary swirl of wind that cleared the air down the center of the street. Five Genos were approaching closely, not more than twenty-five yards away. "Shit, we've got enemy on our doorstop. I'm afraid of shooting and missing—there's no telling where anybody else is in this mix." I had pulled back in, my back against the wall.

"I could get much closer."

I knew what he meant. He'd go out there and pretend to be one of them.

"Not a chance. As soon as they recognize you they will shoot you and if a person should happen to see you first they'll start shooting as well."

"You will stop me?" he questioned.

"I'll shoot you myself if I have to." I peeked back around the corner.

"I think that you would."

"Oh, you can trust me on this one." I was still looking for a break in the smoke. At least the grenade launcher had stopped. They couldn't see a target to shoot at. "I think we need to move further back, something is close."

It had gone from the noise of war to as quiet as a cemetery at midnight. The loudest sound was the crackling of fire from down the street. I saw movement to our left. It appeared that Genos had come up the other side as well. Dee followed suit as I slid slowly down the wall of the house we leaned against, making as small of a target as possible. If we shot at the Genos to our left, the ones coming up on the right would immediately fire upon us. The squeal of a window being raised on the far side, closest to the Genos that had passed, interrupted my thoughts of how screwed we were. I saw the barrel of a rifle poke out.

"No, no, no," I whispered. They didn't hear me. The detonation of the round shattered the quiet. A Geno went down; whatever the person was shooting was a heavy caliber. "Let's go." I tapped Dee on the shoulder.

"What about the human?"

"We're going to have our own problems soon enough." I turned the corner from the ensuing firefight. There was another traditional bullet fired and then the slamming of blue bolts into the wall of the house. Then once again we were cloaked in quiet, except it was not a comforting quiet. The Genos we had spotted earlier were close enough to where I could hear them breathing. I had a feeling from their trepidation they knew they weren't alone.

Dee closed his eyes, simultaneously bringing up his rifle. I would have asked him what he was doing but I couldn't have asked quiet enough to not be heard by others. He let out a soft breath, could have been a sigh, and then fired. A heavy thud landed no further than five feet from my feet. Blue streaks radiated out from roughly the same location. The same soft sigh from Dee as he fired again. This time I got in on the action, although I kept my eyes open. We were so close to one another we could have easily had a knife fight instead. A Geno warrior rushed my location, the barrel of my rifle making contact with his chest when I was able to pull the trigger. I was bowled over and damn near crushed as he landed on me. Dee had reached out and deflected enough of the dead Geno that I didn't become road kill. I really think if I had gone out that way, I would have become a vengeful spirit and haunted the hell out of that corner of the street.

We'd dealt with what was directly in front of us, now we needed to find some cover. There was more rifle fire, which led me to believe the townsfolk had rallied. I was happy for that, but we were in danger no matter which way this battle went. If I could have found Paul I would have just headed further east and out of the kill zone. I wasn't scared of the fight, just the outcome.

"Dee, we have to hole up before someone sees you in this swirl and takes a shot," I whispered to him. We broke into what was once the post office. Not much mail was sent these days. The heavy brick and stone building would hold up well in an assault. I didn't know it then but at that point we were out of the conflict. Now it was just going to be a waiting game.

There were a couple of times I thought we were going to have to get back in the action as rifle fire happened close by. For Dee's sake I was glad that didn't happen. It was Paul and his men I spied first through the window once the dust settled.

Of the sixty-seven or so Genos that had attacked, all of them were dead. Forty-six townspeople had paid the ultimate sacrifice. Paul's gunner had died when a Geno had come out of the mist and twisted the man's head until his neck snapped. He hadn't even enough time to scream from what Paul had told us. A prevailing wind had come in, showing the devastation the short attack had brought with it. Five buildings were destroyed down to their foundations and two more were burning. Large divots on the street were going to need to be filled in before they could be used safely again. I needed to get Dee out of here as soon as possible. If the townies had dislike for the Genos before this last spate, this was sure to ratchet up that notion.

***

We were halfway home. Another shuttle had showed about a half hour after the first had crashed. Nobody had said much. Paul and Dee were both scowling. Dee, I would think because he had to kill Genos, and Paul because he hadn't killed enough. I was trying to forget the events of the day. I'd received a local anesthetic and a couple of painkillers, a medic aboard the shuttle was stitching up my face after cleaning the wound and applying a liberal dose of alien cream. A couple of days and the scar would be barely noticeable. Then I'd have nothing to remember the day by. Cythion would still be dead, though. That was fine with me.

It took a shaking of my shoulder to either wake me up or pull me out of my trance-like state.

"What? What's going on?" I asked, trying to focus my eyes.

"We're almost back to your house," Paul said. "I'll give you a day to say your goodbyes. A shuttle will be here day after tomorrow to pick you up. You're going to put the fear of something into the Progerians to get them to listen. This is your problem now."

"You can't order me around. I'm not in your goddamned army anymore."

"Listen, Colonel, you either deal with this or I'll toss your ass in jail for crimes against humanity."

"Full-bird Colonel? Do I get a raise?"

"Just being closer to me should be enough. Mike, I need you for this. I can't afford to be battling on two fronts. Are you with me?"

I looked into Paul's eyes. "Bud, you know I've

always been with you."

"It doesn't always feel that way." I could see the hurt in his eyes. We'd competed at everything, almost from the first day we'd met, but never over a woman. As far as I was concerned we still weren't, but apparently Paul didn't see it that way. He had been in battle with me over Beth for close to three years and even though I didn't want a thing to do with her, he was losing. Considering I wasn't even trying--that was a blow to him. I wanted to tell him I wanted nothing to do with the psycho-bitch, but that really is a hard conversation starter.

"I'll be ready," I told him as I hopped off the shuttle. The truck ride from the landing strip to home was quiet except for the hum of tires on pavement. Dee looked like a museum statue from the Mesozoic era. It was late afternoon, coming up on early evening. There was plenty of sunlight left and Travis and Tracy were playing in the front yard. Dee got out, walked to his house and slammed the door so hard I thought the thing was going to end up on his lawn.

Travis's arms had been outstretched for his uncle. When he realized that wasn't going to happen he came running toward me.

"Well it's nice to know where I fit in, little man!" I told him as I picked him up. I'd thought about swinging him around, but the pain from my injury said otherwise.

"What happened?" Tracy asked with concern. She came over and grabbed Travis. Can't say that I blame her. I was covered in dirt, mud and a fair amount of blood. My clothes were torn in a dozen spots and I reeked of death.

"War. We're at war with the Genos." I kissed her lightly on the head and walked inside. I was halfway through a scalding shower when I realized just how tired I was. Adrenaline crash can be among the worst. Your system floods your body with a chemical that will keep it at peak performance to preserve its safety. You can see, smell, and hear better. You're muscles are primed to kill or run for your life. It's like having a current of electricity surging through your body. You feel invincible, but like all good things it comes with a price. The drain on your system is tough and you can only sustain the push for so long. When it's run its course you feel as if you've been run through a car wash and forgot to take the car with you.

    I had to lean up against the side of the shower, at some point I just slid down. My knees nearly touched my chest as I scrunched up at the bottom. It was a combination of the frigid water and Tracy pulling at my arm that told me it was probably a good time to get out. My teeth were chattering and I was shivering all over, partly due to the water, but I figured most of it was due to how close, once again, I'd come to losing everything that was dear to me. I kind of remember Tracy drying me off and getting me into some clothes—my brain was as foggy as the streets in Arizona. I shuddered violently as Tracy's voice came in and out in waves. This seemed a little extreme for an adrenaline crash.

Chapter Twelve - Tracy

Tracy had come up to tell Mike that he was about as clean as he was ever likely to get. When she knocked on the bathroom door and heard no response, she wasn't too particularly concerned. It wasn't the first time he'd fallen asleep in the shower. She thought it funny when she'd go to wake him up and he was all folded up like a pretzel. This time was different, though. Generally she'd hear him flop about because she'd startled him. Besides the running water, it was bone quiet.

"Mike?" She knocked louder this time. "I'm coming in." She'd always thought it strange that Mike never locked the bathroom door, now she was happy he hadn't. He'd told her that she was always more than welcome to join him in the shower.

"Haven't you ever seen *Psycho*?" had been her response.

"If Norman Bates has such a personal grudge against me that he comes to my house to try and kill me, then a bathroom door isn't going to stop him," he had said in return.

"Mike?" she asked again. Her hand was shaking as she reached out to pull back the privacy curtain, certain that Norman had done just what Mike had joked about. The ring of blood and grime that outlined his frame on the floor only added to her horror. Mike's lips were as blue as the sky on a summer day. His skin had the pallor of a ripe lemon. She couldn't understand why she kept thinking in warm weather analogies to describe something that looked so cold.

She pulled him out from under the cold water. A large bruise the size of a grapefruit was on his side—fingers of deeper purple radiating from it.

"He's bleeding out," she whispered. She debated calling the base ambulance but knew she would lose precious time while waiting for it to arrive. She knew Dee was angry but this, however, superseded everything. She ran past Travis who was looking on with concern from the bathroom door.

"Daddy?" he asked as she ran out the door.

Tracy slammed her fists on Dee's door. It took moments longer than she'd wished.

"I do not wish to be bothered!" he shouted from the other side.

"Mike's in trouble!" she yelled back at him.

The door flung open, Dee quickly following the retreating form of Mike's mate, grumbling the entire time. "Probably got his foot stuck in his rectum again."

"Hurry! I need help getting him into the car!" Tracy yelled from upstairs.

In two strides Dee was at the top landing. He heard Travis crying and Tracy grunting. Dee took in the scene quickly; Mike's semi-dressed lifeless-looking body was dripping on the bathroom floor.

"He yet lives," Dee said as he scooped up Mike effortlessly and ran back down the stairs.

Chapter Thirteen - Mike Journal Entry 08

I awoke in the hospital tied up to enough machines that it was difficult to tell where they ended and I began. The irritating blips and whistles let me know I hadn't passed over.

"What the hell is going on?"

Dee was sitting in a chair with Travis on his lap.

"It is good to see you awake."

"That didn't really answer my question." I tried to sit up.

"You were bleeding internally, having suffered a hemorrhage where a broken rib had sliced through a fair amount of tissue."

"Felt like I'd broken something."

"You perhaps should have told someone."

"I didn't think there was a Geno or Olde Town doctor who would have been willing to help. I'm not even sure when it happened; it could have been when Cythion kicked me or tossed me off of him. Most likely he'd just set it up for when we crashed."

"This is possibly true."

"How's Tracy?" I was looking over at Travis. He looked fine, the previous events having not affected him greatly. "Did she go to get food or something? I'm starving."

"Are you sitting down?"

"What?"

"Is that not the appropriate expression to say when you have difficult news to deliver? Although I have yet to see anyone swoon from words. Is this perhaps a colloquialism?"

"Dee, I'm not prone to swooning and I'm indeed as

horizontal as I can get."

"Paul came to visit you while you were in surgery."

"Okay," I answered. I didn't yet see where this was going.

"He promoted your mate."

"Great, we'll be able to afford brand name macaroni and cheese. What of it?"

"The Genogerian army is gaining strength and weaponry."

And then he paused.

"Dee, if I have to get up and pull those fucking words from your mouth, I will."

"The doctor said stress would not be conducive to your recovery."

"Me getting into fisticuffs with you would not be conducive for my recovery."

"Yes, you would lose. At least you are at a facility that could help."

"DEE! I thought *I* could dodge a question."

"The Genogerians are marching enforce to California. Paul sent Tracy to head them off."

I would have sat bolt upright but moving more than an inch or two caused severe pain in my midsection.

"I have upset you." Dee stood up to assist.

"What the hell are they thinking? I'll kill them both. Why would Paul do this to me?"

"It was not a decision he took lightly. Your mate *is* a member of your fighting force and a good one at that. With you injured and unable to go on, he requested that she take command of the California defense initiative."

My heart was racing; I heard its skittering on the machine next to me.

"How many men does she have?"

"Two battalions, Michael."

"Three thousand men and women. And how many Genos are heading her way?"

"Perhaps as many as three hundred thousand. Genogerians are amassing all around the globe."

"How can it be this orchestrated? How much of a head start does Tracy have on me?"

"You have been in a controlled coma for nearly a week. Your mate left soon after you came out of surgery."

I winced at his response. I'd been hoping more for something like she just left. "How much longer do the doctors think I need for recovery?"

"Four days."

"Damn you, Paul." I had my finger depressed on the nurse call button. I know, however, those were about as useless as the button on a traffic signal. I'm under the belief that neither of those things is actually hooked up to anything. It just makes us feel better if we think something is going to happen on our schedule. "Dee, could you please get me a doctor and if he won't come willingly..."

"He'll come."

Dee helped me sit up and then gingerly placed Travis in my arms. "Hey there, rugrat." I smiled at him.

We played for a few minutes. Travis was unnaturally gentle, which just isn't in his genetic make-up. Usually I come away with bruises from some well-placed knees and elbows whenever we wrestle. Seems the kid knew more than he was letting on. He sat quietly, which made hearing the disturbance outside our room and down the hall that much easier to pick up on.

"Well, that's your uncle. He's really a great people person."

Travis giggled, that changed to a laugh when Dee walked back in holding a doctor suspended a few inches off the ground. The doc's legs kicked back and forth, furiously attempting in vain to gain purchase on the floor. That was funny enough, however, it was the look of horror on his face that really took the cake. He looked like he thought Dee was hauling him off to be eaten.

"Sorry about the rudeness with which my friend brought you here, Doc, but I'm under a bit of a time crunch."

"Could you please tell him to put me down?" He asked, not daring to turn and look at the ogre holding him. Dee gently placed him down. "As I was telling your…ummm....friend, I'm not your doctor. I work in neurology."

"Perhaps you are the correct doctor then," Dee spoke.

"Hilarious." I told him.

"What is he talking about?" The doctor looked like he was going to make a run for it. Dee had the door covered though.

"I just need to know when I can get out of here."

When the doctor realized he wasn't going to be able to leave he grabbed the clipboard hanging from the footboard. He flipped through a few pages, reading through the notes. "You're actually lucky to be alive," he said as he finally looked up.

"Why does no one answer questions anymore?"

Travis shrugged. I didn't know if he'd meant to but his timing was impeccable.

"Sorry, it's just remarkable. This alien medicinal technology is incredible. Without it, had you even survived, your recovery period would be close to a month. With it, that period is almost reduced by three quarters."

"So in a roundabout way you just said I need to be laid up for another four or five days?"

"I would say so, according to this." He flashed the clipboard. "Can I go now? *My* patients need me."

"What would be the absolute minimum?"

"I just told you."

"Listen, Doc, my wife is out there leading a couple of battalions of soldiers against a vast horde of Genogerians. It's imperative that I get out of here as fast as I can so I can either help here or die with her."

He looked taken aback by that last part. "Mr. Talbot, I

understand how you feel. But if you leave now you will more likely do the latter rather than the former."

"I hate that saying. I can never make sense of it, even when I use it. What's he mean, Dee?"

"You'll die."

"See, Doc? That's all I really needed. Dee, do you have any intel on when they will clash?" I couldn't bring myself to say get "run-over".

"The General has brought them to a place that he feels they can defend. They are digging in and receiving supplies now. The Genogerians will be upon them in approximately sixty hours at their current pace."

I turned to the doctor. "Will forty-eight hours help?"

"Of course."

"Doc, I promise I'll make sure my friend will never bother you again. But I need double doses of the alien elixir."

"Mr. Talbot, too much of a good thing can be worse than too little. It takes a toll on the body."

"Doc, it won't be the first time I've been over-juiced. This has to happen."

The doctor acquiesced. Maybe it was the set of my features that let him know I was serious or it was the heavy breathing of the large animal behind him. Yeah, probably option "B".

Dee moved so the doctor could get by. When the door closed he spoke.

"When do we plan on leaving?"

"*We* aren't going anywhere."

Dee cocked his head. Endearing on a puppy, not so much on a Geno.

"Dee, I know you don't want to fight the Genos and I'm not going to ask you to. And don't give me that honor bound shit. I'm positive I couldn't do it if the roles were reversed and I'd be the biggest hypocrite if I said otherwise to make you come. Before you protest, I'm going to ask you something that is much more important than the protection of mine and Tracy's lives."

Dee closed his mouth.

"I'm asking you to protect my legacy."

"I know not what you are asking, Michael."

"I'm holding it...my legacy, I mean."

"Your son? You wish me to protect your son?"

"I can think of no one more worthy or up to the challenge."

"Is this manipulation on your part?"

"Just a little, but I'm serious, Dee." I swallowed some bile before speaking again. "If I go down and fuck I hate to say this…" I brought my fist down on my thigh, "and...and Tracy as well, you're the best chance of Travis's survival."

I thought for sure he was going to protest to his high heaven. "I would be honored to do this for you, Michael. I believe if I possessed tear ducts that it is possible that the feelings I have now would be manifest in tears."

"I'll miss you by my side, but I will have great comfort knowing that you are watching out for him."

"No harm will befall him. However, your mate made me promise that I would not allow you to follow."

She knew me pretty well; that I was going to follow was a foregone conclusion. I already missed her. "And what of it?"

"If we should meet again, I will tell her that you overpowered me." We both looked at each other before laughing. I had to hold my side it hurt so much. "I knew you would find a way to get to her whether I tried to stop you or not. I did not wish to delay you. In the event you perhaps got there too late, you would never have forgiven me and I could not have lived with that burden of guilt."

"Again, Dee, thank you. How am I ever going to repay you?"

"We will work something out should the time arrive. Michael, there is more. I must admit I have not yet learned all the intricacies with which your kind communicates, especially in the deceptive realms. That such a vast part of your societies rely on this confounds me."

"You're off-track."

"It is about the General. He had valid arguments in regards to sending your wife out there but he had other and better options. I got the impression that he was sending her in the hopes that you would go as well."

"Are you saying that my best friend sent my wife out on a suicide mission knowing full well I would follow? Why doesn't that sound as strange to my ears as it does speaking the words?"

"I do not know this for a fact. He is very adept at hiding the subtle clues in his physiology and he also had on an abundance of cologne, which interrupts my sense of smell."

"This is Beth's doing—all of this can be laid at her feet. I'm not saying she told him to do it, but she may have driven him to it."

"Perhaps."

I really didn't like the sound of that or the implications it could present. I was thinking on that when a different doctor came in with a syringe that looked more appropriate for a hippo.

"Yum, lunch," I told him.

"I'm Doctor Lymond. Doctor Samuels told me of your request and I don't recommend this. However, I know enough about you to realize that arguing would only waste time for both of us."

"Thank you for that." I meant it, even if a part of me wanted him to talk me out of this shit.

"I mixed this with a heavy sedative so that you will get the optimum rest."

"Just keep it coming, Doc. I need to be out of here in forty eight hours."

"Right." He didn't delay as the needle plunged into my arm.

"A head's up would have been nice," I growled. Heat and a searing pain radiated out from the spot of the injection. "Shit, that hurts."

"That's another reason why we generally put people under," the doctor said, although it was already beginning to sound like he was under water, or maybe I was.

"Bye daddy!" Travis was making his fist open and close.

I distinctly said 'bye' but now I'm more convinced it sounded like 'rah'. Then I was asleep.

Chapter Fourteen - Tracy

"You picked a hell of a time to make this request, General. Why me? Certainly there are more qualified people," Tracy said as she bounced Travis on her hip. "Mike is still in recovery."

"I'm not going to mince words with you, Captain. If I had another choice in this matter I would take it. Yes, it complicates matters that you're married to my best friend. The Genogerians are attacking all over the planet. In the U.S. alone there are six major battles going on. I've had to field promote twenty-six officers in the past few days alone. They are over-running everything we put in their path. I can't get close with bombers—their anti-aircraft outclass anything we've ever seen. My next rapidly approaching option is nuclear."

Tracy hesitated. Mike was out of danger but he certainly hadn't cleared the forest yet. "What about my son? I can't just leave him by Mike's side in a play pen."

"He can stay at the base daycare until such time as Mike can pick him up."

"No," Drababan said in no uncertain terms. "I will watch Travis."

Tracy was warming to Dee but the thought of leaving her son with him was tearing holes in the lining of her stomach.

"I will not leave the hospital," he told her, trying to allay her fears.

"General, what can I hope to accomplish with two battalions against so many?"

Paul's head nodded slightly. "I need them slowed down before they destroy what little remains. It appears that they are heading for one of our major fighter manufacturing sights on the outskirts of Los Angeles. I need time, Captain, time to either figure out how to stop them or time to move that facility. That factory is vital to our survival and I cannot afford for it to be destroyed."

Tracy had her doubts and some major ones. She realized she and the two battalions were merely being used as speed bumps and there was no chance, no matter how heavily fortified their position, of holding out against such a vastly superior force. Mike was still injured and she was about to leave her baby with the enemy, albeit a trusted enemy. She was a wife, a mother, and a soldier in a world that desperately needed all three. "When should I be ready for deployment?"

"A reinforcement unit is being assembled and will be ready for insertion within the next twelve hours."

She hoped the look of shock on her face went unnoticed. So little time, she thought, looking at Travis's face. "I'll be ready."

"Good." Paul said not another word before walking out of the room.

Drababan could sense that something was wrong but he was having a difficult time picking up on what it was. Something about the General wasn't ringing true. The curt way in which he left raised more questions than it answered, almost as if he was afraid if he lingered longer he would reveal something he wished to keep in the dark.

"You'll be alright?" Tracy asked Drababan, although she was looking at Travis.

"I will treat him as I always have, Tracy."

A tear rolled down Tracy's face as she looked upon her son. She wiped it away and looked up, saying, "You....you called me by my name again. Why? Why now?"

"What you are doing is brave beyond words. You feel that you will not be back, that you are sacrificing yourself for a mission you know will possibly fail. Yet, you are doing it to protect Michael because this mission should be his. You are also doing it to hopefully protect your son. In the off-chance that you succeed, you will thwart the Genogerians from destroying the facility and thus giving Earth more of a chance of survival when the Destroyer comes."

"Mike always thought you could read minds. I thought he was crazy, now I'm not so sure."

"Oh, I can assure you that Michael is, indeed, crazy. However, I cannot read the thought waves that emanate from your mind."

"Thank you, Dee," Tracy said, reaching up and stroking his cheek. She strode out quickly to go back home and get ready.

She was back at the hospital in under an hour. She had precious few moments left with the ones she loved and she would be damned if she missed the opportunity to be with them. When the shuttle showed up in the hospital parking lot, she kissed Travis and then her husband. "I feel like Snow White in reverse."

"Rest in peace," Dee told her.

"That saying is generally reserved for those who have passed or are near to passing." Tracy said, correcting him.

Dee did not respond and she wondered if that was indeed the meaning in which he'd intended. A cold finger traveled up her spine. A corporal snapped off a salute as Tracy approached. She returned the salute and got into the transport, taking a cursory glance around before she found a seat. "Looks like a bunch of scared kids," she mumbled. "Where in the hell did the General find them—at a high school? Well, at least the pay is good," she laughed.

"Something funny, ma'am?" the corporal who had escorted her onboard asked.

"Nothing worth repeating."

"Do you think we have a chance, ma'am?"

Tracy noticed for the first time how truly young he looked. And scared, definitely scared.

"I wouldn't have gotten on this shuttle if I didn't believe that," she lied. *So that's how Mike does it,* she thought, referring to how Mike would continually and with ease gloss over hard truths with lies and platitudes.

Two hours later the shuttle landed in the old Marine Corps base of Twenty-Nine Palms. The name was a misnomer much like how, according to popular legend, the Vikings named Greenland. Twenty-Nine Palms was a harsh desert environment of dust, sand and scorpions.

"This is our heavily fortified location?" Tracy asked over the din of multiple shuttles in the process of taking off and landing. Soldiers and machinery were moving about in a controlled cacophony.

"Captain Talbot!" She heard her name yelled and it took her moment to find out from which direction. "Captain Talbot." A man pushed his way through the throng. "My name is Staff Sergeant Alex Carbonara and it's my job to get you up to speed."

Tracy looked at the man. She figured late twenties to early thirties, medium build, dark brown hair and a pencil thin mustache which normally she found to be hilarious, although on him it somehow looked right, distinguished even. Here was the first true soldier she'd seen that day. She hoped for all their sakes it wasn't the last.

"I'm listening."

"We've got twenty-seven tanks hidden up on the ridge, camouflaged as best we can, even dug them in a bit. They have the range advantage over the Genos but once they get close those plasma cannons cut through them like they were made out of tin foil."

"Would it not be better to keep them mobile so they could fire and run?"

"They can back out easy enough and that may end up being the case because the Genos also have some decent targeting weaponry. It's much better against aircraft, almost infallible in fact. Something about ground clutter seems to mess it up. I think it was designed for space battle and they've somehow adapted it for ground warfare."

"It seems our guests are properly prepared."

"Too much so. If you ask me, ma'am. We have machinegun nests spread out along the ridge as well to take as much advantage as we can of the high ground."

"What is the probability that the Genos will hit here and not just circumvent our fortifications?"

"It's safe to say pretty high. They've been on a straight line since they left Arizona. Like someone drew a line on a map and the Genos can't deviate even a degree. They've waded through rivers instead of using bridges just a couple of miles away. We've thrown up blockades before and they don't seem concerned at all with engaging even though we were slaughtering them at range."

"How many blockades?"

"This will be our fourth attempt."

"Shit," Tracy muttered. She was feeling as if she was a little bit in over her head here. "What is the effective range of their weapons?"

"It's really not much more than a couple of hundred yards. The problem is they just don't stop. We can't put enough rounds through our barrels. We were completely overrun on our first attempt, lost a full ninety percent of our fighting force in that attack. We've since learned to pull back when they get to that two hundred-yard point. We've got it marked out with some destroyed machinery over there." Alex pointed to a crane that was overturned. "The problem is there's only one more rally point worth its salt between here and the fighter factory. The General wants us to hold this as long as we can before withdrawing."

"How much closer can we allow them and still be able to withdraw?"

"With your approval, I'd like to have the machine gunners break down their gear at the two hundred-yard mark. Once they are secure we'll get the foot soldiers into the trucks as well and then have the tanks cover our withdrawal until we can get out of range."

"What kind of casualties can we deliver and expect?"

"Best estimates have it at ten to one."

"We are killing ten Genogerians for every man?"

"That would be a conservative guess. We just don't have the man power to sustain."

"What is their method of attack?"

"Best I could describe it is 'horde'. There does not seem to be any leadership. They are just spread out, running over anything and everything with a single-mindedness like I've never seen before. We keep our line spread out as thin as we dare, making sure that we don't get flanked."

"Do you have any booby traps set up?"

"Ma'am?"

"Minefields, bombs, fire trench?"

"No, it's all we can do to get the men dug in, get some food in their bellies and maybe a few minutes of shut eye before they start up again."

"How much time do we have?"

"A few days. The only thing that has kept us in this fight is that they don't drive and they don't have air support."

"Do you have two men to a fighting hole?"

"Yes."

"Alright, I want you to get one man out of each hole and get them down here. We are going to lay down as many nasty surprises for those ungrateful bastards as we can."

"Ma'am, I realize you're fresh from a safe zone and have yet to see any action, but my men are tired. They haven't slept or eaten properly in days and..."

"Did I say anything about wanting to hear excuses?"

Staff Sergeant Carbonara snapped to attention. "No ma'am."

"These men aren't yours, Staff Sergeant, they are mine. As for just leaving a safe zone, you're right. I left my toddler son in the care of a Genogerian while my husband recovers in a hospital from life threatening injuries he sustained at the hands of these Genos. Not that I need to explain myself, but I've seen more combat both human and Geno than any man with boots on the ground here. I was on Mike Talbot's extraction team."

"In France?"

"Yes, in France. And I was also one of the original defenders of the Hill. I know how to fight, win, and more importantly, stay alive. I will not have my orders second-guessed, do I make myself clear?"

"You do, ma'am."

"Besides, as my big green friend says, is it not a good day to die?"

"It is, ma'am."

"Bullshit!" She spat. "I want to live; I want every man and woman here to live through this day and the days that follow. That's not likely, but I'm going to do my best to see as many make it as possible. Now do as I ordered, or I'll have you shot and replaced. Or replaced and shot, whichever I can do faster."

"Yes, ma'am." Staff Sergeant Carbonara saluted and ran off.

"I think I've been around Mike too long." She smiled and began to survey the upcoming battlefield. She wished she could sustain that smile as she looked around, but that wasn't to be the case. Yes, the Genogerians would be exposed for close to a thousand yards as they charged at the beleaguered defenders. Yes, they would have great casualties inflicted upon them. She just couldn't get the image out of her mind of so many swarming across the ground like an angry, disturbed anthill. And, like the African Fire Ant, they would destroy everything within their path.

Men were already beginning to come off the ridge top as the Staff Sergeant commanded them to do so. She could tell they were complaining by their exaggerated movements but not a one of them said anything as they passed her by. To bitch and moan while in the service was pretty much a tradition and Tracy had no problem with that as long as they showed professionalism and deference when she was around. That was the sign of a well-run unit. She would make sure not to shoot the Staff Sergeant.

After the battlements were in place, Tracy called for a muster. She wanted all of the troops front and center minus the scouts and the lookouts. It took a few minutes to get all the personnel assembled and a fair amount of griping as well.

She caught snippets as the units streamed by. "Typical officer, doesn't she know we have a battle coming..."

"Probably wants to make sure we have our wills filled in correctly..."

"Think she's going to want us to re-up?"

She heard 'fucking stupid' no less than three times and 'this is bullshit' at least six but she wasn't really counting.

"All personnel present and accounted for." Carbonara saluted and turned to be next to her as she walked down the front line of men and women. Some wore the disgust openly on their features. Others more hardened and used to the typical dog and pony show wore a mask of indifference. The majority looked scared. A crow cawed in the distance, a pack of coyotes yipped somewhere over to their left.

Somehow the animals know something is about to happen here. They'll hang around looking for scraps when it's all over, she thought, shivering. That thought disturbed her more than the Genogerians. Combat was one thing, getting picked clean by a scavenger was quite another.

"My name is Captain Tracy Talbot," she stated, her voice not as strong as she would have hoped.

There was a smattering of laughter as someone shouted out, "Who gives a shit?" Carbonara pulled away from Tracy and was headed towards the malcontent who had spouted off to initiate some fast and furious battlefield justice. She reached out to stop him. She couldn't afford a mutiny; she was on a precipice as it was. These men didn't know her and had no reason to die for her.

She spoke with more force. "I started off much like all of you—a grunt, a foot soldier. I've seen more battles than I care to remember. I've buried more friends than I can forget. Those around me were always dying at the bidding of those that sat safe and warm in their high privileged chairs. As we all know, any true form of government is gone. We fight now for ourselves and the person beside, in front of and behind us. We fight for our families and for all of mankind. This isn't a battle for foreign oil or sovereign lands. This is a battle for the future of mankind. If we fail here in the coming days, we fail for all time. There will be no second chances, no reinforcements, and no extraction. We stand, we fight, and if necessary we die, all in the effort to preserve who we are as a species. The coming enemy cares no more for us than a dog does a flea. Some of you are probably wishing that my husband was leading you in this fight. I love the man but he's about as adept at leading as he is doing the laundry." There was a smattering of laughter.

"I was raised a military brat—I've been around men and women of uniform my entire life. When I was old enough to enlist I did so. I earned my bars on the field of battle, and I know what it's like to be so nervous it's impossible to keep your knees from knocking. I've been in fights where the odds were so seemingly impossible I've said my final prayers. Yet, here I stand. Here we all stand. We will win this day and we will live forever because of it. Your great-great grandchildren will be reading about the Battle of

Twenty-Nine Palms when three thousand soldiers stopped three hundred thousand Genogerians. We will live among the greatest battles of all time; it will be the Spartan 300 at Thermopiles and the Marine 3,000 at the Stumps! Who is with me?!"

For a heart breaking moment all was silent. Tracy did not believe that her words had broken through. She couldn't be sure but she'd bet money that the man who had shouted out in derision earlier was the first to shout out the Marine Corps battle cry of 'Ooooh Rah!', his solitary scream immediately picked up by the rest of the battalions. The thunder of their voices was music to her ears.

"Now get your asses back in position and let's show these motherfuckers what hell looks like!"

Another chorus of 'Oooh Rah!' echoed throughout the valley.

"Dismissed!" Carbonara shouted. The soldiers disbanded rapidly, heading to their respective locations. "Stirring speech, ma'am." The Staff Sergeant had caught up to her as she strode towards her command tent at the top, just behind the ridge.

She said nothing.

"Is that true about your husband, ma'am?"

Tracy turned toward Carbonara, a smile on her face. "He is one of the bravest, craziest, luckiest bastards I've ever known in my life but he couldn't lead a band."

"I'm glad you're here instead."

"You will be. Please let me know when the Genos are within five miles. Right now I want to write some letters."

He looked at her with concern. "These wouldn't be final letters would they, ma'am?"

"Of course not, but I always like to be prepared. Besides, someone needs to keep a record of our victory."

"Very well."

When Tracy arrived at her tent, she saw a small field desk in the middle surrounded by maps, equipment and personnel rosters. She sat down heavily on the folding chair, noticing the slight shaking of her traitorous knees. "Well, that's an improvement over previous years." She began to write.

I wish you were here, Michael, and then again, I don't. Your strong arms around me would crowd out the chill that threatens to encircle my heart. The thought of never seeing you or our son again weighs heavily on me. I'm so sorry I did not get to say a proper good-bye to you. For that, I will always have regret. I hope that Dee holds true to his promise and that you do not find a way to come out here. Just know that with all of my heart and all of my being I loved you and I will always love you. Until we meet again.

Tears running down her face, she moved away from her desk. She didn't want the salted water to make the ink run and give Mike a clue of just how scared and desperate she felt.

She'd thought about turning the General down, but if not her then who? This wasn't the only fight being waged; the human forces were spread as thin as a sheet of paper. To take from one to supply another would only leave someone short. No, she would do her part, some of it would be for the country and her unit but the biggest majority would be for the two she'd left behind. She would do it to give them a chance at a better life, a life without the threat of dominion. "I still wish you were here," she whispered.

She'd been staring off into space, slightly lost in thought, her booted feet resting on the desk, the front two legs of her chair in the air. When the thought hit her, she thumped to the floor as she pulled her legs off the top of the desk. She bolted out of the tent. "Staff Sergeant Carbonara!" She found him looking over the motor pool, their only form of retreat should the need arise and he wanted to make sure all was within working order.

"Yes ma'am?" He turned.

"You said the Genos never deviate?"

"Not so far as we can tell."

"I've got an idea. I'm going to need five hundred men." She laid out the plan to him and waited for his response, gauging his facial movements as he went through the merits of her idea.

"It's risky. If it doesn't work those men will be caught out in the open. Not to mention the fact that you're reducing an already decimated fighting force by a significant percentage."

"Taking all of that into account, what are your thoughts?"

He placed his right hand to his chin and then rubbed his small moustache. "I like it." He smiled. "Nothing else has worked and to be honest I think the Genos are too arrogant to care."

"That's what I'm hoping for."

"I'll go get them. When should we leave?"

"Not you, Staff Sergeant…or should I say, 'Lieutenant?'"

Carbonara looked taken a back.

"You are going to be in charge of the ridge and I will lead the men on this mission."

He opened his mouth to protest.

"I've never been one to idly lead. And you're right; this could go bad in the span of a heartbeat. If I'm wrong and I have sent them all to their deaths, well then, I will lead them on their path to the afterlife."

"This is madness, ma'am."

"You know the escape route and rally point better than anyone here. To take you away from here jeopardizes the lives of those remaining. I cannot risk that. Besides, even if you don't agree, I'm the Captain here."

"And you'll have me shot and replaced if I don't comply."

"Something like that." She smiled.

"Your husband is a lucky man."

"Oh, I'm just as fickle as any woman at home, but this..." She spread her arms. "This is my element. Let me know when you've got them picked, I'd like volunteers first if possible. Tomorrow morning I'll brief them on what I plan on doing." With that, she went back to her tent, wrote a few more notes and got a surprisingly good night of sleep.

That next morning when Lieutenant Carbonara told her they were ready and assembled she went down to speak to them.

"Who here is not a volunteer?" She asked first, there were more than a few that looked over to Alex. Tracy could tell he was trying to act casual but if anyone spoke and said they were not she felt they would instantly be feeling his wrath. "Okay, good, I guess." She laid out her entire plan, which really wasn't all that much.

"Excuse me ma'am."

"Yes Private...?"

"Private Jandilyn Hollow ma'am."

Tracy could see Alex stir out of the corner of his eye.

"Umm ma'am are you fucking crazy?" Private Hollow asked.

Alex was halfway down the aisle way about to throttle the girl.

"It's okay Lieutenant. Let her speak."

"Ma'am you're asking that five hundred of us take on the entire Geno army and out in the open. It doesn't make any sense."

"Lieutenant, you're making me nervous, sit down. The Private is concerned for her safety, as are we all. Listen, all of you, I am not risking yours or my life needlessly. I have reason to believe this tactic will work. If not, you have my word that we will not be sticking around long enough to see just how wrong I was. Is that understood?"

She received nods from the group.

"Private Hollow?"

"I'm on board ma'am."

Tracy spent the remainder of the day getting to know as many of the troops as she could. Talking with them, eating with them, and on at least two occasions getting in on some games of Spades. By the time nightfall came she was more than ready to call it a night.

When first light came Tracy took twelve deuce-and-a-half transport trucks crammed full of soldiers and headed due south.

Chapter Fifteen - Alex

"Well, she didn't stay long. Is that her majesty's personal guard?"

"Excuse me, Corporal?" Alex asked.

"I'm just saying she gives this rousing speech about sticking together and fighting for all eternity and she bugs out. She going to get a nice vantage point a few miles away so she can watch us get slaughtered?"

Alex let him continue.

"Then maybe she can write about the battle for all them books she was talking about."

"You done?"

"Just about. Aren't you pissed?"

"That's maybe one of the bravest women, nope, persons I've ever met. She's risking everything to increase our chances of survivability. I suggest you shut the hell up and get to your post. Or, to steal one of her lines, I'll have you shot and replaced."

The Corporal did not seem mollified but did as he was ordered.

Alex had taken up residency in the command tent, letting his eyes shut for what seemed like only a moment when Private Ackerson rushed in.

"Sir, the forward observation post has sighted the enemy."

"They on course?"

"Straight as an arrow."

"Thank God for small favors."

"Sir?"

"Nothing," he said as he followed the Private out. He grabbed a pair of field binoculars, but he didn't need them to see the giant dust cloud a force of that size was stirring up. "Private, let everyone know the tanks are going to begin firing." With an effective range of about two miles the M1A1 Abrams tanks could deliver a devastating punch from afar.

The ground shook as the tanks began to fire, shells whistling overhead. Alex watched plumes of fire, dirt, dust, debris and, hopefully, blood fly up into the air with each impact down range. From this distance the large artillery shells were about as loud as a party popper when they hit. He knew that would change and soon. The Genogerians would not seek cover from the barrage. They would run headlong into it.

"ONE MILE!" the Private shouted through a bullhorn. The dug-in soldiers checked their weaponry one last time.

Alex was still looking through the binoculars and was now able to see the angry twisted faces of the enemy. It was when he pulled them away he sighed, "Oh, Dear God." The Genogerians had gone from a massive cluster to long lines that stretched from side to side as far as the eye could see. The sight of it was devastating to behold. The tanks were only slowing their rate of fire long enough to readjust aim as the Genos moved ever forward. He couldn't be sure but he thought he was hearing the chatter of small arms fire from far away. That was confirmed when he heard the telltale swish of an RPG.

"You go ma'am! Give them hell!" Alex raised his fist in triumph, a rare display of losing his military decorum. Grabbing Private Ackerson's shoulder, he yelled, "Tell the gunners in those tanks to stay closer to the front ranks of the

Genos rather than the rear!"

"Yes sir!" The Private answered as he picked up the radio mic and relayed commands.

"This one is for you, Marta," Alex said. His young pregnant wife was safe at home and he hoped she stayed that way.

Chapter Sixteen - Tracy

The truck jostled violently as it traveled over the uneven desert terrain. Tracy braced herself as best she could. She half wished she were sitting in the back, wedged in tight with the troops. She watched as the driver more than once slammed his head off the roof of the cab. If his window hadn't been down she was convinced he would have shattered it with his helmeted head as he went from side to side. As it was, she kept one eye on the steering wheel so when he was flung out, she would be able to grab it and hopefully keep them from crashing.

"Do you even have your license?" Tracy asked in one of the rare moments of smoothness.

"I lost my civilian license, ma'am. That didn't seem to bother the Marines much though. I do have my military transport card." He was smiling much like Tracy figured a vengeful demon might.

"What's your nickname?" Tracy was holding onto the dashboard, her feet pushing tight against the floorboards.

"Rut, ma'am. They call me Rut."

"I can't imagine why. Listen, Rut, if you kill me before we even get into position I'll have you cleaning latrines for the rest of your life whether you're in the military or not. Do you hear me?"

"Yes ma'am." A thick black plume of smoke poured

from the truck smokestack as he pressed the gas pedal to the floor. Surprisingly enough the ride got somewhat smoother, at least while the truck was airborne over the divots. However, the landings were merciless on the entire body, from teeth to kidney.

Tracy had Rut pull over for a brief stop. She could see the airborne dust as she stepped from the cab. Joints popping, she groaned as she stretched, hoping beyond hope that she was doing some good in realigning her back. She could hear the troops complaining about chipping teeth or having concussions, one was even joking that he may have been entered involuntarily, his ass hurt so much.

"What now?" Rut asked, coming up next to the Captain.

"Well, I'm going to take a few more steps and make sure my spine hasn't been severed. After that, you're going to get this truck as close to the rear echelon of that advancing swarm as possible.

"And then?"

"Well, at that point we're going to let them know the true meaning of the word, 'Devil Dog'."

"Yes, ma'am!" Rut got that same maniacal smile on his face he had when he was driving.

Tracy smacked the side of the truck as she reentered. "Round two," she shouted to the harried passengers.

"Wonderful. I hope I don't get pregnant this time," said the same Marine that had spoken earlier about his hurting buttocks. A raucous laughter ensued. Tracy could only hope they could still laugh with so much vigor once the day was over, but she held no real illusions of that happening.

Rut found a road for part of their journey, although Tracy was amazed that he still somehow managed to find every imperfection in that roadway.

"Slow up." Tracy noticed that they had not quite gotten behind the Genos. If they were to stay in front they would be wiped out quickly. Rut had no sooner pulled up than the heavy rounds of tank fire began to explode within the ranks of the Genogerians.

"That oughta ruin their day," Rut said.

"I hope so. Let's mount up. Swing further south then cut across."

"Round three!" Tracy smacked the side again.

This time all was silent. The time for play was over and the time for war was nigh. And like a switch had been flipped, everyone grew serious. Tracy hardly noticed this time as she was bounced around. The Genos were transforming from a throng into individual beings. Not one of them was taking notice of the trucks coming up on their flanks and that was just fine with Tracy.

"Get as close as you can without getting run over. Scratch that. Hit one of the bastards and see what happens." Tracy had told the other trucks to hold off until she was somewhat certain of her theory holding true.

"Ma'am?" Rut asked, his eyes growing bigger as they closed the distance. The truck was close enough to see the rippling muscles on one Genogerian's back as he ran toward his destination. His full attention was fixed on everything forward, so much so that even as Tracy urged Rut on and the truck bumper collided with the Geno's heel, the beast never turned.

"I'm going to have to fill out an accident report for that, ma'am," he said in all seriousness.

"Rut, all of your driving is an accident." Tracy leaned out of her window and shot a three round burst. The first hit the Geno in the side, the second hit his shoulder and the third went wide right, but it was enough damage. The Geno slowed and Rut was slow to react. The two and a half ton truck mowed the Geno over. The drive shaft caught him in the back of the skull, cracking it open like an over boiled egg. Rut stopped short. He was in danger of getting ahead of some of the slower Genos. He put the truck in reverse. The Geno's legs were twitching violently. Tracy didn't think it was quite dead yet as he was trying to push himself off of the ground. His left arm was struggling with the task, his right side immobile like that part of his brain had been damaged and he couldn't control it anymore.

Tracy jumped out of the truck and placed the muzzle against the Geno's exposed brain. Matter flew up and over the front of her pants up to the knee.

"Everyone out!" she yelled. "Rut, call in the rest."

His gazed at her uncertainly, but did as she ordered.

"Alright, everyone get in a line and spread out. Keep firing until you don't have anything left."

She received her fair share of headshakes and incredulous looks.

"Do or die I suppose," one of the soldiers muttered as he raised his rifle to his shoulder and fired. Genogerians went down as he blew open skulls or severed spines. The Genogerians were much better prepared for a frontal war, where the bulk of their armor both natural and Geno-made was located. They were not used to running away or being pursued—that was just not in the natural order of things. In almost every planet they'd invaded they'd been the dominant species save one, where only their advanced technology was able to overcome a larger and fiercer adversary. Even then, they had not run. At first, the human firing line was hesitant, ready to bolt at the first sign of the Genos turning. Rut had stayed in the truck and was keeping pace as the Marines advanced, fired, and reloaded.

"Why aren't they turning?" someone asked.

"Who gives a shit? Keep shooting," someone else replied.

"Would you rather they did?" another posed.

The line grew as more troops joined in.

"Get the RPGs up here!" Tracy was motioning with her arm. The Genogerians were being bled but not at a fast enough pace. The smell of iron rich blood intermingled with gun smoke dominated as the desert drank its due. Rockets exploded into the mix sending body parts spurting into the air. Vast swaths of Genogerians were dying and still accumulatively it was equivalent to taking a glass of water out of a swimming pool. Given enough time they could be stopped this way but time was a commodity that was running low as the Genos ran headlong into the booby trapped area.

More explosions rang out as Claymore mines sent ball bearings the size of marbles hurtling into the masses. Legs were shredded, torsos lay open, and faces turned into mashed portraits of their former selves. And still they ran. Lieutenant Carbonara waited as long as he could before he had the hastily dug trench lit on fire, the fuel causing a ten-foot high wall of flame. The first line of Genos had been hesitant to cross but was forced through it from the press from behind. Genos screamed in rage and pain as they burned alive. Rifle fire from the ridge added itself into the fight, mercifully killing those who were cooking alive.

"This isn't really how a crossfire is supposed to work, ma'am," Rut yelled as Tracy came up to his side of the truck. It was actually a fairly dangerous game they were playing, even with taking the Genogerians out of the equation. Marines were at the front firing back and Marines were in the back firing forward. The only thing protecting them was the heavy press of so many Genogerians between them.

"Get on the horn with the L.T. Tell him to withdraw and meet us on this side!" Tracy could tell she was going to be talking with a rasp for a few days—she was shredding her voice trying to be heard. She waited for confirmation before getting back on the line.

"Ma'am, he wants to talk to you!" Rut was handing out the radio receiver.

"Captain, I'd like to leave a few men up here," Carbonara said.

"Negative! They'll be all over your position within the next few minutes, get out of there!"

"With all due respect, ma'am, how fast can you run?"

She understood his inference. If there were nothing to the front slowing the Genos down they would be once again free to run at full tilt. It'd be like a Dachshund trying to keep up with a Greyhound once they were off to the races.

"Get your men off the ridge, we'll figure it out when you get down here."

The Genos had indeed slowed down as they dealt with the fire, claymore mines and the driving fire of the defenders. It even helped coalesce the Genos who seemed to want to be in on the action as opposed to moving away from it. And still, Tracy's unit harangued them from the rear. Occasionally a few Genos would look at what was going on, one or two actually taking a hasty shot, but the only injury anyone had suffered up to this point was a broken ankle when a private stepped into a hole.

The Genos were advancing, albeit slower. Tracy held up her troops as the tanks were still firing into the congealed mass. She felt reasonably safe from friendly fire where they stood. She had a moment to reflect on the thought of "friendly fire". How could anybody firing at you be construed as friendly? *Oh Mike, that so seems like a question you would ask*, she mused. *I hope you're alright and that we'll be together again soon.*

There was a moment when the Genos progress was halted—maybe the span of ten to twelve heartbeats, not much more—then it was like a dam burst. Genogerians flooded up the side of the ridge. The chasers could hear the sporadic fire of M-16s and a tank round from time to time. Tracy just hoped it was part of a strategic withdrawal on Carbonara's part. She knew she'd been disobeyed the moment the firing became more intense. It was the shooting of the desperate.

"Son of a bitch!"

***

Alex had known the only chance his Captain would have to kill more of the Genogerians was to slow them up as much as possible. He sent the valuable tanks and most of the men under his command away. He asked for volunteers, nearly all had said they would stand with him. He chose a hundred or so and said his goodbyes to the rest. Full-throated war cries came forth from the Genos as they ran up the hill. Alex and his men fought savagely, torrents of bullets raining down on the Genogerians.

***

Tracy's forces pushed on relentlessly when they figured out what was happening on the ridge. Their war cry was added to the din.

Tracy saw the column of defenders head south and west, trying to get away from the advancing army in order to eventually swing around and get in behind them. This fight would be long over before they'd be able to help. With so many blue rays being concentrated on the top of the ridge, the rock itself began to liquefy and run down the slope, looking like mini flows of magma.

Return fire began to dwindle and finally stopped as the overpowering force blasted through. Tracy could hear the screams of men as they wept for mercy or their mothers. Neither would be forthcoming. To the base of the ridge they followed, the mass of so many dead Genogerians slowing their progress. Some began to climb the ridge to follow.

"Cease fire! Cease fire!" Tracy ordered. It was long minutes later that the final shot rang out. The last of the Genogerians were clearing the ridgeline. The chasers were drenched in sweat and soaking in adrenaline. Many were hunched over, hands on knees, some evacuating what was in their stomachs due to exertion or the overpowering smell of death.

Rut at some point had abandoned his truck and had

been alongside the others, exacting his own fair measure of revenge for all those he had lost.

"What now?" he yelled, even though it was almost as quiet as a church.

"We wait for the others to catch up, take a small breather and then we chase those bastards into the ocean if necessary."

"Sounds like a plan!" He was shouting again. The top of the mount sizzled and cracked as the rocks and twisted metal cooled. She would have spent the time to bury the dead but that would have meant they found some sort of remains. Tracy had Rut radio to the rest of the battalion to meet them on the other side of the ridge. There was a heavy degree of sadness intermingled with their success as the troops walked over their old encampment. They'd lost friends here yet they had made the Genogerians pay dearly for the ground they'd traversed.

Tracy didn't know if she was more pissed off, saddened or proud when the final tally of those lost was assessed. She'd lost a hundred and ninety two souls that day. Most of the losses had been in a futile attempt by her Lieutenant to halt the progress of the Genogerians. She was going to miss her second in command. She had a conservative estimate that the Genogerians had suffered far more grievously, maybe somewhere in the fifteen to eighteen thousand mark.

"In two hours they lost five percent of their fighting force and they didn't even blink," Rut shook his head as he spoke. "Too bad they don't stop to bury their dead, we'd be able to finish them off completely then. They can't take too many more days like that."

"Neither can we," Tracy said. "Percentage wise we lost more than they did. And we only have a few more days before they get to that factory. Better let the General know that he needs to start evacuating. If he has any troops he can spare, now would be the time to send some."

It took a few minutes until a response came. "He wants to speak with you," Rut told her.

"This is Captain Talbot," Tracy said as she took the receiver.

"Captain, you didn't neutralize the threat?" he asked. He seemed rather surprised to be speaking to her.

She wanted to ask him how in the hell he expected her to do that with the limited resources he'd given her but, unlike her husband, she kept her mouth in check. "No sir. We've suffered some losses and had to withdraw. However, I found a new tactic to deal with the enemy and we've inflicted some heavy casualties on them."

Tracy could almost feel the freeze emanating from the handset. "I told you to hold that ridge at all costs, Captain."

"Sir, it would have been senseless to stay; we could not hold them back."

"Are you questioning my orders, Captain?"

"The term "suicide" comes to mind, sir."

"Your husband would not have abandoned his post."

"You're probably right, sir, and now your best friend would have been dead…was that the point all along?"

"That sounds a lot like insubordination."

"You can call it whatever you'd like, sir. I saw no reason to plant three thousand crosses atop that hill."

Rut had an utter look of shock on his face as his Captain verbally duked it out with the Commander of the Free World.

There was an unnaturally long silence. Tracy thought for a moment that they might have lost comm. After a heavy sigh Paul spoke.

"Can you stop them?"

"Sir, with anything short of a nuke I just don't know. They have absolutely no fear. If it's possible to get more…"

"I can't get you more of anything. We are stretched beyond our means. You'll have to make due."

"Sir, the new tactic…."

The line went dead.

"That went well," Tracy said, handing the mic to an astonished Rut. "Make sure everyone has eaten and then we're going croc hunting."

"Yes ma'am," Rut said enthusiastically and with a new found respect for the Captain.

Chapter Seventeen - Paul

Paul had been thinking about his and Mike's relationship after he'd got off the horn with Tracy. He was realizing just how much of his best friend was rubbing off on her. Paul loved Mike—that was without doubt. He just wished that occasionally he would be more compliant like Dennis had been. Dennis was a true soldier; he'd followed orders without question. Paul didn't necessarily want that all the time but some modicum of military decorum from Mike, and now Tracy, would be acceptable. Mike would get the job done, of that there was little doubt, but the manner in which he did it would always be suspect. He had faith in Tracy's leadership, but he'd just given her a goal that was unattainable.

"Sir, I'm requesting permission to land and I have yet to hear anything from the Guardian."

Paul had come up from the passenger area and was looking at the large ship. "Hail them again."

The pilot did as he requested. There was static, silence and then the dreaded response. "Land and submit," was the terse reply.

"Sir?" The pilot asked Paul, looking over at him.

"We've lost the Guardian."

"Weapons lock, sir. Should I employ evasive maneuvers?"

"No, reply and comply with their demands. I need to get closer."

"Sir?" the pilot questioned but did as he was ordered.

"We'd never get away in this heap. Even if the Guardian missed, her fighters would be on us before we could get back to the atmosphere."

"I realize that, sir, but we cannot afford for you to be captured."

"I have no intention of being captured. Tell them I'm on board and maybe they won't use us for target practice."

"Yes sir."

Paul walked back to his seat, a small satchel that Mike tauntingly called Paul's man-purse on the seat next to where he'd been sitting. "I had hoped to never have to use this." He sat down. "I should be struggling to earn a wage I think is fair and partying hard on the weekends with my friends, not trying to keep Earth from falling into enemy hands."

"Sir, they are awaiting our arrival."

"I'm sure they are."

Paul waited until they were at the appropriate distance. "Open the comm."

"To the bridge, sir?"

"To the entire ship."

After a few moments the pilot gave Paul a nod.

"To the loyal crew of the Guardian, it appears that renegade forces within our military have taken over Earth's only viable means of defense from the Progerian offensive. I cannot allow this to happen and will be initiating Project Mistletoe. It is my sincerest hopes that those of you still alive will be able to get to designated safe zones. For those who cannot, your sacrifice will not be forgotten. God's speed." Paul sighed before depressing the button on his transmitter.

"Sir?" the pilot questioned.

Paul pointed towards the ship, as illuminated panels across the bow went out first, followed by the stern. "I've shut down the ship." Paul sat heavily in the vacant co-pilot seat.

"For how long?"

"Until they're all dead."

"Oh my God…I've got friends up there!"

"We all do. With any luck they'll get to their suits and wait it out until we can get back with reinforcements."

"How long will that be?"

"Our computer models show that the ship's air will last for upwards of eight hours. It's the cold that will finish them off before that. It's almost absolute zero in space and without any heat generated; everything will be frozen solid in few hours. The Guardian is soon to be a floating ball of ice."

"How long are the suits good for?" There was a look of desperation on the pilot's face.

"Three hours. Burn heavy back to earth, we need some soldiers."

The pilot did the math in his head. Best-case scenario put them a half-hour past the deadline. He was going to do his best to push his shuttle past its maximum safe operating limit.

Chapter Eighteen – Mike Journal Entry 09

I probably could have drowned in the amount of alien go-go juice I was receiving. I was feeling simultaneously better and drained. By the time I was done with my new drug regiment I was close to a hundred percent physically, yet I didn't think I could lift a kitten without some help. Although why I'd want to hold a kitten (a known gatekeeper to hell) is just another one of life's little mysteries.

Dee had already brought Travis back to my house. He thought it would be best if the little one stayed in a familiar environment while Tracy and I were gone. Dee hoped he would see the both of us again but he didn't feel all that confident. I told him that he needed to work on his lying skills and we left it at that. I showed up to the base airfield a little after noon, days after Tracy had left. I didn't have orders, didn't figure I'd need them as a full bird Colonel. I was thinking I'd just flash the shiny shit on my collars and people would bow at my feet. If it didn't work out quite as well as I'd hoped I was going to hijack a shuttle if necessary. I think the two escorts I was assigned were catching wind of my intentions.

They stayed close, so much so I'm sure I could have asked one for a courtesy wipe if I had to go to the bathroom. I was thinking of doing just that to see how dedicated they were to their mission, but my priority was getting to Tracy, not messing with those dill-wads. Someone eventually got a hold of Paul and I got clearance to hitch a ride. I was a little annoyed with Paul that he wouldn't speak to me personally but then I figured he might be feeling a little guilty for risking my wife's life. I wonder what he would have thought if I'd done that to Beth. I had a feeling I'd be looking at a firing squad.

"Sir, you can't be up here," the pilot told me for the fifth or sixth time.

"I'll be anywhere I damn please. Can't you make this bucket go any faster?"

"Sir, we're at Mach-5."

"Is that fast?"

He looked at me like one would a particularly slow first grader.

"Listen, I shoot stuff for a living. Just hurry up."

It was an hour later when he called me up. He was pointing through the front windshield.

"Is that a sand storm?"

"Sort of. That's a Genogerian army in full battle mode."

"Holy Mother of God." I absently crossed myself. It had been so long since I'd last done it that I was relatively amazed I still knew how. The shuttle began to veer south. "What are you doing?"

"Can't fly over, sir. They'd shoot us down."

"He sent Tracy to fight that?" I asked, more to myself than to the pilot.

"Sir, are you referring to the Battle at Twenty-Nine Palms and Third Battalion?"

"What? Yes," I said, trying to shake the feelings of dread from my soul.

"The Palms fell in under two hours, sir."

I think I stepped on my heart.

"We've been getting sporadic reports that there were survivors, though."

"Any idea who?" I was being selfish and to be honest I didn't care. The only thing that mattered was Tracy's safety.

"Not really, sir. The General has us on radio silence."

"The better to hide his complicity." I had a slow fury building for him.

"Sir?"

"Nothing. What's ahead of them?"

"Los Angeles."

"Get me there."

***

"Sir, are you sure about this?" the pilot asked as I was stepping out.

"I bet you're wondering what one man can do against so many."

"I am, sir."

"The fight has nothing to do with it. You married?"

"Engaged, sir."

"And if she were in danger?"

He nodded. "I'd do anything in my power to help her."

I dipped my head.

"Good luck, sir."

"Gonna need a little bit more than that, but thank you." I stepped off the shuttle and into the rubble that was East L.A. I turned and shielded my eyes as the shuttle took off. I watched it for a minute as it quickly retreated. I was sorry to see it go--if I found Tracy that would have been a nice getaway vehicle. I got my pack on my shoulders and was on my way to see if I could find where and if Tracy had set up her last defensive line.

The city had suffered some serious hammer blows from the Progerians. Nothing much above three stories or so had survived. Broken glass, bricks, cement chunks and the twisted hulks of cars and trucks were strewn all over the place, making my initial trek difficult and slow to say the least. It was my fourth or fifth street over, tough to tell where one block ended and the next began, when I began to see signs of life. Much like game trails in the woods, someone had cleared paths for people to walk quicker through the city. Although, why anyone would desire to stay here ranked right up there with owning a cat. Sorry, sorry, I'll lay off the cats. Maybe I should have said something like, ranked right up there with seeing clowns at the circus, or how about ranked right up there with desiring a zombie apocalypse. Choose any of those as substitutes.

I should have seen it sooner but it honestly just didn't register, as there was so much assailing the senses. The charred bodies, the devastation, the debris fields, it was so alien in itself to see a city so vastly laid to waste. I guess it can't really be held against me that I missed the gang signs. I think I should have known the fresh graffiti for what it was, though. It was movement in a window across the street that got my attention. The second floor to Eggroll Emporium was still virtually intact, the only reason I was even looking over there was because a damn eggroll sounded delicious about now. I had been wondering if there was a possibility of some having been left behind.

"Long ways from home aren't you, Army boy?" The question was laced with malice. I couldn't hone in on it.

"Marines."

"All the same to me."

"Yeah, it really makes a big difference when you're in. There's the pride associated with your branch..."

"I don't give a shit! That's a nice gun you have there."

"This old thing?" I meant to pull it up as if to show him what he was asking about, when all I really wanted to do was get it into a firing position. If I hadn't been so fixated on food maybe it already would have been.

"Hold on there, we don't want this to get messy."

"Yeah, I'd hate for you to have to wipe my blood off of it before you could use it," I answered.

"That's funny."

I was trying my best to turn my head and get some sort of fix on what kind of pile I'd stepped in this time. Even with only a modicum of success in looking around I saw at least four armed gunmen. I had to figure there was at least that many to my back. They had the numbers and the position. It wasn't going to be Genogerians that did me in but the rather pedestrian gang-bangers.

"Yeah, the rest of my unit thinks that too. They'll really miss me when I don't show up for tonight's show."

I think I gave him something to think about. They had me outnumbered but if my mythical unit did show up he could potentially be in as deep as I was now. He didn't need to know I was slightly exaggerating and that, as of yet, I had not found my unit.

"Flats, you see any sign of this man's unit?" my mystery voice called out.

"Flats?" I mumbled. That didn't seem like a really good nickname to strike fear into the hearts of an opponent.

Flats must have been close enough to shake his head in negation to the question, as I did not hear him respond.

"Doesn't really sound like you have any back up there, Army man," the man who I figured to be the leader said.

"Marines. And you trust this Flats to have the best recon available to him? How far can he really see from his vantage point? You willing to wage an all-out firefight on his limited field of vision?"

"I trust Flats more than I trust you."

"Well, I'm not sure if that's really a fair assessment. I mean it seems like you've probably known this Flats character longer than me. Once you got to know me we could become pretty good friends, besties maybe."

"Doubtful, but I sure do hate to kill such a funny cracker. What are you doing down here by yourself, Army man?"

"Marines."

"I'm getting weary of this and that rifle would make a good addition to my arsenal. We're going to start at the beginning and you're going to assume that we know you got off that shuttle by yourself."

"Saw that did you?"

"Let's just kill him and get this over with!" another from behind shouted out.

"Just wait. I'm curious. It's not like we have anything else going on right now. So do you have a good enough story to save your life, Army man?"

"Marines."

"I told you, I don't give a fuck!" he rumbled.

"Fine. I didn't come here with my unit but I am trying to hook up with them and I have reason to believe that they are in this city somewhere."

"And what would be your reasoning behind that assumption?"

This is insane, apparently I've run into a Yale educated gang member, must have dropped out of law school, I thought. What I chose to say was much different. "They're trying to stop an invasion from the Genogerians before they can destroy the fighter facility north of here."

"Flats?" the man asked.

"There is no one else on the whole east side," he answered.

I didn't know if I should feel despair or elation that she wasn't here waiting to get mowed down by these thugs or by the Genos.

"What about the Allees?" the man asked.

"Allees? Sounds like a pretty blonde's name." I threw my two cents in, which right now was worth about half a penny.

"The fucking crocs, man, we're talking about those ugly scaly bastards." I think it was Flats that spoke.

"I know what you're talking about; I just never heard them called that."

"No Allees," Flats answered the original question posed.

"Listen, whatever your name is. I have no reason to lie at this point. When I was in that shuttle I saw them. Raised a dust cloud that went to the stratosphere, which is not an exaggeration. My guess is there's close to a quarter of a million of them heading this way."

"He's lying!" someone else shouted.

"Listen, you can have the fucking gun, I don't care. Just let me live. My wife is leading a resistance force against them and I either want to rescue her or die with her. That's all I'm asking."

"Can't really ask for anything right now, can you?" Flats said sarcastically.

"Shut up, Flats," the leader replied.

"You can't let him go—he'll bring his friends back here," someone else piped in.

"Listen, in the grand scheme of things how important do you think East L.A. is to me or anyone in the military? Most likely everyone in that battalion that survived Twenty-Nine Palms is going to be wiped away, and pretty soon. It's not me you have to worry about—it's the Genos heading your way. From what I've been hearing they don't let much stand in their path."

"Your wife a pretty special lady?" the leader asked.

I thought that a strange question in our particular version of détente, but it was a crack and I wanted to exploit it. "Yeah, she's saved my worthless ass a couple of times."

"Are you Michael Talbot?"

That question I was not prepared for. There were some gasps and 'no ways' from around me. I didn't answer. Didn't matter, the leader did.

"Your wife—she's the one that rescued you in France, right? You were fighting the Allee champ. Sorry to say it, man, I think he would have killed you. I wanted to bet all my money on him but no bookie would take the action, the odds were that bad against you."

"Oh yeah, he definitely would have killed me. And if I had any money, I would have bet it on him as well."

"This whitey ain't Michael Talbot, that guy's like 6'5", two hundred fifty pounds, used to play pro football or some shit."

"You're probably thinking of Durgan," I said.

"He don't look like no living legend," someone else said.

"Listen, I'm not. I'm just a regular guy with some irregular shit going on around me. I've been lucky, maybe a little too lucky. Plus, I have some incredible people around me, including that big green guy that wanted to kill me, Drababan."

"You are *friends* with that thing? I thought that was all a publicity thing or something," Flats said.

"No, we are most definitely friends. In fact, you might not believe this, but he's watching my kid while I'm off trying to save the little one's mom."

"Bringing a tear to my eye." It was that same asshole behind me spouting off. If anyone needed to get shot today it was him. If I could neutralize that one's mouth I might get out of this.

"I'm going to move real slow and take this gun off. Then I'm going to put it on the ground and leave, hopefully to never return again. Are those acceptable terms?"

No answer. I slowly began to move the gun over my head and was about eye level with the barrel when a shot ricocheted by me feet. It would have been difficult to squirt out any more adrenaline than was coursing through me at that moment. My instincts screamed to dive, roll and come up firing. Some higher level of reasoning told me this would be my undoing. No matter what the leader thought, he would have to kill me if only to defend his role or potentially his life.

"Annie Oakley you aren't," I said as I bent over and

put the gun on the ground.

"Fuck man, he didn't even flinch!" Flats yelled out.

"We good?" I stood back up, hands above my head.

"Strings, go get the gun," the leader shouted out.

"Why me, man?"

"Well, you shot at him and you apparently want him dead. Go make it happen. Tre, get Strings' gun first, though."

"Come on man, that's not right," Strings entreated.

"Come on Strings, you beat the Earth Champion you'll be a legend," Flats said.

What the hell was going on here? I was at the mercy of this gang and I was losing precious time while they played cat to my mouse. "If you beat me, how many people are going to want to try and kill the man that killed the Earth Champion? It'll be a vicious cycle you're starting."

"I'm keeping my knife! And I'm going to give him a Nigerian necktie!"

"I thought it was Colombian?" I answered.

"Go." I think Tre was ushering Strings along.

I turned when I heard the crunch of glass underfoot. Strings was not much like his namesake, sort of like when a fat man is called Slim. I'm thinking he got the nickname when he was a gangly youth and had sprouted up faster than his body could keep up with. I think a more fitting name would have been Straps. He was bigger and stronger, doubtful that he was meaner than me, though. I was still coming off the after-effects of the alien meds although I had been eating vitamins like candy since I'd left the hospital in an effort to combat those ill effects. Speed was my best option. I could only hope that the gut ache I had from force-feeding supplements had been worth it. I looked down to my gun as casually as I could.

"Don't even think about it," the leader said.

"How the hell can I not?"

"Valid point. Don't act on your impulse."

"Okay, that's fair."

"I'm going to cut you." Strings was building up his nerve.

I tried to act as nonchalant as possible. "Oh, is that why you're carrying that knife? Do you think maybe we could do couples therapy? See if maybe we can work through some of our issues? You know, try and salvage what's left of our relationship?"

"What's wrong with you?" Strings was advancing, albeit slowly and warily.

"The doctors used a lot of fancy medical terms but when I asked them to use layman terms, the word 'nuts' came up a bunch followed almost immediately by 'crazy'. I think 'psychotic' made an appearance or two, I can't remember. By then the lithium had kicked in and I was drooling pretty heavily."

"Shut up, man!" Strings had the knife out in front of him. He looked like he knew how to use it.

"I'm going to fuck you up, Strings," I said menacingly and for his ears only when he was in range. I got down into a fighting stance and awaited his lunge.

He looked around, probably wondering if he could get away.

"Just me and you champ, isn't this what you wanted?" I asked him. I think he would have taken a hot coffee enema over this right about now.

"Gut him Strings! Cut him up!" Things along those lines rained down from the peanut gallery. Surprisingly, I heard little from their leader.

Strings swiped with the knife. I moved back and almost fell over a brick when I put my foot down wrong. If I hadn't been wearing boots I would have rolled my ankle. As it was the stumble gave Strings a false sense of superiority, and he followed quickly. I regained my balance and gave him a kick to the shin that had him swearing up a storm as he stepped back.

"There's no kicking! What are you, a girl?" he asked.

I think he was debating if it would be safe for him to lean over and rub the smarting area.

"You have a knife. I seriously doubt you're a chef."

"I don't need this!"

"Then get rid of it." He didn't. A boy can dream, can't he?

This time I moved towards him, he backed up.

"Come on Strings, twist it in his stomach. Make him bleed!"

"Yeah, Strings, stick it in my stomach. Not going to be able to do that if you keep going that way."

"He's fucking crazy, someone just shoot him!" Strings begged.

"Anyone shoots him, I'll shoot them," the leader rang out.

Strings looked pretty pissed.

"So much for back-up, Champ."

"The name is Strings."

"Don't need names where you're going."

He swiped again, slicing the sleeve of my jacket open. That was a little closer than I would have liked.

"Got you, motherfucker!" he shrieked.

"Yeah, you destroyed my military-issued clothing. No worries, they'll get me another."

Strings came in again, I pivoted my body, both of my hands wrapping around his knife wielding hand and quickly rolling his forearm across my abdomen. I managed some upward torque as I planted my right elbow on his forearm. The snap of his bones made a resounding crack. The knife fell to the ground but I didn't hear it as Strings screams of pain dominated all.

Strings was leaning up against a wall cradling his arm, pathetic moaning coming from him. I reached down and grabbed the knife. "I think your dog is out of the fight…can I go now?" There was silence, I mean except for String's sniveling. "Oh yeah, I've decided I'm taking my rifle as well just in case there are more assholes like you."

Well, this is it, Talbot, I thought as I strode towards my weapon. *I'm either free or dead. Although, there is a lot of freedom in death so that's not really as bad as it sounds.*

"Hold on!" the leader yelled.

I was halfway bent over, my fingers tantalizingly close. I stood back up. "Oh, for the love of..." And then he came out a doorway, not more than ten feet away. "Holy shit," I mumbled out loud. The only human I'd seen as big as the man that came out of the building was Durgan. "Oh well, the bigger they are the harder they fall. I'm not sure how that's supposed to be a comforting saying to the opponent. I mean, really it's just bolstering up the bigger guy because it's saying it's going to be tougher to take them down."

"I believe it refers to the part where someone bigger will make a larger impact when they hit the ground."

"Well shit, now *that* makes much more sense."

"My name is BT." His hand was extended.

"This a trick?"

He stepped closer. I was beginning to feel slightly cooler as he blocked out the light from the sun.

"Shake my hand or it's going to look bad."

"Must be a bitch finding clothes that fit."

He ignored my taunt. I shook hands with the giant; it was like a kid shaking hands with his dad. I kept expecting him to squeeze harder and prove dominance or maybe just bear hug me to death.

"I wanted to say thank you."

"You're thanking me? You've got to realize how fucking strange this is from my point of view, right?"

"Naw, man. I'm talking about sticking it to the Allees like you did. You saved us, man, you saved us all."

"Not sure if you're going to have that same sentiment later tonight."

"I think we can help."

"PT?"

"BT."

"Is that short for Bad Tempered? Forget it, sorry. You realize I just broke one of your men's arms, right?"

"He's an asshole, he needed a lesson."

"What if he'd killed me?"

"Well then, I guess I would have known you really had gotten lucky in all your travails."

"You really know how to lay on the comfort."

"Do you want my help or not?"

"You really think you can pose any type of threat to that many Genos?"

"I didn't say we were gonna go toe to toe, but I owe it to you to at least try and get your old lady back."

"Old lady? Shit, I'd love for her to hear you say that." I was going to turn his offer down. He was a wild card but something in me decided against it. At the very minimum he'd be able to get me through the city faster. He whistled and some thirty or so of his gang came out from where they had been. I was thankful they hadn't just killed me—the odds had been more skewed then I had initially realized.

"Flats, bring Strings to Hernandez and get his arm slung. Why didn't you just kill him? He would have killed you if he could have."

"I've killed enough men, kind of sick of it."

He looked at me then nodded. I guess I answered the question correctly or at least to his liking.

"How many of you are there?" I asked as we made our way through the area.

"Enough."

"Enough" was a vague answer. Enough to defend his turf, defend against the Genos, or attempt an overthrow of the government? That last part made no sense since there wasn't much left to take down. A well-armed Girl Scout troop might be able to do that.

"How long have you been here?" I tried another question. For some reason I felt the need to talk, maybe it was a nerves thing. I wasn't too big on having this many men following me and not know their intentions. Although if he'd wanted my gun why the charade? He could have taken me out a dozen or so times. This time I didn't even get a one-word response.

"Why are you helping me?" I had waited a bit before trying again.

"You sure do ask a lot of questions."

"That's not really an answer."

"I know that."

And then we were once again traveling in silence, well, at least verbal silence. Our footfalls echoed off of the remnants of buildings. The devastation was awful. I can't even begin to imagine the loss of life that must have happened here in one fell swoop. I'd finally decided that I was not going to calm my nerves with idle chitchat, at least not with him. I could probably pull off a full conversation with myself but I didn't want them to think I was any more unstable than maybe they already thought.

"Hold up," BT said as he put his forearm against my chest. I'd seen smaller tree trunks.

"Sure thing." I winced as I tried to get air back into my lungs after he'd knocked it out.

There was a series of whistles and hand gestures.

"All clear," BT said after a moment. "Check point." He explained before I could ask.

We had gone maybe another mile. I was looking around for any signs of life.

"No more questions?" he asked.

"Well I'd love to, but you don't seem like much of a conversationalist."

"You asked why I was helping you."

"I did."

We must have walked a quarter of a mile before he spoke again. Maybe to figure out the answer himself. "We don't have much here."

That was an understatement, I kept my mouth shut. Whatever the reason they stayed here, he found value in it.

"This is where I grew up, right over there in fact." He pointed to what I guess was a house lined street at one time. Now it looked like something you would expect to see after a tornado has ripped through a mobile home park. There were stacks of crumbled two by fours intermingled with pieces of furniture and hunks of drywall everywhere. Occasionally a personal item like a picture frame or a stuffed animal could be seen but really for the most part it looked like mountains of trash.

"I was away while it all happened. I had gone to take my police entry exam, if you can believe that."

"You're shitting me?"

"What's the matter, you don't think I could be a cop?"

"No, I don't think they'd been able to find a uniform big enough."

"I'd had enough of this gang bullshit and I'd somehow managed to keep a clean enough record. I've done some stuff, petty larceny, stole a car or two. Never got caught. I guess I had the luck of the Irish."

"Irish? Sure, why not. And was the car a Volkswagen Bug? Because that would have been kind of funny trying to see you fit in one of those."

"You're making me regret my decision."

"Sorry, my wife tells me I don't have much of a filter from brain to mouth. Part of it is being raised in Boston, the other might be lack of proper medication."

"Anyway, I never killed anyone, at least up until the Allees came. By then it was out of necessity. Kill or be killed."

"I can relate to that."

"I figured you might. That's why I'm thinking we could be kindred spirits or something."

Personally, I was thinking he was nuts. Those of us

who are precariously holding on to our sanity can spot this in others. He was tough to read but I was thinking his killings weighed as heavily on him as mine did.

"Is everything they say about you true?" He had turned to look into my eyes as he asked this.

"Not sure if that's a fair question. I don't know who you were listening to and what they said. For all I know someone might have told you I shit gold coins."

"Well, if that was the case it really would have been a shame if Strings had killed you. I'm talking about what happened aboard that ship." He pointed but did not look, as if to do so would summon its wrath.

"I'm not proud of it."

"I didn't say you were. You did what you had to do. From what I can tell, you held on to at least a little of your sanity, enough to snow a woman into marrying your ass, anyway."

"And having a kid."

"And a kid. Impressive."

"I know—I'm already saving up to put his therapist's kids through college."

"All I'm saying, man, is that me and a lot of the guys behind me are thankful for what you did."

"I honestly didn't get that feeling."

"We're a gang. There's not much room for social graces or the expressing of one's true feelings."

We were coming up on the outskirts of the city and the debris field was slowly diminishing. This was not a fact I registered until I finally looked around and realized the ground was scraped nearly clean, leaving only the remnants of foundations or pavement as the case may be. "What happened here?" All I could think was that it was part of some rebuilding effort.

"You'll see."

He wasn't kidding. It took another quarter mile and then there it was—Los Angeles's own version of the Great

Wall. Mountains of trash were piled twenty to twenty-five feet tall as far as the eye could see. "What the...? How?"

"We got a hold of a few bulldozers and other construction equipment and have crews working around the clock."

"To what purpose, keeping people in or out?"

"Not people."

"We know about the Allee city and if they attacked, this is the most likely avenue of approach."

"That's not going to stop them," I told him as we approached closer. "Slow them down a bit, maybe."

BT looked undeterred. "Oh, I think you and the Allees are going to be a bit surprised. Follow me." He began to traverse the hill.

"Whoa, I'm not sure if my tetanus shot is up to date."

"It's mostly stable."

"Wonderful." I walked in his footsteps figuring if he hadn't caused an avalanche I should be all right. "Is that cement?" I was looking down at my feet and noticed the material between cracks in beams and twisted metal.

"We put as much cement on each layer that we can."

"Where are you getting these kinds of resources? Nothing against you, big man, but this seems pretty industrious. Wouldn't just heading to a safer place be a much easier proposition?"

"This is my home, I am not leaving it again," he said defiantly. "You might want these." He handed me a pair of black sunglasses as we began to crest the top.

He had donned his and then stopped, motioning me to move ahead of him. *Well, here it is*, I thought. *He's going to push me over the edge and out of his life.* I was a fraction of a second too late putting on the glasses as sun glare nearly melted my eyeballs. I clamped my eyes shut and put them on, which I now realized were welding glasses. Only the most intense light could make it through and still it looked like noon when I dared to open my eyes. The beginning of a headache from where I'd singed my cortex was flaring in the middle of my head.

"I...I can't make out what I'm looking at." The side of the hill facing away from the city was ablaze in white fire. As much as I was drawn to the shiny shit I couldn't take the intensity anymore, even with the glasses on. I turned and walked back towards BT, pulling the shades off and rubbing my eyes furiously. I was thrilled I could still see, albeit everything was a little washed out with giant blue spots floating before my eyes.

"It's glass and mirror fragments from the skyscrapers mostly," he said proudly.

"To what purpose?" I was pinching my nose again. "If it's to blind the enemy then fucking congratulations, although I would have loved a heads up."

"I gave you the glasses, it's not my fault you didn't put them on immediately."

"Fine. What if they attack at night?"

"The glare, although it is effective, is not the primary reason for the glass and mirrors."

"I'm listening, sort of." My head was throbbing. Whatever fire had been unleashed in my skull seemed to be catching and laying waste as it moved rapidly through the folds of my mind. I was sort of hoping it would incinerate some of my shittier memories. Lord knows I had enough of those.

"The glass absorbs a fair amount of the alien rifle fire."

So lost in my minor misery, I didn't process what he'd said immediately. "Wait...what?"

"The glass..."

"I heard you."

"Then why did you ask again?"

"I just really enjoy your voice. It's sort of soothing, like Barry White or something."

"You realize I could just pick you up and toss you

over the edge, right?"

"How? How do you know this?" There was more going on than he was letting me know. "And how effective is it?"

"I don't have percentages if that's what you're talking about. But that blue shit just kind of dissipates when it hits that much of the material. There's some blow back but not much."

"This is unreal…I'm sort of speechless."

"From everything I know about you I'll take that as a compliment."

"Funny." My head was finally beginning to feel relatively normal. "So, now what?"

"We wait."

"My wife is out there."

"Listen, I said I'd help, but leaving our only means of defense was never an option. If she's alive and she comes this way we'll get her. Sorry, man," he added when he saw my reaction. "If your old lady is anything like you she'll be fine."

"Shit, she's twice the man I am."

BT laughed. "Then I'm looking forward to meeting her."

I don't know what message BT had spread but more and more men and women came to man the wall. It was easy to see at one time these were multiple gangs. Some wore blue, some red, while others had leather vests with their name or colors. Others were tattooed on their faces with their particular gang sign. But each person had on a black bandana armband to signify his or her allegiance to BT and to whatever his higher purpose was.

"Here, put this on." He handed me an armband.

"I follow my own orders. I'm sick of taking shit from others."

"I understand. Just consider it a piece of armor—when the bullets start flying you don't want to be misconstrued as an enemy."

"I'll take my chances. Last I checked I wasn't anywhere near eight feet tall, green and scaly."

"Suit yourself." He stuffed it back in his pocket.

There was a silence between us, but not an uneasy one. It felt good being around this giant of a man, like maybe I was supposed to be. I don't believe in that alternate reality bullshit or past lives or any of it to be honest. Which in and of itself is kind of strange that this is where I decided to draw the line. I mean, I'd seen Debbie's spirit when she died and aliens were attacking us. Plus, I was fairly certain Beth was the anti-Christ so there's that. But the alternate reality stuff? That's all bullshit. Although I don't know why I felt like I already knew BT somehow.

"What does BT stand for?"

BT looked over at me. "That's the question you have for me?"

"Right now, yeah. I think on very basic terms. Next will probably be, 'Do you have any food?' "

"Let me know when you get to the self-actualization level."

"Are you talking about Maslow's Hierarchy of Needs?"

"I wouldn't think you were educated enough to know that."

"Don't let the fact that my knuckles drag on the ground fool you. So I know self-actualization is the highest level—I get that. And esteem is the second highest; I have a fair amount of that, maybe more than the average soul. But I'm also racked with self-doubt and paralyzed by past actions so that is a tenuous level for me. At the bottom is physiology, right? Besides not being able to get enough sleep, whether due to my boy waking up or being in battle, the next thing I do is stuff my face whenever possible, which is not always easy. Then comes safety, something I haven't felt since early in my freshmen year at college when the only thing I was really worried about was contracting some new and rare STD. Then at the mid-range is the social aspect. Look at me man…do you really think I'm going to get past that roadblock any time soon?"

"You're a funny bastard. BT stands for Big Tiny."

"Of course it does. Is that your birth name?"

"I didn't realize you were going to show your social ineptitude this quickly."

"We are who we are." I smiled proudly. "See, that's esteem."

"Only my mother knows my real name and I'm not going to tell the likes of you."

"Eugene?"

"What?"

"You look like a Eugene. No? How about Maurice? Am I getting close?"

"Listen, I realize you talk a lot when you get nervous, but how about you try for some quiet solitude, otherwise…"

"Yeah, you're going to toss me off this glistening mountain of trash. Speaking of which…"

"Shit." BT pinched his nose. I think I was giving him a headache.

"How did you come to realize the glass absorbed the rifle energy?"

"If I tell you, will you shut-up?"

"There's no guarantee."

"We have a few of their rifles. While we were practicing with them we noticed that the damage done when they hit glass was far less than other material like wood or metal. So we experimented, putting in more and more glass until finally it was like hitting it with BBs."

"How thick?"

"About a foot and a half."

"That's genius."

"See! Look at you already working and improving on your social skills."

"Why this mound and how? Nothing against you and your umm...associates but this is a serious undertaking and for what reason? The Genos were seven hundred miles away and peaceful for the most part."

"And now?"

"I mean I see your point and I'm thankful someone took the lead on this project. It's just surviving right now is a full-time job."

BT was reluctant to answer any further. If a big man can be described as squirming then that's what I think he was doing. There was more here, but like his true name he wasn't going to tell me. I was hoping I had the opportunity to wear him down.

Someone brought some food around. I guess that's what you could call it. The pouch of sand-food they handed me made military MREs look like fine dining. I had a plastic spoon and was on my third bite of chalk when BT looked over.

"You do realize you're supposed to put water in there, right?"

"Jerk," I mumbled, dust shooting from my mouth as I spoke. I added some water and retried. "Not bad."

"I should have just let you eat the whole pack like that. It's the quietest you've been in hours."

I was about to say something witty I'm sure, when my glance caught the horizon. All water in my mouth dried. It was like trying to swallow pebbles. I pointed.

"Whoa," was BT's response, and it was as good as any. I'm sure had I been able to talk I would have had said something laced with a liberal amount of profanity. BT stood. "Tell everyone to man their posts."

The Genos were still miles off and I'd swear if I'd been able to still my heart I could have felt the ground shaking from their running. Maybe if this had been a cheesy sci-fi novel their accumulated mass and footfalls would cause a rift in the tectonic plates and a giant earthquake would swallow them up. I could live with cheesy right now.

BT got back down beside me.

"Why, man?"

"Why what?" He looked a little perturbed.

"Why are you doing this for me?"

"You really do hold yourself in high regard, don't you?"

I shrugged.

"Contrary to popular belief, it isn't all about you, man. We didn't build this wall or come here for you. This is about defending our turf."

"This is a gang thing? You know if you just melt back into your homes they'll pass right on by, right? This isn't their objective."

"They took my home. And I'm not about to let those ugly bastards just waltz down my city streets like they own the place!" He was hot now.

"Look around, man, there's not much of a city left."

"And who's to blame for that?" Others had stopped what they were doing to see what was happening on my tiny little piece of real estate. "Listen, man, if this is too much for you and you don't want to fight, you're more than welcome to leave." He was breathing heavy, his fists curling and uncurling.

"I think you've forgotten why I'm here."

His eyes were blazing as he looked at me, his eyebrows furrowed. I thought for sure he was going to take a swing and if he connected, I was pretty sure I'd miss the festivities to come in their entirety. Slowly the rage began to leak from his features. "You're an asshole." But it contained no animosity.

"I've been called worse." While we waited, more and more gang bangers began to show up. I felt like I was in the *Warriors* movie remake. "Where's Cyrus?" (The de facto leader of all of the gangs of New York, although it was a short lived reign.)

BT palmed his head with his hands. "I think there's room if you would rather stand over there."

The Genos were starting to gain definition. It was getting easier to see them as individuals as opposed to one massive giant green blob.

"Do you hear that?"

I cupped one ear, then both when I couldn't make anything out. "What?"

"Small arms fire," BT said. "Are they using firearms?"

"Doubtful, their fingers are too big."

"We have help then. Is that your wife?"

"God I hope so." I began to hear tiny pops way in the distance, it sounded like someone breaking bubble wrap from across a football field. I didn't see any blue rays, which would have been easy enough to pick up as they refracted off of the dust storm. It seemed like whoever was attacking had caught the Genos unaware and they'd as of yet not had enough time to fight back. "Please let that be Tracy."

BT's hand clasped my shoulder. "It is, man."

"I said that out loud?"

It was beginning to darken and the Genos did not appear to be coming any closer. In fact, they had set up camp. I don't think I'd ever realized that the Genos didn't like to fight at night. We could hear tank rounds and grenades going off in the distance. More than once, BT had to put a hand on my shoulder to tell me that going out there was tantamount to suicide. Even if it was Tracy (IT IS TRACY! I was holding on to that thought), she was on the other side of a hostile army. I had to believe she knew what she was doing. The Genos did not seem to be attacking her, although we had seen a few blue flashes. Was she somehow routing them? I couldn't even begin to imagine any advantage she was finding in the open field against such overwhelming odds.

"If that's your old lady, her balls are bigger than yours." BT was looking through the binoculars.

"I don't know about bigger. It's actually pretty close."

"Why aren't they attacking en masse?"

"Really?"

"Sorry, just a question worthy of an answer."

The fighting stopped after fifteen minutes, and then the silence was absolute. I watched as long as I could to see if they were going to approach. When I figured they were settling in for the night I decided to do the same.

"I'm going to get some shut eye."

"You're kidding, right? They're not more than ten miles from here and you're going to take a nap?"

"Oh, not a nap. I plan on getting a good six or seven hours of real sleep."

"What the fuck is wrong with you?"

"The Genos don't have a stealthy bone in their body, and apparently are scared of the dark, which leads me to believe they are hunkering down for the night. And do you want to know what I've learned since this shit began?"

"Enlighten me."

"That once the bullets start flying, getting some rest will be impossible. Any soldier will tell you that if the opportunity presents itself, you take it because you may not get another chance anytime soon."

"Your wife's balls may or may not be bigger than yours, but I'm just hoping the screw loose in her head isn't as wobbly as yours."

"Good night…could you please have room service wake me at dawn?" And with that I rolled over onto my side.

Chapter Nineteen - Tracy

"What the hell are they doing?" Tracy asked aloud, although she was talking to herself. She handed the binoculars back to Rut.

He immediately looked through them. "Looks like they're making camp."

"Look over to the left…do you see that?"

Rut shifted. "You mean the Genos with the giant packs?"

"That's their supply line."

"Oh."

"Tell the tanks to target that area as best they can. Let's make them a hungry bunch."

"You want me to get the machineguns up in there as well?"

"No, I don't want any personnel too close. We know they don't care about their flank when they're on the move, but they've posted guards since they stopped. I think they'll be more inclined to fight."

It was a few minutes later when a small circle of hell was unleashed on the Genogerian "supply-train" as heavy blasts from the tanks ripped through the ranks of food bearers. That was immediately followed by multiple 'whooshes' as RPGs set the encampment ablaze. Then came the "whomps" as mortars rained down from above.

"That got the hive buzzing, didn't it?" Tracy was watching through her field glasses. Death came in swaths—with them packed so tightly it was impossible to miss. Fire began to spread from being to being. There was confusion where the impacts were hitting, that was without a doubt. There was something else as well; they were mustering.

Tracy saw them gathering. "Get them out of there!" she yelled a little too loudly as she watched the Geno detachment rapidly form. "Now, Rut."

"Withdraw, withdraw, withdraw!" Rut shouted over the radio. There were a few more rounds expended as the order was being relayed.

Tracy watched as her men headed back toward the trucks. She realized her mistake just a moment too late. The men shooting the mortars were fine at an effective range of almost three miles—they were in a field next to the trucks. They'd already broken down their equipment and placed it in the back of the deuces. The RPG crews had hitched a ride with the tanks. They were only good from about five hundred yards away.

"Too close, dammit." The majority of her tanks had withdrawn. Two were racing to pick up the men shooting rockets. Genos were in pursuit. She could not afford to lose those tanks. Each round took out anywhere from twenty to thirty of the enemy. Blue rounds were streaking outwards looking for targets. The "loaders", men who placed the rocket in the tube for the "launchers" had set up a line of covering fire with their M-16s.

The tanks were firing with precision as they made their way to the line of men. The hundred or so Genos that had peeled off from the main group had halved the distance and were firing with effectiveness. The M-16 line was being torn to shreds from the ferocious blue flames. Tracy wanted to stop watching but forced herself to look on. She owed them at least that, to watch as they died following her commands. The turret of the tank closest to the men exploded in a shower of blue and red as it took a direct hit. Slag from molten metal dripped down the sides and even into the tank itself. This became evident as screaming, burning men exited the cavernous hole the Geno rifles had made.

"Oh, God." Tracy placed her hand over her mouth. She'd just sent so many sons and daughters to their deaths.

The second tank used the first as a shield and what was left of the RPG crews scrambled on board. The tank hit its full speed somewhere in the fifty mile per hour range.

"Come on, come on," Tracy urged. The tank hit something and bounced. The men clinging to her frame rose up with it. One soldier was not lucky enough to keep his grasp. It was with horrifying slow motion that Tracy watched his ascent and subsequent descent. He hit the ground and rolled to a stop, unmoving.

"Engage! Engage! Let's go, Rut!"

"Yes ma'am." Rut stepped heavily on the gas.

Even as they sped out Tracy knew they were going to be too late. The Genos were nearly on top of the fallen soldier, who had just begun to stir. He sat up slowly and was attempting to dust away the cobwebs. Something must have clicked in his mind because he spun quickly to see the advancing enemy, but he was out of time. He had no sooner raised his weapon than the first Geno got to him. A heavy fist smacked into the side of the helmeted soldier, the impact planting his head firmly into the ground. The Genogerian then picked up the man. He had one hand wrapped around the soldier's upper torso, the other around his knees, and began to bend the soldier backwards.

The soldier, unconscious after receiving the strike, was now fully awake and screaming in agony. The Genogerian roared as he snapped the soldier's spine, tossing the broken, useless body to the ground. Tracy leaned out her window and fired; her shots made hastily and in a bouncing truck did not find their mark. Other Genogerians came to the site of the dead body and began to take out their frustrations.

The soldier was tossed high up into the air and batted around much like a balloon. Arms and legs were torn from sockets.

"Captain," Rut said with some urgency. The trucks were coming dangerously close to enemy range and the original Genogerian had his rifle up, ready to shoot.

"Captain!" Rut was tapping Tracy's leg. Blue bolts were now heading their way.

Tracy screamed a war cry as the Genos ripped the head off the torso. One of them held it high, his deep throated cry of triumph cut short as a sweeping burst of Tracy's rounds hit him in the belly. The soldier's head rolled away like a discarded soccer ball. An explosion of dirt in front of the truck pulled Tracy from her partial loss of control.

"Pull back." She sighed as she came back into the cab of the truck.

Rut cut the wheel so hard he was in danger of overturning the vehicle. Tracy was nearly in his lap from the force of the turn. Covering machinegun fire erupted from their left as the Genos were now in pursuit of their retreat. When Rut was fairly certain his passenger side wheels were once again firmly on the ground he pushed the gas pedal down as far as was allowable by the floorboards. The rear of the truck rocked as shots came dangerously close. He watched the chase in his side view mirror. The cutting machinegun fire kept the Genos from following for too long.

"I think I might need to change my pants," Rut said as they pulled away. His Captain was lost in sour thought. "Captain, you alright?"

Tracy looked over at him. *Fuck the blue bolts, that look could melt a man*, he thought. *And not in a good way*. It was an icy cold gaze his Captain gave him.

"I'm going to kill them all."

"I have no doubt of that, ma'am."

***

It was a few hours later when Tracy emerged from her tent. "What's the sitrep?"

"They look pissed," Rut told her.

"Can you be more specific?"

"Sorry ma'am. We've been watching them with the NVGs (night vision goggles) —there's been a lot of fighting amongst them. We did some serious damage to their chow line and I think the natives are angry about not getting fed properly. It's hard to tell but it doesn't seem like there's much in the way of leadership over there. It's possible we killed their leader and now they're trying to decide who is next in line."

"Well, we've figured out, albeit at some cost that they don't adapt well to change on the battlefield. They've been told what to do most of their lives. Leadership, and what to do with it, are cultivated over time. Maybe we killed him, but more likely they were given a specific set of orders from the Progerians and that's all they really know. They can't deviate from that plan because they don't have another one. Their inflexibility is their weakness and I plan on exploiting it until the end."

Rut didn't know if she meant the end of the Genogerians or their own. Right now he wasn't sure if his Captain knew the answer to that either.

"How long until dawn?"

"About four hours."

"Get some sleep, Rut. In the morning they're going to wish they'd never set foot on this planet."

"Ma'am, I'm pretty sure they're thinking that now."

Chapter Twenty - Paul

Three shuttles loaded with troops cautiously approached the Guardian. It was twelve minutes until the life support systems in the space suits expired. The Guardian stood as a silent sentinel seemingly long forgotten in a world gone cold.

"Sir?" the pilot asked.

Paul was looking for any sign that this was a ruse and that the Progerians had somehow figured out a way to reestablish power to the ship. He knew it was possible; the engineers' computer models showed that it was. During fully seven percent of the simulations they had got the ship back up and running. Paul could only hope this was one of the other ninety-three percent. Replacing the human personnel on the ship was going to be extremely difficult given that anyone with serious knowledge of how the thing ticked were dead or dying onboard.

"Everyone suit up, we're boarding," Paul announced.

Paul pushed the transmitter button, giving the ship the signal to come back up. However, this was another concern. During the thousand or so simulations they'd run the ship had simply failed to come back online sixty times, the cold having damaged something in the extensive network of electronics and equipment. The delay in the ship's exterior lighting turning on had Paul convinced he hadn't even depressed the button—obviously that was much better than thinking he'd lost the men and women of his command and Earth's only hope as well, for nothing. If the ship became nothing more than a new cold celestial body, all he'd done would have been for naught and he was not sure if his psyche could take that. The shuttle was about two miles out looking at the closed hangar bay.

"Come on," Paul mumbled.

Blinding light pierced the cockpit. The Guardian's 'running lights' had illuminated.

The hangar doors began to open too agonizingly slow for the pilot's liking. By his reckoning they were down to mere minutes if they wanted to try and save anyone. As the ships pulled in, an eerie heavy silence awaited them, the sound of the skids making contact with the deck the only noise. A bevy of guards stepped out first followed immediately by the General, who did not wait for an adequate perimeter to be set up.

"Sir." One of the guards pointed up to the deck above them that overlooked the hangar. A row of armed Genogerians stared down at them, forever frozen in their stances, their weapons pointed down at them.

Paul's heart skipped a beat until he realized they were dead. "Eject them out into space."

"All of them, sir?"

"Every goddamned single Genogerian and Progerian, I want the stain of them removed from my ship."

"Yes sir."

"Corporal Tennons, what's our temperature?" Paul was walking around, taking in the surroundings. He'd been warned not to touch anything because there was a real possibility it would shatter.

"Negative one hundred and twelve, sir." said the Corporal holding different monitoring equipment.

"Alright, before we head up to the bridge I want those extra suits taken to the quarantine area next to sick bay. If anyone survived that's the most likely spot." Fifty men surrounded Paul as they made their way to the helm. The contorted visages of Genogerians, Progerians and humans awaited them at every turn. It was the third hallway they entered where the caravan stopped, blocked by a large group. Apparently the Genos had rounded up all the humans they could and had been herding them off to the brig. Chief among them was Paul's Science Officer, two of his most experienced engineers and Corporal Jackson, one of his first recruits in the mountains above Aspen. The man couldn't shoot an elephant with a torpedo but he had been getting pretty good at steering the Guardian.

"Dammit. Make sure these men get proper burials." He angrily shoved through the Genos, pushing more than a few over with a grunt. "I should have never trusted Mike," he mumbled.

Paul looked around the deck—blood was everywhere. Looked like the Progerians had been in the midst of conducting ad hoc tortures to the human crew in the hopes to extract information that none of them possessed. He figured the Progs would get desperate. It wasn't like they contained much love for the human race anyway. Someone behind him vomited in his suit.

A small warning alarm went off; the man was in serious danger of asphyxiation. The man's hands went to his throat. A couple of the guards raced to get his helmet off.

"Hold off on that."

"General, he's choking."

"I understand that, but if you take his helmet off now his lungs will freeze. Corporal, what's the temperature?"

"Negative eighty, sir."

Paul shook his head. The guard's face was reddening, pronounced purple blotches rapidly spreading.

"Negative seventy five."

The guards were looking from the Corporal's countdown to their failing friend and back to Paul, repeating the cycle every few seconds.

"Get him down to sick bay. At negative fifty or when he stops breathing you can take off his helmet." Three guards grabbed the downed man and raced off. "Go with them, Corporal. When it gets above freezing call me on the comm."

"Yes sir." The Corporal departed.

"Anyone else feeling a little sick just step outside. I don't think at this point there's much need for an escort." No one moved. "Sergeant, assign your men to each deck and look for survivors."

"Yes sir." His Sergeant saluted and grabbed his men, giving them their assigned areas.

There were scorch marks on the hull. Paul couldn't tell if in a last ditch effort the Progerians were trying to sabotage the entire ship or more likely there had been a brief firefight. Paul paced, waiting impatiently for his intercom system to be restored. A crackle over his head caught his attention.

At first the Corporal sounded like he was under a thick layer of ice and then he was able to break through. "Thirty four degrees, sir."

Paul pulled his helmet off, a plume of breath rising around his head. "How's the guard?"

"Dead, sir."

"What about the quarantine room?"

"Four survivors, sir."

Four out of seventy five. His grief at the loss was intense. He'd had dozens of survival suits placed in the room along with battery operated heaters. He'd briefed the entire human crew on what to do should the Mistletoe order come down. They'd done some mock drills off-site. He could only figure that the ship had been nearly under Progerian rule when he'd executed the order. He'd sealed the fates of seventy-two men the moment he'd pressed that button, and quite possibly destroyed any chance of Earth's survival.

It was hours later when the ship was finally at a

comfortable life-sustaining condition. Paul had shuttles waiting back on Earth loaded with anyone and everyone who had knowledge of how the ship worked. He hadn't wanted to bring them along until he'd received the okay that all of the Genos and Progs were dead and jettisoned into open air.

"Savages," he said as the bodies floated by.

The blood stains of the humans tortured on the bridge were being mopped up just as Beth entered.

"What are you doing here?" Paul asked.

"Is not my place by your side during a time of crisis?"

"For fuck's sake, Beth. This is a military crisis, not the mourning of the loss of a statesman or something."

"Mike went after Tracy."

Paul looked like he'd just swallowed something that didn't necessarily agree with him. "How do you know?"

"That disgusting giant green friend of his." It was lost on Paul that Beth had left to visit Mike. "Can you believe he's letting that monster watch his son?"

"What? I'll have Drababan arrested immediately."

"On what charges?" Beth asked curiously.

"Does it matter? He's a hostile alien and has no rights here."

"Michael will not be happy."

"Mike was dead the moment you convinced me to send Tracy in his stead. I don't know why I listened. I thought that maybe you'd love me for it I guess. All I've done now is added him and his wife onto the list of those whose deaths I'm responsible for."

Beth was silent, but inwardly she smiled. If she couldn't have Mike then no one could. She knew inherently that something had been damaged within her during her trek across the country. She just couldn't find it in herself to care. Her entire existence revolved around getting to Mike and the protection he afforded her. His spurning had snapped that which had frayed. Finding out about Tracy had only added salt to a weeping wound. She'd cared about Paul at one time in her life but that was long before the aliens had come. He was merely a tool to be wielded—she would forge a new reality, a reality she wanted, using him. When Mike had been injured, sending Tracy to command the doomed troops seemed a brilliant stroke.

She wanted to be the one to tell him the news about his fallen wife, then to comfort him at his lowest. She was convinced he would have been like putty in her hands. *Oh Mike, we could have been so good together. You just had to go and do something so stupid. That alien medication will eventually kill you…and for what purpose?* She knew he was as good as dead, just like his bitch of a wife.

"You're a General and a leader. You will always be tasked with sending other people to their deaths and you will have to get used to it."

"Including my best friend and his wife?"

Beth scoffed.

"We're going to have to take his son in, raise him as our own." Paul sighed.

"We'll do no such thing—he is not our blood."

"The blood of his parents is on my...our hands. It's the right thing to do."

Beth did not agree but felt it wise to keep this to herself. She would find a way out of this responsibility, but not while everything was so fresh in her husband's mind.

"Someone call down to the base and have Drababan arrested. Any force necessary is authorized. He has Mike's kid with him. However, if he resists and that baby is injured I will suspend the offending party by his balls with barbed wire."

"And if it's a woman?" Beth asked in jest.

"This funny for you?"

Beth smiled slightly and walked away. She would not be adverse to Drababan and the baby taking friendly fire.

Chapter Twenty-One - Drababan

Dee watched as Mike entered the shuttle, Travis fast asleep in his arms. He walked slowly back to his house, occasionally receiving an astonished stare as people noticed the package he was carrying. His home now seemed anything but—his friend and his friend's mate were gone and the chances of either or both returning were infinitesimally small. A strange sensation he'd rarely felt, the humans called it guilt, coursed through him. No matter how he thought about his predicament he could not think of an outcome that would sooth his tortured mind. To stand with Michael, his friend meant going against his people and not even just that, it meant going against his species.

The alternative was to join his people and war against the humans who had helped to free them and now harbored them on their shores. To do so would show just how little he appreciated all that the humans had done for him. And he knew the fates would not be kind. A time would come no matter where he inserted himself into the war where he and Michael would have to square off to the death. He would kill the man if he had to, no matter the sadness it would inflict upon him. Now, though…now what? Michael had made him promise that he would keep his son safe. Dee loved the boy like no other, regardless of species.

Paul was not to be trusted, he knew that. Where could

he go? Certainly not a Genogerian settlement, but here, when Mike wasn't around as a buffer, he stuck out among the humans. He was debating what to do when his doorbell rang.

Beth stepped back as Dee opened the door.

"Is Michael here?" she asked, backing up even further.

Dee could smell the stink of fear on her and something else. He thought it was a sliver of guilt, just the smallest touch.

"Do you wish to come in and talk?" Dee no more wanted her inside than she herself wanted to go in, but it was a social custom he was adapting to.

"I just want to know if Michael is here. I went to the hospital and they said he left after trying to overdose on whatever your people created."

He was going to tell her it was not the Genogerians who had created the medicine and it would be extremely difficult to overdose, but he wanted to talk to her as little as possible. For all her seemingly human beauty, she smelled wrong, as if something inside of her had rotted and was already spreading its fingers of decay throughout her. "Michael has left to join with his mate on the battlefield."

"What? He's not supposed to...I mean...he can't do that! My husband never gave him the orders to go!"

"I do not believe the lack of a verbal command from your mate would have been sufficient to keep him back. Actually, I do not know of much that would have stopped him. Death perhaps, although he most likely would have found another realm to travel through to get there." Dee was pondering that.

"What? What are you talking about?"

Travis took this inopportune time to cry out.

"Who is that? Is that his son?"

"Yes, that is Travis. I have been tasked with the responsibility to keep him safe until such time that Michael or his mate come back to claim him."

"That cannot be! You are an alien—you can't watch the child. What happens if you get hungry?"

"I can assure you that I AM watching the child and that I can. If I get hungry there are bigger meals," he declared, taking a small step in her direction. He thought about licking his teeth, but he'd conveyed the message he had wanted to. Beth was halfway down the walkway.

She turned. "I'll be speaking to my husband about this."

"Michael does not love you."

Beth paused, fury usurping fear in the matter of a heartbeat. "Maybe not…but he will." And with that she left. Dee knew now without a doubt that at the very least his freedom was in question and more likely his life. He had promised Michael he would keep Travis safe and he would. He had, however, not promised where he would do that. He could fly a shuttle but those could be tracked. There were a couple of Hummers retrofitted to accommodate the much larger Genogerians. The motor pool had two on base that he knew of. If he'd had the time he would much rather walk away but he felt that Beth was going to do something and soon. He'd driven before but it was not something he was accustomed to, nor did he enjoy it. Mike had brought him out a few times for lessons and generally had laughed the entire time, once stating that now Asian women were the second worst drivers on the planet. Dee did not know what that meant but he was certain it was a slight.

He looked in on Travis. Taking him to the motor pool with all the supplies he could carry would arouse suspicion. Travis was peering at Dee as he debated on what to do.

"It is nap time!" Dee said, trying to inflect as much mirth into his voice as he could.

"Trobbit!" Travis replied.

Dee knew this meant the boy wanted him to read a story first. *The Hobbit* was a story they both loved. It had happened quite by accident. Dee had been reading the tome on a night that Michael and Tracy had gone out. Travis had woken up, as cranky as he'd ever seen the boy. Dee had attempted to amuse him with toys and then some of his picture books. When that had not worked he sat him in his lap and rocked. That seemed to work somewhat, but it was when Dee picked up his copy of *The Hobbit* that Travis had stilled, as if the book itself had cast a spell on him.

    This was not lost on Dee. He began to read aloud. Travis had sat still for a solid two hours, his eyes becoming wide as Dee told the tale. He'd finally succumbed to sleep when he could no longer keep his eyes open. From that point on, Dee read him the book before the boy fell asleep. He was on the third retelling. It had been his goal that next month he would try to move on to *The Lord of the Rings,* if Travis would allow it.

    "Peep now?" Travis had asked in an unusually short amount of time.

    "Yes, sleep now. Are you picking up on my feelings little one or do you somehow know the importance of leaving now? Either way marks you as your father's son."

    Travis let the giant place him in his crib where he dutifully laid down. As soon as Dee walked out of the room Travis stood and looked out his window.

    Dee signed the vehicle out with not a hitch. Most wanted as little interaction with him as possible. Sometimes this affected him but right now, it was a blessing. He had been gone no longer than twenty minutes. He nearly ran from the vehicle to Travis's room to see how the toddler was. Travis quickly ducked down and lay on his mattress as he watched Dee pull up and exit the vehicle that was much the same color as him.

    Dee let out a heavy breath of relief as he checked on the boy. "I promise that will be the last time I leave you behind." He grabbed all his food stores, Travis's toys and then his books and stuffed them into the back of the Hummer. He debated on leaving a coded message for

Michael to find in the unlikely event his friend did indeed come home. He could think of nothing that Paul would not be able to decipher as well. He wrote a quick note and deposited it on the table where it was sure to be found.

"I will miss this place." He closed the door behind him.

"Trobbit?"

"Yes, it appears that we are also going on a quest."

Chapter Twenty-Two - Paul

"Sir, the alien is gone." Corporal Akers had the unenviable task of telling his General.

"Gone? Gone where?"

"He left a note, sir. Says he'll be in touch."

"Is the baby there?"

The Corporal asked the question over the radio. "No sir," he relayed.

"I told you he was dangerous, now he's gone and taken that poor baby!" Beth said with added drama for effect.

"Sir, it appears he has a Hummer."

"Son of a bitch. How much of a head start does he have?"

"Motor pool says he checked the Hummer out at thirteen hundred yesterday."

"He's got close to thirty hours. He could just about be anywhere in the United States."

"Don't be ridiculous—he has to sleep," Beth chided.

"No, Beth, he doesn't. The only thing I can hope for is that he gets in a serious enough fender bender to disable the Hummer without harming Travis. Corporal, get an A.P.B. out to anyone who will listen. Shit." Paul ran his hands through his hair. "I've really let you down this time, buddy," he said softly. "With friends like me who needs enemies?"

Chapter Twenty-Three – Mike Journal Entry 10

"You alright?" BT was looking over at me.

I was staring up at the sky. I'd slept funny—kind of tough to get comfortable using construction debris as a bed. My healing rib itched like a bugger but was sore to the touch. So it was kind of like a horny woman wearing a chastity belt. You can look but can't touch, no relief coming your way. "Just an injury I incurred while on a peace making trip to the Genos."

"You visited them?"

"Yeah—right before they completely lost their minds."

"I've been around you long enough that I think I should ask this question."

I waited until the stitch in my side subsided before I sat up. Actually I stuck my hand out and BT pulled me into a sitting position. "What's that?" I asked when I got into a reasonable facsimile of comfortable.

"Did you cause them to go all rogue?"

"Always a distinct possibility. Whenever I'm in a social setting a riot can be the inevitable outcome. This time, however, no. This stinks of the Progerians, through and through. They found a way to really shit all over everything. They have contacts in the Guardian. They're softening us up for the next wave of attacks from above, although I don't know why. We're about as solid as Jell-O."

I had my back to the front as we spoke. I heard oohs and aaahs and the occasional gasp. Looking around, I noticed men that had been playing cards or eating or just about anything else now had their attention completely pulled to the front.

"Shit," I said. As I began to turn around I didn't even need to know what I was going to see to know it was bad.

"Fuck me." BT was now looking out. "Looks like they're coming."

"What? Did you think maybe they decided against it?"

"You're an asshole. And what would be wrong if they had?"

"Absolutely nothing. I'm sort of attached to this life and it would be nice to hold onto it for a little while longer."

"Whoever is behind them is firing again."

I couldn't tell if I was happy or not. Happy that the soldiers had survived the night, but now I wish they'd go on the sidelines and watch the rest of this play out, especially if Tracy was in the mix. No that's a lie, ONLY because Tracy was in the mix. We were going to need their help that was for sure.

BT was standing up. "Get the rail guns up here!"

"Both?" someone shouted from below.

"One there and the other a hundred yards further down by the mercantile!"

"Rail gun?" I asked when he looked down at me. I noticed how uncomfortable he looked from the question, squirming was almost a better word. Why though?

"Yeah...umm, we found them in the rubble."

"A rail gun? What is it?" All I could figure was it was big—so big they needed to lay a track down to move it. When the first one rounded the bend on the back of a pickup truck it certainly was big, but not that big. Four men each grabbed a handle and muscled it up the side of the hill. It was unlike anything I'd ever seen. Its name must have been derived from the fact that the barrel was shaped like a piece of train track. Instead of a round hole though, where the bullet would come out, there was what looked like an upside down 'u' or an 'n' without the little burr on top.

The front or business end rested on a heavy stock tripod and where the trigger and the shoulder stock should be was just a box. It had some lights and three clear tubes that ran from it to about midway up the barrel. Where someone's shoulder should go was an opening, the only one on the whole contraption, it had to be the ammunition port was all I could figure. Once the gun was in place the men raced back down and grabbed what looked like ten-foot sections of metal.

"What is that?"

"Aluminum," BT explained.

The gun turned on as a man pushed a rod into the back of it. I could hear the heavy hum of it.

"What is that thing and how do you fire it?" I wanted to know.

"Show him," BT told the gunner.

He opened a box and pulled out what looked like a small flat screen television with a joystick attached to it. He flipped a switch and the screen came on, revealing a dust-laden sky. He fiddled with the stick and the front of the weapon came down until he was about chest level with the Genos.

"That's incredible. Where did you really get this?" I noticed the strained look the gunner gave BT. "This some top-secret military thing or something?"

"Or something," BT said.

"What's the range?" I honestly didn't give a flying shit where they got the thing, if it could deliver even half as much as it looked like it could.

"A couple of miles."

"That piece of aluminum flies for two miles?"

"Not the whole piece, not at once anyway," the gunner said. "There's a mechanism inside that cuts the rail before sending it out. You can adjust the thickness depending on the target. Don't need much more than an eighth of an inch when you're only dealing with flesh. An inch will go though most tanks. A couple of inches will go through a steel reinforced bunker."

"What the hell would happen if you shot the whole rod? Is that even possible?"

"We've been warned not to do that."

I was so enraptured with the gun it took me a moment to process his words. "Warned? Warned by who? Or is it whom?"

"It's whom," BT said, giving the gunner the stink eye. He pulled me away. "It's time to get ready."

"There is so much more here you're not telling me. You know if there was still a government, I'd be an employee, right? I'm sure I have whatever secret security clearance you need so you can tell me."

"I promise if we make it I'll tell you."

"Well that's incentive enough."

"And what about your wife?"

"Shit, mental lapse. Don't tell her about that."

Pebbles of glass were beginning to vibrate and slide down the hill as the Genogerians approached. They stretched as far as the eye could see. This wall was going to be about as useless as a shore bound wave breaker during a tsunami. Genos were going to pour up, over and around it. And then the rail gun nearest to me kicked on. If I hadn't been looking I wouldn't have known it because from where I sat the gun made hardly any noise, although it would have been really hard to miss the glowing balls of green that blew out the front.

Genos were folding in on themselves as the rounds struck. It was shooting projectiles so fast it looked like a laser stream. The front waves of enemy combatants were being disintegrated—it was a death-dealing machine like no other. I heard the tapping of metal. One of the men that had been carrying the gun was now responsible for loading it. The other two were shuttling up more tubes.

"Does it overheat?"

"It can shoot five rails and then it needs to reset, that's why we have the second one."

I could almost feel pity for the Genos. I said almost. It didn't stop them any as they weren't even slowing. And that gun had to be killing them by the hundreds. The round was passing through multiple Genos. I would imagine the smell of burning meat was prevalent down on that field.

"Stubborn bastards, aren't they?" BT asked.

"Yeah. They don't really know a different way."

"Whose bright idea was it to let them on our planet, anyway?"

"Must have been some idiot politician." I sure as hell wasn't going to step up and take claim for that. Yes, I'd been in on the discussion and yes, I had wanted the Genogerians to have a new home. I'd also advocated that we keep the Progerians—lock them away, sure, but don't kill them. I'd been outvoted on that part. "We must study them," they had said. "We must befriend them." I'd argued that we must put them in a large box, preferably on a deserted island. I knew they weren't going to sit idly by and watch the earth spin. I can't imagine that anyone truly knew they'd be capable of launching a full-scale war. Or maybe somebody did. When and if I got back I was going to go over the meeting notes and see who fought the longest and hardest for the Progerian settlement accord.

"Yeah, you never do see the idiots that make the decisions on the field of battle, do you? They get to make the boneheaded choices but then everyone else has to pay the price."

"That's what I'm saying," I agreed a little too vehemently.

"You didn't say anything."

"I meant to."

"Do you always make so much sense?"

"Oh, you'd be amazed. We should probably do less

debating and more fighting." I steered him off the conversation as deftly as I could. It was far from subtle. But we had bigger fish to fry right now, so I figured I was going to be able to skate under the radar for now. The Genos were still coming and we needed another thirty of those rail guns to really swing the momentum. They were beginning to come into effective range of our more conventional weapons. I'd say they were still more than a mile out but that didn't stop some of the defenders from popping off some rounds.

I can't begrudge them that, seeing so many of the Genogerians running full tilt was unnerving. "Will any of your men run?" I asked, once again checking my sights.

"They're not all my men. And no, losing face among their gang would be worse than anything they could do." He was pointing towards the Genos.

"Well there's literally losing face and then figuratively, so I'd have to disagree on this one."

"That's some scary shit out there."

"Approaching five hundred yards. Game on." I took a deep breath and exhaled slowly. There was no guarantee I'd take another one. "Oh yeah, before we begin shooting and I can't hear you…do we have a fall-back position?"

BT merely smiled.

"I'll take that as a no. Please be out there, Tracy. I love you, Travis." I took my first shot but it was tough to say if it was a confirmed kill. The Geno went down hard but was completely swallowed up as the herd passed him by, most likely trampling him to death and finishing what I had started. That was also fine with me.

BT was shooting a fully auto AK, the heavy rounds nearly twice as loud as the borrowed M-16 I was using. The bullets were slamming into the ranks of the Genos. We stayed to the right of the rail guns' field of fire, doing our best to suppress the enemy's forward progress.

"Four hundred yards!" someone shouted. The Genos had passed another threshold. In two hundred more yards they would be in range with their own weaponry and then I would switch back to my original rifle. Right now it was a wholesale slaughter. Our entire line was firing, blood sprays lifting into the air like a fine mist. It was impossible to tell the damage we'd inflicted as the Genos just kept advancing.

No one needed to announce the two hundred yard marker as blue rounds headed our way. Most fell short or ineffectively into our glass barrier. When the rounds hit it sounded like someone putting a cigarette out in a toilet—just a short 'fzzt' then nothing. The screams started as the Genos found targets, which is no easy feat considering they were running at full tilt. At a hundred yards the horror of it really slammed home; their army was vast. I think even the men at the Alamo would agree that we were at much worse odds than they had been and they'd all died to the last man.

We had about eight seconds of life left, doesn't sound like much when you say it like that. I looked over to BT. He was calmly shoving another magazine into his weapon. I turned back to the enemy and could most assuredly see the whites of their eyes now. Even when I was a kid and I'd read about the Revolutionary War and that famous command to wait until...well you know. Screw that, if I could have kept them far enough away that they stayed a faceless, bodiless blob that would have been better, much, much better.

I think the Genos had begun to realize just how ineffectual the majority of their shots were. A good number of them were screaming in rage, their rifle carrying arms over their heads. They weren't going to shoot us when they arrived—they were going to beat us to death. There are a lot of ways to leave this earth and I think that would rank up there as one of the worst. Slow roasting might be the only one that would beat that. I'd had to switch trigger fingers as my index finger was beginning to cramp from the repetitive movement. If I lived I was going to file a workers' compensation claim.

"Might want to duck down!" BT shouted.

I wasn't sure how that was going to save us and then I quickly looked around. It had gone mostly quiet. Those around me were slightly pulled back and covering their faces. "What the hell?" I don't think I got to the 'hell' part. I might have more or less thought it by then. There was a white flash like you see from fireworks right before the explosion, only this was much more vast. I kept waiting for the resultant explosion, like you do when you're far away from where the rockets are going up.

I noticed pressure in my ears began to increase and small debris around me lifting off the ground. I mean like hovering, not as if it had been lifted from percussion. And then, as if someone had shot these small pebbles and shell casings, they flew towards the Genogerians, who I noticed were all standing stock-still. Whatever was going on, they were as freaked out about it as I was. Along with the debris, the air was also pulled away from my lungs. For three or four terrifying beats of my heart there was no life-giving air. It had been sucked away from me as effectively as if I'd been submerged in water.

"Get down!" I could tell BT was yelling, but in a vacuum there can be no sound. Reading his lips was easy enough. I was curious and scared as hell, but not stupid. Well, not completely stupid anyway. I ducked and covered, my chest hitching as it begged for air. Right now I wouldn't care if it was a crappy diaper laden toke, it'd be worth it. How many times had I pulled my shirt over my nose when I changed my son's diapers? Right now, I'd breathe deep.

My ears popped, as did my jaw. It'd been about twenty seconds since my last breath, which doesn't sound like much. Give it a go sometime without taking a large intake of air first AND while you're heartbeat is at an accelerated rate because you're in the middle of a deadly encounter. Twenty seconds is an eternity; it's all relative. How long is a day with your loved one? How long is your day when you lose a loved one? Same physical time, perspective-wise they are worlds apart. The mind is a funny thing.

I knew I was a few seconds away from tunnel vision as brown/black spots began to form in my field of vision. Next came the explosion—like a giant bubble bursting. It was more of a 'popping' sound. Air, blessed air, blew past me. I gulped deeply nearly drowning in it. This was followed immediately by all manner of debris including but not limited to the pebbles and brass casings that had been in such a rush to leave. I thought at first leaves were flying past, until I noticed they were wet, red wet. Sheets of blood blew over our location, the leaves were hunks of skin ripped clear from their hosts. Then came the really disgusting part as body pieces, eyeballs, fingers, feet and maybe even some unmentionables bombarded us.

It was like someone was using the world's largest cheese grater, but instead of a nice parmesan they were using Genogerians. I gagged as I took in some bio-matter, it was much easier on the psyche to call it that rather than what it was. BT tossed me a bandana, this time I took it. Fuck it if it made me look like a gangbanger. I placed it over my mouth and nose and hurried to tie a knot behind my head. BT was covered in blood, and I imagine I was the same. I could tell from the crinkle next to his eyes he was smiling but I did not see the humor in our situation. When the carnage finally stopped we both looked to the battlefield. A significant number of the Genogerians were now racing to their maker. It was going to be a busy day up there, with all the calculating and weighing of souls.

But much more importantly, the remaining ones weren't moving. Shock, perhaps? Then I heard fighting again, small arms and tank rounds. Whoever was behind them was still firing.

"What was that?"

"A bomb." BT was still smiling.

"That was not a conventional weapon, man! Are you

going to tell me what the hell is going on here?"

He put his AK back up and starting shooting again. His non-answer was answer enough. And then something I hadn't been expecting at all happened. The Genos were pulling back.

"Three hundred yards!" Then the call came for five hundred and finally at a thousand yards it went quiet again. Even those that had been pursuing them had taken a reprieve, probably to get away. I'm sure the Geno retreat had caught them as much off guard as it had me and they were scrambling to get out of the way. My only hope now was that the Genos weren't turning their attention that way. That was answered soon enough as the entire Geno line, at least that I could see, had just stopped. A low, mournful sound arose from them. It was a heart-wrenching wail.

"Never heard that before." I stood to survey what had happened to at least gain some semblance of understanding. The ground where the Genos had stood had been wiped clean. The ground had been stripped at least two feet down. The topsoil, along with any vegetation was gone. It was as close to any photo I'd ever seen of an off-world site like the moon or Mars, devoid of any resemblance of life. Bedrock was showing in some places. The wailing stopped after an indeterminate amount of time and was replaced by a chanting. I knew what that was.

"What are they doing?" BT had risen and was standing next to me.

"They're praying for their dead and chanting to their god for our deaths."

"Those savages pray?"

"You'd be amazed how very similar they are to us."

"Oh yeah…you have a pet one."

I laughed, thinking of Dee as a pet. "It's probably the other way around, but yes, I've had a lot of contact with them and that one in particular. And I consider him more of a friend than anything else."

"You're kidding, right?"

"No." I shook my head. "Are you going to tell me what that was?" I turned so I was facing him.

He pulled his bandana off and wiped the blood off of his face. If anyone looked the savage I would have to say it was the both of us as we were covered in viscera.

"We've had some help."

That was obvious—a couple of bulldozers had not created the wall. The rail guns were light years ahead of anything our military was working on and the bomb, if that's what you could even call it, was not of earthly origin. "I'm listening."

"Ever heard of Stryvers?"

"Unfortunately I have. I was aboard the Guardian, on one of our tours I believe, when our guide told us about the war they'd had with a species called the Stryvers. Neither the Genos or Progs have much good to say about them. Another alien race hell-bent on world domination and destruction, right?"

BT nodded reverently. "The dust had just settled over L.A. I'd come back trying to find out if any of my family and friends had somehow survived. There was nothing, man, not even a stray dog. I rounded a corner and there it was, a ship. I ran toward it, I didn't even have a gun, I bent down and grabbed a chunk of something. I can't even remember what it was. I didn't care I was ready to kill something. They had just killed everything! My city was gone." BT was choking up.

I knew the feeling well enough, upon my first glimpse of what used to be Boston the despair had settled so deep I thought it would weigh me down forever. It had threatened to shove me to the floor and maybe through it. I would have put my arm over his shoulder if I could have reached.

BT continued. "I don't know what I was thinking, or even if I was thinking at all. I wanted revenge. What stepped out of that ship, though…*that* I hadn't been expecting."

"More crocs?"

"Not even close. These things made the Allees look like cuddle pets."

"You're shitting me?"

"Do I look like I am?"

"No, I just wish you were."

"I've seen them four or five times now and it's all I can do to keep my gorge down. They're something like a spider mixed with a yeti."

"What?" My fear of spiders is only eclipsed by my fear of cats and clowns.

"They have these four thick legs covered in this coarse brown hair that they travel on. And then the torso comes up at a ninety degree angle from the body."

I was having a hard time visualizing what he was saying. "Like a Centaur?"

"Something like that, I guess. The two halves are about the same size although the body is bulbous like a spider. The things had to have been about nine feet tall with four arms, two of which were recessed back…didn't seem to be used much, almost like they were vestigial. I stopped short when I saw it holding something. It didn't look like a gun but I was pretty sure it could kill me. I could hear it crackling like a taser."

"What the fuck did you do?"

"I was frozen, I couldn't do anything. I'm not proud to admit this, Mike."

"I won't tell anyone. I'm pretty sure I would have just crapped myself and balled like a baby."

"I don't really believe that."

"You have more faith in me than I do then."

"Its head though, if that's what you can call it, was just more of an extension of its upper torso. I can unequivocally tell you that it was the most terrifying thing I'd ever seen. It had eight eyes and they were all as black as night. Then it spoke."

"It spoke?"

"Sort of, it had some sort of mandibles and they were moving but it seemed to be projecting thoughts in my head, telling me to calm down and be still. The funny thing was, I did."

"Is that some sort of predatory thing on its part? Make you calm just before eating you?"

"It may be, would be pretty nice if the stuff you were hunting just stopped and waited for you to kill it. But I'm still here so..."

"You're killing me, what happened?"

"It expressed sorrow for the devastation. Then it showed me images of its home world. There were these huge misshapen towers and his people walking all around doing whatever it is his kind does. He showed me images of great land battles. They were giving as good as they were getting from what I could tell, maybe even winning and then he shifted to a later time that had a strikingly similar quality to what we're looking at. The towers were gone, replaced by rot and ruin. The Stryvians were gone, and he stood upon the remnants of his world much like I had been here. The Progerians had developed a new technology."

"Those city-busting bombs?"

BT shook his head. "Biological weaponry that specifically targeted them."

"I've got so many questions I don't even know where to begin. Why...why are they here?"

"He said that they trail the Progerians when they can, doing raids and striking at their flanks whenever they can cause some damage. Anything to help pay back the vast debt of death the Progerians inflicted on them."

"The rail guns...the bomb? This hill?"

"Them."

"Are they here?"

"They're pretty gun shy for good reason."

"So they're willing to help but not get their hands

dirty? Did you get any sense of who started the war between the two?"

"I didn't think to ask, I suppose he implied it was the Progerians."

"What if they're here to assist until we win, or lose I suppose, and then swoop in to take out the victor?"

BT was silent. "Were you a government conspiracy theory kind of guy?"

"The question should be, 'Weren't you?' "

"I guess it's possible. But why bother helping at all? We'd be dead by now if not for their help."

"That has merit. I'm not convinced, not by a long shot, but it has merit. And they're not here now?"

"No, they've attempted contact before but they realize what the sight of them does to us mentally and psychologically. They even evoke a negative physical response."

"I can't imagine why. Why did they seek you out then?"

"Maybe they thought I wouldn't turn into a girlie man."

"Or they were desperate. That makes more sense."

"I like you man, I don't know why. I feel like I've known you a lot longer than I have and that somehow you should be here. Just don't push it."

"I've really only just begun."

"Wonderful."

"Want some food?" I pulled a Pop-Tart from a cargo pocket.

"You said food." BT's nose wrinkled at the sight of the foil packet.

"What are you, a foodie?"

"I just assumed that when you had some food that it would be edible."

"The gods shined their heavenly light down upon us when these were created."

"Did you know that nutritionally speaking the box is better for you than its contents?"

"Yeah, but does it taste like blueberry goodness? My wife's been trying to wean me off of these since she found my stash."

"Your stash?"

"I came across a packaging plant. I filled a shuttle with pallets of them."

"Pallets?"

"Yeah, had to get a storage locker to hold them all. Would have been more but there were a lot of cherry flavored ones. Those I burned."

"You burned the cherry flavored Pop-Tarts."

"It was for the betterment of mankind. They are the root of all evil as we know it."

"How long have you been delusional?"

"I would imagine it came with my 24th hit of acid."

I could feel BT's intense stare on me, I didn't care. I was eating. Next time he'll be more careful whom he hitches his cart to.

Chapter Twenty-Four - Tracy

"What is that?" Tracy was holding up her hand to shield her eyes. The glare from the L.A. wall was blinding even from three miles away. From this distance it looked like a giant white fire. Rut had just come back from a scouting mission.

"Well, it's a mountain of glass."

"Glass?"

"Yeah and it's huge, stretches at least three miles long, ma'am. Has to be fifty feet tall in some spots."

"Who built it and for what purpose? Do they think the Genos are going to stop because they cut their feet?"

"Tough to say, we couldn't get too close. It's manned."

"Military?"

"Not military ma'am and if I had to hazard a guess I'd say gangs."

"Like gangs of people or Bloods and Crips?"

"Bloods and Crips."

"What the hell is going on?"

"I don't know ma'am, but maybe that's the anvil to our hammer."

"Yeah, unfortunately sometimes it feels like we're swinging plastic toys. How close are the Genos to that thing?"

"Gotta be about a mile now."

"Let's pursue, when the tanks get in range they have the command to fire at will."

It was a few minutes later when the tanks opened up a fresh barrage on the backs of the Genogerians.

"Rut, get the Captain on the horn!" Tank Commander Sergeant Drake shouted, his voice barely audible over the din of war.

"It's Sergeant Drake." Rut handed the radio over.

"This is Captain Talbot. Everything alright, Sergeant?"

"Can you see this from your location?"

"Going to have to be more specific, Sergeant. What are you seeing?"

"There's some sort of green fire coming from the ridge."

"Chemical?"

"I mean rounds coming down range."

"Tracers?"

"I don't think so, Captain. I've never seen anything like it. It looks like they have two positions set up with this weapon and...and it's cutting rows and rows of Genos down."

"Is your position in danger?"

"No it's concentrated on the front ranks."

"I can't see it. I'll have Rut get me closer."

"Yes ma'am," Rut answered before he was asked, the truck already rolling.

It didn't take long to spot the line of green fire shooting down the hill, which was accompanied by a multitude of small arms fire.

"Looks like whoever is up there is pretty dug in." Tracy was looking through her field glasses. "What do you make of it?" She handed the binoculars to Rut.

He was silent for a moment. "Laser?"

"It could be, but I've never seen one powerful enough to do that and I think I would have heard about it."

"Whatever it is, it seems to be working. We might have a plastic hammer, ma'am. But that anvil is all metal."

Tracy got out of the truck and went to the front. She climbed up the bumper and onto the hood.

"Ma'am?"

"Something's happening."

Rut joined her up on the hood. He found himself being overly protective of his Captain, although if there was anyone he'd ever met that didn't need his protection it was she. "They're moving towards the gaps. I don't get it."

"I can't say that I do either, but it seems that they are filling in their lost ranks."

"That's crazy. Why would you subject your troops to that kind of abuse? They could just go around."

"They don't know any other way. Head down and forward seem to be their modus operandi." Tracy had one hand on her hip, the other shielding her eyes.

"Huh?"

"M.O., Rut."

"Oh." He still didn't get it.

Tracy was looking off to the north at the vast Geno line.

"Down!" Rut had seen the brilliant flash of white light. He grabbed Tracy and even through her protests tossed her off the hood. She landed with a loud 'umph' and was about to put a round in his ass when he jumped down next to her and shoved her under the body of the truck. He immediately joined her and did his best in the limited space to cover her body with his.

"Rut, what the fuck?"

Debris blew past them, pinging hard off the front of the truck, the windshield exploding under the assault. Tracy threw her hands over her head and dropped her head down. The truck stopped most of the fragments from hitting them but still some hit hard against her exposed fingers and hands. Blood began to fall from her, she wondered briefly if that would make it easier for the radiation to seep into her system.

As a violent wind blew past, both expecting to be seared and forever become a shadow emblazoned on the hard packed ground. When Tracy realized it was over, she rolled out from under the vehicle.

"Nuke?" Rut asked, looking up at her from below.

"You can come out now, I think it's safe. It wasn't a nuke. And before I forget to tell you…thank you."

"You're welcome. So, no nuke?"

"If it was it was unlike anything I've ever seen."

The radio squealed. "Genos turning, Genos turning! Retreat!"

"Time to go, Rut," Tracy said as she extended a hand down and helped her driver up.

Ten minutes later the small force had pulled back to relative safety. The scouts reported that the Geno horde had stopped moving in any direction. Tracy had unfolded some maps of the terrain but not really focusing on what she was looking at. Her main thoughts were on who was manning that ridge. They had now used two weapons she'd never seen and for the first time since this had started, the Genos had stopped their forward progress. She looked up when she heard the low keening.

Rut was outside the truck trying to smoke a cigarette, his hand shaking too violently for him to get a proper drag. The new alien sound did little to quell his nerves. Tracy came out as well.

"What now?"

"Well it isn't a battle cry, so that's good."

"I suppose, ma'am."

Tracy reached over and steadied Rut's hand. He thanked her silently as he took in a big pull.

"Now what, ma'am?"

She wanted to keep pummeling the Genogerians, especially now that they seemed in such disarray. Two things kept her from that decision. The first being that when the

Genos stopped they seemed more willing to come after her men and she would not sacrifice any of them needlessly. And second, she couldn't be sure but the Genos sounded like they were grieving and she couldn't bring herself to attack them while they mourned.

"We'll pull back a little further, set up guards and get everyone fed and rested."

Rut hoped that they went far enough away so as to not be able to hear that discordant sound. It stirred something primal within him and he didn't like it one bit.

The mourning howl turned into a chant sometime later that night. Tracy had been awakened in her tent by the noise. She quickly dressed and went out.

"Sure does seem like they're revving themselves up, ma'am." Rut was never more than ten feet from his Captain's tent.

"Don't you ever sleep, Rut?"

"I think, ma'am, the question is how could you? I mean...I mean with all the racket." Rut looked like he had just slapped a grandmother.

"Relax, Rut. When I sleep I get to visit with my child and husband...much more comforting there than here."

"Yes ma'am."

"And Rut."

"Yes ma'am?"

"Call me Captain. I feel like an old woman when you say that."

"No ma'am, you certainly aren't an old woman."

"Fine, we'll do this your way. What time is it?"

"Nearly 5:30."

"Sunrise in about a half an hour. Get the troops up. I've got a feeling that dawn is going to be very eventful."

Chapter Twenty-Five – Mike Journal Entry 11

I slept a little that night, the dreams tending to be on the bittersweet side. I saw Debbie—she looked so sad. Dennis and I had gone up to Indian Hill long before the war. We were joking, drinking Moosehead beer if I remember correctly, when a girl appeared on the other end of the expansive field. Even in my dream I felt a cold wind rush by me.

"Who's that?" Dennis asked. "Do you think she needs help?"

At first I thought it was Beth and I was going to warn Dennis that she most certainly did not. And then as she moved closer, I noticed she was floating above the grass rather than actually touching it, which should have been enough to have me running. Instead I took a long pull from my beer, maybe in hopes of shoring up my courage to stand my ground. Her left hand came up and extended towards us. When she had halved the distance between us she stopped moving, though her long dress continued to billow in the wind, her features seemed frozen. There could have been a sad smile there but I wasn't sure.

I reached out to try and grab Dennis's shoulder when I realized he was moving towards the vision. I tried to move and stop him, but my feet were mired in the ground, ropy green vines ensnaring them. I was rooted to the ground. I broke the beer bottle and was going to slash through the growth when I realized the green tendrils were hands—Dee's hands to be specific.

"WHY?" I cried.

"Because it is not your time," was his response.

"Dennis, stop!"

"It's alright, man. It's supposed to be like this!"

"No it's fucking not!" Even in my nightmare I knew I was tearing up my vocal chords.

Dennis brought his arm up and took Debbie's hand.

I went to my knees. "No, man, no please don't go, I miss you so much, I miss you both so much."

Dee was now standing next to me, my feet no longer cemented to the ground. I tried running again. The air might as well have been made of molasses. It had a physicality to it I could not push through. I went to the ground, my hands reaching out and grabbing turf. I was hoping I could pull myself forward.

"Michael, they no longer travel this realm." Dee was watching as Debbie and Dennis began to fade into a colored mist.

"What do you know?" I had rolled onto my back, the day turning to night just as fast. Stars were blotted out as something moved across the heavens.

"Mike! Talbot!"

I awoke with a start, sitting up rapidly. I was disoriented in the dark.

"You alright, man?" BT asked, "You were making some pretty weird noises in your sleep."

"Am I still here?"

"Where else would you be?"

"Sorry, sorry, um, just a little out of it."

"Who's Debbie?"

"You make it a habit of eavesdropping?" I said it a little more harshly than I'd intended. I still hadn't shaken the memory of the encounter from my mind.

"We're in the same fighting hole you and I, in case you hadn't noticed. It was my shift to stay awake. It would have been harder not to hear you."

I took a breath or two to calm down. "I'm sorry, man.

It was a pretty intense dream. Debbie was on the ship with me."

I was glad I didn't have to explain further as the Genos cries turned into something much more ominous.

"That's a war chant."

"You sure?" BT asked as he shifted so he could look forward.

"Get your men ready. It looks like the dawn is going to be eventful."

"Eventful? You call a full scale war eventful?"

"I can think of other more descriptive adjectives. Do you really want me to use them?"

"No, eventful will work."

The chanting was rhythmic, hypnotic and about as peaceful as it was going to get for a while. The sun had no sooner broken over the horizon than the chant became a single unified explosive scream. It was deafening. If my hands weren't plastered to my rifle I would have covered my ears. "Here we go," I said through gritted teeth.

As the Genos started at a full run, the rail guns went off again, followed almost immediately by gunfire around me. Something had shifted. Yesterday had been measured controlled bursts; this was frenetic wild firing. The chanting had seemed to sap our wills while bolstering theirs. Then the Genos did something I'd yet to see. Their front lines began firing. With us up high they weren't in danger of shooting the one in front of them. The effect was dazzling brilliant, with so many rounds coming at us it was impossible to see the Genos through it, like someone had pulled a blue tarp over them.

The glass sounded like rain falling on fire. Then the screams of men were intermingled as the impossible barrage began to find targets.

"What are they doing?" BT asked as he fell back into our small depression.

"Winning."

It was then we heard the heavy rounds of the trailing tanks start hitting. "Yeah!" I pumped my fist. "Whoever you are, I love you. Fuck them up!"

Chapter Twenty-Six - Tracy

"Oh my God," Tracy said as she watched the battle begin. It was awe-inspiring as the Genos raced across the field oblivious to the deaths they were suffering. They had made their fear go away. And then they'd opened up with a salvo that no opposing force could withstand. The air crackled with the charged rounds. It was a blue canopy of light—any thicker and it could have been a curtain.

"Rut, get those tanks firing, get everything firing. If it's in a box and it shoots something I want that as well. The men on that hill are screwed if we can't help. Tell the men to fuck them up!"

"Fuck them up?" Rut wanted to tell her those poor souls were screwed already but did as he was ordered.

"Those words exactly! Get it done."

The Genogerians paid absolutely no heed to what trailed them. Tracy was convinced she could have tapped them on the shoulder before putting a round in their ugly faces. And she just might have proved her point if she could run that fast.

Chapter Twenty-Seven – Mike Journal Entry 12

The rail guns were still doing damage. I can't imagine any other enemy would be willing to or could sustain and still they made progress. They couldn't have been more than fifty yards from the base of our mount.

"Any more bombs?"

BT shook his head.

"Pity." I was switching between hands to keep pulling the trigger as fast as I could. I could feel my fingers wanting to curl up like a ninety-year-old severe arthritis sufferer. Then the Genos added a new wrinkle, hurling something that looked like metallic Frisbees. The sky was littered with them, had to have been hundreds. They were coming from the Genos so I knew they couldn't be good. I started shooting at them. It was a lot like skeet shooting, although not hitting a target in this game most likely meant death.

Some others got the idea and began shooting at them as well. It was a no-win situation, though. It just gave the Genos a breather to come closer. The first of the discs opened up about halfway up the hill and bloomed like a deadly rose. I figured it was going to shower the area with metallic fragments, but instead a yellow beam as thick as a tree shot down from the bottom. The ground it hit blew apart and away from the force. A crater the size of a truck was left behind. When the other "spinners" reached the crest of the hill, we took our heaviest losses. Explosions rocked the terrain, I was pushed over onto my side just in time to see the rail gun closest to us turn into a twisted pile of exotic scrap metal.

My hearing was shot. I think for that I was happy.

When the spinners stopped I knew the Genos would be close behind. I righted myself and propped up my rifle. I hate being right sometimes. The Genos were hissing and I could see their teeth through the snarl, they were that close.

"BT, we have to fall back!"

He was shoving rounds in a magazine. "How much time?" He hadn't stopped.

"You won't finish that!" I grabbed his shoulder. I'd like to think I was so strong I pulled him up effortlessly but more likely he was already on the move. Whoever was still alive on that ridge must have gotten the same memo as we had. They were in various stages of exiting their holes with some of the luckier ones halfway down the slope already.

Men were screaming as we ran in a full on retreat. To the left and right they were falling, burned in half by the Genos. One skidded to a death-stop not more than ten feet from me. We were three quarters down, I wasn't holding on to much hope of survival as targets were rapidly being diminished. In all of my encounters with Death, this was the first time I felt his icy finger upon my forehead as if to say 'Over here! This one next!' Unlike my earlier dream/nightmare my legs were pumping faster than they had a right to as they were aided by gravity and adrenaline. I was in very real danger of falling over as I haphazardly sped down that slope. In fact I was teetering when Death reached out and snagged my shoulder, righting me.

Okay, so it was BT, but I didn't know that at the time. "This way!" he yelled.

Fear had tunneled my vision, all I could see was the burned out ruins of a home that may have been done a favor when it was razed. It would afford little cover if we decided to turn and go out firing. Bolts began to fly all around us and it was only a matter of time until I smelled my own cooking flesh. Again I felt Death's hand upon me, but it was BT. You can call it melodramatic if you want but I have never been so afraid in my entire life. It's one thing to face your fears—that takes a depth of courage. It's a whole other to run from them, to open yourself up to it. It becomes unbridled and will quickly gallop away from you.

BT flung me through an opening I wasn't sure a child could have made. I suffered a few abrasions; it would be hours before I noticed. Boards shifted as BT forced his way through.

"Crawl, man, crawl!" BT screamed.

I wanted to ask him where because the light was too dim for me to see much. Then I made out what was once a hallway leading down to what I guess were bedrooms. Shards of glass and splintered wood made putting my hands down a painful experience, again something I would consciously notice later, if that mythical time ever came.

"Left! No, left!" He smacked my foot when I started to go right. For some strange reason I'd never been able to ascertain I'd always had a difficult time distinguishing my left from my right. Strange, I think part of it has to do with my ambidexterity or maybe I just fried that connection under a marijuana-induced haze.

"Man, I don't know about this." I was in the opening to the room, although using the word 'room' seemed like a pretty big exaggeration. The hall was cramped, I was on all fours and if I raised my head up I would have hit the collapsed ceiling. Crawling into the bedroom was going to be difficult.

"Go! In the back on the left wall next to the bed you'll see an opening, leads to a crawl space," BT urged.

I wanted to tell him I *was* in a crawl space, although my movement in the bedroom was more of a low slithering. I clamped my mouth shut when I heard the harsh Geno-speak outside. I pushed my rifle ahead of me and did an arm over arm creep. My breath was getting short from the panic I was feeling. Had never been particularly fond of tight spaces, especially the ones in which I was most likely going to be entombed. I was focusing on the dark hole that was my target, envisioning it opening up into a grand cavern. I lost hold of my rifle and it clattered to the ground inside the cavity. I didn't dare breathe, waiting for the Genos outside to hear it.

After what I felt was a safe amount of time, I began to move again, pulling myself into the hole. It wasn't quite the cavern I'd been hoping for, although I could almost stand and right now that was like Grand Central Station. BT handed me his weapon and was through a few seconds later. I was going to say something until he pointed over into the corners where there were air vents that led directly out. We could see shadow play as Genos ran past.

I sat down heavily on the dirt floor. I didn't realize just how much adrenaline or fear I'd had coursing through my body. That became abundantly evident as I looked at my shaking hands. On reflection the hole couldn't have been too small because the behemoth BT had made it. Claustrophobia is a bitch.

"You alright?" BT whispered.
"Never better. How'd you know about this place?"
"Friend owned it, he grew weed down here."
"Any left?"
"Are you serious?"
"I can think of no better time that one might wish to escape their present reality."
"You've got a point, but no."
"What now?"
"We take a break, wait for them to pass by I guess. Then we go to our secondary rally point and see who survived."

The house rumbled, dust falling in copious amounts on our heads as Genos thundered by. We heard sporadic fighting from time to time. But this hill had fallen. There was nothing between the fighter facility and the Genogerians now. Whoever had spun them up and set them loose had done it masterfully. It was a half hour or so later, BT and I hadn't said much more than a handful of words. I'm sure he'd lost a fair amount of friends today and he would have to get used to bearing the weight of that. They say time makes it easier, I'm not so sure about that. Maybe you just get used to the pain of loss, but I can't say it ever diminishes. It's cumulative so that every additional loss just gets added to the pile until finally one day you can't prop it up anymore. Not sure what happens at that point…rubber room and crayons would be my guess. I hear the purple ones taste pretty good.

"You ready to get out of here?" he finally asked.

"Never really wanted in, but yes."

"Follow me." BT had to crawl, I was able to hunch over. We went to a small bulkhead. BT turned to look at me. I checked the safety of my rifle and put it on "fire". Light flooded into our small haven and I squinted, trying to hold on to some semblance of sight. BT opened the door completely as I thrust the barrel of my weapon out and swung it from side to side looking for a target. Then I cautiously went all the way through. Nothing. The Genos had swept past like an ill wind, leaving nothing but destruction in their wake. The smell of burning everything was in the air. I reached a hand down and helped BT up.

"Didn't even leave with so much as a kiss goodbye," I said.

"Your wife must be a saint. Let's go back up the hill and see if anything from the rail guns is salvageable."

The hill looked like a volcano getting ready to erupt, as smoke and fire poured from the top of it. It seemed highly unlikely anything of value was still there. Bodies littered the ridge and slope like discarded trash. BT stoically avoided looking at any of them, I would imagine because he didn't want to see anyone he knew and cared for. As we crested the hill the sight on the other side was breath taking, but not in a scenic awe-inspiring way. Thousands, no, tens of thousands of Genogerians were on the ground, large birds of prey and scavengers alike assembling to begin the process of reducing them to bones. In some places the bodies were three to four deep, stacked almost with care.

I would have liked to have said it was victory of sorts. But we'd lost a significant part of our force. We'd been overrun and the damn Genos were still going to complete their mission. It had been a complete and utter failure. I could have stayed home and played Legos with my son for all I'd done to help turn the tide.

"You hear that?" BT asked.

"Tanks." I couldn't see them yet, the smoke rising from the battlefield making an effective screen.

It was sickening to hear as the tanks rolled up and over the Geno bodies, the grinding of bones into dust should have held some measure of satisfaction, it didn't. Slowly through the mist the tanks' long barrels, turrets and bodies revealed themselves. I noticed with a small amount of trepidation that those same long barrels raised up when they saw the hill or us.

"Wave, man," I told BT, "before they mistake you for a small Geno."

There was a chance he was going to hit me, but at least he waved without any additional prodding. "Friends of yours?"

"Friends of both of ours right now."

"Do not move!" Came through a loud speaker somewhere on the first tank.

"Doesn't sound very friendly."

"On this I'd have to agree. Just remember they were involved in the same attack we were and I'm sure they're still a little hopped up."

"Do I look like a fucking Allee to them? I just lost hundreds of men!" BT was working himself up into a rage.

"Listen, man, they just want to talk."

His grief was close to the surface and it was manifesting as anger. It was much easier to deal with—the white-hot burn of being mad rather than the long, slow, steady smoldering of sorrow.

"Put the weapons down!"

"Well how in the hell are we going to do that if he told us not to move?" I queried BT.

"Nobody's shot you yet?"

"Oh, I never said that."

We both leaned over real slow and put our respective rifles on the ground. Dodging a tank round was not on my 'to-do' list for the day. Trucks and then foot soldiers began to cautiously materialize through the wispy shield. Foot placement on dry ground seemed to be of more importance than actually looking for an enemy. The Genos were miles from here. The tanks stopped near the base of the hill. I'm thinking they were hesitant to scale it, not knowing if they would sink up past their treads in the material it was constructed of.

"Identify yourself," came another command. It was not a request.

"I'm Ponch and this big guy here is Avilla!"

"I don't know him!" BT shouted, taking a step away.

"Fine! I'm Colonel Talbot and this big brute is BT!"

"Did you say Talbot, sir?"

"You're famous?" BT said.

"Infamous is more like it."

BT snorted.

"Do not move, sir. We've got someone who is sure going to be glad to see you."

I thought my knees were gonna go weak. There were only a handful of people on the planet that would be happy to see me and only one in this zip code, if those things even existed anymore.

A troop transport truck came racing over from the left. I thought it was going to be in some serious trouble from overturning the way the driver was slamming into Geno bodies. Gristle and blood were spraying over the top of the hood. The truck had no sooner come to a stop than someone I knew and loved deeply jumped from the passenger seat. Her booted feet were already moving before they touched ground.

"Your wife?" BT asked. I was already running down the hill.

I had so much momentum built up by the time she was getting close that I was in real danger of passing her by or slamming her into the ground as I used her like a backstop. I don't think it could have worked out any better as I yanked her up off the ground and spun her around. The only thing that would have made it better was if her helmet had flown off, her red hair fanning out. Yeah, that would have been a movie quality scene. I'd have to be content with her sigh and kiss. And then she seemed to remember where she was and what she was doing.

"You should maybe put me down."

I kissed her again and set her down easily. She adjusted her camo blouse, trying to look like she had not just completely lost her military decorum. Her huge smile gave the ruse away though.

"What are you doing here?"

"Saving you," was my response.

"Looks a little bit like the other way around."

"To-may-to, to-mah-to."

"Travis?"

"He's with Dee."

Her eyebrows furrowed for a moment.

"He'd die ten times before he'd let anything happen to our child."

"I know, I know. It's just that I have been seeing the Genogerians in a different light lately."

I nodded. The man who had been haphazardly driving my wife was running up the hill to keep an eye on his charge.

"Colonel, this is Rut. He's not much of a driver but he's a hell of a bodyguard."

I extended my hand. "Rut? Thank you for keeping an eye on the Captain."

"She didn't really need it, sir, but it was my honor."

BT had come down to us by this time.

"BT, this is my wife, Captain Talbot, Tracy. And her driver/bodyguard, Corporal Rut."

"Captain." He shook her hand.

"This is my bodyguard, he's bigger than yours," I told Tracy.

"It's always about size with you, Mike," Tracy said slyly.

BT outright laughed. Rut looked about as embarrassed as a nineteen-year-old Corporal could.

Tracy, myself, Rut and BT sat in the back of her truck eating a couple of MREs while we both recounted our sides of the story. I was simultaneously full of pride for what my wife had done and horror at the danger she had been in. She excused herself to get the men assembled so that I could see them.

"How'd you manage that?" BT asked as Tracy left.

"A lot of skill, man, and a little bit of luck."

BT was looking at me.

"Fine, some skill and a decent dose of luck. Stop looking at me, man. It was all luck. She thought the world was ending."

"There's the answer I knew was there."

"Kiss my ass."

"Beauty, brains and a killer attitude. She's a triple threat. You up for the challenge?"

"What do you think?"

"I didn't think so."

"Sir." Rut came running up to the tailgate. "The Captain will have the men assembled on the hour and wants to do the transfer."

As the senior officer in the area the men would now fall under my command and this was just a little bit of pomp and circumstance. I'd told Tracy that she'd more than deserved the right to keep leading them and with the way they were looking at her they'd follow her just about anywhere.

"Tell her I'll see her then. Thank you, Corporal. What are your plans?" I asked BT when Rut bounded off.

"Well, I've got to see who's survived and then I wouldn't mind exacting a little more revenge on the Allees."

"You've done more than should be expected."

"So have you, are you going to stop?"

"I can't, I'm still in debt for the military duds. They take so much out of my paychecks each week to pay it back."

"Let me go and see who wants to come along. When are you planning on pulling out?"

"If I said 'never', would that make me a coward?"

"Naw, man, it makes you a father and a husband who doesn't want to lose what he lucked into."

"Hurry up or I'll leave without you."

"Glad I never joined the military," BT said as he extracted himself from the truck. "These MREs suck."

"You're not supposed to eat the package." I told his back. He flipped me the finger.

I kept my speech short. I'd learned that one of a military man's least favorite activities was standing in formation. I'd gleaned all the information I needed when I first walked in front of them anyway. They were battle-hardened, tired but not exhausted and they were ready for more. Paul, um, General Ginson loved the dog and pony shows; he would keep his troops out in formation for hours. I could see the constant shuffling as the men tried to get comfortable while they stood and listened to his speeches. The man liked to talk, of that there was no doubt.

"My name is Colonel Mike Talbot." There were a few murmurings but not much, word of my presence had probably spread before I'd even showed. It was a mystery how information could pass so quickly among the ranks. "I am now your commanding officer. This might be the only time I can call Captain Talbot my subordinate." There were some snickers throughout the ranks. "I would like to finish what my better half has started. But just know that there will be no fresh troops coming, there will be no air support coming, there will be no Calv..." Rut tapped my shoulder and pointed to the ridge. Men began showing up on the top, at first only a few handfuls, then a few dozen and finally a force that rivaled ours. BT was at the helm. "Well, okay, scratch that. There will be a cavalry." More and more of my men were turning as they heard the clatter of moving glass. The gang members came down to join us.

I waited until the gang got into a reasonable facsimile of an assembly. There were some uneasy glances from the two sides.

"This is BT," I said, introducing the big man. "He is the leader of these men here. Don't let the colors of their clothing fool you. They, like you, are part of a battle-tested hard group of men and women. They are not apart from us. Not anymore. This isn't about the Bloods or the Crips or the Barrio 72s or the Marines and Army. This is about humankind. Every one of us here has lost someone or something—loved ones, homes or even just a way of life. The Progerians and Genogerians took it from us. They came from some shitty little hole in the universe and just took it. Didn't matter to them if it already had a rightful owner. However, this planet is ours! Who wants to take it back?!" There was a smattering of "Ooh rahs". "I fucking asked, WHO WANTS TO TAKE IT BACK?!" This time I got the response from both sides that I'd been looking for—the heavy stomping of boots and the screaming reply of "We do!"

"Mount up, then. They were wailing for their losses last night, let's make their grandmothers light candles tomorrow!"

"What's that even mean?" BT asked, leaning in. The men and women were still cheering.

"I was going with the church thing and lighting a

candle for their souls. Wasn't sure if it was going to work but it sounded good. Thank you, by the way."

"I wouldn't miss this for the world."

"That word play? Because that's what we're fighting for."

He smiled.

"You have rides for all of them? I could fit a decent amount in some of the trucks but not all of them."

"We've got rides."

"Yeah, probably not a good idea to mix them just yet. Just because they have a common goal doesn't make them friends. That will change quickly enough once the lead starts flying."

"You're not half bad."

"You haven't known me long enough. I'm assuming your rides are on the other side of the hill, so where should we rendezvous?"

"The hill goes for another two miles, we'll be there."

I shook BT's hand. "I can't thank you enough."

"When this is over I want Wyoming."

"I'll see what I can do."

BT nodded and he and his men went back up the slope.

***

"Well, at least I now know why they call you Rut," I said, one hand propped on the dash and the other on the roof of the cab. I was trying desperately to keep myself from being tossed around like a sneaker in a dryer.

"Sorry, ma'am. I mean sir!" He stumbled over his apology. Tracy was just smiling.

"This funny to you, Captain?" I asked.

"Actually, yes."

"How are you not bouncing around like a super ball?"

"It's called a seat belt. Maybe you should try it

sometime."

I started looking for this magical device.

"Umm, sir, that belt is broken," Rut meekly said.

"Of course it is. Do the men in the back actually survive these rides?"

"Only six concussions to date," Rut said proudly.

I could hear moaning coming from the back of the truck. If I hadn't of known better I would have thought we were transporting zombies. Looking ahead I saw that BT had beaten us to the gathering point.

"School buses?" Tracy asked questioningly.

To say it was an odd means of transportation, especially considering whom the passengers were, was an understatement. It was like looking at nuns in a hot tub. Great, now I had visions of Sister Mary Elizabeth half naked, oohing at the sensation of jet nozzles on her ass. Pretty much just punched my ticket to hell.

We drove past, BT's men followed. We'd been on the road for a while when we finally started to see the Geno horde. I had Rut stop, BT swung around the military column and pulled up alongside.

"Nice ride," I told BT as I quickly got out of the death machine Rut was driving.

"These were the only things available. Found them in a garage in South Central."

"Got any room?" I was looking back over at Rut, who may or may not have sprouted horns.

"What's your plan?"

"Plan? I don't really like to have one. That would mean I've thought out what is going to happen and then I wouldn't be flexible enough to change should the need arise."

"Uh-huh." BT wasn't buying it.

"Right now I don't see any reason not to follow the design the Captain has already laid out. Getting in front of them doesn't really pan out so well."

"You going to be able to stop them before they take out that plant?"

"No," I finally answered. "I'm going to have to warn the people there, though."

"Don't they know?"

"I don't know. Tracy says she has not had comm with the Guardian in a couple of days and they'd be the ones to relay updates around the globe. Shit, I should have thought of warning them earlier."

"Don't beat yourself up; you've been a little busy."

"I've got to go up to the factory."

"You just gonna go around the whole Allee army?"

"Well, if anyone can do it, it'd be that guy." I was pointing at Rut who was mouthing the word 'me' in question and pointing at his chest.

"I want to come."

"What about your men?"

"I don't really lead them; they're doing what they're doing because they feel the same as the rest of us."

"This is going to be pretty dangerous. I can't ask you to do it."

"Yeah, because nothing we've done up to this point has been dangerous."

I went back to the truck. "Captain, I'm requisitioning your truck and your driver."

"The hell you are." I wasn't expecting that. "And don't pull that rank crap on me. What are you thinking?"

"I need to get ahead of the Genos and warn that plant to evacuate."

"I'll come with you."

"And who are you going to give command of your unit to?"

"Technically, *Colonel* (there was a definite sneer added to that word), you should be assigning me to the mission while you lead the main force."

"Tracy, these guys love you. They're not my men—

they're yours. You've found a way to win an unwinnable battle, a battle that you were basically left to hang out and dry in and you're winning." I don't think I was convincing her quite yet. "Plus, you know I don't play well with others."

She nodded in agreement. "Talbot, I just got you back…I can't stand the thought of you leaving again."

"Rut, how far to the plant?" I asked.

"Maybe four hours or so, depending on the terrain, sir."

"And with you driving?"

"I can do it in three, sir."

"The Genos won't make it there tonight. I'll be back before they even start up in the morning."

"Rut, anything happens to him you'll be digging latrines with a spoon." Tracy kissed me then ushered her men out of the back of the truck.

"I didn't think she was going to let me go."

"Me neither, sir."

"Let's get that seatbelt fixed. My big friend has decided to come with us and if he's hopping all around the front of the cab he's likely to squish one or both of us."

BT grunted and then went to tell his men what was going on.

Within fifteen minutes we were back on the road. I didn't know if having the seat belt on was better or worse. It was cutting through my midsection every time Rut tried to launch us into the air.

It didn't take too long until we began to see the Genos in the distance again, beginning with the voluminous dust cloud. I had Rut turn sharp right when we could make out actual bodies through the haze they kicked up. They weren't nearly as large a force as they had been when I'd flown over them. But it still took a mile and a half driving perpendicular to them before we were able to get around them without going through. I had Rut go another mile or so just in case they put patrols out that far. I didn't think they would but caution seemed prudent. Once we got past them and they were no longer within sight of our rearview mirrors, I could feel the pressure within the cab begin to ease immensely. The drive was even beginning to be soothing. We were on a stretch of highway even Rut couldn't find a hole in, and for him that was pretty amazing.

"How long have you known the Captain, sir?" Rut asked.

"Seems like forever."

BT was looking at me.

"I mean that in a good way. Like we were meant to be together. I don't know how to explain it. But it's like I've known her spiritually all my life and it's just a matter of me physically finding her or, more likely her finding me. Does that make sense? There was a connection the moment her eyes met mine, even if she wanted to kill me."

"The Captain wanted to kill you? I wouldn't want those hazel eyes to look at me that way." Rut was staring through the window and I was not convinced he was looking at anything. Fairly scary proposition when that's your driver.

BT nudged me in the shoulder and was smiling. "I think our boy Rut here is crushing on your wife!" He was laughing.

Rut's face turned candy apple red. I was afraid it was going to blow up like some cheesy special effect.

"Got a thing for older women?" BT was taunting him.

"That's...that's not it." Rut was stammering.

"Isn't fraternization illegal or some shit in the service?"

"Article 12, section 37 b," I added, although I had no idea. "I think I can have him court-martialed and shot. Or shot and court-martialed."

"Sir, I'm not in love with the Captain!"

I figured it was time to stop before he had an aneurysm. "Just messing with you, Rut. She's a special woman no doubt, how the hell I ever ended up with her is open for debate."

"You got money?" BT asked.

I shook my head.

"Well it's not like you're movie star handsome, so that's not it."

"Thanks, man."

"You packing?"

"You really think I'm going to get into a discussion about what is or isn't in my pants?"

"I'm gonna go with a 'no' there as well. You do have the 'saving the whole world' thing in the bag. That is probably a positive."

"Appreciate the vote."

"Is that Beth chick as big a bitch as she looks on television?" he asked, switching gears.

"You have no idea."

"Was she worth fighting for?"

You would be hard pressed to find someone on the planet that did not know my story. A decent part got sensationalized but the main premise was still there and people loved hearing that the aliens could be defeated. "She was, at least at one time. I'm not sure what ultimately happened to her. She wasn't always an evil bitch." I paused. "Shit, maybe she was. I was pretty much enthralled with her, she could have probably crushed rabbit skulls in front of me and I would have thought that was just the cutest thing."

"You had it bad for her, man. Can't blame yourself, happens to all of us."

"Thanks, man."

"Not to me, I mean. I'm a real man, but to lesser guys like you that kind of shit happens."

"You'd have to be with a woman before you could understand," I retorted.

"What the fuck you laughing at?" BT asked Rut angrily. Rut's smile vanished quicker than a nut at a squirrel convention. BT again nudged me and smiled. Rut's face had taken on a pale hue. I shook my head and smiled.

We went on like this for most of the ride until Rut pointed out a building not too far ahead. Night was coming quickly and the thing was lit up like a Christmas tree, like it was begging for something to come along and destroy it, with a huge "HERE WE ARE" sign emblazoned on the roof. All it needed was a few spotlights and it'd be perfect. There were thick plumes of smoke coming from circular smokestacks. That would be more than enough.

"They're still there. Shit. Rut, make this bucket go faster."

The parking lot was full of cars. Light streamed from every window, and we could hear the heavy sounds of industrial work going on inside. I jumped out, heading for the front door.

"Hold on, Mike," BT said, looking around.

"We've got to warn these people." I was a little peeved he was wasting my time.

"That's the thing of it Mike…what people?"

And then it hit me. What people? A factory that had a parking lot full of cars and apparently three shifts that worked 24/7, yet there was no one milling around, nobody going to or from their cars, no one out front smoking a cigarette. No security guards patrolling such a high security area.

"…the fuck is going on?" I brought my rifle up. Rut and BT followed suit. "Rut, you stay out here and keep a watch on our six."

"Yes sir."

"You ready?" I asked BT.

"Looks like fun."

I pulled the front door open. The lobby was small; it had a little table with magazines from the Nixon era if the settled dust on top of them was any sort of indicator. The receptionist desk was empty and also coated in the same thick layer. I walked across the room and pushed against the heavy double doors. After doing a quick scan I let my rifle down. BT did the same. There was nothing and nobody here. If this had ever been a fighter plant it had been stripped down to the beams. I walked further in. On a small table to the left was a stereo system I would have loved to own. I hit the power button and all the fake factory sounds ceased.

There was a huge furnace on the far side of the factory and that seemed the next logical destination.

BT gave it a once over. "Oil fed. It's just burning oil to make it look like something is happening here. What's going on, Mike?"

"The whole thing is some sort of elaborate set-up."

"Set-up? For the Allees or for you?"

That was a good question and I told him so.

I walked around most of the factory floor looking for some clue as to what had happened or what was going on. It was BT who found it. He'd opened a maintenance closet.

"Mike, you might want to come here."

"You find a mop?" I'd asked when I saw the sign on the door. He was standing stock still, as if touching that handle had frozen him in place. "What's the matter..." I stopped talking when I came around and was now looking at the same thing he was. I grabbed his shoulder and spun him around.

"Let's go Rut." I said tersely when we got back to the truck. I was pushing BT along as fast as I could. Rut was asking questions as we headed back to the truck.

"What's going on, sir? I heard all the work stop, everything alright in there?"

"Rut get in the fucking truck and I want you to break all land speed records getting away from here, you got it?"

"I've got that, sir."

We were on the move when BT spoke. "That a bomb, Mike? Was that a fucking nuclear bomb, Mike?"

"There's a nuke in there? Oh geez." Rut found a gear I don't think even he knew that the truck had.

I was pissed off to a degree I don't think I'd ever been. Paul had obviously been planning this the whole time. Why the charade, then? Why let so many good men die? Why put my wife in jeopardy? This just couldn't all be because of his wife or me, could it? I would pummel the answers out of him if necessary.

"How...how far away do we need to be?" Rut asked.

"Twenty miles minimum, fifty would be better," I told him. It was late night by the time we saw signs of the Genos again. They had hunkered down for the night with some fires going. We didn't get close enough to run into any patrols. Ten miles later we were back in our own encampment.

I was in Tracy's command tent along with BT. I told her everything we'd discovered there.

"It makes no sense, Mike! He told me directly he didn't want to use nukes on American soil," Tracy said as she sat down.

"I guess he changed his mind."

"Who is going to trigger that thing? Did you notice if there was a timer?"

"I saw some lights on it and once I figured out what it was I thought it would be a good time to go."

"It must be booby-trapped somehow," BT said.

I shuddered just thinking about it. Maybe if we had opened the left double door instead of the right we might have been vaporized. Probably wouldn't have even known—BT and I would just have kept trading barbs in the metaphysical world, maybe occasionally wondering why we were never hungry or had to go the bathroom.

"I think we should pull further back."

"Mike, we're close to sixty miles away from there," Tracy said.

"It's a nuke, Tracy, how close do you want to be? I have no idea how big the thing's yield is. What if it's alien technology-enhanced?"

"I'll get the men up and moving within fifteen minutes."

That was the answer I was looking for. She left the tent.

"So what about the Allees?" BT asked.

"Looks like they're going to meet a fiery end. Whether we're there or not doesn't matter much. Wasn't like we were herding them."

BT nodded. "Well, I might as well go tell my men." I was alone. That's never really a good thing. Thinking isn't my strong point. My fucking best friend had set me up...twice, maybe three times. This mission had been doomed to failure, so why bother throwing troops in the mix at all? Can this really all come down to his wife wanting me? It can't...I wouldn't believe that. And once I'm done making him bleed he had better have a really good explanation.

I heard trucks and buses cranking up. I walked out of the tent expecting at any moment that the night was going to light up like there was a noonday sun.

"Mike, we've got a problem," Tracy said as she headed my way, map in hand.

"Like you and me or in general?"

She looked at me. "Why? What have you done? Should I be concerned?"

"Well, I'm just trying to cover all my bases. I usually do something wrong at an abnormal rate."

"I'll give you that but I was talking about in general."

"Whew, dodged that bullet. Okay, what is it?"

"My mother told me you were going to be more problems than you were worth. We'll talk about that later. According to my scouts, there are settlements around that facility."

"How close?"

She opened the map to show me. "One is no more than ten miles and then one more within twenty-five."

Absently I tried to run my hand through my hair and

ended up jamming my fingers on my helmet. "What time is it?"

"It's three."

"Makes sense."

"What?"

"That's the hour of the dead. Sorry. We have about three hours before the Genos begin moving and they have to cover what, fifty miles? They travel about ten miles an hour or so. We've got seven hours. Where's Rut?"

"He's coming. He was making sure everything started up."

It was another minute before he came running up. "Everything's good to go ma'am, sir, they'll pull out on your order." He was looking back and forth to see who was going to give it.

"Rut, I'm not going to order you but I'm looking for a volunteer. Lots of danger, probably cumulating in death."

"I'm in, sir."

"I haven't even told you what's going on."

"If the Captain's going, so am I," he replied.

"You do know she's my wife, right Rut?"

His face turned deep shades of red again.

"Mike," Tracy chastised.

"They're not going to listen. The townies I mean," BT added, walking up to us.

"Even if they do we're not going to get anywhere near a hundred percent compliance." That was my cynical side speaking.

"We have to try. There're mothers and kids, we have to make them listen."

"I know honey, I know. I'm just not holding out on much hope or how much good we're actually going to do. And we have our own kid to think about." Nukes scared the hell out of me, maybe it was growing up with the constant threat of them hanging over our heads. You couldn't hide from one and you couldn't outrun one. Even in the off chance that you survived the initial blast and weren't incinerated completely, odds were you'd lose all your hair and teeth and die a horrible death, wasting away from the inside.

"We should get going." Tracy was heading for the truck. The chance of anymore debate was pretty much done. The troops and the gangs were heading back to L.A. I'd tried to contact Paul again. Sure I wanted to beat the shit out of him, but if he could bring a shuttle down in the meantime it would give us an immeasurable amount of safety to get done what we were attempting. It had been like sending a message into a black hole. Something wasn't right. Well, a lot wasn't right and that was just an added wrinkle.

Chapter Twenty-Eight - Paul

"Sir, long range scanners are picking up a signal." Paul had been sitting on his bunk, trying to remember a simpler time when the message intruded on his thoughts. He knew that wasn't good; there was no earthly vessel out in deep space or ally coming to help. No, it was the Battle Cruiser and they wouldn't be able to catch this one off-guard. Even if they could, they had nothing to hurl at it. The Guardian was running on the absolute minimum staff that could be mustered, and most of the personnel were pulling double shifts attempting to learn their new stations. A few had been on leave and recalled immediately, but the rest were not just wet behind the ears, they were still leaking.

Hitting the respond button, Paul asked, "How long?"

"Weapons range in seven hours at present speed and course, sir."

Paul arose and went to grab his uniform pants.

"Where are you going?" Beth was on her side and propped her head up on her hand.

"I'm going to figure out how to save this ship."

"One more time before you leave?"

"Did you not just hear what I heard?"

"Of course I did. I just thought it would be fun. You know, under the threat of the gun and all."

Paul put his pants and shoes on. He grabbed his shirt

before turning to face her. "Mike was right to leave you." He walked out.

"I LEFT *HIM*!" she raged.

Paul walked onto the bridge and immediately over to the scanner console. "It even looks big on a twelve by twelve screen."

"The ship has been picking up speed, sir," the technician said. Paul could see the sweat rolling down the man's neck.

"Prepare to buckle." Paul was moving towards the Captain's chair. There were glances thrown around as people tried to figure out what was going on.

"To where, sir?" the Chief Engineer asked. Last week the Corporal had been at school learning about this equipment. Now he was in charge of it.

"Plot any course; just get us out of here."

"What about Earth, sir?" The Corporal turned to look at him

"We can do it no good if we are scattered all over it."

"But Sir…"

Lieutenant Braverly took a step towards the Corporal who immediately turned back around. "Yes sir," he stated instead.

Paul had no plan other than to leave. It wasn't like he could go to the planet next door and ask for help—they were alone out here. The men and women might get more proficient at their jobs but they were still dangerously thin on positions. He could count the number of fighter pilots on his hands and have a couple of fingers left over. It wasn't going to get any better. His best option was to stay and fight. He knew it and the men knew it. There was a minute chance they could inflict some sort of damage on that Destroyer before it reached Earth and that was better than running with their tails tucked between their legs.

Paul sat back. No one on board had ever been through a buckle. He heard the sensation was akin to being on a falling elevator. He gripped the handholds; his stomach feeling like it was rising and trying to escape through his mouth. "I'm sorry, Mike." And then they were gone.

Chapter Twenty-Nine – Mike Journal Entry 13

"Fuck, Rut, they should have called you Crater." Even with the seat belt on I thought I was going to get tossed from the truck with the whole seat. "Did you purposefully have the leaf springs removed from the suspension?"

"Sir, I didn't have the truck modified in any way," he said in all seriousness.

"Don't listen to him, Rut. He likes to be pampered," Tracy said. BT snorted.

"You do realize I have to put on an air of authority here, right?" I asked my wife.

"You keep trying." She smiled.

We were trying to lighten a heavy mood. It's amazing what you can accomplish if you just put the thought of a many megaton nuclear bomb going off in a few hours out of your head. We got to the first settlement. For a second I thought I was looking at a movie set. Large metal doors easily twenty feet high were the only ingress into a walled city. I'd not been out much past the military bases in a long time. To see how far we had regressed as a civilization was shocking. This was obviously a community that had a healthy fear of outsiders; my guess was for good reason. Gun turrets dotted the fence every hundred feet or so and from what I could tell they were all manned. Why bother going through all the trouble of walling yourself in and then not protecting it?

"Rut, stop here," I told him when we were about fifty or so feet away from the entrance. I put my rifle down and got out.

"Do you know what you're doing?" BT asked.

"He never does," Tracy explained.

"Nice vote of confidence." I walked toward the doors, my hands about halfway up.

"Don't get shot!" she yelled out.

"Best piece of advice I've had all day," I mumbled.

"We don't want whatever you're selling!" a guard posted next to the gate shouted down.

"I need to speak to the leader of this settlement." I was looking up and shielding my eyes because the sun was right behind his head.

"Yeah, know what I need? A shower and a steak dinner. Doesn't look like either of us is going to get what we want."

"My name is Colonel Michael Talbot."

"Yeah and I'm Pope Francis."

"Really? I've never met a Pope. Do you take confession?"

"Are you an idiot? I'm not really a Pope."

"And yet I'm still Michael Talbot, so it seems our relationship has gotten off to a rocky start. I mean with you lying to me and all."

"What would the anointed one want with us lowly peasants?"

"Anointed? Really? You have no idea the shit I've been through this last week. If that's part of being anointed I want nothing to do with it. Listen, we could trade taunts and jests all day—it's kind of what I'm famous for—but I've got an urgent message for your leader that pertains to the safety of this entire place."

"We're doing fine, don't you worry your pretty little head over it."

I turned towards the truck. "Tracy, he's not listening to me!"

Tracy came out to stand next to me. "Get your damn leader out here NOW! Please."

The guard looked down at her, shocked maybe to hear such a loud yell from someone so diminutive. "Yes ma'am."

"How the hell did you do that?" I asked.

"It's all in the inflection."

A couple of minutes later the door cracked open just enough to let three men out. Two trained their weapons on us while the third patted us down.

"Hey, man! Watch where you touch her. She's my wife."

He looked apologetic. "Just a precaution. They're clean."

One of the gunmen waved us through.

A few feet through the gate we met one of the leaders. He couldn't have been more than 5'2", with wire-framed spectacles that held thick lenses, made his eyes look like an owl's. His nose was the biggest thing on him. He was what I figured an IRS audit manager might look like. I thought I'd dislike him immensely, it was quite the opposite. A group of people came to see what was happening. I didn't get the sense that it was with hostile intentions, even though most of them were armed. It was more of curiosity. I had to bet they didn't get many visitors.

"My name is Harold Treemont. Welcome to Safeville." He extended a hand, first to Tracy and then to me. We made our formal introductions. "I am part of the community leaders. I'm sorry for all the security. One can't be too sure about a person's intentions these days."

"You've got that right," I blurted out. I was still pissed about Paul.

Harold looked at me a little funny, which was a sight I was used to. "So *you* are Michael Talbot. I hoped I'd one day be able to meet you."

"Really?" I asked.

Tracy kicked my shin. "Sorry, what he lacks in manners he completely misses in charm."

It took me a second to catch it. "Hey!"

"And smarts. Mr. Treemont, we came here with some news that I'm sure you're not going to want to hear. Do you have a place we can talk in private?"

"We've decided, Captain, that unlike governments of old that all information will be available to everyone. We have nothing to hide here. Perhaps if the old regime had thought the same way we would have had more of a chance to prepare for what was coming."

I doubted that but I had finally learned to keep my mouth shut.

Tracy held no punches, she couldn't afford to. "Four miles from here there's a nuclear bomb we believe is set to go off in about five hours."

Treemont looked like he was going to pass out. I reached over to steady him.

"Yield?" he asked, taking off his glasses to wipe away the condensation that had just formed.

"We don't know, sir. Big enough so that four miles isn't going to make much of a difference." There were gasps at first and then people ran off in different directions.

"Can't you disarm it?"

Tracy shook her head.

"Harold, we've been fighting a Genogerian army for the last few days." If I thought he'd paled earlier, his pallor now resembled bleached flour. "Our mission has been to stop them from getting to the fighter plant north of Los Angeles."

"The...the factory?" he was sort of in a daze. "That place hasn't been operational for six months. Why would you possibly need to defend it and why would the Genogerians want to destroy it?"

Tracy and I looked at each other. "Mr. Treemont, for reasons my husband and I don't understand yet we weren't given that information. We were told to protect that facility by all means necessary."

"And you decided a nuke was the best way to go about it?" he questioned.

"We didn't know about that either," I filled in. "When we realized we wouldn't be able to stop the Genos we went to warn the factory that they needed to get out. All we found was a ticking nuke."

"Dear God."

"Mr. Treemont, you and your people need to leave," Tracy said tenderly.

"This is our home." He was looking at both of us as if we could do something to prevent the horror coming.

"I'm sorry. I truly am," I told him.

"How far is safe?"

"I'd say twenty to twenty-five miles north. Stay away from prevailing winds. To be honest, I'd keep driving the entire time until it went off and then some more."

"We don't have enough transportation. Are more of your trucks coming for an evacuation?"

"Shit." I rubbed my hand over my face.

"There is no one else coming. How many people do you have here?" Tracy asked gently.

"Four hundred and twenty-six."

It was a pretty specific number. I guess in a small closed society like this every birth would be celebrated and every death mourned by the populace.

"How many can you move?" I was going into salvage mode.

"We have a school bus and eight cars we use for scavenger runs."

The bus crammed to the gills could probably take a hundred people, the cars another fifty or sixty. Nearly three quarters of this community were up shit creek. And not only did they not have a paddle, they didn't even have a boat. They were just wading in crap up to their necks.

"If you get moving now those vehicles could make that round trip in under an hour."

"If we go the minimum safe distance away."

"Mr. Treemont we're not experts, but twenty five

miles is a significant amount of distance away. However, you have to start now to ensure your people make it."

"You...you don't understand. There are other things and other people out there that we need to protect ourselves from. Without these walls we'll be vulnerable."

I got blunt. "You stay here and you need not worry about anything anymore."

"Mike!"

"Tracy, it's the truth. They're going to have to deal with one problem at a time."

"He's...he's right. I'll set it up now."

"Bullshit, Harold! He's going to wait until everyone is out of here and then just move in. Take over all the hard work we've been doing for the last three years."

"Fuck, man. Why is there always one asshole in the crowd?" I asked. "Tell you what, *you* stay and make sure that doesn't happen. Me personally? I'm getting the hell out of here. We've got one more township to talk to then I'm having my crazy driver get us as far from here as possible. Then tomorrow I'm heading home so I can see my son again. And then I think I'm going to retire from this shitty military life *again* and go underground."

"That sounds like the best plan you've ever come up with," Tracy said as she leaned into me.

"Good luck, Mr. Treemont," I said. I shook his hand and headed back to the door.

"You can't just let them go!" I think it was the same jerk, but who knows? When one is quiet another village idiot is always willing to step up and run with the torch.

"We're leaving. We don't want your home and we have other people we need to warn before time runs out."

Harold stepped in front of a man twice his size and stopped him. I nodded to him.

"Good luck and God bless." And then we were out, headed for the truck and the next stop. I thought I heard engines as we pulled away and I could only hope it wasn't wishful thinking on my part.

"They leaving?" BT asked.

"Seems that way. One down one to go."

The ride was mostly quiet except for the tortured metal of the truck as it was bent and twisted into agonizing shapes from Rut's harsh driving. I felt for the inhabitants of Safeville. It was not going to be an easy road for them to start over. Just one more thing I needed to talk to Paul about.

The clock was ticking and we were in the neighborhood of three and a half hours until presumed detonation. What the hell did we know, though? The Genos could have double-timed it and be pulling up now to the factory or the thing could be rigged to go off when they were ten miles out. We had no clue and having the threat of a mushroom cloud forming over your back was intimidating. The next place we came to, that was all I could really call it. Settlement would have made it sound like they had their shit together. This place was mostly cardboard boxes and sleeping bags. A homeless person under a bridge was less transient looking than this motley crew. But they were armed…oh yes, they were armed. This was evident when we were close enough that they pulled their guns out. We were about a hundred feet away, enough to realize that the barrels of those weapons were huge. Although really anything pointing at you that can shoot a projectile seems huge.

At first two of the grubbiest men I'd ever seen were standing side-by-side, guns trained our way. They quickly garnered back-up with the rest of the group and began to advance. I'd swear as if it was on cue.

"Back up, Rut," I said softly.

"Mike, we have to tell them," Tracy intoned.

"Rut, now." I turned to Tracy. "If we can we'll tell them from a safer distance."

As he ground the truck into reverse, bullets began to fly. I heard the chatter of an AK, which has a very distinctive heavy percussion sound to it. A line of fire came our way. I could hear bullets as they whined off the ground or slammed into the grill of the truck. The engine was getting banged with rounds. Then they raised their muzzles, figuring if they couldn't disable us then they'd kill us, I suppose. Our windshield blew in, a bullet lodging into the back of the cab in between my wife and Rut.

Red flares of anger ignited in my mind. For me to get shot at was one thing, but for someone to shoot at my wife, well, that was a completely different animal. If it had been possible, lava would have flowed from my ears.

"Fine, fuckers! You want to play?!" I ripped the seatbelt off, leaned back, pulled my foot up and kicked out what remained of the windshield. I blasted blue rounds down range. BT was already leaning out the window, his own AK sputtering in his hands. Two men were blown back as I hit them with a volley of shots. It was amazing to me how quickly their attack ceased once they started taking casualties. Out of the nine, five were dead or dying. I'd taken out the initial two grubbiest to the sheer delight of germaphobes everywhere. BT had unloaded an entire magazine and taken out an additional three men. Rut was still driving backwards, but looking forward, his eyes wide trying to register what was happening. We were now more in danger of him than anything else at this point. I'm guessing the vast majority of his military career had not entailed fighting his own kind. I think he was more in shock that they were firing on us than scared of the bullets.

Genos are huge and vicious, but man is more cunning and devious. If Rut was going to survive the upcoming harshness of the new world it was a lesson he'd better learn soon. The truck was still going backwards, a heavy ticking coming from under the hood, thick black smoke beginning to leak out.

"Rut, you might want to look at where we're going," I said, looking at the side view mirrors. A bend in the road was up ahead with a healthy drop off if he stayed his present course. I was fairly confident we wouldn't die down at the bottom of the gulley but it didn't look like a fun ride either. Plus, if we lost our wheels the odds we could escape the nuke had gone to virtually zero.

"Right," he said without looking.

"Rut, man, the friggen mirrors man, use the mirrors!" BT was getting in on it.

The rear of the truck swung to the right as Rut somehow managed to turn with the road. I was still wondering how he'd managed to do that, when the ticking became more of a knocking. It literally sounded like someone was hitting the engine with a tire iron. In the span of a few seconds we went from loud hammering to near silence as the engine sputtered and ceased.

"Out!" I ordered. We hadn't put more than a quarter mile between the Dirty Dozen and us, my guess once they realized we were out of commission was they were going to come and check it out.

"I can fix her," Rut said sadly.

"I'm sure you can, Rut, but not in three hours," Tracy put her hand on his shoulder.

Three hours? I kept the thought to myself but she was being pretty liberal with that precious commodity. We had three minutes.

"The gully…come on," I told the group. It offered the best protection for what we had on hand. There was a small copse of woods behind us with some scrub brush to our exposed side. We'd no sooner got into our positions than we saw them coming. This time it looked like the whole unkempt lot of them was heading our way.

"Warn them, she says. We've got a duty, she says."

"You do know you're talking out loud?" BT said.

"This isn't the time, Mike," Tracy said.

"Who knows when I might have another? Dumbasses to our front, radioactive destructive fireball to our rear."

The men to our front fanned out. Apparently our spot

was not so secret.

"Before you start shooting, hear me out!" I yelled after making sure I didn't expose any part of me.

"You're kidding right? You kilt..."

"Kilt?" I mouthed.

"...five of us."

"In all fairness they shot at us first."

"True 'nuff. Say your piece fors we start the killing."

"We came here to warn you."

"Funny way of showing it."

"Again, man, they fired on us first."

"I'm still lissnun."

"There's a nuclear bomb at the fighter facility not more than fifteen miles from here. It's set to go off anytime within the next...(I am almost said 'couple of hours' but that would have given them enough time to kill us and still vacate the area) ...few minutes."

"Seems mighty convenient, now that we gotcha surrounded."

"I'll admit it does. That doesn't change the fact that if we all stay here we're going to become crispy critters."

"They probably like crispy critters," BT said.

"Not helping."

"Movement to our right," Tracy said softly.

"Listen man, we need to...we *all* need to get out of here as soon as possible."

"Why would someone want to blow that place up? Been nuttin' there for months."

"There's nothing there now, but soon enough there will be an entire hostile Genogerian army in the parking lot. It was set up as a trap for them." *And for us I guess as well*, I thought. But why? This made about as much sense as Cherry Pop-Tarts, which basically meant not at all.

"Bullshit. Them ugly bastards are holed up in 'Zona."

"Not anymore."

"Tell you what, as soon as we're finished here, we'll

go check it out, I promise."

"Well, that makes me feel better," I yelled to him. "You got a shot on whoever is trying to come up on our nine?" I asked Tracy.

"I think I'll smell him before I can see him."

"BT, anything?"

"They're pretty stealthy for a bunch of hick looking motherfuckers."

"No, really, don't hold back on my account."

"You of all people, Talbot," he said, looking over.

"There's a house back there." Rut was looking through the small woods.

When I looked I saw what he did, but the thing had to have been five hundred yards away and a good three quarters of that was in the wide open. Still, it was something to keep in mind if we made it through the next few minutes. If it had a basement that would offer some measure of protection against the blast and the assholes.

A lone shot kicked up dirt right above my head. It was safe to say he had a pretty good bead on me. He should have just waited and I would have popped up eventually, like a prairie dog. He should know how to hunt those—odds were they were a large part of his diet.

"You planning on shooting any time soon?" I asked BT.

"Why don't you get your ass up here and help?" BT grumbled.

I heard movement on our left. It seemed they were going to cross the road and strike from three sides. I was able to take one out but at least two more had gotten across. Now it would just be a matter of time until they got into position.

"It's fallback time," I said.

"Mike, we haven't even begun to fight," Tracy said.

"Yup, aware of that, pulling a tactical retreat while the opportunity is still afforded."

"I'll stay for a few seconds and lay down some

suppressive fire. Rut, you keep an eye on our front, Tracy your right and BT your left. This isn't a discussion, it's an order. Well, I mean except for BT—he can do whatever the hell he wants."

"Come on, ma'am." Rut got up into a crouch, as did Tracy.

"This one time I'll let you tell me what to do. But no more." BT stuck his meaty finger in my face.

"Fair enough." As soon as he stood I blew all manner of shit up—trees, old cars, squirrels (no on the squirrels, it just sounded funny). Fire, sparks, and splintering objects needed to be big enough distractions so we would be able to get away clean. Tracy and BT started firing, whoever was on our sides quickly became privy to our plan and I guess they weren't on board with it. We had the element of surprise for a second anyway.

Rut had spun to help Tracy. I was shooting and pulling back, constantly looking over my shoulder to make sure I didn't fall and trying to see where I was in relation to everyone else. What happened next went by so fast, it looked like one of those damn targets that pops up on a shooting range. The bad guy was right in front of Rut, could have poked him with a stick if he'd wanted to. Blood sprayed from the exit wound in Rut's back. He barely had enough time to register the fact he'd been shot and turn to see his killer before he fell over. I turned completely, firing and walking my shots right into the assailant. He had little time to savor his victory as I pretty much cooked him alive.

Rut was still. I don't think Tracy even knew he was down yet, as she was fighting to hold her position and not get overrun. Bullets were whining around. I could feel the displacement of air around my head.

"BT, Tracy, run!" An orderly withdrawal was not going to be possible. BT swung, still firing to his side but running towards the house. I saw Tracy take a quick look to her left. She saw that Rut was down and was moving towards him.

"Too late, let's go!" I was almost running into her.

She knew enough to trust my assessment. I'd never leave a wounded person behind no matter the diminished chance of survival, even if it had meant I had to sling him over my shoulder. War came down to two principles: survive being the first and make sure the enemy doesn't being the other. It was really that easy. Now doing those two things, well, that's the difficult part. Watching those you care about or are in command of die around you...that's why they say war is hell. The men who created the mythos revolving around hell had never been on a battlefield. If they had, they would have realized they didn't need to make up a place to torture the souls of the damned because we'd done a good enough job all on our own. I don't think I'll ever understand the defect in man that makes us want to kill each other. If God truly made us in his own image, he missed a couple of brush strokes or he's a really pissed off being. *Rut, if I can bury you, I will*, I thought as I stepped over his prone form. Chances were he was going to get one hell of a Viking funeral in a little bit anyway. We all were.

BT yelled. I saw a flap of his pants flutter to the ground. A bullet had caught him in the thigh. He was either pumping on adrenaline or it had passed through a meaty portion because he barely slowed. I did my best to shield Tracy's back with my own. My left foot nearly flew out from under me as a round caught me in the heel. It felt like I was stepping on hot coals as I brought my foot back down. I think it had hit my boot and scraped across the bottom of my sole. I felt a squishing sensation as I ran. I was bleeding but not terminally. Tracy's head whipped violently to the left. I thought my heart was going to burst. I damn near tossed my rifle thinking I was going to have to grab her body as it fell.

Her helmet spun to the ground. A round had carved a crevice in the top, ripping it from her head. I turned back towards our attackers. I'm pretty sure I was yelling all manner of expletives. My mouth open, I blanketed the entire area in rounds. I'd caught two of the fuckers completely unawares. They'd been in full on chase mode when I'd spun around.

"Mike, come on!" Tracy was urging.

I turned back to see BT staggering. I think he'd taken another hit. We were still a couple of hundred yards from the house. I garnered us a second or two reprieve as the assailants regrouped but even at world class speed, we were twenty seconds away. And at the rate we were moving that travel time was much closer to a minute. *What a strange place to die*, went through my head. My biggest hope was that I would go first. That way I wouldn't have to watch the love of my life fall. Selfish, I know, never said I was perfect. I'd wait for her on the other side though, if such a thing existed.

Then I heard it in the base of my skull, like a low level hum, something you might hear if you were close to an electricity transformer or something. My short hair was rising like I'd rubbed a balloon on it. Static electricity. I mistakenly assumed it was the forerunner of the bomb. I could only wonder what a wave of heat hot enough to evaporate me would feel like. Would I still be screaming as I crossed over? Would I in perpetuity think I was frying? Someday there would once again be living beings in this clearing and they would hear my haunted hollow screams. I was going to turn and drape my body over Tracy's to protect her, maybe if we were that close when we died we'd be forever inseparable.

"What is going on?" She was about ten yards closer to the house but had turned and was coming back.

The men that had been trying to kill us were now hauling ass away from us. I shot one of them in the back before he could get clear. I did not feel guilt. He'd been trying desperately to do the same to us. I may have just saved someone else that might unluckily stumble across his path. I lined up another shot.

"Mike," Tracy said, trying to put the voice of reason into me.

Fuck reason, I shot him. Ended up in his buttocks. You might think getting shot in the rear end is funny, like what they show in the movies. It's actually a very serious wound and more painful than people could imagine. The chances for complications are extremely high, not that the guy I'd shot was going to have any of those. I hadn't shot him with a traditional round. His right leg was almost severed clean from his body. He fell over, gouts of blood pouring from the seven-inch long trauma I'd administered.

I heard a grunt near me. BT was attempting to sit without falling. That got me moving. Tracy and I helped him as best we could to get down without any more damage.

"I think my leg is broken." He pulled his hands away from the injury. They were covered in blood.

I ripped open his pants and saw three holes. Two from where a bullet had gone in and out and a third that must have struck bone. If his femur was indeed broken, of which I had no doubt, then he was one of the strongest individuals I'd ever come across or possibly shock was setting in, because he should have been screaming.

"Tracy, you got a knife on you?"

"What are you going to do with it?" Both could have asked that question but ultimately it was BT as Tracy handed me her Ka-Bar.

"I need to get that bullet out."

"You need to do no such thing!" BT moved his hands to his leg, where I'm positive if I had strayed within his grasp he would have crushed the encroaching body part. "You a doctor?"

I shook my head.

"Medic?"

I shook my head again.

"Ever done this before?"

"Not so much."

"Come on, man! Throw me some sort of bone."

"Got nothing for you."

"Then just let me be. I'll say my goodbyes and just wait."

I sat down next to him.

"You two get to know each other, I'm going to see if there's a car at that house."

BT and I looked at each other. "I probably should have thought of that," I said.

"No, you were too busy wanting to carve me up like a Thanksgiving turkey."

"I don't like dark meat." And then we both started laughing. It was wrong but it felt right. We had barely escaped death and even now it was probably circling back around to finish, but right now, RIGHT FUCKING NOW, we were still alive and I would laugh in its face right up until I began to cry. I turned to look at Tracy and saw she was half way between the house and us. She had stopped moving, her rifle down by her side, her right hand shielding her eyes as she looked up. I followed her line of sight.

A shuttle! Hope surged within me until I realized it was like no shuttle I'd ever seen before, like no ship I'd ever seen. "What the hell?" I asked as I stood. BT was now looking. He was quiet but I didn't take note of it then. The flying object looked like a hockey puck; it was round and thick all the way across. The edges did not taper like I expected an alien spaceship did, at least back before I knew better.

Dread quickly replaced hope. I think Tracy felt it too because I saw her trying to decide in which way she was going to run. I would not have held it against her in the least if she chose the house. I'll admit I was happy though, when she started booking it my way. When my mind was working correctly again I thought the ship was from the Progerian Destroyer, even if the design made absolutely no sense. There was a chance it was new technology, a probe or some sort of devastating weapon. None were great options. Who knew? The next option would be worse.

The ship hovered over our location for a moment then moved a bit south to land. Tracy had reached me just as the machine came to a rest. The grip I had on my rifle was about as tight as I could manage without melding to the thing.

"Put it down," BT said, with no small amount of resignation.

"You crazy, man? Thing is probably full of a hundred Devastators," I retorted.

"It isn't."

Part of the ship turned from the matte black it was, to more opaque looking. It was roughly the size of a double door. And then something stepped out of a nightmare I'd not even dared to have yet.

'We are Stryvians and we mean you no harm.' The words entered my head as easily as if I'd made the thought. I began to experience a sense of well-being but I knew this for the falsehood it was. Whatever that creature was, it was messing with my brain juices. I'd done enough drugs to know I was being altered.

"No, no, no, no, no," I muttered over and over. I was about as close to babbling as I'd ever been. "What do you want?" I shouted. It seemed to recoil from my words as if they were too harsh or loud. Or maybe the thing was just getting ready to spring like those damn jumping spiders. I think I would have been too petrified to even shoot.

'We cannot process sound through the airwaves. All communication must be done through telepathy. Do not kill us, Michael Talbot.' The voice sounded like rocks rolling on the bottom of a fast moving murky river, watery and full of death for anything that resided there.

I was about to ask how it knew my name but what was the point? I didn't want to think that those things had been watching me. I'd thought that BT's description of them might be slightly distorted and embellished. He'd done nothing to capture the hideousness of the creature. I was going to tell it to go the fuck away and then my mind started to get crowded. That's as accurate a description as I could muster. I heard multiple voices now. For ease of reading this journal I will highlight the text I think I was supposed to be hearing.

'Does it not understand us?'

'Is it injured?'

'The reptiles are nearly in place, we must go.'

'Get at least him aboard, Inruk. The rest kill if he will not comply.'

I got the distinct feeling I was not supposed to be hearing all the layers and depths of their conversations. I got the sensation that they had a particular frequency (for lack of a better term) that they used to communicate with humans and then a variety of others that they used to communicate amongst themselves. So not only was I hearing what Inruk had to say, I was also getting the side conversations that were going on all around him. Some private between individuals and some meant to be heard by their shared oscillation.

"Mike what...what is that thing?" I'd never seen Tracy that scared in my entire life.

"That's a Stryver," I managed to choke out.

"It says it means no harm, do you believe that?" Her gun was coming up. She might be scared but not too scared to act, unlike her husband.

'We can help the injured one.' Another spoke. **'Yes, we can make him better.'**

'Kill the injured male, kill the female.'

"They say they can help BT. Can you hear them?" Tracy asked.

"I can, and..." I was trying to see if Tracy heard the others talking without letting the Stryvians know, just because they said they couldn't 'hear' communication, didn't mean they weren't lying. For all I knew they could maybe read lips.

"And what? If they say they can help BT, I think we have to take it no matter what they look like. Looks can be deceiving." She was saying the words but she wasn't convincing either of us.

'It is suspicious.'
'We cannot trust him.'
'We know the truth.'
'He must never know.'

One of the things came out. ***'I am medical, I will help.'*** It said as it moved towards BT. I didn't know whether to grab Tracy and run for the hills or get in the thing's way before it got to BT.

BT was the largest man I'd ever seen. Drababan was just about the biggest Genogerian I'd ever seen. And neither of them was as big or devastating looking as this creature. And then it dawned on me with a hundred percent certainty why the Progerians had created the Devastators. They were roughly the same size, not the same shape, though. For the life of me I couldn't figure out why the Progs hadn't just turned their ships around when they caught wind of this abomination.

'It is scared.'
'It might do something.'
'The device is armed.'

That last sentence snippet caught my attention. How was I going to play this out like I wasn't hearing everything they were saying? And more importantly, why the fuck was I hearing it? Hadn't they ever heard the saying 'ignorance is bliss'? And to top it off and not for nothing why were they speaking in English? Now I know the English empire in its time spread far and wide, but I'm thinking not quite as far as where these things were from, though.

"Alright, help him," I said, although I'm pretty sure I couldn't have stopped them. BT went rigid. He looked pretty resigned that they were going to be so close.

'There is no need to speak verbally,' the initial beast

said.
'Humans are stupid. It does not understand.'
'Must get the weapon away from it.'
BT cried out in pain. I instinctually raised my rifle pointing it at the barbed hairy back of the medic.
'Administering medicine.'
The needle looked like something my folks used to baste a turkey with.
'We must go Michael Talbot. Others are coming.'
"Others?"
'Its voice grates on my sensory lobes.'
'The death dealers have returned.'
'The hostile ones.'
'Murderers.'
'Marauders.'
'Defenders.'
I wanted to tell them to shut the fuck up. It was already busy enough in my head without all of them spilling their guts. "The Progerians are back?"
'Yessss.' That 's' sound trailed entirely too long, striking a discordant chord deep within me. My evolutionary biology was screaming at me to end this meeting and with unchecked hostility. These things were dangerous to not just me but all life on this planet, all life on any planet. **'Your guardian has left as well.'**
My first thought was they were talking about Dee. I'll tell you what, that went all the way to the bone to think they were spying on him and my son.
"How...how do you know that?"
'Easy to detect buckle with correct instruments.'
"Oh, the Guardian, it left? Where?"
'Ship left, yes.'
'One less to deal with.'
'Fall.'
'Cannot detect location.'
'Running.'

'Destroyed.'

I looked over at the medic carrying BT as if he were a baby. "Where are you taking him?"

'Ship. He needs more assistance than I can give here.'

"What are your intentions?"

'To heal, to mend.'

"I'm talking to Inruk."

'To help, to aid in your war against the aggressors.'

'He does not believe you.'

'It is as disgusted with us as we are with it.'

'Must not know the truth.'

'Fifteen seconds to detonation. If it will not come aboard kill the female and grab it.'

"Well I appreciate the help, let's go," I said, grabbing Tracy's hand to pull her on board. She was doing her best to not drag her feet, and so was I.

"Mike, are you sure?" Tracy was stumbling as I nearly dragged her.

"Trust me on this one."

"You know something I don't?"

"I do." That seemed enough to placate her.

As I approached the ship I shouldered my rifle, making any attempt to grab it from my hand hopefully unnecessary as I boarded. By the time we got in, BT was already strapped down on a platform much too big for him. The interior was bigger than I would have imagined from the outside yet entirely too small with seven of the Stryvers there as well. The spaciousness was due to the fact that there were no furnishings or instruments for that matter. The platform had either slid out from the wall much like a hidden cabinet in an RV or it was created by a force field.

Lights crawled along the smooth walls like spider webs. There was no way, none that I could discern, to see outside of the ship or control it for that matter.

'Prepare for flight.'

The Stryvers spread their four bottom legs out wide for stability. I noted that they were all facing in the same direction.

BT was secure, as were our hosts. Tracy and I were in danger of rolling around the damned thing like a marble inside a can. Bringing Tracy with me, I went to the far wall and sat down on the floor. The ship was extremely quiet except for BT's labored breathing and the rustling of our clothing.

'We must accelerate, the bomb has detonated.'

I could feel the pull of inertia as we began traveling faster. There was a slight rumble as what I believe was the bomb blast washed over us and then all was quiet again.

'Radiation levels are within normal.'

I was saddened that a nuclear device had been exploded in the States but I won't lie; I was happy it had killed all the Genos. Although as funny as it might sound, I wish they were here right now rather than the ones that had "saved" me. Now I had to figure out why and for what purpose.

'We are safe now.' It was Inruk. I could only tell the difference in voice as his was marginally less frightening.

"From what?" I needed to play dumb. Not really all that big a stretch for me.

'The Genogerians have detonated a device to destroy your factory.'

Well that was an out and out lie. "Wow, must have been an incredible bomb if we were threatened this far away."

"Mike is he talking about..." I put my hand across Tracy's mouth so fast it could have been construed as a slap if seen from a distance.

"Yes, um, he's talking about the Genos' city busters."

'He knows.'

'He cannot know the truth.'

'He is dishonest.'

Tracy was quiet, thankfully, although she did smack my hand away.

"How did your kind survive the Progerian attack?" I wanted to distract them from their current thoughts.

'Our planet is much hotter and hostile than your home but it is still conducive to Progerian and Genogerian colonization and depletion of our resources. They came in their mighty ships. We had not learned flight yet as our populous had never seen such things. This threat from the sky was unheralded.'

'From the sky they came.' I got the distinct feeling this one was shivering as he recited the words.

'They destroyed our aboveground cities. We hid deep within the bowels of our planet as death rained down. For five of your Earth years we hid, never venturing out into our sun. We bided our time and then they came. The monsters set foot on our planet and we struck back.'

Images of those powerful mandibles and forearms shredding into unsuspecting Genogerians began to dominate my vision. It was repulsive. These things not only tore the Genos apart, they drank the blood greedily like a famished vampire. The Genos had been completely unprepared for the savagery they met when faced with the Stryvers. I saw vast battlefields where hundreds of thousands of combatants had died from both sides. Stryvers were striking out from holes in the ground, ripping and tearing into Geno ranks before going back down to their lairs. More ships came, indiscriminately raining down destruction on friend and foe alike.

'We were winning. The master race could not supply enough of their slaves to bend us to their rule. They tried, for eleven years they tried. Finally when it had not become worth it for them anymore, they poisoned our planet. Billions of my kind perished. We went ever deeper to escape. Twelve more years we spent down there, surviving on little more than deep-earth worms.'

Their story was horrible. The Progerians were every

bit the monsters I believed them to be. Our paths were similar, except for the winning part. Like them, we also went underground, the Indian Hill bunker being the most famous. But it was still hard to elicit pity for something as ghastly as the creatures in front of me. Ever felt bad for a grub? Yeah, me neither, and I'd adopt a carload of them, even set them up with their own bedroom in my house rather than keep this proximity to the Stryvers.

"How did you get flight?" From the images Inruk showed me it didn't even look like they had hit the equivalent of our industrial age. Their "cities" seemed more like huge earthen works.

'Colonists had begun to populate our world. OUR WORLD!'

Yeah he had pretty much screamed in my brain, I'm surprised the ugly thing didn't cause an aneurysm in my head.

With the threat of the Stryvians thought to be completely wiped away the Progerians began to settle the planet. The colonists, however, were not prepared for the onslaught, as legions of starved Stryvians descended upon the many communities. In less than a year they had taken back their world and with it all of the technology left behind by the invaders.

'We did what your kind did and reverse engineered their ships and weapons, adapting them to our use. We went from a civilization living in the shadows to star-faring conquerors.'

'Do not tell it about the worlds we found.'

I caught images of many planets flitting through its memory, some with no intelligent life, and others with beings that looked surprisingly human. Many of them contained Progerian settlers, though. Those they destroyed with a crazed zeal.

'When our great enemy discovered our revenge they paid us back with a retribution we have as of yet not been

able to reciprocate. They did not poison our planet this time, but they had found a way to peel the atmosphere away. No living creature was spared. Our oceans have evaporated and boiled away and nothing, not even the lowly deep-earth worm, has survived. Our planet revolves around the sun, cold, hostile and indifferent to all life. It will most likely never sustain life again. We have battled them long and hard to hold on to our victories, but one by one they have taken them back. Not by conventional means but rather what you call "scorched earth." They would rather completely destroy a planet than let us have it. Twenty-six planets have now suffered the same fate as ours.'

To think of my home as barren, devoid of all color except the browns of rock, affected me more than I can express. To never see anything move along its surface was disheartening. Here were two enemies so hell-bent on destroying each other they would take the cosmos down with them. The Stryvians were no better than the Progerians, not now anyway. Once the battle for Earth was decided and we won or the Progs won, the Stryvers would bide their time and strike. Then the process would repeat itself here like it had in so many other places. Was I aligning myself with a demon to beat the devil? They had a ship, a much larger one somewhere. I knew enough that for whatever reason, to complete a buckle a ship had to have a certain mass and contain the means to produce enough energy to propel through it. This ship lacked both.

"Where are we going?" I asked with dread. This was the time they all decided to go with "mums the word". For the last hour they'd been chattering up a storm, now I could fucking hear crickets in the distance. I mistakenly thought the ridge in L.A. was the worst the day was going to offer. I now found myself aboard a ship with monsters indescribable, heading towards a much larger ship with more of them. My son was on a planet about to be barraged from the sky and the only chance we had to make it had buckled away to who knows where. Could it get worse? I'm sure it could, I just don't know how.

I was pissed the Stryvers weren't here to help. They were just setting up a mutually assured destruction between the Progerians and us. They'd given us just enough weapons to make a decent showing of a stand. They'd set us up perfectly; with the rail guns and the bomb BT probably figured he had a chance. He got the gangs unified and exposed. All it had done was get a lot of them killed needlessly. The Stryvers knew the nuke was in place and that the Genogerians were going to die either way. And what of Paul? That nuke was an Earth born weapon and he had to have known that facility was empty. Was it possible he was in collusion with these things?

One thing was for certain: there was no motherfucking way I was staying with them for any extended amount of time while they figured out how to claim the planet. And of what possible good could I be to them?

Chapter Thirty - Drababan

Drababan had initially thought about going to Indian Hill. It had been almost entirely vacated when it was once again "safe" on the surface, but there was sure to be at least some maintenance personnel and some officers and crew to keep an eye on things, especially now that there was a very high likelihood that it was once again going to be needed. His next thought was the remote mountains of the Ozarks. He was not concerned that he would not be able to provide for Travis but he felt the boy needed to be around others of his own kind as well. Living in the rugged area with only him as a friend would be to deprive the youngling of a proper upbringing. He knew what he had to do; he was just wondering how he would be accepted.

The crunch of gravel was loud as the wheels of the Hummer slowly traversed the unpaved road. He pulled up to a modest home shaped much like a barn hewn from logs. He stepped out of the car and then leaned back in to undo Travis's safety straps on his car seat.

"Stop right there!" He heard the ratcheting of a bullet into a rifle chamber.

"May I stand?" Dee called out, still hunched over inside the vehicle.

"Just let me see your hands when you do so!"

Dee came out of the car holding the baby.

"Pop, Pop!" Travis exclaimed.

Tony, Mike's dad, immediately put the safety on the rifle and placed it down on the porch as he quickly came down the steps. Travis's affectionate name for his grandfather was 'Pop, Pop'. They'd tried to get him to say Poppa, but he'd just always preferred the former and it had stuck.

"Dad, what's going on?" Mike's sister Lyndsey was next out.

Her father obscured Travis and she didn't see him when she first stepped out. She gasped when she saw him racing to the beast in the driveway. For a split second she thought he was charging the much larger Genogerian and was about to have his head removed from his body.

"Ron, get out here!" she screamed.

Ron, Mike's brother, had been sleeping but barreled down the stairs in record time, desperately trying to get his head through an arm hole in his shirt. He quickly tossed it to the side when he saw the Genogerian and then his father with Travis in his hands. He was thrilled to see the boy, but his parents were nowhere in sight.

"What is going on, Drababan? Are you alone?" Ron asked.

"I do not bring good tidings, sibling of Mike."

Dee related everything he knew. He told them the Genogerian uprising was most likely caused by the Progerians and that Paul had sent Tracy to deal with them because Mike had been injured on an emissary mission. Lastly, he let them know Mike had gone to join his wife on the battlefield. All of this was told with a heaviness upon his heart.

"I fear that they could not have possibly survived against such grievous odds." His head dipped down. "Michael made me promise to care for Travis. I would have done so without the oath. I have a depth of love for the youngling that I cannot express in words. When Beth threatened to have him taken away, I ran. I do not know if it was the right thing to do but I felt it was right."

"Pop-Pop." Everyone turned to look at Travis, who was showing his grandfather his muscles.

"You did the right thing," Tony said, his eyes shining with the happiness of seeing his grandchild.

"What now, Drababan?" Ron asked.

"I am torn. My word is honor-bound to Michael, yet I feel that I must go to his aid should he still need it."

"A lone Genogerian traveling across the country during a time of war is not that good of a decision," Ron said.

"And if the Progerians will soon be here you will most likely be on their most wanted list," Lyndsey added.

Tony could see the pain in Drababan's eyes and was going to do his best to alleviate it. "You made a promise to my son. He would want you to keep it no matter the circumstance. That boy's entire life has been about escaping dangerous situations. When he was just a little older than Travis, he pushed a screen out of one of the bedroom windows. Crawled his little ass right onto the roof."

"You never told me this, Dad!" Lyndsey exclaimed.

"I never told anyone." He smiled. "I was watching him while your mother had you two out getting school clothes. I was watching the Red Sox and got a little wrapped up in the game. I should have known something was up by how quiet he had gotten. By the time I figured to go and look in on him, he was halfway down the roofline. I thought my heart was going to burst. I called to him as I started to crawl out the window. He turned to look and lost his footing, toppling over on the roof and rolling off. I almost ran off the roof to go and check. I think I missed the entire staircase on the way back downstairs."

Lyndsey had her hands to her mouth.

"And you know what? He was fine. He'd landed on the damn trampoline we had. He was laughing up a storm when I grabbed him off that thing, like he'd just been on a carnival ride. I think my heart had finally calmed down by the time the three of you got home. I made sure from that point on to never let him out of my sight. He's been doing stuff like that ever since. Whoever his poor guardian angel is deserves overtime and hazard pay. I'm just thankful he or she is so vigilant. So you see, Drababan, as much as I am concerned for the safety of my son and daughter-in-law I have to believe in my heart that if there is some way for them to survive, he will have been shown that way. You will stay here and watch his son like a Guardian Angel. And as for Mike…he will find his way back here. That's what I choose to believe."

"I will do as I promised and as you have requested. I thank you for that, Sire of Michael. You are indeed wise."

"I'm not sure about wise, Drababan. I just know my son."

Epilogue

Commander Pandreth sat in his chair on the bridge, looking out at the bright blue-jeweled planet that was causing his kind so much strife. They had found the Progerian settlement the previous day and had been shuttling its inhabitants from the surface ever since. He'd learned about the Julipion falling into the hands of the enemy, the revolt of the Genogerians and the alliance they had made with the humans. That two species so different could align themselves was a mystery. Unlike a good number of the ruling Progerians, Pandreth knew the Genogerians discontentment with their lot in life had not died with their last failed uprising. Those feelings may have been covered over, but they were far from buried.

What was much more unsettling was that some of his kind had sided with the humans and had even helped train them on how to use the equipment and even build fighters. He had taken over command of the Earth mission when the Cruiser and the flagship Destroyer had been annihilated. That the humans had violated all manner of law by hitting a ship in buckle told him just how dangerous and unpredictable the hairless mammals were. He would show them no quarter in his dealings. The immediate problem was now coping with the 'wild' Genogerians that still roamed the planet's surface.

I hope you enjoyed the book. If you did please consider leaving a review.

For more in The Zombie Fallout Series by Mark Tufo:

Zombie Fallout 1

Zombie Fallout 2 A Plague Upon Your Family

Zombie Fallout 3 The End....

Zombie Fallout 3.5 Dr. Hugh Mann

Zombie Fallout 4 The End Has Come And Gone

Zombie Fallout 5 Alive In A Dead World

Zombie Fallout 6 Til Death Do Us Part

Zombie Fallout 7 For The Fallen

The newest Post Apocalyptic Horror by Mark Tufo:

Lycan Fallout Rise of the Werewolf

Fun with zombies in The Book of Riley Series by Mark Tufo

The Book Of Riley A Zombie Tale pt 1

The Book Of Riley A Zombie Tale pt 2

The Book Of Riley A Zombie Tale pt 3

The Book Of Riley A Zombie Tale pt 4

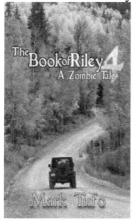

Or all in one neat package:

The Book Of Riley A Zombie Tale Boxed set plus a bonus short

Dark Zombie Fiction can be found in The Timothy Series by Mark Tufo

Timothy

Tim2

Michael Talbot is at it again in this Post Apocalyptic Alternative History series Indian Hill by Mark Tufo

Indian Hill 1 Encounters:

Indian Hill 2 Reckoning

Indian Hill 3 Conquest

Indian Hill 4 From The Ashes

Writing as M.R. Tufo

Dystance Winter's Rising

The Spirit Clearing

Callis Rose

I love hearing from readers, you can reach me at:

email
mark@marktufo.com

website
www.marktufo.com

Facebook
https://www.facebook.com/pages/Mark-Tufo/133954330009843?ref=hl

Twitter
@zombiefallout

All books are available in audio version at Audible.com or itunes.
All books are available in print at Amazon.com or Barnes and Noble.com